**DAW BOOKS PRESENTS
CAMILLE BACON-SMITH'S
NOVELS OF URBAN DEVILTRY:**

DAEMON EYES
(includes EYE OF THE DAEMON and
EYES OF THE EMPRESS)

A LEGACY OF DAEMONS

A LEGACY OF DAEMONS

CAMILLE BACON-SMITH

DAW BOOKS, INC.
DONALD A. WOLLHEIM, FOUNDER
375 Hudson Street, New York, NY 10014

ELIZABETH R. WOLLHEIM
SHEILA E. GILBERT
PUBLISHERS
www.dawbooks.com

First Printing, May 2010
1 2 3 4 5 6 7 8 9

DAW TRADEMARK REGISTERED
U.S. PAT. AND TM. OFF. AND FOREIGN COUNTRIES
—MARCA REGISTRADA
HECHO EN U.S.A.

PRINTED IN THE U.S.A.

To Erik and David
and to my sisters, and my brothers too!

ACKNOWLEDGMENTS

Thanks pour out to Barb and Hilary, the best beta-readers ever, and to Paul W., who answered my questions about what Det. Mike Jaworski could do. Thanks also to Mike Jordan, on Jeweler's row, for letting me see the shop and the tools of the trade. The mistakes in police work and gemstones are all mine!

Prologue

The universe comprises seven spheres, of which the outermost is the abode of the Archangels. There follow the seraphim, cherubim and thrones, the minor angels in which group are included those Guardian Angels, and the Princes, who reside in the second sphere, closest to man who holds dominion over the first sphere of creation, that of all matter in the universe ... As there are seven spheres, so of Princes there be seven in number. Ariton most often allies with Oriens and Amaimon, and likewise Azmod most often allies with Magot and Astarot. In battle alliances may change, except that Ariton never allies with Azmod, nor Paimon with Magot. Each Prince comprises a host of lords of daemonkind, each with its own powers and enmities. To call upon the powers of a Prince of daemons, the host must convoke in quorum.

"LIKE A PATCH ON A LEAKY BOAT." Count Alfredo Da'Costa, lately of Venice, poured jewel-red wine from a battered carafe. He wore a crisp summer suit and admired the wine, a house Bordeaux, with a bland expression in his hawklike eyes that Brad—Badad, daemon lord of the host of Ariton—didn't trust one bit. He took the glass anyway, no reason to waste the afternoon. The wine was a simple pleasure, like the afternoon sun on the Seine rolling below, but he didn't know why he was drinking it at a sidewalk café on the tiny Ile St. Louis with the Guardian from the third celestial sphere. He was pretty sure Da'Costa hadn't pulled him off course to admire the view, or the wine, and waited for more explanation than a very old argument about the end of the universe. They were all still here, and Brad had a date.

"How's Evan?" Da'Costa sipped, waited for a reply while Brad wondered why his half-human son was suddenly an issue when they'd called a truce just weeks ago.

"He's fine. Recovering. Lily's on it."

Da'Costa raised an eyebrow at that, but Brad let it slide. They both knew Lily—the daemon Lirion in the second celestial sphere. Da'Costa knew her a bit too well to be having this conversation with Brad again. He didn't need the warning, or the veiled threat.

The first time Da'Costa brought out the patch story, he'd been explaining why Evan Davis had to die. The spheres didn't mix well. Weren't supposed to mix at all, but they had, originally out of misplaced curiosity. The third celestial sphere had punched a hole between universes that almost ended them all. The material sphere, where they sat drinking wine and enjoying Paris on a sunny afternoon, had formed like a patch in what humans called the Big Bang. Alfredo Da'Costa was a Guardian, left behind in the explosion to make sure nothing broke the fragile patch that held it all together. It all worked as long as everyone stayed where they belonged.

The material sphere was the weakness between them. A handful of humans in each generation, sharing the curiosity of the third sphere that formed them, exploited that weakness, learning the names of the daemon lords, summoning them from their home and binding them to a human will for profit or pleasure or malice. Evan Davis was the child of malice and Ariton. Brad—Badad of the host of Ariton— should have saved the universes and himself the trouble and killed the boy when he first raised a ripple in the second celestial sphere. He hadn't done it then, or when Alfredo Da'Costa had pointed out the danger of keeping him alive. Because he was half daemon, Evan could enter the second celestial sphere at will. If he somehow breached the patch in the other direction, taking his daemon nature into the third celestial sphere, he'd bring those incompatible universes together again.

Evan had been a prisoner then, of humans bent on treasure that didn't exist and of daemon lords of a foreign prince that hated Ariton on principle and Badad in particular. Between them, they'd pointed Evan at the spheres and mindlessly beat at the patch on Da'Costa's leaky boat of a universe. At the very least, they'd have lost the patch, Evan's world, and the universe he knew as home. Maybe the scar that the material sphere left behind would seal the damage again, but Da'Costa had been pretty sure that he'd take the other spheres with him.

Evan was going to kill them all if he didn't get a handle on the power of his daemon side, and it didn't look like that was going to happen any time soon, let me kill him now, I'll make it easy ... Brad knew all the arguments, had considered them a few times himself. Nothing about Evan was easy, but Da'Costa had to learn that the hard way, like everybody else.

In fact, he'd proved more difficult to kill than any of them anticipated, even Brad, which he found a little odd, given Evan's propensity to suicidal gestures. Evan had fought a war between Princes to a standstill long enough to take himself and his preferred daemon kin out of the conflict. And he'd learned to control his power. Had saved Brad and possibly all the spheres on their last case and won a grudging reprieve from Da'Costa and yet another set of concessions from the Princes.

Brad was still stuck in the material sphere until Evan died on his own or Lily killed him, but he had free run of the planet now, and so did Lily. He was on his way to Singapore to make use of the freedom when Da'Costa sidetracked him to Paris. The city was beautiful in late spring, but he was done fighting for Evan's life regardless of the setting. Evan was a big boy, he could do that for himself, and Brad had much better company waiting for him. Mai

Sien Chong had promised him a chessboard, and a bed covered in green silk sheets.

"Evan doesn't need siblings." Da'Costa sipped his wine. "I really can't allow two of them."

Brad wondered what that had to do with him. "It seems unlikely, frankly, but I think that's his mother's decision. I don't know that much about human relationships, but I'm pretty sure Evan won't have anything to do with it."

"No, he wouldn't. I'm not worried about Evan's mother."

That left Brad, which explained the timing of this little chat.

"I'm not a fool." Brad set down his glass and pushed back his chair. Maybe it was a lie, about being a fool, but he'd figured out how to make children not happen long before he stepped into Mai Sien's bedroom, and Da'Costa really couldn't stop him. So he stood up, gave an abrupt nod of farewell, wandered into the shadows of a building as old as the city, and disappeared.

Chapter 1

EVAN DAVIS USUALLY LOVED HIS JOB. He knew he'd been damned lucky, could have been dead or still locked in chains, tortured in two universes and not a partner in the most prestigious recovery and investigation agency in Philadelphia. But today the cool blue-and-white Federal period elegance of the Society Hill offices of Bradley, Ryan, and Davis did not fill him with the usual pride of accomplishment.

He was one part angry and one part—okay, just angry—and trying not to lie about it to Khadijah Flint, his lawyer, who passed him a notarized contract for a security check they started next week. The agency mostly worked with digital contracts, but the client in Barcelona wanted paper this time, so she got paper. The contract went on the low stack of documents growing on the antique Hepplewhite desk, followed by the notice of final disposition of a forgery case he'd done some expert testimony for, back before his father tried to kill him. Good thing Brad had changed his mind about the killing part, or Evan would be sleeping with the roses while his mother wept over whatever ashes he left behind. And Brad would be stuck with the paperwork.

When he came back from that thought, Flint was waiting with the last file. She'd noticed that she'd lost his attention, handed over the half-dozen stapled pages, but he knew he'd hear about it later. "The agency's police statement on the art museum case. I made a few changes

to protect the agency—the usual. Sign here and here—"
She tapped the lines at the bottom of the pages with the
blood-red, high-gloss tip of a fingernail.

Evan took the statement, noted the passages she indicated where she'd hedged things a little—good—and one
place where an entire paragraph seemed to be missing—
better. It hadn't added much to the specifics of the case, but
it might have given the FBI a wedge to ask more questions.
No one, including Evan, had expected that Brad would do
the security walk-through at the art museum in the middle
of the night, or that he'd arrive moments after the thieves
had stolen the Dowager Empress' crystal ball. They had a
contract with the museum, so it hadn't made his father the
prime suspect until Police Detective Joe Dougherty had
blown in from Evan's old neighborhood. Dougherty was
on a mission from Evan's mom, and he had a folder full
of research showing that neither his father, Kevin Bradley,
nor Lily Ryan, the Bradley and Ryan of the agency's name,
had existed until four years ago. He wasn't wrong, but that
didn't make him right. If Khadijah Flint hadn't been there
to get his father out of his little misunderstanding with the
Major Crimes Unit, Philly would be a hole in the ground
by now.

She didn't know that part, and he planned to keep it
that way, so he signed the statement with a flourish in both
places, said a perfunctory "Thanks," and signed the next
copy she slid under his hand. He owed her more than that,
though, for the part she did know even if she didn't know
the rest.

"If I didn't thank you before for your help—"

"I talked to my accountant this morning, and your thanks
are in the bank." She gave him a wry smile, a conspiracy of
friendship and concern. Last week's braids had given way
to a cluster of short dreads. It should have looked softer,
but somehow, it didn't. The warriors printed on tan, peering
out at him from the open jacket of her dark red suit, just
made him nervous. Truth in advertising—he was glad she
was on his side.

She signed as witness after him and made more of a job

than she needed of slipping the stack of papers into a manila envelope. "I'll have one copy messengered to Major Crimes and the other to the FBI this afternoon."

They were done. Evan was halfway to his feet, but Khadijah Flint appeared to be settling into that deliberately uncomfortable spindle-back guest chair. The hair might be new but the glance over the top of her reading glasses wasn't. He tried for mildly surprised though he'd been dreading the questions he knew were coming since she'd called to set up the appointment.

"Was there something else?"

"Minding the shop on your own today?"

That was one. He didn't sit down again, but waited her out while she studied his bruises: the green faded to yellow on his temple that the daemon Lirion had put there in her wrath, and the purple streaks that his father, Badad of the host of Ariton, had scored across his cheek. Evan had cut his hair short to blend the shaved spots growing back where the stitches had come out on his temple and at the back of his head, but he knew she was thinking about that too.

As it happened, they'd had good reason for what they'd done and most of the time he was just glad they hadn't killed him. The official report said "unknown assailant." The police suspected the Chongs. Evan pretended not to remember. The truth would give him a long-term rental on a padded cell.

Khadijah Flint called them Lily and Brad, didn't know about the daemon part. Wouldn't have believed him if he'd told her, and wouldn't be his lawyer anymore if he showed her. Humans didn't take to the knowledge well. He sure hadn't, so he kept it to himself.

"Yeah, on my own today. Not exactly the face I'd like to show the public, but Lily's working an estate case." Lily was in Hokkaido, stealing a netsuke, a small lacquered lion, from the brother of their client. The agency had charged a lot more for the job than the netsuke was worth, but the client had a copy of his father's will, a picture of the little carving, and as Lily had pointed out, a bank balance with more zeros than this universe had stars. Which might have been an exaggeration, but probably not by much. "I expect her back later today." They had their own ways of traveling, and Lily didn't leave fingerprints.

Flint accepted that with a slight nod, little more than a tilt of her chin. Lily wasn't the point of the question, and Brad should have been covering the desk, not Evan with his multicolored face. "I do not want to know where your father is, or who is with him." Evan really hated it when she looked at him that way, as if she knew the answers already but wished she didn't. That look always meant he was in deep trouble. "For both our sakes, I'll pretend he's around here somewhere—he is coming back, Evan?"

They'd found most of the Philadelphia Museum of Art's stolen property and broken up a plot to overthrow the Chinese government. But one of the suspects, Mai Sien Chong, had disappeared, and so had Evan's father and an alabaster figure of a kneeling child. No coincidence, and it narrowed the "wheres" considerably. If his lawyer had guessed that much, Interpol probably had it figured as well; Evan just hoped Brad was wearing a different face while he consorted with a known criminal. It wouldn't matter if they never left the bedroom, of course, which creeped him out more than discovering his unknown father was a daemon. Brad avoided human entanglements, didn't date. Certainly didn't have sex with humans. Except for that once, when he hadn't had a choice and hadn't much liked the consequences. Evan put a big "no trespassing" sign on his father's sex life and left the thought as fast as he could.

Like Brad's whereabouts, that was information their lawyer didn't need to know, so he answered her with the bland smile she'd seen right through the first time he'd met her. "Brad's away for the weekend. Of course he'll be back." Which was no certainty. Brad warned him often enough, and so did Lily, that he was a curiosity, an experiment. If he kept putting human emotions on that, it was his problem, not theirs. He jammed a hand into hair that wasn't there anymore, felt his fingers slide over still-healing gashes. Knew it for a tell when her eyes widened. Well, shit. She didn't call him on it, though, and he pretended not to notice.

"What do you need from him?"

"The FBI wants his personal statement, not just the agency's official report."

Sid Valentine, she meant; prime pain in the ass. Sid had taken a special dislike to Bradley, Ryan, and Davis. He still suspected the agency as accomplices in the art museum thefts.

"I'll let Brad know. And now, I have another appointment—" Another estate case. Evan came around the desk, holding a smile in place. Thirty seconds, he figured, and Khadijah Flint, with her sharp, knowing sympathy, would be out of there.

A soft chime announced the arrival of the new client in the outer office.

"I'm sorry I took so much of your time." Khadijah Flint closed her briefcase and stood up, but hesitated a moment. She looked a little worried. Brad's absence might look suspicious to the police, but the alabaster figure wasn't worth that much, comparatively speaking. If he wanted one, he could afford to buy it. Khadijah Flint had a list of personal motives that fit her client better, starting with Mai Sien Chong, and only half of them were likely to get him arrested.

"I'll let you know when the results of your DNA tests come in." And there it was, the point of all the less-than-subtle questions. "Brad should be here as well. He's assured me that the legal side will not be an issue, whatever the results of the tests. But—"

She was wrong about this part of it, at least. His father hadn't walked away over a question of paternity. He'd already seen to the DNA match, simple enough for a daemon lord who created a physical body out of the tides of the universe, but he couldn't tell her that.

"In the meantime, call if you need me. Your father keeps me entertained, but I worry about you, Evan." She patted his arm, offering comfort as they crossed the elaborate medallion at the center of the pale blue Aubusson carpet and he took it, pretended for a minute just to be human.

"I'm fine."

He opened the door to their small waiting room. "Fine" might have been premature.

Chapter 2

"**Y**OU'RE UNINVITED," HE SAID and slammed the door against the thing dressed as human on the other side. Or tried. A steel-toed boot slipped between the jamb and the door, while over his shoulder Khadijah Flint gave him a politely curious raised brow.

"Use the door behind the desk," he muttered under his breath, hoping the creature with the twisting amber flames in its eyes didn't hear him. "Go out through the gate in the garden. I'll call later." He'd owe her an explanation, but she'd already seen the shambles they'd made of the inner study during the last case. He didn't want to explain a fight with a daemon lord in the middle of the Aubusson carpet.

Khadijah Flint had her cell phone out and wasn't moving.

"Don't call 9-1-1," he said, trying to limit the collateral damage. "I'll be fine. Just, go. You don't have to call the police."

"I'm not here to hurt you." The daemon hadn't tried to break the door, which he might have done. Evan had denied him entry but that wouldn't have stopped Brad or Lily. He didn't own the daemon, couldn't command it. There were protections worked into the floral patterns of the plasterwork in the ceiling, a pentagram in a circle carved into the elaborate design, but Evan was outside of it, and so was his lawyer.

The not-a-man said. "It's a straight deal. I'll pay like

any other client." He looked to be in his early thirties, which meant nothing, with hair a nondescript brown brushing the tops of his ears and falling into his eyes—eyes with flames burning at their centers that marked a daemon lord on the material sphere. He wore a pair of paint-spattered jeans and a flannel shirt hanging open over a dusty gray tee that made the part about paying like any other client doubtful. His eyes glinted with amber fire.

"Evan?"

Probably safer to deal with the creature *under* that ceiling. It was there for a reason, after all. "It's all right, 'Deej," he told her, "But you've really got to get out of here." Out of the corner of his eye, he saw her nod. She was looking at him like he'd taken off a mask, which he figured he had. Didn't have time to play innocent youth while he dredged through memories of night terrors and battles in a place where humans weren't supposed to exist at all. Lords of the host of Ariton, like Brad and Lily, manifested in blue eyes a little darker than his own, and the eyes of Azmod, his personal enemy and the sworn foe of Ariton for longer than Earth had existed, burned green. He didn't know the name of the Prince this one belonged to, or if it was friend or foe to Ariton in the alliances that the hosts of heaven forged for the wars they waged among themselves. He just knew it had tried to kill him once.

"I need your help. There isn't anyone else I can ask."

Evan heard the soft thump against the door. A head, he figured, leaning for support, and to hide the fact that his last hope was leaking away. Evan had felt that, was having a hard time remembering this thing was a monster and not necessarily friendly to his own preferred brand of same. Shit.

"Please, 'Deej. I'll call you later. Right now, my client needs a little privacy."

She gave him a long, calculating glare, but finally let him go. "Apparently, so does mine. But I *will* call later."

"Thank you." He waited until she had gone through the side door that led her away through the house, and then he opened the door. "Matt Shields, I presume? You couldn't show up in a suit and tie?"

The daemon followed him past the sideboard with Brad's bottle of scotch in it that they used for a credenza, onto the carpet and under the circle carved in the plaster overhead. Funny thing about those circles—they could keep an enemy out, or hold one in. Evan felt the wind at his back when Shields realized he couldn't close the distance to the desk. "You are starting a war you won't live to see," it said. By then Evan had reached the other side. It was a lousy way to start a business relationship, but he didn't see much choice. In his whole life he'd never met a daemon who hadn't tried to kill him—including the one he slept with on a fairly regular basis.

"It's just a precaution, until we resolve why you are here—preferably without starting any more wars. Ariton is pissed off at me already. Have a seat." Pointing at that uncomfortable spindle-back guest chair that hadn't stopped Khadijah Flint, he gave the daemon his best effort at the new-client smile—comforting, he reminded himself—and sat behind his desk. "We'll start with who you are."

"I'll never tell you that." Amber flame licked the chair. The daemon curled his lip in a white snarl, pressed as close to the antique desk as the pentagram in the ceiling would allow him. "And my 'never' is a lot longer than yours."

"Look, the last time I met a Prince the color of your eyes, it tried to kill me. I thought that was done with, then you show up at my door. Maybe you are willing to sit in that chair until Badad of the host of Ariton comes home and takes care of the situation his way, but I'm not stuck in there, you are. So unless you came here to start a war with Ariton, you are going to answer some questions."

"Good to know that I'll be doing my Prince a favor when I kill you. Nice look, by the way. Did we do that? Or was it Ariton, freak-boy?"

The bruises. Evan had known this was a bad idea from the start. No part of this argument felt new. Daemons were touchy, including his own relations. He *knew* better than to escalate an argument with one of his father's kind. Planets could die because his anger at his father colored every word he said to this thing. Or, his own world might survive because he was cautious about his bargains.

He tried to think of the thing in the chair as a man. At the door, Shields hadn't looked angry—he'd looked desperate, trying to bluff through how much he had on the line here. Evan really didn't want to think about what it would take to make a daemon desperate enough to ask for help outside his own host, but he was going to have to, if he wanted a world to stand on at the end of the conversation. Smoke was already rising from a circle of charred carpet around the creature. He wondered if he could add the price of a new one to the bill.

"Okay. Let's start over. I'm Evan Davis." He stood up and reached a hand across the desk. Dangerous, if the daemon meant to harm him, but a risk he had to take if he wanted to get this conversation back on track.

"What?" The daemon looked at Evan's outstretched hand like he was trying to calculate the danger from his side of the desk.

"Do over," Evan explained. "I'm Evan Davis, you're Matt Shields. Your real name, up there, is off the table. I get it."

"It's not up," the new client grumbled, but he took the hand Evan offered and shook it, letting go quickly, like he was afraid of catching something. "Matt Shields. Do I get out of the circle now?"

That was the trick question, all right. Evan had thought about it from the moment they'd added the words "cases involving the occult handled with discretion" to the agency's ad in the yellow pages. Pentagrams were useless against humans, but they'd stop the supernatural if you were strong enough to hold your lines together. In or out, didn't matter. With daemons, it was always about the intention and being on the other side of any line you held.

So, the ad had changed—they didn't go looking for occult cases anymore—but not the answer to Matt Shields' question. "You can leave by the front door any time you want. All you have to do is swear not to harm this house or the people who live in it, or their connections freely given. And to take no retribution on this world or the universe it resides in. Your own enemies are your business. Anything more is by mutual agreement, but some things I have to know if we are going to work together. Not your name, but your Prince, to start with. I won't cross Ariton, or cause harm to Ariton's alliances, or aid Ariton's enemies. It's a family thing." He gave a little shrug, knew he sounded pompous, but daemons were legalistic by their nature and he'd been sitting with his lawyer all afternoon.

Matt Shields considered the questions for so long that Evan thought he might refuse. Then he held out his hand. "Paimon," he said, "Not an ally of Ariton, but not an enemy either. We pick our side based on the fight. And yeah. I agree to the terms of leaving the circle."

Evan accepted the hand, an idea starting to take shape. Risky. He usually kept out of politics between the Princes. It was sort of like juggling the orbits of planets—he probably could if he tried hard enough, but that didn't mean it was a healthy thing to do. Which had never stopped Evan before.

"How about some pizza? Negotiating the fate of the known universe always makes me hungry." He wasn't really, but the daemon, Matt Shields, looked like he could use something to defuse the tension. And, stranger yet, he looked like he hadn't been eating regularly. Which— daemons didn't have to eat. The body was a construct. Something was really wrong here. Evan made the call—"no anchovies" changed to "one with and one without,"—and pulled a tablet and a file folder with Matt Shields' name on it out of the side drawer in the desk. While they waited for the delivery, he brought up a standard contract on the screen of his laptop. This was going to be anything but standard, but they had to start somewhere.

"When you called, you said you wanted Bradley, Ryan, and Davis to agent the acquisition of an art object at the Grayson Donne estate sale."

"That's not exactly what I said."

"That's contract talk for 'Grayson Donne's estate is being sold off and I need somebody to buy a box at the auction.' Given that you pick your side based on the fight, and that you appear to be stuck on this ball of rock I like to call 'home,' I think you understand about contract language."

Matt Shields glared at him from under the flop of bangs that obscured the amber flames in his eyes. "Assuming we come to an agreement on terms, I want Bradley, Ryan, and Davis to agent the acquisition of a piece of art at Grayson Donne's estate sale. Now it's contract language. Pending terms, of course."

"Of course." Evan remembered the precision with which his father had confirmed the one command he'd ever given. It had almost killed him, but he did understand about daemons and contracts, had to stop slipping between what he knew about the creature in the chair and the contradiction of the clothes, the slump of shoulders. "What exactly do you want us to acquire?"

"A box."

Chapter 3

"A PARTICULAR BOX, OR WILL ANY BOX DO?"

Matt Shields frowned like he'd never heard sarcasm before, and took a breath, then stopped, a question in his eyes that cleared suddenly. A little twist of smile turned the corner of his mouth. "Ariton always did have a lousy sense of humor." But the tension in his shoulders shifted into new patterns, at once less desperate and more alert.

"This box," he said, and hunted around in the breast pocket of his flannel shirt until he came up with a picture, much folded, torn out of a catalog. A bit of the trailing page at the bottom said "Sotheby's."

The photograph showed a wooden box bound in a metal too tarnished to identify, with the legend, "14th c. French strongbox, 27 in. x 18 in. x 27 in. high, oak panels with iron strapping, elaborately decorated. Locked but empty. No key. $10,000–$35,000."

Evan made a few notes on the tablet in front of him, mostly because it reassured the client. Medieval objects had never been his specialty. They weren't particularly fashionable, and never had been with Bradley, Ryan, and Davis' usual clients, so he'd spent only as much time on them as it took to get out of grad school. But something didn't make sense. He didn't do medieval furnishings, but he had worked with Sotheby's before. They were as thorough as it gets.

"Why didn't they open it? Wouldn't that be usual?"

Shields twitched an I-don't-know shoulder, but Evan couldn't tell whether he meant that he didn't know auctions or didn't know about the lock. Either way, he expected the lie and waited it out.

"The key is missing. They had a locksmith look at it, but he couldn't open the lock without destroying the mechanism. The auction house had some tests done, and they say it's empty, so they are selling it as is."

Closer. Evan made another note. He'd have to see more than the picture from the catalog to be sure, but it looked like Kabalic symbols worked into the metal. Which maybe helped explain why Shields wanted it, but not how much he'd pay to get it. The ad had a valuation that Evan didn't trust at all. He could have priced out a painting of the period for himself with a little research and not much trouble. An empty strongbox? Not so much. "How much interest in the box are you expecting? How much are you willing to pay for it?"

Shields gave him a closed-off shrug obscured by the inward curl of his shoulders. "There'll be interest because it was Donne's, but for the box in particular, I don't know. As for the other, I'll do whatever it takes to own that box."

"Not sharing much here, are you?" Evan rubbed his hands over his face, remembered why he wasn't supposed to do that. "Okay, first—money. Do you have any? Because unless you are the eccentric branch of the family, you don't look like you can afford the catalog at Sotheby's, let alone the opening bid on this box. And then there's a matter of our fee. We're expensive, and you don't get the friends and family discount. Friends don't get the friends and family discount, and you don't come close to qualifying as a friend."

"Money?" Wrinkled brow, like he'd never heard of money. Lily never lied to Evan—early on, she'd explained in that off-hand way that he wasn't worth the trouble. But their kind did lie, frequently. Matt Shields was lying now.

"No, but I have these." Another mining expedition, this time into the front right pocket of his jeans. Evan was ready

to ask if he wanted some privacy for that when he pulled
out a soft leather pouch and dropped it on the lined tablet
at the center of the antique desk.

The pouch settled with a little clink. Evan tore off the
page where he'd been writing notes and scattered just a
few of the gems on the blank tablet. Cut rubies. All sizes,
including one as big as Evan's thumb. Okay. Maybe. The
smallest ones weren't worth much, in the scheme of Sotheby's auctions and Bradley, Ryan, and Davis' fees. But
the largest one, if it was real, was worth millions. The office
sat a block from Jewelers' Row. With a little help at agency
prices, Shields could have it appraised and sold in a private
auction by morning, if they were pressed and didn't mind
selling at emergency prices. If it was real. If, if, if . . .

"Where did you get them? Are they natural, or did you
take a little corundum, a little chromium, and squeeze?"

"They're mine. I bargained with Donne for a single perfect ruby as payment for each task he required of me. I've
been collecting them ever since. I have the original documentation for each of them, but Grayson Donne had them
all appraised and collected on one certificate of ownership
about twenty years ago. He was particular about keeping
the paperwork in order."

Evan took the photocopy, which was in the condition
he'd expect given the pocket it came out of, and scanned
the page and a half of identifications. Weight, color, grade,
estimated value—most of the gems came from the Mogok
Mines, in Burma. A few had names and histories. Donne
was this particular about his paperwork, but didn't have a
will? Shields may not have killed him, but Evan didn't ask
the obvious next question. Didn't want to know something
he'd have to give the police when the agency's part of it
ought to be simple, fast, and lucrative. Except that making
a deal with a Prince of the second celestial sphere *who was
not Ariton's ally* was not in the least bit simple and might
still get him killed.

None of this fit Evan's knowledge of daemons, and
he studied Matt Shields across the antique desk, trying
to figure what was wrong with this picture. Those rubies

represented bargains for a hell of a lot of tasks. Shields had been really busy or somebody had bound him here a long time.

Evan knew the name on the Sotheby's catalog—would have to in his business. Grayson Donne's obituaries had swept the chat rooms where high-end arcana traded for large sums of money. Eccentric recluse, upstate New York, died without a will. Things had gone quiet while the state ground through the investigations and searched for heirs, but they hadn't found anything. The market was lining up for this auction. Evan had a copy of the catalog in the back office somewhere. Hadn't given a glance at that strongbox, though. The key word in all of this was dead. Donne was dead. In Evan's experience, daemons didn't collect souvenirs. They departed, sometimes leaving a hole in the ground that raised questions for centuries. So, why had Matt Shields hung around for almost three years instead of heading right for the second celestial sphere as soon as Donne died?

"Why do you need the box? Why don't you just go home?" Evan leaned back in his chair and gestured at the ceiling.

Shields twitched a bit at the questions, and Evan figured he was still deciding how much truth to mix in with his lies. But lies could be telling as well. "Donne was a Magus, and careful. He knew if I ever had a chance at escape, I'd kill him. So he bound me to the box. I need to find it, own it, destroy it, and then I can go home. I've already done the first part. It's up to you to do the second part. I can take over once I own the box."

"Fair enough, but why us? You've already said that Paimon is no ally to Ariton, and your Prince tried to kill me not that long ago. We seem an unlikely first choice."

Shields had a laugh like broken glass. "If I walked into any other agency with $15 in my pocket and a bag of rubies, they'd want to know where I got the rubies. You want to know why I don't have a million dollars in the bank, and you don't expect me to tell you. Who else can I tell the truth?"

Not all the truth, but more than either of them had expected. It explained the symbols on the strongbox, and why he was here. Evan nodded and put the rubies back in their pouch, all but the one the size of his thumb. "Does anybody else know about the box?"

"I don't think so."

That was a lie. The rest had been omission. He figured some answers would have to wait until they had a contract. "You'll need to liquidate this one for the sale," he said, holding up the ruby. "It should cover the auction and our fee—once we have a contract, we can help you sell it. If anything you haven't told me costs time or effort, we revisit the stash. The price goes up if bruising is involved." He'd meant it as a joke, but Shields nodded agreement. Dangerous, then.

Evan considered the standard contract, thinking. "Our usual rates shouldn't bother you. We charge a bidders' fee of 15% of the value of the acquired property. There's a $10,000 retainer up front, but you'll get some of that back if we acquire the object for less than the estimated value. Provenance doesn't seem to be an issue, but if you need investigative work, protection of the object, or other services related to the purchase, our rates are $700 per hour, plus expenses, with a $20,000 retainer, nonrefundable. It's an open-ended contract—we guarantee success, but not the time it takes to accomplish it. So, if you lose the bid, we'll negotiate a private sale, however long that takes, at our standard hourly rate, plus the bidder's fee for the final sale value. You can cancel and walk away at any time, but that nullifies the guarantee."

"I have the money," Shields said tartly, dropping the handyman pose for a moment. "Or, I will have it as soon as we sell some of these stones." Amber fire flickered in his eyes, but he seemed more amused than annoyed. "I'm not going to need it where I'm going."

"About that—the rubies are yours, and you should clear quite a bit from the sale of this one. If you want it to go to someone in particular when you leave, we can include that in the contract. Our lawyer can take care of the transfer of ownership, we can make sure they get where they are going—"

"For a small standard fee, I am sure," Shields added.

"Not small, no. But for a standard fee."

Matt Shields stared out the window, focused on the day-lilies in the side garden, while he thought about the question of his rubies. "Carlos Sanchez," he said, coming to a decision. "He was Donne's gardener. Has a daughter at SUNY and another heading there next year. Donne left him nothing."

Donne had left nothing to anyone—thus the auction of his property. Or so the State of New York seemed to think. Evan made a note of Sanchez's name on the contract. "One more thing," he said, and the hairs on the back of his neck came to attention. This was the part that could get him killed. "We have a deal between Matt Shields and Bradley, Ryan, and Davis. Of those names, mine is the only one that is real. 'Matt Shields' doesn't want that box—a daemon lord who wants to go home does. If Brad was doing his job, he'd know your true name, and this would all be much simpler. But he isn't, so we have to go with what we have. Money is nothing to your kind. You trade in favors, and that is the bill. I want an agreement, your Prince to mine. Paimon will owe one host-debt, payable when called upon by Ariton, for any need or conflict. And Paimon will refrain from attacks on my life for ninety years. Humans don't usually live that long, but I don't want Paimon looking for a loophole either." Evan added the clause, obliquely phrased as a "reciprocal support agreement," printed out a copy, and signed at the bottom of the one-page contract, with fees attached. Then he pushed it across the desk and held out the pen.

Flames rose in Shields' eyes, as if his gaze could burn its way past the deal to the trick behind it. Evan let him look. There wasn't any trick as far as he could see, just a wild-ass shot at a binding contract, assuming Shields was free to make a contract and not lying about that as well. The daemon laughed softly, shook his head, but took the pen Evan offered.

"*Badad's* job is to kill his misbegotten spawn and go home. You most assuredly do not have the authority to bind a Prince of the second celestial sphere to a human contract. But if you do what you promise, Paimon will owe you." He signed on the solid line, because the desperation was still there.

And then he screamed.

Chapter 4

MAI SIEN CHONG HAD SKIN THE COLOR OF SUNSHINE that felt, under his human fingers, like the waves of the universe at home. And her hands on this body . . .

Something not-home caught at Kevin Bradley's attention with an almost familiar dread. This world could never be home, but on a quiet street in Philadelphia, in a house he shared with his son and with Lirion, daemon lord and host-cousin, something had gone seriously wrong. Evan was at the center of it, bleeding panic into two universes like he hadn't learned anything at all about control in the past four years.

"Evan's in trouble," he said, and reached for his clothes because he liked that jacket. Through an expanse of glass the Singapore night glittered, light from the city bouncing off the darkness. On the other side of the world it would be well past noon.

"Evan can take care of himself, and most of the known universe when he puts his mind to it. His competence cost me my home. Both of them—I can't set foot in Philadelphia or Vancouver without getting arrested, thanks to Evan." She swept her long, black hair over one shoulder, raising her arm in a way that lifted her breasts like they were reaching for him. The body he wore reached back. She laughed and let him kiss her. "But I suppose you're going anyway."

Her lips didn't really taste like honey, but he thought

of honey when he kissed them. So he did it again. But the universe was gushing panic at him, so he pushed himself away with a promise, "I'll find you when I'm done." Then he vanished with the image of her naked sprawl on sapphire silk sheets to take with him.

He abandoned human form and in his own true essence as Badad, daemon lord of the host of Ariton, he followed the disturbance into the second celestial sphere. He thought he might slip through undetected, but it didn't work out that way.

Paimon came at him out of the dark, blazing amber fury. Already the lords of that Prince had gathered in quorum: Paimon, Prince of the Western Quarter, swept over him in a tower of twisting flame. Badad fought to escape the tongues of amber fire. A forced merge—there couldn't be any other kind with a foreign Prince—would first rip his mind from him and then tear him apart.

Ariton's lords massed to defend its own, rose up in a wall of blue fire in darkness to repulse the threat. Each side attracted its allies—Oriens and Amaimon, Astarot and Magot—though Ariton had no defenders in this fight. Azmod fell back, but all the princes knew the grudge he held against Ariton's half-human monster. Badad fought the pull of opposing forces, thought they might tear him apart anyway, but he held onto the vortex of his scattered thoughts.

Lirion joined him then, unhappy with Evan and with him, but she wouldn't let that turn into an affront to Ariton.

"Your monstrous spawn declares war in the name of Ariton!" Paimon's knowledge filled him, a blaze of outrage that had nothing to do with human language. Rage kindled, a galaxy exploded, but Badad didn't care. The thread of a binding spell led to Earth. To Evan, who had promised never to bind a daemon to his will again. A lie, apparently. Badad determined that this time, he would kill the creature that had caused so much misery.

Except. Time didn't exist in the second celestial sphere. It was always *now* for the Princes and their daemon lords, but Badad had learned to recognize the signs in Evan. He saw it in the binding that held Paimon's lord. The thread of that spell might lead back to Badad's half-human son, but it was an old spell. Older than Evan, whose panic had mutated into an equally familiar emotion. Worry. Not for himself, but for Paimon's daemon lord inside Evan's circle. Parmatus, the shield of heaven—Badad plucked the name from the gathered host of Paimon.

Evan was worried about Parmatus. He knew the touch of that feeling, had long thought Evan a fool for it. Daemon lords of the hosts of heaven did not need a human's pity, or his anxiety. The daemon lord of a foreign host needed only as much thought as required to assess the danger. But panic still pulsed through the spheres. It wasn't Evan and, following the binding back to its source, he found that Evan didn't hold the lead. The knotted tangle of the spell led to no living force that Badad could find in the heavens or in the material sphere.

"Evan didn't summon Paimon's lord." He let the Princes feel what he knew. "Your lord freely sought Ariton's aid, freely entered into an agreement with my son. Princes must rule on the agreements made, but Evan did not initiate this contract. He's really not that crazy anymore."

He remembered a time when Lirion had said the same to him. It hadn't been exactly true, then, but Evan still wore that lesson on his face, and he hadn't spoken the words of a summoning. Badad would have felt it if he had and he couldn't, at the limit of logic or imagination, believe that Evan would ever bind a lord not of Ariton. Bindings worked both ways. Odd as the boy's mind worked, Evan knew that Ariton would not tolerate a violation of host-loyalty that bound him to a lord not of his own host. Earth would already be ash, and Evan would be dead. So. It had to be something else.

"Evan had a new client today," Lirion showed him. "you were supposed to take it, but you had sex on your mind." Lirion thought his sudden interest in the mating practices of humans was funny. "I was in Hokkaido. Evan was alone."

None of it should have been a problem, and wouldn't have been, until a lord of the only Prince who kept his options open on matters of alliances had walked in the door. "Parmatus has done this, and I trust his Prince that he has acted out of ignorance." He showed the gathered lords his certainty, and the sense of panic that Evan was leaking into the spheres again. "But if he kills my son, you will have the war you have prematurely called to Ariton's account."

"Ariton will owe us a host-debt for removing a problem his own lords could not."

But Ariton had reached a quorum; enough of the host of 833 daemon lords had gathered to become their Prince. Badad felt his identity swallowed into the whole, sensed Lirion become a part of him, with her knowledge of Evan both shared and different. Caramos, wise and joyous, plucked sex from their joined minds. What shape, he wondered and, would Evan show him? Did it really feel that good and, what did "feel" mean?

Sched burned with a terrible female power. She knew humans, had been a goddess once, leaking milk from huge breasts to bless the land, but was curious now about Evan's dual nature. She had propagated her own children on that world, before civilization had blinded it to the sacred female. Anader, cold and cruel, with no love of the material, wanted Badad's half-human monster dead, but would allow no interference in Ariton's prerogatives. Sibolas, Harumbrub, Erdulon, and hundreds more of Badad's host-cousins merged their minds into one thought. Curious or not, the lords of his own host would have killed Evan and been done with him. He had proved himself a part of that host, however, and none but his own had the right to move against him, except in declared warfare, though he'd proved elusive in that arena as well.

Ariton spoke in blue flame, Prince to Prince: "The monster is Ariton's. If harm comes to it, Paimon will have an enemy forever."

"You put yourself at disadvantage," Paimon answered with cold amber fire. There were seven Princes, evenly divided in their alliances—all but Paimon, who chose.

But Ariton laughed. "Your lord Parmatus came to us. Who is at disadvantage here?"

"One way or another, the problem will be solved." Paimon withdrew too quickly, not sharing some knowledge that had made a sham of his challenge. But Badad's monster remained, sending waves of anxiety through the spheres.

"Go. Fix this." Dead would do. Ariton cast him out and Badad fell, into the eternal gravity of the material sphere. He felt Lirion at his side and realized that he had a side again, a body that had picked up his clothes along the way.

Chapter 5

PARMATUS, WHO PROBABLY HAD A HUMAN name here, lay curled in a writhing ball in the center of the office that the agency used for client meetings. The carpet was burning, amber flame rising in a circle defined by the protections in the ceiling, which had already grayed with the smoke. The pale blue walls above the pristine white wainscoting seemed fine, though. Assuming they stopped the blaze before Parmatus dropped them into the basement, the damage should be limited, all things considered. Not counting Evan, of course, who was inside the circle, on his knees beside a daemon lord of a foreign Prince. Parmatus had no reason except the one that brought him through the door to hold to the contract that protected Evan. And Badad had already promised a war on Ariton's behalf if anything happened to his misbegotten son.

"Get out," he said, and took Evan's place at Parmatus' side. Evan leaped out of the circle, his relief so palpable that Badad winced. He was going to have to stand, though, because Lirion had taken his chair and watched with narrow-eyed attention the disaster that Evan had managed this time.

Badad took Parmatus' chin in his hands, turned the daemon lord's human face to look at him, but he spoke to Evan first. "What in the name of Ariton have you done now?" —because that seemed the easiest way to get him thinking.

"My job," Evan answered, just as Parmatus gasped out, "Contract."

"He signed a walk-away contract; it should *not* have done this."

Parmatus' eyes were glazed with pain, but rage percolated just beneath the incapacitating anguish. "Does he understand that?" Badad insisted, and Evan answered, "I *told* him. I spelled it out. He can cancel the contract at any time, verbally, in writing, or he can just stop paying the bill. I'd never—he's not even Ariton. I would *never* bind this agency to anything except a walk-way single task contract with another Prince. I haven't been insane in a long time."

That last was Evan-speak for humor, but it was probably true.

"We know that," Lirion said, though Badad wouldn't have told him so. "But did you add anything to the standard contract?"

"I didn't limit the walk-away clause, not in any way." Evan was looking guilty now, and that was never good. Badad held his human shape steady by force of will. "I added a rider, a host-debt. Paimon will owe Ariton for this. He said if we succeeded he would anyway."

Lily came over the desk, into the circle, adding blue flame to the amber and not even trying to hold her human form together.

Badad still didn't quite believe it. "You asked a boon between Princes? Of my *son*? He's human, you fool!"

"He's more than that," Parmatus gasped out.

Then Evan was inside the circle again, the buzzed hair lifting in a halo of blue flame. "Enough. The rider is no more binding than the rest of the contract, unless we get the damned box back. I need him calm, not burning down the house. Lily! Please! I *like* this house!"

Parmatus said, "Who's Lily?"

"Who do you think?" Lirion bent to glare eye-to-eye with the daemon lord on the floor. "Now pull yourself together. You are shaming your Prince in front of Ariton, and if you burn my house down, I will declare war myself."

"Can't. Can't."

"What's the matter with him?"

"Evan," Badad grated between clenched teeth, "Get out of the circle. We're at war if he kills you."

"Good to know." But he stepped out of the circle. "It's the box, isn't it? The contract set up a conflict."

Badad didn't know what box he meant, but he remembered that tangle of a binding that no human had a hand on. Evan snatched a piece of paper from the desk and tore it in half. "No contract," he said, and crossed back into the circle to stuff one half into Parmatus' curled fist. The edges crisped with the heat and Evan pulled his fingers back quickly, shaking out the pain where his fingertips had blistered "An agreement between Princes it is. But you're still paying our standard rates, and the carpet and cleaning will be included in the bill for expenses."

"Yes." Parmatus sighed, and the tension drained away, dropping the flames with it and leaving him limp on the smoldering carpet. "Take whatever you need from the stones. I don't want them—only asked for them because they were hard for Donne to get."

"Deal," Evan agreed, before Badad could ask what stones.

The doorbell sounded while Badad was dragging Parmatus to his feet. Evan looked startled, but only for a minute. "Pizza," he said, and then made introductions all round. "Lily Ryan, Kevin Bradley—I call him Brad, and the pizza guy knows that, so don't look surprised. And this," he said for Brad and Lily, "is Matt Shields. Lunch, anyone?"

Chapter 6

IN THAT FROZEN INSTANT, with the sound of graceful chimes still fading on the sooty air, Evan considered pretending no one was home. Then he pulled two twenties out of his wallet. He figured he could keep the delivery guy in the outer office and give everybody a chance to regroup before they sat down with a questionable ally to cement an alliance he'd made in a place where he had no standing. If things went badly, he objected on principle to starting a war on an empty stomach. He kept his client face on while he was doing his thinking, but Lily wasn't fooled. She didn't like this case, or the mess it had made of their office—he could tell that and didn't really blame her. But him? She was laughing at him.

Shields, on the other hand, looked like he just might live another day if he could get to the pizzas on the other side of that door, which made no sense in a daemon lord. Some effect of the strongbox in the Sotheby's catalog, he guessed, and found that he really hated the guy who would strip one of his father's kind of its most basic nature and just leave it trapped that way. He liked his job, but restoring valuables to the careless rich didn't usually make him feel like a hero. Strange as it seemed, helping Matt Shields—Parmatus, if he'd heard his father correctly—did.

"This is going on your bill," he said, before he started hearing anthem rock in his head, and opened the door.

Detective Mike Jaworski, Philadelphia Major Crimes

Unit, hadn't waited on the steps outside. "Anchovies, Evan? I thought you hated anchovies. I, on the other hand, love them, so you are going to have to share."

He was taller than Evan, barrel-chested, and he'd been in the Marines. "You're uninvited" wouldn't work on him any more than it had on Matt Shields. Tempting to try, though. During the Empress case, Jaworski had turned out to be a good friend, but he was a better cop and the smoldering carpet wasn't exactly a subtle clue. He walked into the office with two pizza boxes and a bag of paper plates and napkins balanced on the palm of his left hand. His right hand rested casually on the butt of his gun. The flap on his holster was unsecured.

"Where do you want these?" He looked around for somewhere to put the boxes that wasn't an antique Hepplewhite desktop, and took in the damage. His eyes caught on Lily—kept going. Didn't look real surprised until he noticed Brad. "I thought you were on vacation."

"Couldn't stay away," Brad answered dryly. Evan winced and hoped he'd kept it on the inside. Since Lily couldn't decide whether to laugh or glare at him, he figured not.

Jaworski nodded, acknowledging that he'd heard but not necessarily that he believed the answer, and completed his examination of the perfect circle—charred wool carpet on the floor and smoke-grayed medallion on the ceiling—that had contained the fire. "Did you ever get the office in the house cleaned up? Your repair bills for this place must be astounding."

"I can pay in work," Shields interrupted. "Paint, cleanup, minor repairs. I have references if you want them." Which was just so wrong that Evan couldn't wrap his head around it. It had shaken Brad and Lily as well. His father pushed Shields down, onto one of the two guest chairs for clients, and let go of his arm with a muttered, "Son of a bitch."

Mike Jaworski was watching it all, and not missing anything. Whatever he saw brought him off high alert, though. He slipped the pizza boxes onto the remaining spindle-backed guest chair and turned for the door. "I'll get some more chairs from the waiting room," he said, ignoring the fragile antique in the corner, and added over his shoulder, "And I'll stand-down the guys outside."

"Khadijah Flint called you, didn't she?"

"Not me. She called the lieutenant. The lieutenant sent me."

Lieutenant Ellen Li played chess with his father, which had come as a surprise. He wondered if she cheated at that too.

Jaworski said, "You owe me forty bucks for the pizza."

"I guess that means it's on his bill," Shields observed. He didn't wait for an invitation but slid two pieces of anchovy onto a paper plate, picked up the first piece and folded it deftly before taking the first bite. Wherever he'd been for the past three years, they had pizza.

Jaworski came back a minute later carrying one chair from the outer office, which he sat in before helping himself. "Are you going to introduce us?" he asked brightly, and looked from Matt Shields to Evan with the unspoken question Lieutenant Ellen Li had sent him in to answer.

"I'm fine. And if you are going to eat the anchovies, you are going to pay your share. I don't put the police on my clients' bills. It gives the wrong impression."

"So far, I'm down forty, so pony up a twenty and call it even. I'm starving. And, by the way, you're not fine. You're covered in bruises and soot, and one side of your pants leg is burned to the ankle. Not a good look on you."

"Accident with a cigarette," Evan answered blandly.

In response, Mike Jaworski glanced pointedly at the perfect curve that separated crisped black carpet from untroubled blue, that followed exactly the circle defined by carved plaster and soot on the ceiling. No need to mention the absence of a cigarette in all that mess. Jaworski wouldn't have missed that. He finished his slice, wiped his hands carefully on a paper napkin, and stood up. "Dougherty is an asshole," he said, all the humor gone. "But he's not stupid."

Evan agreed with the asshole part. Sergeant Joe Dougherty swore that Brad and Lily were criminals who had brainwashed a troubled kid into becoming the innocent dupe in their nefarious schemes. The only thing that had kept him from figuring out the truth was a lack of imagination that had dogged him all through high school. Jaworski, on the other hand . . .

"I lied about sending the backup away. If you walk out with me now, we can protect you."

Shit. Without even thinking about it, Evan moved—not toward Jaworski or his father, or even Lily, who tended to be his gravity in most situations. Two steps toward the desk and he'd taken up guard duty at Matt Shields' side. Shields looked confused. Lily looked amused. And Brad looked at his watch.

"I hope I didn't make things worse for you." Jaworski raised his hands, palms out in surrender while the puzzle pieces shuffled themselves in his eyes. Still wasn't seeing the real picture, thank God, but he did not suffer Dougherty's lack of imagination. "If you turn up dead, I will hunt your killer down. The case will be solid, and we *will* go for the death penalty."

Which wouldn't matter in the least to any of the possible suspects in the room, but did, for some reason, make him feel better. Jaworski didn't wait for an answer. "I'll be around," he said, and let himself out.

"Wasn't that special." Lily wrapped an arm around his neck and used her free hand to wipe the soot from his mouth before planting a kiss. "Evan has a friend." But she didn't seem displeased.

Chapter 7

BRAD LEANED AGAINST THE DESK, watching Ellen Li's policeman offer promises of retribution he couldn't keep. Ellen trusted him not to do anything stupid, and given the provocation, he'd behaved with remarkable restraint. But it was time to end this charade. He looked at his watch. It was the middle of the night where he'd left Mai Sien Chong waiting naked for him on a silk-covered bed, so he wasn't really interested in pizza and chat. Fortunately, it looked like Jaworski was going to leave now. He might salvage something of his night after all.

"I hope I didn't make things worse for you."

There it was—a few threats the stalwart policeman couldn't act on, not against anything present, at least. If something else killed Evan, there wouldn't be enough of it left to arrest, so that was all right. Gone. Good. Now, to get rid of Parmatus—Shields, he guessed it would be, in this world.

"I need coffee," Lily decided, and vanished, returning almost before she'd gone with a carafe that didn't look like the one in their kitchen. "Need cups," she said, "couldn't carry them." Evan ran a hand across his buzzed scalp and flinched at the discomfort, but he went.

"How did you do that?" Shields asked, staring at Lily as if she'd grown a second head.

"There's this little dive on Second. Food's awful, but I like their coffee, and the stuff in the kitchen is from this morning." She shrugged like all of that should be obvious, but Matt Shields was looking at the ashen circle in the center of the ceiling. Shields wouldn't be sitting there calmly with a plate of pizza in his hand if he didn't have a way out—the crispy fried rug attested to that much—but he could leave only in one direction, if Evan was the smart boy Brad knew. Lily was moving in and out of the circle like it didn't exist.

"It's our house," Brad explained. "We own it, and everything in it, including the protections. It has no hold over us." Which wasn't entirely true. Evan's human will had opened all his traps for them, but he still had his moments. And the house itself, it turned out, created its own connections. The Princes had backed off their earliest limitations on where they could keep Evan, but the house held them here anyway, with promises of comfort it generally kept, and safety that it hadn't, really, with a volatile Evan Davis in residence. All of which were human things he'd gladly abandon for home when Evan was dead, but he'd grown to appreciate them in the now.

Evan returned with cups and sugar, no cream. None of them took it—if Shields didn't like it, too bad. But Shields took two sugars, and gladly. Brad turned down a cup. He still had hopes for the rest of the night, and some of that included sleeping. "It's getting late. I don't think we can do anything else today. Find a room or something, and we'll figure this out tomorrow."

Shields stared off into a distance that, apparently, included calculating the contents of his wallet. "Fourteen dollars, thirty-five cents," he said, "One washer, and an allen wrench. Do you know anyplace I can stay for that?"

For the first time all afternoon, Lily looked upset. "Is that before or after our retainer?"

"A temporary shortage of liquid assets," Evan explained, and added, "show them."

Shields did. Shiny. Lily always liked shiny. "I'll take this one," she said, and plucked a five-carat stone from the palm of Matt Shields' hand. "I'll have it appraised in the morning and deducted from your bill. You do own it?"

"Yeah," he answered, "until now."

"While you're at the appraiser's, see what he has to say about this one," Evan suggested, and Shields dutifully dug out the thumb-sized ruby. "We need to sell it to fund a purchase at the Grayson Donne auction at Sotheby's next week."

Lily took it and gave him her "clever boy" smile. "Give the nice client Greg's card. We can put him up at the B & B for now."

Evan reached around the desk and pulled the card from the top drawer. He gave it to Matt Shields, along with the forty dollars he'd gotten out for the pizza and dug in his wallet for a credit card. "Greg Rush runs a Bed and Breakfast a block from here, on Eighth. The address is on the card. Tell him to put your room on our account. Do you have anything else to wear with you?"

Shields shook his head. Of course not. He just wandered the city with odd change and hardware in his pocket, along with a ransom in rubies. Evan gave him the credit card. "Get some clothes," he said. "There's a Macy's on Chestnut Street, and Greg can give you a list of other places. You're an anonymous buyer for the strongbox, so you don't need to appear at the auction. Buy whatever makes you comfortable."

Brad felt comfortable in a suit hand tailored for him by Carlo Pimi in Milan, but didn't offer Shields that option. He wasn't Ariton, and Brad still didn't trust him—he had an uneasy feeling about that strongbox.

"Why didn't you come to us sooner?" he asked, and could tell from the way Evan's eyes widened before he brought his reaction under control that he'd thought of the question, certainly, but hadn't asked it for some reason. Lies, maybe.

"The box has a radius. I tried to walk away, but once I reach a certain distance—roughly ninety miles—I found myself back where I started. Yesterday, the estate agents moved the box to New York City."

Not a lie. But not the whole truth. He wouldn't work with Paimon's lord, would not allow his human offspring to bind Ariton to a host-debt, without the truth. "Can't you use a telephone?"

Brad saw the moment when he almost said "no"—

almost told the lie that would put him on the street, agreement void, all promises off. Then he slumped in his chair, defenses down for the moment.

"I felt it when he bound you, and then, for a long time, nothing. That made no sense. Why do something as dangerous as a binding spell, and then ask for nothing? After the first day, you didn't fight the binding, not either of you. I didn't trust it, and then last week I felt the terror and fury of a binding command filling this world. I knew the feelings, had them myself each time Donne sent me to perform some task for him. No more than I'd expected all along but, hey, not my Prince, not my problem. I was stuck in New York anyway.

"Then he let you go. He didn't have to do it. You didn't trick or threaten him. He had to know you were likely to kill him, but he set you free. And you let him live. It still didn't make sense, and I didn't know if your agency would perform a service for a lord of Paimon, neither Ariton nor an ally. But I thought, finally, there was someone in this universe I might trust with my story. Then, I walked into this—" he gestured at the smoky circle. "So maybe I've made my worst mistake since that bastard trapped me here. But I've got nowhere else to go."

"You're lucky Evan had the desk today." Brad conceded very little, unwilling to offer consolation to a creature not of his own Prince and a bit put off by the whole case. Shields should have been raging at his own captivity, haughty in need and powerful in his resistance. A daemon lord was, of all things, proud. Parmatus—Matt Shields—disgusted him a little. But Evan was determined, and Lily wanted the ruby. Paimon would owe Ariton a host-debt if they pulled this off, which would raise his own status with his Prince. All in all, it could be worse.

"Go—rest, shop, whatever." He waved a hand in the general direction of the door to the outer office and the street. "There's nothing more we can do today, and I have an appointment elsewhere."

He didn't wait to see what happened next. Mai Sien had fallen asleep, but she was still naked, and the sheets were almost as perfect as her skin.

Chapter 8

"**D**ID YOU GET THE NETSUKE?" Evan was alone with Lily, Jaworski gone to report to Ellen Li, which might be trouble later but not tonight, he thought. Matt Shields had wandered off to find Greg Rush's B&B and a fresh set of underwear, and Brad—Evan skittered away from that thought.

He didn't think she had room even for something as small as the little carved lion in those clothes, though he'd be happy to help her look and made the offer. Lily went with tradition for breaking and entering. She wore a sleek black warm-up jacket and snug black pants though she could move in and out of any vault undetected. The clothes suited her, matched the black of her hair that she wore pinned up for a little B&E, so the blue of her eyes hit him like an electric shock.

"You're not going to find it there." She slapped his hands away from the zipper on her jacket and plucked a stick out of her hair. He'd been right about the clothes. Lily had threaded the carving onto the stick by the holes bored into it for the sash strings. She set it on the desk to free both hands and shook out her hair.

Oh, God, he loved her hair, leaned in to smell it and touch—

They'd lost the sun, so the office lay in cool shadows. Nothing lurking there but the spiraling ash that used to be a wool carpet.

"You really made a mess here."

Lily pulled away, just a movement of her neck that kept her body close enough to share heat, and swung her hair back into order, Ariton fire sparking her eyes. She cut a disapproving glance at the ceiling, her mouth pursed like a kiss. "It's coming out of your share."

"It always does." *Matt Shields can fix it,* he thought, *he even has references.* But he didn't say it, didn't want to spoil the teasing mood she'd set. To reward him, she flicked a spot of nonexistent dust off the jacket she wore, drawing his attention to the curve of her shoulder, the vee where the zipper on her jacket had slid down, not enough to expose her breasts, which was a shame. He reached out, carefully, and gave the zipper a nudge.

"Not here," she said, and grabbed him by the tie. "Bring the rubies." Then she was leading him by a Windsor-knotted leash through the house, past the study. The service had cleaned up the worst of the mess, tight-lipped and wearing silver crosses around their necks, but they hadn't had time for repairs since . . . another thought he skittered away from. Lily had done that, and his father, trying to kill him. They'd changed their minds about the killing part, but not before he was unconscious. He'd imprisoned his father with a word, though, and was lucky to be alive after that. He couldn't do worse and didn't plan to do it again, so he figured he was safe for now. And Lily—just thinking about her made him sweat. Hell of a family.

Through the open living room with its vaulted ceiling and the sofa that looked like Jackson Pollock had used it for a drop cloth. She didn't turn for the floating staircase to the bedrooms at the front of the house, but slid the doors open to the garden, where the late afternoon sun cast yellow light against the brick of the garden wall. In the back corner a fountain trickled with a sound like jewels falling into his palm.

"I want them on my skin, like rain," she said, and grinned at him, hungry.

"On your skin, he agreed, and parted the zipper, ran his hands up under her breasts and pushed the jacket away, let it fall. She didn't wear anything under it, and he scooped her up, buried his bruised face in her breasts. She growled low in her throat when his mouth followed his hands and he would have swallowed her whole, but she pulled away, gasping, "Skin, skin." Then the tight black pants were gone and she was pulling him down, her dark hair spread in a pool among the daylilies they crushed with their bodies. He couldn't get out of his clothes fast enough, didn't have the knack of sending them off somewhere in the void the way Lily did when they become inconvenient. But that was okay. Experience told him he'd do anything she wanted: wherever, whenever, however—any ever she chose. But if he could do it without exposing his backside to the neighbors' scrutiny, that would be good too.

He'd slipped the ruby into his suit pocket and he drew it out now before tossing the jacket into the azalea bushes, held the jewel to the light.

And there it was—the reason she'd dragged him into the garden—the ruby caught the sun and fire like a daemon's soul flashed at its heart. Lily tilted her head to follow the fire in the ruby. "Daemon's blood," she said, and shivered, though the day was warm and full of the scent of daylilies and the rich loamy smell of earth.

"Beautiful," he agreed. He wasn't looking at the ruby, so he saw the moment when secrets lowered her lashes. More than beauty, then, but he hadn't been talking about the damned stone anyway. He didn't, when it came down to it, find anything beautiful in the price of a daemon lord's freedom. Not lately. Couldn't help imagining some pervy old bastard buying pieces of Lily's soul with bits of stone. Grayson Donne was lucky he was dead.

"On my skin," she ordered him, and he didn't tease, because the need in her eyes was more than sex and crossed with sorrow. She was wearing a few scraps of lace—the bra hadn't been there a minute ago, but she thought he liked that sort of thing and, yeah, he did. The lace was white, and he set the ruby over her heart, stark as a wound above the pure snow of the lace.

Then it seemed to melt into her flesh, welling lambent blood with each beat of her pulse, flowing with the light.

His imagination. Had to be, product of a guilty conscience. Evan tried to make it casual, but his fingers trembled when he brushed the stone away. Let her think he trembled for her. He did. Just—

He kissed her where the ruby had lain—kiss it and make it better—red lips on white flesh. He felt the beating of her heart in his kiss, felt it when the rhythm became more urgent.

"Beautiful," she sighed, and he didn't mind the little tug of pain when her fingers carded through the remains of his hair, skimming the cuts and bumps that hadn't healed yet. Her eyes, when he tore himself away from her breast, glittered with Ariton's blue fire.

"You're still dressed." She disapproved, and he didn't care when buttons went flying everywhere. Not like it was the first time—his tailor had threatened to fit his shirts with Velcro. Out of it; the stupid tie was too complicated, so he left it, draped over one shoulder and she was laughing, tugging at his belt, his zipper, and the lacy bits were gone— he'd really have to learn that trick.

He was usually good at making decisions, but for a moment she stymied him—lips, breast, belly? Behind her knee? Top of her hip? Circling the tastiest bits because all her bits deserved his attention.

"All that appreciation is flattering," she said, "but this isn't a museum," and tugged his mouth down in a kiss that examined his tonsils and gave him a clean bill of health on his wisdom teeth.

"Ung," he answered when they broke for air. He still had too many clothes on and he fought his suit pants, glad for once that he wasn't wearing jeans. Denim was a bitch to get out of in a hurry. "Want your tits," he said, and winced at his own utter failure at subtlety, but he wasn't feeling subtle and her laughter jiggled the objects of his attention in a way that kept his brain so far out of the loop that he couldn't have coughed up his address at the moment, though he was becoming an expert at Lily's geography.

She wrapped a leg around the small of his back, and—

"Evan? Evan!" The gate didn't creak, so it gave them no warning. The voice in his garden sent him diving to cover Lily, which he was sort of doing to start with, and she didn't need his protection anyway. Then his brain kicked into gear, and he recognized the voice. God, no. Harry.

"Nobody answered at the front. Are you here?"

Professor Harry Li. Evan had nightmares, in grad school, of showing up naked when he had to present an assignment. Didn't expect grad school to show up in his garden, though he should have expected Harry. He was married to Lieutenant Ellen Li of Major Crimes, who'd sent Mike Jaworski in with the pizzas.

"Go home, Harry!"

"Evan. There you are." Footsteps on the brick patio, coming closer.

"Stay there!"

Lily bit him, just below the collarbone, sank her sharp whites in, to smother her laughter. He twitched before settling into the little pain, dislodging his tie, which fell across her nose. If she'd been human, she would have choked to death on that muffled snort. She didn't conjure up any clothes, though, not even those scraps of lace.

"Ellen sent me," Harry admitted. "She was worried about you."

"I'm fine, Harry."

"Mike Jaworski disagrees."

"Didn't he tell you that Brad was home?" And then he figured it—Mike was outside the gate, probably waiting in the car. "Tell Mike to go home too."

Lily had that dangerous, gleeful look in her eyes. Modesty was a foreign concept, but embarrassing Evan, she had a PhD in that. She let go of the hold she'd had on him with her teeth and sat up, laughing out loud. He figured Harry had a prime view of her breasts between the low azaleas. "Go home or get naked, Harry," she told him, half a pout, all challenge. "You are spoiling my afternoon."

Harry coughed into his hand, doing an awful job of pretending not to laugh. By the end of this day, Evan wouldn't have a shred of dignity left.

"I think I'll go home, thank you, Lily. And Evan, I'll tell Ellen that I left you in good hands."

Could it get any worse? . . . Mike. In the car.

"Just don't tell Jaworski."

"I'm afraid I can't promise that. But I will keep him out of the garden. You just go back to whatever you were doing . . ."

Footsteps, then, going back the way Harry had come. Evan rolled onto the bed of daylilies and dirt beside Lily, staring up into a cloudless sky deepening to indigo with pink around the edges. He'd get the mood back any minute now. But the mosquitoes were coming out—the garden was not going to happen.

"Evan—" Lily, lips to his ear, a question in her breath. He was definitely getting the mood back. "What did you do with the ruby?"

Jesus. He'd brushed it from her skin, just wanting the image of blood gone, and hadn't even noticed where it had fallen. It was a dark stone, on dark ground, and they'd lost the light.

Chapter 9

HALF AN HOUR AGO, BRAD HAD BEEN finishing dinner over a game of chess set up on a coffee table in a four-star suite looking out over the China Sea. He'd traded a last speed game for a fresh suit out of his own closet. The speed game was never the way to go with Mai Sien Chong. Now he sat in his tapestried wing chair, assessing his partners and the lingering damage to the private study at the center of the house on Spruce Street. The wreckage was gone but there were still gaps in the furniture.

Lily sat curled in the corner of the wine-colored leather sofa and Evan perched sideways on the camel saddle in the corner, although the executive desk chair and a second wing-back sat empty. It set him below them, where he belonged, but gave him a view of the whole room, including the door. He looked about how you'd expect given the state of their study. His bruises had turned yellow—Brad didn't regret it, not the bruises or the empty space where the desk used to stand. He did miss the desk, though.

Evan could fix the bruises, but wouldn't, for reasons he would babble at length if Brad looked like he might listen. Under the bruises, though, he looked pale and a little shaky. He balanced his elbows on his knees, his chin propped on his fisted hands, hiding something. Black dirt grimed his fingernails and the skin of his knuckles. Lily wasn't showing anything, which warned Brad more than a flame-throwing tantrum that something was up. But she wasn't worried. So.

"Where is our Mr. Shields this morning?"

"Taking in the sights," Evan dropped his hands between his knees. His upward glance would have hidden his eyes behind a tumble of unruly hair last week. He hadn't quite internalized its absence and was showing a lot more than he knew. "He called this morning, asked if we needed him. Lily told him 'no.' He said he'd check in this afternoon."

Not Matt Shields, then. Brad took that in, moved on. "I called Bill about appraising the ruby. Didn't tell him much, just that it's big. He can see us this morning."

He wouldn't have thought it possible, but Evan paled even more. The last time he'd seen his son that color, he'd been unconscious and bleeding all over the floor. This time, he sat up, looked Brad straight in the eye, and took a deep breath. This was going to be bad—

"What time?" Lily pulled a velvet gem bag from between her breasts and held it up so that Evan could see it.

"How long have you had it?" Air pressure in the room was rising, a sheet of paper abandoned in a corner of a bookcase lifted, fell back.

"Evan—" Brad couldn't decide whether to calm him down or watch him blow for the entertainment value. Lily went for entertainment.

"Since last night. We find things. That's what Ariton does. It's why you humans bind us here."

"That was never why—"

Or maybe it had been. He'd gone looking for a father and found Brad, which merited more thought.

But Lily was going somewhere else with it. "That's why we're in this business instead of trading stocks or assassinating foreign dignitaries for multinational corporations. Because we're good at it." She tossed Evan the bag with the ruby in it, and he fumbled, caught it in grimed hands.

"And you didn't think I might want to *know*?"

"That we find things? Check the ad in the phone book."

"That you had it. "

"You didn't ask."

Brad thought there might be an attempt at conciliation in her tone, but Evan didn't hear it.

"I don't ask." He surged to his feet like somebody'd run an electric shock through his butt. "Asking for something nearly got me killed, so I don't ask for a fucking thing."

It could've happened, Brad figured. He hadn't exactly asked politely, and Lily'd come damn close to ending the experiment of Evan less than two weeks ago. He wouldn't have stopped her, but when it came to it, they both chose not. Near thing, though, so Evan knew the difference between a simple request and a binding command. Not much difference to a daemon lord, really, between "pass the butter" and "let these humans chain you to a table in a tiny box of a room." Could that daemon lord say, "No?" That made a difference. Which wasn't exactly true. He'd rather pass the butter if those were his choices. Close enough, though, and Evan knew it, had been demanding things of them pretty much since they'd met him.

But Evan never let them know what he was really arguing about—he was throwing his cuts and bruises out there to deflect them from something deeper he thought he was hiding.

Evan dropped the gem bag on Lily's lap and headed for the door. "I have work to do."

"It was a joke," Lily said.

Not about life or death, then. Brad understood hurt pride better anyway. "Where are you going?"

"Out. I need to get some air." Between one step and another he was gone.

"Well," Lily said, "you can't say he's boring."

Chapter 10

HE HAD MOST OF THE SOURCES he needed in reproduction in his own library, but that wouldn't have solved Evan's first problem, which was to get away from the house, away from Lily, who hadn't bothered to tell him she'd found the damned ruby. When his own thorough hands-and-knees search had turned up nothing but bruised flower petals and bent stems he'd figured they were screwed. The rational part of his brain told him he should be grateful she found it. The irrational part was still ringing from the hit it had taken from the edge of a flat-screen computer monitor and not up to a daemon lord's sense of humor. So he left, heading for the place that had become a second home while he'd been finishing up his degree at Penn.

Henry Charles Lea's personal library of medieval and early modern books and papers had become a part of the University of Pennsylvania some time in the twenties. For most collections, that would have meant the books, but for the Lea Library, it meant the whole deal—books and papers, and also the dark wood paneling from the walls and the library cases that held the books, the rolling ladders, and the steep spiral staircase that gave access to a narrow iron balcony on a mezzanine level of more books in the high-ceilinged room. Walking into the collection from the modern library stacks that surrounded it always dropped him a century into the past. The books, more centuries than that. Even for a library that specialized in magic and witchcraft, though, most people used the door. So, appearing out of the air in the middle of a library dedicated in good part to magic and witchcraft probably wasn't the smartest thing he'd ever done. He was mad enough not to care until the girl with the long dark hair and the short jeans skirt looked up from her book with a suppressed gasp.

"I didn't hear you come in." She twitched her nose to nudge her glasses up and brushed at her book apologetically, as if she'd been caught scattering crumbs rather than reading.

"I'm sorry. I didn't mean to startle you."

"Not your fault. Happens all the time when I'm working." Evan thought her ears must have popped from the disturbance in air pressure but she didn't seem to connect that with him.

She wasn't on staff—they all knew him and would have noticed something like an appearance without benefit of the door. In fact, she didn't look like she belonged here at all—too young to be an independent researcher, and he didn't think any of the first summer session classes called for the use of the collection, even if there'd been time to get into it, which there hadn't. "Were you looking for something?" she asked helpfully when he didn't comment.

He remembered the grime on his hands, then, from digging in the stupid garden. "The men's room, actually." He plastered a look of lost innocence on his face. "I took a wrong turn."

"Understandable. It's that way, I think." She pointed in the general direction of the door, which wouldn't have helped if he had been lost. He wasn't, and found his way easily enough, cleaned up carefully before he headed back to the books.

She was gone, and he took a look at the book she'd left on the mahogany reading table. *Treatise on the Names of the Angels, and Their Various Homes in the Heavenly Spheres*. He knew that one. Fifteenth century, and closer than most to the truth as he knew it. Close enough to make him nervous. Summoning spells made up the back third of the book and he determined to check with Maggie in Collections to find out who she was and how she'd gotten access to the collection.

He took the spiral staircase to the mezzanine and found the book he wanted quickly enough. Magical objects. The *Key of Solomon* talked about binding demons to chains of fire, a metaphor for hell, he'd thought, until Joe Dougherty had handcuffed Brad to a table in the interview room at Major Crimes. The cuffs had left burns he didn't want to think about, so he slipped the picture of the strongbox from his breast pocket and spread it on the table. Three iron bands wrapped the box lengthwise and three across its width, with the lock worked into a sigil on the center band. Agrippa's *Occult Philosophy* noted that the number three added power to a binding spell—thread wrapped three times, or in this case, iron bands. The pages were old under his fingers. Not original by any means—those were locked away—but still, a hundred years of researchers had turned these pages. The book smelled comfortingly of dust and age.

Iron related to fire, and would have been used to both draw and block the escape of a creature that the conjurer thought had come from hell. He didn't know that it had any effect in particular on daemons without the intent and the words of the spell, though. Sure didn't stop Brad from driving the BMW, though he might make a case that the transformation from iron to steel robbed the metal of its magical properties.

None of the references he checked said anything particular about boxes, though oak was considered magical by the druids. He'd have better luck with the sigils at home— download the photo from the online catalog, blow it up, and compare the imprints to his growing collection of pentacles and other signs spanning a millennium or more. Modern conjurers had an advantage over their ancient brethren—they googled their spells when they wanted to reach into another world. But Evan would bet his share of the agency that Grayson Donne hadn't pulled his spells off the Internet.

And, he'd bet that Donne had used a fire spell. Iron was the fire metal, and rubies were its stone. Definitely a fire spell. Why was a given: power. But how long had Donne held a daemon lord his prisoner? He kept bumping into the same thought there: Matt Shields had a lot of rubies.

His temper had cooled before he ever sat down at the mahogany reading table. Nothing but momentum kept him away from home, and he had work to do. He owed Lily an apology, too. Of sorts. If he ever wanted to sleep with her again. It made him uncomfortable to realize that his temper came from the daemon side of the family, but at least Lily understood it. Expected it. But she'd expect an apology too. Daemons had strict rules of courtesy.

Chapter 11

JEWELERS' ROW HUDDLED ON A NARROW street between Walnut and Chestnut, about two blocks from the agency as the daemon walks on a bright morning at the tail end of spring. Brad enjoyed the sunshine, already warm enough for summer, beating on his shoulders. They passed Washington Square, where the trees had fulfilled the hazy promise of spring, settling into rich greens against a sky so sharp a blue it left nicks in even a daemon's soul. Beside him, Lily tucked her hand into the crook of his arm.

"It's not home," she said, and grinned up at the sun. "But it could definitely be worse."

It had been worse, for both of them, but agreement might tempt fate. He didn't trust this case. Wasn't sure he trusted Paimon, and certainly didn't trust Matt Shields' motives. Daemon lords never told their whole truth. He just hoped Shields' secrets didn't bite them in the ass. Or something. He didn't have all the specifics of ass-biting, except that he'd kind of liked it when Mai Sien Chong did it, but figured Matt Shields might want a bigger chunk, without dinner first.

They passed into the shadows when they turned the corner onto Sansom Street. Newer shops at street level shouldered narrow storefronts crammed into old brownstones, half a flight up, half down, a shop in each direction. Hundreds of shops crammed onto one narrow block and spilled over at the cross streets. Over his head neon diamonds wider than the span of his arms hung over half the storefronts. The other half, wholesalers and traders and appraisers, all the business of a market in gems that fueled the glittering retail stores, hid its less public face behind smudged and grated windows.

Brad stopped at a brownstone halfway down the block and followed Lily up a half-flight to a door with no handle next to an empty display window with "Appraisers, Buyers, Sellers, Family-owned since 1851" printed in gold leaf on old glass.

The receptionist greeted them from behind bulletproof glass and pressed a button under her desk to allow them entry into a narrow passageway where Bill Sanders waited with a smile and an outstretched hand. He was short and balding, with a rumpled shirt and glasses with special lenses propped on top of his head. Brad had worked with him before, so he wasn't surprised by the callused grip. Bill knew gems from the mine to the ring finger.

Lily worked with him more often and gave him a kiss on the cheek. She had convinced him she was European—"not from here"—with a wave that could have meant anywhere, including the second celestial sphere, he supposed, but Bill had settled on France, and complimented her American accent. She was the agency's expert in colored stones and took the lead, which suited Bill just fine.

"We have two today," she told him when they had settled across a narrow gray counter with a microscope and caliper on it. "We are agenting the better one for our client. We've accepted the smaller one as partial payment for the sale and we need to value it for his bill before I have it set."

"So you're not selling it?"

Lily handed him the five-carat ruby with a shake of her head. "I'm keeping it, for a necklace." She never wore rings. Brad had never asked her why, and didn't intend to do it now.

"Beautiful stone." Bill held the ruby up to the light. "And this is the smaller one?"

"It probably won't cover the commission on the whole contract," Brad answered.

Bill nodded, taking it in, but not really, Brad knew. However well they prepared him, he wouldn't be ready.

"Provenance?" he asked, and pursed his lips in a silent whistle, looked at it through a loupe and then under the microscope. "The condition isn't perfect, some minor abrasions. And it's a cushion cut. That cut went out of fashion more than a hundred years ago. It's back, by the way, which increases its value, but this is not a new stone. A lot of the older stones were recut into ovals or rounds, so a stone this size in its original cut is exceedingly rare. If we had the provenance, we could certify when and where it was mined, maybe even who cut it, and who he cut it for. All those things add to the value."

Matt Shields had said he had the original documentation for Grayson Donne's transfer of the gem as payment for tasks performed, but he'd been less forthcoming about what that documentation showed. That was one more mystery Brad wanted answered before he went much further. "He has proof of ownership," he said, "but the documentation we've seen is contemporary, a bequest of sorts."

Bill nodded. "I should send this to the lab," he said. "They can look for signs of heat treatment and give us a definitive report, but I'd guess you are looking at about $50,000 for this stone, as is. An interesting history might bring four times that much at auction. You may owe your client a refund."

Brad just smiled at that. Lily drew the second ruby from the velvet bag.

Chapter 12

THE HOUSE WAS EMPTY, except for the restoration service, who had set up their ladders in the circle of charred carpet. The woman in charge wore a functional navy business suit, flat shoes, and a pentacle on a chain around her neck. She had chin-length red hair, freckles scattered lightly across her nose, and eyes almost the color of Ariton's fire. Not a daemon, though. He could tell the difference by the prickle of his skin now, didn't need to be trussed up like a lamb to the slaughter and thrust screaming into the second celestial sphere to figure it out. Fortunately, he'd come through the door this time.

She shot him a calculating glance and wrapped her hand around the pentacle she wore around her neck. "Claire Murphy," she said, and called the workmen down from their ladders. "Break. Half hour for lunch." When the men had filed out, she turned back to Evan.

"I sent the day-jobbers home with full pay. It's on your bill." She was nervous, and maybe he understood that, but not why she was angry. "We'll clean it, but we won't fix it, so don't try to use it."

"I didn't know it was broken. What's 'it,' by the way? And how many people who aren't working today did you just put on my payroll?"

"Two." She answered the last question first. "If that isn't satisfactory, we can pack up and be out of here in ten minutes."

Evan considered leaving and coming in again, but he'd

already used up his do overs for the month. He couldn't figure out why she was pointing all that righteous indignation in his direction anyway.

"Crack in the third arm of the pentagram." She gestured at a spot the workers had already cleaned. "Don't use it again. Next time it won't hold. You'll wind up dead, and I'll just have to clean the grease off your ceiling."

He didn't see the crack but took her word for its existence. Matt Shields was just the most recent of half a dozen cases that could have damaged the plaster one way or another. But they'd had the original work done by two separate contractors so that neither knew the whole design hidden in the scrollwork. Claire Murphy shouldn't have noticed it either. Except, he did have a perfect circle burned into the carpet. And another perfect circle where the pentagram in the ceiling had contained even the smoke from the blaze.

She was wearing a pentacle. Sigh.

"It's not what you think."

She didn't answer that, just looked up at the ceiling.

He didn't talk about agency business outside the agency. Ever. But she'd already drawn her conclusions. Maybe he could turn the argument—or add some damage to obscure the pattern and start over with a new restoration service. He could find somebody in New York, but he wasn't sure the people he needed didn't have some restorers' graffito tag to warn each other off the strange-o clients.

"It has two uses. You could summon something, if you were that stupid." He'd done that, once, sort of. Had to, and on balance it could have worked out worse than it did. But it wasn't his gig. "Sometimes, it's just protection—it can stop a misunderstanding from turning into a funeral."

She stared up at the ceiling some more, processing that. "Somebody named Matt Shields left a message. Asked if you wanted him to fix the bell." She nodded once, like that answered the question of the misunderstanding, which it did, but she shouldn't have known that. "I think you'd better get hold of him and tell him 'no.' The tourists like it cracked."

Evan closed his eyes and counted to ten. When he opened

them again, she was looking at him, stunned. "You're not just some weirdo freak, are you? You're the real deal."

"Not mutually exclusive categories," he said, but he wasn't stupid enough to give her an answer.

She jumped when the door opened.

Not Lily. A split second of gratitude for that. Matt Shields wasn't much lower on the "trouble" scale, though. He was wearing new jeans, a clean tee, and a fresh flannel shirt. Same boots. Smelled better. Stack of comics tucked close under one arm with B.P.R.D. , "Bureau of Paranormal Research and Defense," on the top. Evan stifled a snort he'd rather not explain to Claire Murphy. Given the option—and Matt Shields had a pile of rubies in his pocket that gave him plenty of options—daemon lords of the second celestial sphere didn't usually dress like lumberjacks or collect comics in which superhero demons saved the world.

Shields tilted his head back to examine the ceiling. "You need some fill over there," he said, and pulled his free hand out of its pocket to point at the third arm of the pentagram. "If you've got some plaster mixed, I can take care of it."

Claire Murphy must have recognized the voice from the phone message; she beat Evan to the question he wouldn't have asked in her presence—"Did you fix the bell?"

Raised eyebrows. Shields was trying to figure where she fit. Evan held up his hands, stop or surrender, he wasn't sure himself which, but his head was starting to hurt and this time it had nothing to do with a computer monitor to his temple. "I just got here," he said, "She was working on the ceiling when the call came in."

A little shrug, then. "Too many people around," he said, "and they seemed to like it that way. It's not like you can ring it, where they've got it."

Evan pointed his index finger at his temple and twirled it, but Claire Murphy wasn't buying that explanation. She still might bolt, but for the moment she looked sort of like she had a handful of fireworks in full bloom—caught between terror and fascination.

"I could help you with this," Shields said, "And then, maybe—"

"Yo!" Evan suddenly had the full attention of the room. "Let the lady do her work. You're paying her; that's all the help she needs. You're going to get me sued for sexual harassment here!" He pointed with his thumbs in the general vicinity of his shoulders, hoping Claire Murphy thought he was gesturing about her imaginary lawsuit when he really wanted Matt Shields to remember what happened when daemons and humans hooked up. Lily never kept the same actual body long enough to get pregnant and he figured his father had worked out his own solutions before he... didn't want to go there, but he was sure his father wouldn't risk another Evan. But Matt Shields had been living in a freaking box.

Whatever message he got, it took him off the hunt. "Are you hungry? I'm starving. There must be lunch around here somewhere." A few blocks over, the bell of St. Peter's Church rang out the time—noon. And yeah, Evan was hungry. But Matt Shields was a daemon lord of Paimon, and Evan owed his allegiance to Ariton.

"You're my client, not my friend. I can give you a list—"

Claire Murphy's expression closed right up, but Shields read him just fine, turned his head so only Evan could see the amber fire in his eyes. "Allies, though. Right?" he said, all business. "That's the contract."

Evan knew what it meant to be the only one of his kind in the universe, knew what that isolation must feel like to a daemon lord who, in his natural home, joined with hundreds of his host-cousins to become the single mind of his Prince. Lily and Brad had each other, and they could go home briefly whenever they wanted, permanently if they wanted it badly enough to kill him for it. They had their own connections in this world as well. But Matt Shields had lived in a box. The church bell rang again. "Box," it rang in his head, "Box."

He figured they both could use a friend. They had a contract, after all. "How about a cheese steak?"

"Cheese on a steak?"

He really had been living in a box. "Not that kind of

steak." Evan took the books and put them on the desk—a copy of *The Goon* slipped out, and he wondered again what kind of life Matt Shields had built for himself in the shadow of the thing that bound him to this world. Not one with cheese steaks in it, apparently.

"It's a sandwich," he said, "You'll love it," and nudged him toward the door before the daemon lord could object in a way that would be hard to explain to Claire Murphy. "It's just a few blocks. We can walk."

"Okay, but then I have to get back to Greg's. I promised to tighten up some loose doorknobs, fix a leaky faucet. Gotta pay for my books!"

Bemused, Claire Murphy stopped them at the door. At least she wasn't angry anymore. "Misunderstanding?" she asked.

Evan didn't answer, just swept a hand over his forehead, pushing hair that didn't exist anymore out of his eyes while he tried to figure out how to get Matt Shields out of there without any more questions. It seemed to be all the answer she needed.

"We'll take care of the break in the plaster." She studied him for a minute, frowning slightly. "You're not what I expected. I thought a Magus would be, you know, scarier?"

"I'm not a Magus," he objected, but Matt Shields laughed at him.

"He is," Shields said, but not to Evan. "He just doesn't realize it. But you're wrong about the scary. He's that too."

Claire Murphy gave him another close look. "He doesn't realize that either, does he?" Again, not talking to him.

"Nope," Shields confirmed, though how he'd come to such a sweeping conclusion on just one—okay, memorable, and maybe scary—meeting. So, not a fruitful line of objection.

Evan wanted to say, "Hey, you're conspiring with a daemon here—I'm the human!" but he kept his mouth shut. It was only partly true, and he didn't want to freak her out again. Not while she still had work to do on his ceiling. So he fell into the banter with all the good grace he could manage. "I'm not. Really, I'm not."

"Yes, you are." Both of them. Together. For a guy who'd been living in a box, Matt Shields seemed more human than Brad or Lily sometimes.

"A magus would already have his cheese steak," Evan pointed out.

"I can take a hint." Claire Murphy turned back to his ceiling, letting him off the hook for now. Evan nudged Matt Shields toward the door before they decided to pick up where they left off. "Come on, Hellboy. Let's get out of here." Shields laughed, but he moved.

Chapter 13

LILY SET THE SECOND RUBY ON A VELVET cloth. "We are looking for a private sale for our client," she said, and added, "as quickly as possible. He has his eyes on a new home."

"Does your client have provenance on this one?" Sanders didn't touch the stone.

Lily leaned forward, elbows on the counter, and gave him a conspiratorial smile. "If he does, he isn't sharing it," she said.

Brad figured her efforts were wasted this time. Sanders couldn't take his eyes off the ruby. "I'm not qualified. You'll need a good lab report and a well-advertised auction. If it's a known jewel, it could be priceless, but that doesn't mean you can sell it fast or for what it's worth. It may not move at all."

The stone would move; it was just a question of when. In the meantime, they might have to buy the damned strongbox themselves. They could write a check for the appraised value out of the agency accounts, but if there were buyers out there who knew about Matt Shields, appraised value might mean nothing at all. So Brad ran the agency's assets in his head, calculating how much they could liquidate on short notice. Evan must have run the same numbers this morning, without the hope of recouping the loss.

"Can you at least size the stone for me?" Lily asked with a smile that Brad knew better than to trust on any day. "And confirm that it isn't manufactured?"

She nudged it with one well-manicured index finger, no color on the nail, just a finish like a pearl that set off the deep red of the ruby. "I need to know whether the stone is worth the trouble or if we're looking at a con," she said, with "help me" in her voice.

It was an out—all Sanders needed. He snapped on a pair of latex gloves and took up the calipers in one hand and the stone in the other. A fake had never been in question. Man-made? Maybe. But some stones had a life of their own. Saunders measured, punched the numbers into a calculator, added a factor for hardness and density, and scrawled the answer on a slip of paper that he pushed across the counter.

"A bit over 85 carats. The value per carat increases with the size of the stone, and its cut and clarity, of course. The last significant ruby sold for about $200,000 per carat. That was 17 carats, so your stone should be worth quite a bit more per carat, but only the sale will tell you how much more. Buyers always weigh the rarity of the gem, including its history, with the amount they are willing to pay for a stone of any size."

He slipped a loupe over one eye and looked into the stone. Silence for a moment while he studied the gem. When he looked up, the color in his face was shifting alarmingly from pink to gray. "You don't have a good stone." He set the ruby carefully on the velvet bag on the counter. "You may have one of the great missing jewels of history."

Sanders went to a battered filing cabinet in the back of the room. From the top drawer he pulled out a journal, old by the look of it, and leafed backward through the pages. Then he pulled open a draw overstuffed with dusty folders full of crumbling pages. "We've been putting this stuff on the computer, but it hasn't been a priority." A minute more of shuffling through the folders, and he found the one he wanted, drew it out and brought it back with him, turning the yellowed pages as he maneuvered the cramped space.

When he found what he wanted, a page with acid burn that deepened at the edges, he set it on the counter. In the top right corner of the page was a set of measurements and a description of the cut, the same description Sanders had just measured for Matt Shields' ruby. At the center of the page, a brief paragraph described the history of a lost gem.

"There's a published index of lost diamonds," Sanders explained. "For colored stones we keep our own journal. Some of these jewels may never have existed outside of a travelers' legend, but this one has real history. It originated in the treasury of a prince of Kashmir and made its way to France via the Silk Road. In 1356, a broker sold it to an anonymous buyer, listed only as 'Donne de Lyon.' At roughly the same time, the Black Plague broke out in a nearby village. Wiped out everybody and set off a wave of witch trials in the surrounding province." The story left no doubt about the identity of the stone, or of Grayson Donne, for that matter. But Brad didn't like the way the math worked out. The *Black Plague?*

Sanders' voice was tight with excitement. "Assuming, just for argument's sake—and I am giving no opinion on the possibility—that your client could prove this is the lost Lyon ruby? It's priceless. A sale to maximize your value will take time, but if you need a fast sale, the firm that sold the ruby back in 1356 is still in business. As of 1983, they were interested in reacquiring the jewel. The standing offer then was five million dollars, but that was 1983 dollars. If you can give me a few hours, I'll find out if they're still interested. They'll need evidence, of course, but they'll send someone of their own to examine the stone."

"What do you need?" Lily asked.

"Photos." He reached for a digital camera on a shelf behind him and stood up, snapped, snapped again. "Turn it, please?" And Lily did, knowing the poses. Sometimes she actually bought the baubles she collected.

While she worked, Brad thought about Sanders' story. How long had Matt Shields lived in that box? And why hadn't he destroyed it and gone home a long time ago?

Chapter 14

"THIS IS SOUTH STREET," EVAN SAID. When he was a kid he used to come down here at night on the El for a slice of pizza or a cheese steak or just to hang out at the comic book shop on the corner, losing himself in a crowd that didn't know who he was and didn't think much past the next drink, which had been fine by Evan. Nobody had looked at him like he was a freak here. Or, not more of a freak than the rest of the skinheads and skaters and day-trippers, just part of the entertainment, now move along—

Daylight didn't do it justice. At noon on a weekday the street was still asleep; sidewalks empty, cars off somewhere else. Without the streetlights and marquees pushing back the darkness, the traffic and the gawkers to hide behind, the shops that crowded the pavement looked run down and kind of sad.

"I don't come here much, except for lunch, but you might want to try it after dark. Friday's the big night, but there's always a crowd in the summer."

"Vampires or zombies?" Shields asked, mock serious, and Evan thought about those books they'd left behind on the desk. "Zombies," he said, and laughed. "Definitely zombies."

They were heading east past Garland of Letters, where they'd been selling fairly harmless kitchen magic, crystals, and new age music for thirty years or more—longer than he'd been alive—and he figured somebody in there must take it seriously or they wouldn't have stayed in business. He avoided the magic thing as much as he could, had gotten over thinking of the daemon side of his nature that way and didn't need props anyway. When the job required it, he did his business farther up the street at Harry's, where the tourists never went.

The street had all its usual smells—exhaust and exhalations from the sewers and a whiff of urine strongest when they crossed an alley. Incense when they passed Garland, but mostly food—cheese steaks and pizza and fries, barbecued ribs and burgers. Greek when they passed South Street Souvlaki, and he almost turned in then, but kept on going because a steak at Jim's was a rite of passage.

Matt Shields didn't seem to mind it. He ambled along, checking out the windows, taking in the outrageous with the just plain shabby. "I like her," he said, and Evan had to run that one back a minute to figure out who he meant. Claire Murphy.

"Just keep that thought in your pants, or you'll be babysitting your half-breed monsters for the next hundred years," Evan pointed out. The shop windows were full of wrought iron crosses and stone gargoyles, and he wondered about that. Figured he ought to be glad he looked human at least but couldn't quite work himself up to a "thank you" for it.

"They wouldn't be monsters if they were mine." Matt Shields sounded halfway serious, which scared the bejesus out of Evan.

"You might want to ask my father about that." And that was a conversation he never wanted to hear. Couldn't imagine Matt Shields initiating it either, so they were all probably safe, at least from the birds-and-the-bees talk. He kept walking. "The auction is in three days. You'll be free to go home."

"Yeah." Matt Shields grinned at that. "She liked you best anyway," but that was just trash talk, and where he'd learned that easy give and take was a big hole in his story. He stopped, stared past a pair of open iron gates to the shop window beyond. "Is that a condom shop?"

"Says so on the door." Evan kept on going. "I've never actually been in most of these places."

"Huh." Matt Shields matched him step for step past two bars and a pizza joint with a spray-painted sign offering tattoos and piercings on the second floor, but he'd gone quiet and Evan had a feeling that wasn't a good thing.

"So. Lily." There it was. Not really a question, and Evan wasn't answering it anyway. He hadn't thought it was that obvious, but Lily was Lily, and Evan was human—partly at least, and that part couldn't have said "no" to her if the fate of the known universe depended on it, which it sometimes did. On days when he was thinking with his daemon side, he couldn't imagine a reason why he would try.

Shields took his silence for all the answer he needed. "Lily wouldn't like condoms," he said.

No, she wouldn't, but he had no intention of discussing his sex life with a daemon lord of a foreign Prince—not with anybody, really. He was saved by a Duck, an amphibious landing craft full of tourists who honked their duck callers at them and passed on down the street while the driver blared, "and those are the famous South Street gum trees," through a loudspeaker. And that, thankfully, gave Matt Shields something to think about besides Evan and Lily getting naked.

"What *is* that?" Matt Shields looked first at the nearest tree, then down a row of them lining the sidewalk.

"It's gum."

"*Chewing* gum. I thought he meant a kind of tree!"

"Nope." Evan studied the tree, its trunk covered in bright, pointillist dots of used chewing gum, with a combination of pride and distaste. "This is Philly's Bourbon Street," he said, with a twitch of his hand that took in the crush of bars and shops, "which means most of its traditions start with too much alcohol. It's sort of disgusting, but on the other hand, it keeps the gum off the bottom of your shoe.

"This is it." He stopped in front of a low building that looked like an art deco diner and tugged the door open. "Jim's Steaks. Don't let anybody tell you Pat's are better!

Shields looked from the chrome-framed windows to the gum tree and back again. "I think I lost my appetite."

Evan pushed him through the doorway. "Ask for wiz and fried onions. You'll find it again."

Chapter 15

EVAN CAME HOME TO A DARK AND EMPTY house. He'd dropped Matt Shields at Rush's Bed and Breakfast—Greg Rush had greeted him with a big smile and a bigger "to do" list of minor repairs—and headed out for a few appointments he'd moved because of the workmen in the office. He didn't think he was avoiding the apologies he knew were due. But the sunlight had gone while Evan found another reason not to go home, and another, until here he was, alone at the desk in the agency's office, listening to voice messages in the dark. First up, Sid Valentine stumbled through a threat to have Brad picked up off the street if he didn't come in and provide a statement voluntarily.

The police had officially cleared the agency, Brad included, and the authorities in three countries were fighting over the right to put the Chongs in jail. China had first dibs, with executions in mind. That didn't mean Brad had gone back to chess on Wednesdays with Lieutenant Ellen Li. At least, not yet. But the FBI had nothing and Evan had learned his lesson. Brad could do whatever he damned well pleased about Sid Valentine. Evan wasn't going to stop him.

He erased the message, and the earlier one from Shields. The Liberty Bell was still cracked, and he was starting to figure out that Matt Shields had a weird sense of humor. Claire Murphy's bill lay on the desk, with a note scrawled across it—"Fixed the crack." It wasn't often a civilian put him on the side of the angels. He laughed a little remembering that the character reference of a daemon lord had tipped that scale, and realized he wanted to live up to the faith she'd put in him with those three mundane words. He was considering knocking a hole in the wall just to hire her back to fix it when he felt the hairs rise on the back of his neck.

"Lily?" He made it a question, though he knew her touch in all her forms, even the whisper of a breeze in his ear that raised gooseflesh on his arms and other things in his pants.

Soft blue flame enfolded him, licked at lips, at his lashes.

"Lirion," he said, because sometimes he needed her to know that he loved her for what she was, not just for the body she wore in his world. He couldn't tell her those absurd but true things—that he loved her fiercely, beyond all reason. That losing her was unthinkable, would be unsurvivable. Men had said them to her before, made a prison of the words and died for it. He didn't think she'd kill him for saying it, but she wouldn't believe he meant it as anything but the same old prison either.

He knew she didn't feel love the way humans did. Tolerant affection for his human side—she did that. She liked the sex, he could tell that much, but she just didn't get that fierce roil of emotions he felt when he thought about her, or the deeper tie, steady and absolute beneath the turmoil. She knew him body and soul in his world, and in hers where his mind was as open as a bleeding wound, and she didn't walk away. Didn't strike him dead for that matter, but sometimes, the thought that she might just made him want her more. And how screwed up did that make him?

His whole body ached to get his arms around her. But he didn't think that was going to happen until . . .

"I'm sorry," he said to the flame that lifted his hair, and licked a bead of sweat from his lip. "It's just a stone. I'd trade a hundred of them for the light in your eyes."

"Wow, Evan." Suddenly, his lap was full of Lily, solid and laughing, her arms wrapped around his neck. Her dark hair

tickled when she leaned in to press a quick kiss to the tip of
his nose. "That's the dumbest thing I've ever heard you say.
It's not just a stone, it's a perfect 85-carat ruby. There probably aren't five of that quality on the whole planet. You just
have no sense of humor."

It wasn't his sense of humor in question, and Evan knew
it. Trust was always on the table.

"I may not be a lord of Ariton," he said, "But I'm close
enough. If the ruby'd been lost, I'd have found it." He knew
it was true—he'd always had the knack, even as a kid. It
made him good at the job. He hadn't trusted it as part of
his nature, though, hadn't put that together with the side
of himself he never looked at too closely. Lords of Paimon
carried secrets—he'd done the research, wondered what
secrets Matt Shields had carried for Grayson Donne. Ariton found the lost and hidden things.

But that question always lay between them, woven into
the trust thing like the medallion burned to char on the
Aubusson carpet—was he Ariton, or was he human?

"Come on," she said, and slid from his lap. He groaned,
reached out to bring her back, but she took hold of his
hand, tugged him out of his chair.

"God, Lily, I'm not going to make it up the stairs!" he
complained.

She laughed, turning into flame, and then she was away,
drawing him with her into the second celestial sphere, his
body falling back into his chair, and that seemed to be the
way she wanted it for now.

Lily filled Evan's mind with the strangeness of her
thoughts—countless ages in the eternal now of her kind,
freedom that held the whole radiant universe in its grasp.
He'd been here before, sensed those things from a distance,
been terrified of them, and later, learned to navigate them,
find his way home. More often than not now, sex wound up
here. It was the one thing he could give Lily that none of
her other human lovers had—the daemon side of his nature meant he could move with her when she wanted more
than a shell of flesh could give her. Best of both worlds, he
liked to think, which made her laugh. But there were usu-

ally orgasms involved, and lots of touching, as improper as either of them could make it. He'd been hoping for some of that improper touching now, but that didn't seem to be where this was going.

Others of her kind had gathered, knots of flame in the darkness that he felt rather than saw, because he had no eyes in this place. Ariton, his own Prince, didn't like him much. Evan reached out, looking for his father because he needed all the allies he could get. But Badad wasn't there.

Chapter 16

BADAD MOVED THROUGH THE SPHERES with a quiet rage. Ariton had barred his presence from the gathering of the host. Something blew up behind him—maybe not so quiet—but it wasn't where he was going, so he didn't look back. He thought about where he wanted to be, considered his current mood, and rejected the house on Spruce Street. They'd just gotten the place patched up and Lily would be seriously unhappy if he accidentally blew it up before they paid the bill for the last time.

He was still surprised at the things he'd put up with for his misbegotten son. More surprised at what Evan would risk for a daemon lord who'd fathered him as someone else's revenge, and who'd left him half-mad and alone among humans for most of his life.

Lily would take care of him. He thought she could sway the daemon lords who would challenge Evan, could protect him enough to bring him home whole. But if the lords of Ariton merged, became their Prince, Lily would lose her singular purpose to the group mind. He didn't think Evan would survive another meeting with Ariton. He just had to trust that Lily wouldn't let that happen. In the meantime, he needed a distraction.

There was pleasure to be had in a luxury suite looking out over the China Sea, and he would doubtless visit Mai Sien Chong again sometime, for chess and other contests. But she was not Ariton, and he could not feel for her the things that Lily felt for Evan. So, not Singapore.

New York, he decided. Sotheby's had Donne's estate on exhibit in their galleries for a week before the sale. He wanted to get a look at the box that Parmatus—Matt Shields—wanted so badly. Brad found the place easily enough; Shields wasn't the first client to want anonymity when he bought expensive toys. The auction house was dark, but that didn't matter, any more than the security. He knew his way around the galleries and didn't need the light anyway.

The Donne estate was large, and Brad passed from room to room, not quite corporeal, taking the measure of the dead man by the objects he'd left behind. Without a will, which seemed shortsighted for a man of Donne's obvious wealth, a man who'd managed to devise a trap to hold a daemon lord even after he was dead. He passed a room that held bits of furniture, chose instead a small alcove with a fourteenth-century silver chalice, French, and a curved silver knife, not French, probably Moroccan, resting on a velvet-draped pedestal. The knife looked decorative, except that Brad sensed blood and darkness when he drew too close.

Three years ago, Evan had bound his father and his lover to protect them from a nasty piece of work named Franklin Simpson. They'd agreed on the need, but Brad's innate rage against the violation might have killed a human purely of the material sphere. Evan hadn't even had the sense to stay in his own circle. But he was more than human and had drawn on Ariton as much as the relatively benign spell to stay alive and bind not one but two daemon lords.

Grayson Donne had neither a daemon heritage nor permission, and there had been nothing benign about his spell. Someone had cleaned the chalice before sending it to auction, but there was blood mixed with the silver. Brad took a moment to identify the lot number. He'd take personal pleasure in making sure no one ever used those pieces to summon a daemon lord out of its home again.

It wasn't his reason for this after-hours visit, however.

The next room held Donne's library furniture: glassed cases and small antique tables. No books, though. He hadn't seen any books in the catalog either. So where were the books that used to sit in those cases?

The strongbox sat on a pedestal next to a small seventeenth-century desk that had its own lot number, but Brad was only interested in the box. The symbols worked into the iron bands made him uneasy even from a distance. The nearer he got, the more the box filled him with dread. He would have sworn it was screaming, except that Matt Shields was tucked up in an antique bed under the eaves at Greg Rush's Bed and Breakfast, as bound to that body, and the need of flesh for rest, as he was bound to the box.

By the time he'd got close enough to recognize the symbols, he was having trouble focusing at all. He recognized some of the marks—locks, every one. The screaming didn't stop, just rose in pitch until he thought it must have woken the entire city. He expected the police at any moment, but this time nothing bound him to stay.

He couldn't make his escape through the second celestial sphere yet, but he didn't have to hold a human form. Within limits, he had some flexibility of movement. Singapore was out of reach, but Philadelphia was just an hour down the road by train. He latched on, a low-burning flame, and let it carry him home.

Lily and Evan were still gone. He wasn't worried, just bored, when he called Harry Li. The coffeemaker was set to brew and he turned it on while he waited for Harry to pick up.

"Brad?" Harry's voice was foggy, thick with sleep. "Is something wrong?"

"Not really, just wondered if you were up for a game of chess."

Harry didn't answer right away. When he did, Brad couldn't quite sort the exasperation from the concern. "So I gather your vacation was not in this time zone. Do you know what time it is?"

"Time?"

"One o'clock in the morning, my friend. An odd hour for the first time you've ever called for a game of chess. It's not even Wednesday." Another pause, then, "Where's Evan?"

"Evan and Lily are out. Working." He didn't mention the screaming box.

"Ah." He could hear Ellen in the background, Harry's answer to her muffled by a hand over the phone, then the sound of movement. "Undercover? I didn't know the agency did that kind of work." Brad didn't correct him, and the exasperation was still there, but understanding too. "I know how you feel. Ellen gave me a few sleepless nights before the department promoted her to a desk. But they're both good at their jobs. They'll be fine.

"Look, try to get some sleep—they'll be mad as hell if you're waiting up for them like they were a couple of teenagers on their first date. In the morning, get Sid Valentine's interview out of the way. Then meet us for chess at seven. Winner pays for dinner."

"I thought it was loser pays?" Brad accepted the offer, even though it came with a tacit promise to answer Sid Valentine's questions.

Harry laughed softly. "Only when I have a chance of winning," he explained. "Go to sleep, Brad. They'll be home in the morning."

"I know. Tomorrow, then." Brad hung up, but he didn't go to sleep. He took his coffee into the study, turned on the lamp behind his tapestried wing-back chair, and stared at the empty space where the desk used to sit. *Have to replace that,* he thought, and settled in to wait.

Chapter 17

EVAN FIGURED HE WASN'T GETTING LAID IN either universe today. Okay, take that back. The celestial family reunion didn't matter.

Lily was part of him, merged with his mind as she might with a daemon lord of her own host, and he felt her pleasure as somewhere nearby suns exploded in the nexus of their own energy. Waves of power rushed through him, filling him everywhere, and he filled the universe, felt its movement in the beating of a heart he no longer had as he tried to make sense of an experience he wasn't built to survive. A human thought clung for a moment, hope that it hadn't been his own sun dying, then the rush swept even that thought away.

He spread the stuff of his daemon nature as wide as he could make it, catching the sensations of the universe in chaotic motion. Later, when he managed to pull a coherent though together, maybe he'd remember to feel guilty that the death of stars felt this damned good. Right now, he was wondering if he could make it happen again. Which, okay, right there? Time to back away and ask himself a question. Until now, Lily had protected him from the full effect of this. Brad had. Something had changed, and it wasn't just his death wish.

"Someone wants to meet you," Lily said, from inside his mind, so he knew she'd seen everything. If this was a test, he thought he might be failing because he couldn't rein in thought or feeling, knew he was sending his own obliterating responses back out into the universe and gathering a crowd. Blue, though, and he thought that was okay. He might be embarrassing the relatives, but he hadn't started a war yet which, for him, was a good day.

He wasn't exactly afraid that he'd wind up in the middle of the daemon Prince that formed when enough of its lords merged into a unified being. Ariton didn't like him, and he figured the gathered lords would make sure that didn't happen. But there were a lot of them. Flames passed through his mind, not cautious what they took. The closest he'd come to this feeling before, he'd been laid out on the floor at the Black Masque, strangers touching him, crooning worship into his ear, incense and the smell of blood and Omage's smile, colder than the marble beneath him, all of it heightened by the drugs Omage had fed him. That was before they'd snapped on the chains and ridden him into insanity.

He didn't think that would happen here. He trusted Lily, really. But—oh, God—he thought he would die of the overload and reached for his father. Still not there. In all that gathering mass of daemon lords, he could not find his father, and he was pretty sure no one else would protect him here, now. He'd thought Lily, but she was withdrawing from that open connection they'd formed between them. He still felt her presence—still there, but not interfering while daemon lords pulled his mind apart like the seams of a cheap suit, unraveling the threads of him into the universe. *Carlo will be furious,* he thought, but his tailor couldn't help him here. He would never gather the pieces of himself up again—he would die, his body cooling in his office on Spruce Street while his mind scattered itself among the energy waves of dying stars.

Then something pulled his attention, one lord in particular who poked around where Evan really wished he wouldn't, except that he needed the focus right now. Definitely a he, sort of, though Evan had never figured out how he knew, or what difference it made in an existence with no body, no young. "Caramos," this one introduced itself. "Tell me about sex."

Caramos tugged on a memory, and Evan thought, "Ungh."

The daemon lord didn't take that for an answer, but rummaged around in Evan's memories, pulling out kisses, his mouth holding onto Lily's breast like he would die of thirst without it, Lily's hip, her thigh, Evan's hand between her legs, his mouth there, and Evan inside of her, feeling the softness surrounding him, sweat and slide and arms tangling, her heels dug in—

Another mind slipped into his, and another, and he felt— a density that was not physical, not his body, but something he knew he couldn't hold. He was human, not Ariton, but Caramos laughed, growing breasts and learning kisses. If Evan had a body, he would have blushed, but he didn't, and Caramos plundered all his memories of pleasure, and one laying close to the surface, speculation.

"Who's Claire Murphy?" Lily tickled his mind with the question. "Does she like girls too?" Evan hadn't gotten that far—didn't know if she liked guys yet, let alone him. He wanted to hide those thoughts from her, because he knew his attraction there was just a carrier signal for his regrets. Not human, not daemon. What was he?

Another, who called herself Sched, poked at years of terror brooding below the surface of the new life he'd built. She plucked out memories of Omage, a lord of Az-mod, who had tortured Evan into insanity, and Pathet, of that same host, who had murdered Evan's only friend in his own kitchen.

"Make more friends," she told him, and plucked at the memory of Claire Murphy looking up at his ceiling. "Make babies." No sympathy in her, but terrible understanding that she held apart from him a little, the only grace he'd been given in this place. He could sense its presence, knowledge as dangerous as she was herself. She knew humans intimately, profoundly, read him more clearly than Caramos had, realized where his feelings led. He didn't think he'd survive her knowledge. She read that in him too, and didn't deny it.

"Find a human woman," she said, "The heavens are not for you."

Evan wanted to hide his thoughts from Lily, who slipped in and out of flesh and its inconveniences at will. He was a monster and would never have children, refused to bring another monster into the world to suffer the confusion and terror he'd suffered as a child.

"Our monster," Sched said. Evan lifted an image from her mind and knew it, had seen it carved in stone a hundred times or more—wide hips, pendulous breasts—behind the glass of a museum shelf. Ancient fertility goddess, the legends on the cards below the carvings always said. She answered the thought. "Armies of our children have walked your world, but that was a very long time ago, as humans and stones measure such things. Now they are stories and a whisper of power between women. But no one really believes in us anymore, not even the evil old men with their spells and bindings."

"I believe in you."

"I suppose you would, under the circumstances," she reminded him. Hard not to believe when his body was cooling without him in some other universe. He wanted Lily with his whole heart and soul. But he wanted home more.

"I can't do this," he said. Ariton was a part of him, and he hoped that the daemon lords, host-cousins, saw their Prince in him, knew host-loyalty tied him as much as a half-human monster could feel it. But he couldn't live here. Didn't want to, and would die if he tried. And he needed the solitude of his own mind. Without Sched's questions to focus him, the cacophony of cousins overwhelmed him.

Lily had gone from his mind. He couldn't find her, and that terrified him more than anything since he'd arrived without his body. She wouldn't abandon him, and she'd helped teach him how to find his own way home anyway. But, "I can't . . ."

He reached into the material sphere as Brad and Lily had taught him, turned for home, and wrapped his body around him like a new suit. He had a bed and he found it, fell facefirst into the pillows, and let a million thoughts that were not his own bleed away into the darkness. Five years ago, he'd have been reaching for the gun he'd kept under his mattress for just such an occasion. The gun stayed locked in a safe in the study now; he hadn't touched it since they'd put it there, years now, and he had no desire to go looking for it. Figured, on the edge of sleep, that he'd have to pick up a few new skills for dealing with the cousins, because he wasn't having Caramos rummaging through his sex life again.

Chapter 18

LILY WAS BESIDE HIM WHEN HE WOKE a few hours later. Her eyes gleamed in the darkness, and he reached out, found her breasts with his fingertips, reading her nipples like Braille. "So we have a pervy uncle," he said.

"Caramos is just curious." She grinned. "Very curious. But he's a good friend, and has no malice in him, which makes him unique among us, I think."

"Be nice to Uncle Caramos. I can do that. As long as he doesn't ask for lessons."

She turned to give him better access to her breast, wrapped long, tapered fingers around the back of his head and pulled him in—it was where he wanted to go anyway—he felt the slow glide of her skin against his, felt the breath catch in his throat the way it always did when she touched him. He couldn't talk with a mouth full of Lily, and didn't want to, certainly not about Caramos.

"You have a deal," she said, her voice breathy. "Ariton will accept Paimon's debt."

Tomorrow he would care about that, but now he just wanted to hear her make that noise—there, that one—and pull his head up to kiss him slow and deep. She didn't grin at him like she usually did, but he recognized the glitter in her eyes, pleased that he'd put it there.

"Don't do it again." Lily told him, and held his head away so that he would pay attention to what she was saying. Since the rest of his body was pressed as close to hers as it could get in this reality, it didn't stop the shutdown of his higher brain functions. But he was still sensible enough to take her at her word when she said, "If you try something like that again, Ariton will kill you. Your explanations will die with you, unspoken."

"Got it. Won't. Do it. Again." Between tiny kisses, he dropped the words like promises on her breasts. He didn't ask where his father had been. Instinct told him he didn't want to know right now, didn't want to spoil the mood. He'd think about it tomorrow, when she didn't have her warm soft body wrapped around him.

Sometimes sex between them was wild, almost a battle, and sometimes playful. Tonight he was counting up his losses. "Make babies," Sched had told him, but he never would, had known that since he was a half-mad kid and didn't mourn something that was never meant for him in the first place. He took his consolation in the curve of her hip, the feel of her waist circled by his hands, the arch of her back as he traced the body he held.

"I love you," he whispered into the low swell of her belly. She wouldn't hear him, but he needed to say it, to the inside of her thigh and the back of her knee and the soft flesh at her ankle. Then he followed the curve of her leg home. They would stay where they were tonight. Evan felt the pull of Earth, or maybe he was hiding from her world, and she seemed to think that was a good idea right now. But it was enough.

When he woke up, she was still there. Not for long, though. "Daddy's called a meeting," she said, and nipped at his chin to cut through the fog in his brain.

The sun had risen, but his room didn't get the eastern light the way Lily's did, so no patterns of light shifted across her skin. It was bright enough to know he'd slept late, though.

"Is he all right?"

"Pissed off, but not at you, for a change."

"Then—"

"Ariton," she answered, before he had worked out a diplomatic way to ask where his father had been last night, given no life-or-death appointments elsewhere.

"If Ariton had decided to kill you, your father could not be trusted to allow it."

"Oh." Evan thought about that. The lords of his own host believed that his father might put the life of his son above the will of his Prince. He'd figured that Brad would prefer him alive to dead, all things being equal. The equal or not part came as a comforting surprise.

On the other hand, Lily had been there.

"It was a good deal." She slid out of bed, not bothering with clothes. "I thought we had a pretty good chance that the host would agree. And Caramos was predisposed to like you. But there was always a possibility that things would go the other way. Since no one wanted to deal with the consequences of a rebellion, Ariton banished him to Earth until the lords had made their decision."

She stopped in the doorway, a last thought. "I told them they were wrong about Badad, but they didn't want to take the chance."

He was still working that around in his head when he heard the hiss of the shower in the next room.

Chapter 19

BRAD DIDN'T HAVE TO WAIT LONG. Lily had stopped at the Café du Monde on her way down to breakfast and dropped a bag of beignets on the breakfast bar. Evan had detoured through the study and wandered in a moment later with his computer tucked under his arm. "There was a message from Bill Sanders on the phone. Said the buyer he had in mind for the ruby is in New York on business." He slid the computer onto the counter and picked up the coffeepot but Brad had used the morning coffee set up last night. His nose twitched in distaste at the stale grounds but he cleaned them out and started a fresh pot while he finished the message. "Her name's LeRoux. She's interested, but wants to meet in person, around 3:00 this afternoon if you're available. Let Bill know before noon if you're not." Evan slouched onto a stool while they waited for the coffee to finish dripping like any morning, give or take a donut or two, kitchen or study.

Three o'clock would do. Evan was mad about something, but the fact he was alive at all meant Ariton had agreed to the deal, which had been the only logical outcome. Logic didn't always rule business between Princes, but Evan's contract left Ariton in a good position and didn't cost anything. Except, they had to free Matt Shields, which had looked like a simple job until yesterday.

Waiting through the night in the shadowy light of the single reading lamp, Brad hadn't made notes—not that much to remember, and he wasn't likely to forget it anyway. Evan did have notes, though, and pulled them up on the computer while they waited for the coffee.

"I'm sorry I got you into this," he said, and Brad noticed that he didn't apologize for his own involvement in the case. "I was thinking about the advantage if we succeeded. It hadn't crossed my mind that we might not." He lifted one shoulder in half a shrug.

Brad knew how to read that gesture now: a little embarrassed, but still preoccupied with the stuff in his own head. So he wasn't surprised when Evan said, "I started to put it together yesterday at the library, then Lily had new information about the ruby."

"And?" Brad pulled thick blue mugs from the cabinet over the coffeemaker and filled them because Evan had his nose stuck in the laptop.

"The catalog says the strongbox is fourteenth-century French. The three iron straps in each direction are consistent with early modern instructions for binding spells—thread, anything, but wrapped three times. I can't say definitely that the instructions go back as far as the box, but Agrippa wrote about it in the sixteenth Century, said it's earlier knowledge."

Brad waited while Evan absently sipped at his coffee, took a long draw of his own, savoring the hit of it going down. Not as good as scotch, or a good brandy, but like the best of human things, it was an acquired taste with a bitter edge, reminders of mortality.

"Rubies are the fire stone, iron is the fire metal." Evan had that faraway sound in his voice, which, oddly, meant that he was talking to himself, had pretty much forgotten his audience. "Matt Shields had the one in his pocket and the other wrapped around the box he wants us to buy on his behalf. And Lily says the ruby disappeared in the fourteenth century, in France. So. . ."

"Grayson Donne is not immortal," Brad stopped him there, gestured at the computer with the thick pottery mug over the breakfast bar. He pretty much agreed with where Evan was going, but Donne had died an old man at ninety.

"He was a recluse as an adult," Evan read off his screen, "but his birth certificate is on record. He graduated from Yale. After that, not much. Lived quietly on his family money until his heart gave out from what anyone can tell.

"There's some chatter on the feeds about the auction, but it all sounds like speculation. I've been watching for keywords related to the box and Matt Shields. So far, nothing. If anybody knows what Donne was up to, they're not talking—not publicly, not privately."

Which meant that Evan had been digging deeper than was legal. Sid Valentine might be the least of their problems if Homeland Security caught them tapping into the major data collection centers. Didn't change the fundamental truth of the case, though.

"Donne is dead," Lily sipped her coffee and Brad figured she'd smooth that frown line the next time she passed a mirror. "Parmatus—Matt Shields —is still here. So it didn't have to be our Donne."

"Six hundred years?" Evan asked, "Is that even possible?" He flung himself off the bar stool and paced the kitchen, running his fingers across his scalp like he was looking for the tangle that wasn't there anymore. "There's something wrong here, and not just with Donne. Donne's been dead for three years, apparently with no heirs. If nobody owns the box, why hasn't Matt Shields found a way to destroy it and go home?"

"Why isn't he rich?" Lily asked. "He has a fistful of the most valuable rubies in the world, with proof of ownership—where are the yachts, the houses, the women or the men, or both? I like both!" She grinned brightly at Evan, but he didn't rise to the bait.

It didn't take very long for a hostile binding to drive a daemon lord insane. Franklin Simpson had driven Omage mad in less than twenty years. They all knew it, were just avoiding putting the words in the room, where they'd be real. But they had to ask themselves, was their client insane? And how? Or, more Brad's concern, was Matt Shield's personal kind of crazy a danger to them? Not just some frantic self-defense when he thought he'd been caught in a trap—was he running according to some logic that was going to rock this planet on its axis, or hurt Ariton's interests in the second celestial sphere? Parmatus didn't *seem* to be thinking ahead that much, but they didn't know that for sure.

"Why did he show up here offering to pay our bill with repairs and pretending he doesn't know anything about money?" Evan pursued Lily's question. "He's been on the outside of that box and living in upstate New York for the past three years, so that's bullshit." He hrmmed a little huff through his nose, which was a sure sign he'd come to a conclusion that didn't make sense to him. "He's keeping something from us, which is no surprise. But, he's not real subtle about it for a daemon lord whose special skill is keeping secrets. It's as if he can't tell us, but he wants us to uncover it for ourselves."

When they started the case, Brad hadn't considered trying to figure out Matt Shields. They had to sell his ruby and buy a box for him at a fifteen percent commission on both transactions. Money in the bank, end of story. But he was starting to wonder if even that would be enough to send Shields home. "I checked the box last night," he said. "The symbols in the iron strapping are seals, locks."

"At least he's not lying about that part of the job," Lily agreed. "Whoever initiated the spell made the box as a prison."

Evan stared into the distance for a minute, and Brad had no desire to follow him into whatever memory had caught hold of him. It didn't take much of a stretch to guess it anyway. His son could heal the scars his own captivity had left on his skin. He had that skill now but refused to use it because it made him something other than human. Which had been the point in the first place.

Evan brushed off the moment, but his voice shook a little when he said, "That's not a very big box."

"No," Brad agreed. "And it's not happy. I could hear it screaming."

"An alarm?" Lily asked.

"No one came," He said. "It sounded like a voice, rose in

volume and pitch when I approached it, but I'm pretty sure no one else heard it. I didn't touch it."

"So the box isn't empty after all," Evan breathed.

"I'd say not."

"Shit." Hand across his close-cropped head again. Evan didn't take the news well.

Lily grinned. "I think we should revisit Mr. Shields' bill." But her teeth seemed particularly sharp when she bit into her beignet, and blue fire burned steadily in her eyes. Brad thought Mr. Grayson Donne was a very lucky man, because he was already dead.

"I'll take a look at the house." Evan grabbed his coffee mug on his next swing past the breakfast bar; trying to pretend everything was normal just made him twitchy. "See if they left any clues when they cleaned the place out for the estate sale."

"See if you can find the books while you're looking. Donne had a lot of bookcases, but none of the books are up for auction." It wasn't what he wanted to say, but last night Ariton had agreed to a bargain with Paimon that had taken "walk away" off the table.

Brad wasn't afraid, he really wasn't. Nothing to be afraid of anyway. Donne was dead, no heirs. And he trusted Evan completely, if that meant to do something stupid again and maybe get himself killed over it this time. But if Evan hadn't owned them, bound with a spell he shouldn't have been able to pull off at all, Franklin Simpson would have had them. He'd be a prisoner still, driven as mad as his nemesis.

Evan had kept his promise for the most part, not to use the binding against them. He'd screwed up there at the end, but he'd fixed it, and anyway, Brad had gotten used to being rich and pretty much free, didn't think he'd handle well six hundred years as a handyman. They had an agency contract that spelled out the business shares in money, but it didn't cover eventualities like Grayson Donne. He thought they ought to fix that, and he figured they could do it so that Evan didn't have the option to screw it up this time.

"Before you go, we should probably add a rider to our own contract."

"No." Evan's coffee mug hit the floor, bits of dark blue pottery skittering across the pristine white tiles. It looked, for a minute, like he was going to join them, little bits of broken Evan everywhere, but he pulled himself together. "That didn't work out very well the last time."

The doorbell chimed, but no one moved to answer it.

"Apparently insanity is contagious." Lily set her own mug more carefully on the breakfast bar. "You can go, Evan. I'll change his mind while you're—somewhere else."

"It wouldn't be like last time." Brad was pretty sure of that. "A one-way contract, like the one you offered Matt Shields. For as long as we mutually agree."

"If you recall, that didn't really work out well either. I tore it up."

"That's because he's already bound to something else."

Another chime of the doorbell. "I won't do it," Lily said, and Brad answered, "You don't have to. It's a one-way contract. Walk away at any time. Or you can take your chances with six hundred years in a box. It's up to you."

Evan's eyes had rolled back the way they always did when he was treating his brain like a badly organized computer, shuffling through folders in his head. "It could work," He finally agreed. But they were too late to answer the door.

"Hello! Is anybody there?" Mike Jaworski wandered into the kitchen.

Chapter 20

DETECTIVE MIKE JAWORSKI HAD A TALENT for interrupting at exactly the wrong moment, but Brad did not stoop to the level of exasperated sighs like the one his son delivered. Lily smiled like she'd just beaten him at chess, and held out the plate of beignets.

"Where do you get these? Jaworski asked around a bite that left powdered sugar on his tie. "They're fantastic."

"We have them flown in from New Orleans once in a while." Evan poured him a mug of coffee, handed it over when the beignet had disappeared. "Wanna go private?" Shards of blue pottery still littered the floor. Evan didn't move to pick them up. Jaworski pretended not to notice.

"Ask me again when I have my twenty years," Jaworski said, pretending to think about it. Then, "On second thought, don't. I'm not willing to trade my salary for your bruises. Which reminds me—don't you people ever lock your doors? Big city, house broken into regularly: what part of security don't you get?"

The gate had a warding spell, locked to everyone but the half dozen or so people they'd allowed access, and with a suggestion that the random canvasser or burglar didn't really want this house after all. They didn't need burglars—they wreaked their own personal havoc from the inside.

Jaworski didn't know that, of course. Easier to blame

the Chongs for a tossed study than explain that Evan had bound his father to a tiled box at Major Crimes and his father hadn't liked it. The handcuffs still burned when he thought about them, though he'd healed the flesh a week ago. Brad felt the air pressure building, controlled the impulse before he did something spectacularly stupid and turned Ellen Li's policeman into a really unhappy true believer. Safer to let skeptics lie, especially when they carried guns. A bullet in the head didn't do any damage he couldn't repair, but it hurt like hell on entry.

"Detective. Did Lieutenant Li send you again, or are you here on your own?"

Jaworski smiled, fake as Brad's own polite air. They didn't, when it came down to it, trust each other—smart on both their parts. "I'm just here for the donuts," he said. "But since I was dropping by anyway, Ellen thought you might like a ride to Sid's office—a familiar face and all." He was talking to Brad, but studying Evan for signs of more damage.

"I'm fine, Mike, really." The laugh wasn't convincing, but Evan didn't sound worried. Regretful, maybe—Brad had heard that one before. Couldn't figure out why now. But ridding his kitchen of Ellen Li's policeman was his top priority.

"I called my lawyer; she'll be all the familiar face I need, thank you."

It answered the question Jaworski had bothered to ask out loud. He didn't much care about the ones conveyed with meaningful glances. He didn't *get* the whole silent communication thing, but Evan would doubtless enlighten him later, earnestly and at maudlin length.

"Okay." Jaworski took a swipe at the powdered sugar on his tie, made a face when it smeared. "I'll tell the lieutenant that you're good. Can I drop you anywhere, Evan?"

"I'm fine. Clumsy, but fine." Evan waved at the floor, finally acknowledging the mess. Jaworski nodded, accepting that for now.

The doorbell chimed again, at the front. "That's my lawyer." Brad started moving, crowding Jaworski toward the doorway. "Nice to see you again, but I have to go. Sid Valentine is waiting."

He headed for the hallway that led to the front office, herding Mike Jaworski a step ahead of him. Neither of them spoke until they reached the front office, where Evan couldn't hear them. Then, Jaworski stopped and turned, dropped a hand on his shoulder.

Brad considered his options. He wasn't sure chess with Ellen was worth putting up with her policeman, but killing him would interfere with the business at hand. Since it had now become Ariton's business, he waited with a show of long-suffering patience for whatever the man had to say.

"I read the file Joe Dougherty put together on this agency," he said, and was diplomatic enough not to say, "on you," the way Sergeant Dougherty had. "Evan says you couldn't have committed any of the crimes in there, that you'd have to be in two places at once, thousands of miles apart, to have managed it. That logic is hard to beat. But you're his father—nobody who's seen the two of you in action has a single doubt about that, no matter what Dougherty says. Have you ever considered taking jobs that don't come quite so close to getting him killed once in a while?"

He'd expected threats of some sort, not—whatever this was. Evan didn't have friends, or hadn't until they'd gone hunting the Empress Crystal. Just like him to start with Ellen's policemen. If there was a way to complicate their lives, Evan always found it.

Jaworski took the hand back, but Brad stayed put. Hell of it was, he had a point.

"They don't usually start out that way. He has a knack." He sounded like Evan—so rueful even to himself that he just shook his head.

A knock on the inner door started him moving again. Khadijah Flint waited in reception, briefcase in one hand, fist raised to knock again with the other. "I was about to go around to the back," she said, "Oh, Detective. Should I be sitting in on this conversation?"

"This one is personal," Jaworski answered, and turned for a last word. "Get him over it, will you?"

"I thought you *knew* Evan!"

Jaworski actually laughed. "Yeah, well. Tell him it looks bad on his permanent record. And Joe Dougherty is still checking it." He ducked out the door, not waiting for an answer.

Khadijah Flint watched him go with a wry smile. "Evan has needed a friend for a long time," she said. "And speaking of friends, Sid Valentine is waiting, and there will be no chess for you until you get this over with."

The Lis were not friends. Daemon lords did not build relationships with humans. They played chess, and sometimes did favors to smooth the way to Wednesdays. The scales were badly balanced in his favor already, but Ellen saw this interview as a part of the most recent favor, so he went. But he'd have to give Mike Jaworski more thought.

Chapter 21

WE NEED THE OXYGEN. Driving through miles of dense forest, trusting the painted white line there'd be road on the other side of the next hairpin curve, Evan tried to think good thoughts about the trees crowding him on either side. He was born and raised in the city, went to school in the city. As a kid, he'd never spent more than a field trip or two in the woods. He hadn't missed it and couldn't figure out why every evil son of a bitch they ever tangled with lived in fucking nowhere.

Three and a half hours on the road didn't help. He'd asked Shields if he wanted to come along, but Shields had declined. Planned to spend the day at the art museum, he'd said, but he'd call Carlos to let him in. Which was fine, really. Evan had wanted to interview Carlos Sanchez since Matt Shields put his name on the table. But he hadn't seen a real town since he'd turned left at Newburgh, heading into the Catskills

His GPS was running out of map, and the gas gauge sat on empty. Evan stopped for gas and directions at a strip of narrow storefronts huddled around a supermarket with a quaint brick exterior and a pump out front about a mile from "here there be dragons" on the GPS. He tried a few questions, but the kids behind the counter at the Dairy Queen just shrugged—didn't know Grayson Donne, didn't care. He used their bathroom and bought a coffee anyway. The woman at the dry cleaner was older and about as helpful as the kids, at first. She gave him a funny look when he walked in and he remembered his fading bruises. "Accident." He told the lie easily. "I stopped on red, the other guy didn't."

"Ouch." She offered sympathy back. But she'd known of Donne, filled in the directions where his GPS sputtered out once he'd spun her a story about buying the old house.

"Don't miss the entrance, or you'll be in Albany before you know it," she said, drawing a stick-map on a piece of scrap paper. "Though you'd be better off if you kept on going." She hadn't said much more—refused to speak ill of the dead—but gave him a warning, "Funny things went on in that house. It gives a place a bad feeling."

Evan knew what she meant, but pretended he didn't. He thanked her for the directions and got back on the road. It was a genuine clue, and it should have cheered him, but it didn't. It wasn't the place or the drive that bothered him. Evan knew that. How could his father drop a bombshell like that on them and just walk out?

All right, they had to get the FBI off their tails so Brad could get back to his no-longer-secret life playing chess with the police. But they needed to talk about this. Or not talk. Just. Shit. He couldn't shake the memory of Matt Shields screaming and burning in the middle of the agency's office, but he figured he would, eventually. The burns on his father's wrist, where Joe Dougherty had snapped on handcuffs, were going to stay with him forever. That's what came of a binding spell. Unforgivable, inexcusable, and he couldn't believe that his father had suggested that he bind them again.

Except, of course, his father was suggesting something else. Trust, in his goodwill if not good sense. Ariton thought a daemon of its own host had a divided loyalty. Lily, not so much, which didn't surprise him. He knew beyond thought, in the place in his gut where "family" and "lover" tied him in knots, that she would protect him against any external threat. But she wouldn't cross her own Prince for him, and she would retaliate if he pissed her off too much. Alone in the BMW and miles from home, he could laugh at himself for pushing that line, over and over again.

But his father— Not *human* feelings. Evan knew better than that. Badad of the host of Ariton had no loyalties to humans, though apparently he enjoyed the company of a few. He could no more stand against Ariton than a human could cut off his own head and go on breathing. Which could only mean that his father had accepted him as Ariton, not a daemon lord, but still a part of the host that made up their Prince. That was something to digest. Something to treat with care. And the threat was gone—Grayson Donne was dead.

It hadn't freed Matt Shields, though, or whatever else Donne had locked in that box with him. Old Magic, from when it was new, but some of those rubies had laser IDs. So Donne had held the key until he died. Evan wondered about that—an actual physical key? How were they going to find it? Did Shields even want them too, or would he be happy to leave whatever it was trapped inside the box forever, as long as he got himself free of the material world?

Ariton found things. It was the special talent of his Prince's daemon lords, but Brad hadn't recognized a key in the lots on display at Sotheby's. Maybe it was still in the house, maybe gone forever, but he'd find out soon enough. Donne's estate had to be here somewhere. Special talent and all. . .

The two piled stone pillars that marked the entrance to the private road appeared on his right. He made the turn, barely—almost hit the far pillar but righted the wheel before he put the beemer in the drainage ditch. Another half mile and the forest opened up to a broad lawn that sloped gently toward the house, a Victorian monstrosity of stone and clapboards that sat atop a rise with the shoulders of the Catskills hunched low on the horizon. Gardens with tightly constrained yew hedges flanked the house. It looked more like a reformatory for wayward girls than a country estate; Evan pulled up in front next to a white Prius and got out of the car, tilted his head far back to take in all the dark and turreted glory at the center of Grayson Donne's web. Maybe a walk-away contract wasn't such a bad idea after all.

Chapter 22

BRAD HAD RECOGNIZED THE NAME—
LeRoux—in Bill Sander's file, had drunk the company's wines on occasion, and he'd checked out the address, standard precaution. The discreetly elegant pied-á-terre in Lyon led him to a hulking castle surrounded by working vineyards. If Evan didn't get himself killed in the short run, he figured he might like something like that for himself one day, but this wasn't the time. Lily was waiting for him at home.

The lords of Ariton found things, hidden in an attic or a database, it didn't make much difference. Lily was as good as Evan with a computer and neither of them worried about the legal niceties, so he wasn't surprised when he found her sitting on the burgundy leather couch in their private study, the laptop computer open on the beaten brass coffee table.

She handed him a list of businesses, including a small but exclusive trade in gems, that the LeRoux family had its hand in one way or another. They'd sunk most of their money into the grapes, though.

"They have a website." She turned the computer so that he could see the screen, filled with an interior shot of the castle, sepia tones with a splash of light on a display case. The company had a small museum and gave public tours of the vineyards on Tuesdays and Thursdays. She clicked a link to a general inquiry for a short list of artifacts spanning centuries. No arcana on the list, and he didn't see Mark Shields' ruby on there either, but the museum's web page had a contact number and a general request for information leading to the acquisition of objects with a connection to the company's history. All very public and aboveboard, but Lily wasn't finished.

"Numbered Swiss bank account, which isn't much of a surprise," she said. "The bank is private and goes back a lot farther than the Banking Secrecy Act but the account seems to have been dormant for at least twenty years. Until today. No movement yet, just a notice that the bank should expect to move a large sum."

They knew the LeRoux name had ties to Grayson Donne's line going back to the Black Death, so Brad hadn't ruled out trouble as an option. But humans had short memories. Donne had been dead for three years and the company hadn't renewed its inquiry on the ruby for a lot longer than that, had given no indication that it was aware of the recently deceased Donne at all. An inquiry going back more than twenty years didn't even make it a coincidence. Nothing out of the ordinary except the wine and that notice of an impending transfer of funds. But he wasn't taking any chances.

The limousine pulled up at the curb at precisely three o'clock. Lily waited in the Federal period office where they met clients. In his daemon form, Badad watched from the general direction of the corner of Spruce and Seventh Streets, above the house. Evan had told him once that they sometimes made a ripple in the air like heat rising from the roof, but the day was warm so that shouldn't matter.

LeRoux Cie could be exactly what it seemed, a company with a long-standing policy of buying back its history when the opportunity allowed. Bradley, Ryan and Davis had a few of them on their client list. Maybe after today they'd have another one.

Or, maybe not. The driver stepped away from the limousine, alert, with one hand brushing his jacket near a suspicious break in the fall from the shoulder. If he was going to carry that much firepower, he needed a better tailor. The second bodyguard didn't pretend to be anything else. He stepped out of the front passenger-side door and glanced up and down the street, a narrow, tree-lined mix of sixties modern and age-softened Federal that had been there since George Washington had walked the city, which seemed to mean a lot to Evan. Brad hadn't ever met the man, but he liked the comfortable way the street had settled into itself. The bodyguard just seemed annoyed by all the trees.

He wasn't sure why LeRoux was expecting mayhem on a quiet city street. Wednesday, midday, there were a few students heading for the medical school with their own purposeful strides and one deaf old neighbor navigating the rumpled brick sidewalk to water the flower baskets hanging from the Franklin lampposts. Normal. The second bodyguard let his hand fall from the holster at his belt, opened the limousine's back door, and waited.

A black walking stick with a brass grip appeared first, planting a firm hold on the street. Then a small, frail-looking old woman with pure white hair followed. The bodyguard took her arm to help her over the curb; it seemed to distress the woman, but he didn't let go.

A priest climbed out after her. Middle-aged, close-cropped steely hair. Might have been a soldier once. He had Jesuit eyes, glanced around to take in the neighborhood, and looked up—stared right at the space Badad had taken for perspective. That was trouble. The priest said nothing, gave no indication that he'd seen anything, just took the guard's place at the woman's side and helped her up the two low steps to the door.

Badad decided it was time to become Kevin Bradley again. Lily was going to need backup. Or maybe the priest would. He knew the suit he wanted, and the shirt and tie, let Carlo Pimi's fine tropical wool settle him into his wealthy businessman identity. Then he opened the door from the house to the formal office, back to its spare but gracious order yet still smelling faintly of paint.

Chapter 23

"PLEASE, HAVE A SEAT." Lily offered a chilled version of her usual professional smile.

"Thank you for seeing us." The old woman sat at rigid right angles in her chair, sunlight from the garden window glinting off the white of her hair. She wore a dark green suit too warm for the day. Brad recognized the tailoring as couture, not new but probably worth more now than when she bought it. She faced Lily with a level gaze over the smooth expanse of antique desk. In the chair beside her, the priest fingered the cross he wore at his throat. His gaze had sharpened when Brad entered from the house. This close, it was easier to see the family resemblance. No bodyguards, but Brad heard breathing in the outer office, so they hadn't gone far. It didn't look like either of them was going to hurry things along.

Brad stood behind Lily's chair, feet planted, arms crossed, with a slight, ambiguously non-threatening smile. Not even a priest could recognize a daemon lord's corporeal form from a wavering heat pattern over the house. It was impossible. But this priest saw something, studied him with narrow-eyed calculation. For a moment, light flickered in his eyes and Brad wondered. . . . But it was just sunlight glancing off the garden wall.

The old woman gave them both a puzzled look, but when no explanation was forthcoming, she returned her attention to Lily, who offered a frost-tipped smile and a hand across the desk. "Lily Ryan," she said. "And this is my partner, Kevin Bradley."

"Bertrande LeRoux." The woman clasped Lily's fingers briefly in a gnarled hand, her smile more polite than Lily's, and more strained. "And this is my—Father Michel. Father Michel LeRoux." She touched the priest's sleeve, a proprietary gesture.

"Thank you for coming on such short notice, but you needn't have made the trip. We could have come to you." Lily leaned over the desk and offered a bit of cleavage when she extended her hand to the priest. He didn't take it. Not the hand or the glimpse of Lily's breasts. Didn't take his hand off the cross at his throat.

"Do we have a problem here?" she asked him. Beneath her professional cool smoldered a rage that never boded well for any of them. Brad didn't think that either LeRoux had seen it. They didn't know she hated priests. A priest had bound her once in a Russian forest and she had little faith in any of them.

Madame LeRoux briefly tightened her hold on Father Michel's arm, restraint or reassurance, it was difficult to tell, but she let go to wave away Lily's earlier concerns. "It wasn't far—we arrived in New York last week. When I heard that the Lyon ruby had surfaced, it seemed like fate. We could not stay away." Her accent was thickly French, her grammar flawless. She hesitated over the word "fate" but moved on quickly. "Mr. Sanders said that you have it? And you are willing to sell?"

"For our client, who wishes to guard his privacy," Lily agreed. She didn't pull out the velvet-lined box, though, and Brad wondered if the agency could afford to buy the stone if Lily decided to keep it out of the hands of humans. They couldn't incur a host-debt over it, so they'd have to pay fair value.

The priest was looking up, tracking the outline of the pentagram hidden in the ornate plaster medallion on the ceiling. "Interesting design," he said, interrupting with a passing glance at Lily and a more pointed one for Brad before he returned his attention to the ceiling. "And recently repaired. Did your client do that?"

"He offered," Lily confided, and it didn't sound quite as true as it actually was. "He's a bit eccentric that way. But we felt his efforts were better spent elsewhere."

"I meant the damage."

"It's an old building." She blinked and looked more convincingly confused.

Brad couldn't help wondering what the priest would make of Matt Shields. Didn't, on reflection, want to find out.

But Lily waved off any further discussion of the ceiling. They had a deal with Paimon that required, as a first step, exchanging Matt Shields' ruby for a large sum of money. The agency did well, but they couldn't come up with that much in the time they had, so Bertrande LeRoux's money would have to do. "Would you like to see the stone?"

"You do have documentation?" Madame LeRoux leaned forward, eager. The priest flicked a glance over Lily, but he seemed to decide his charge was safe in that direction and returned to mapping the protective seal worked into the plaster on the ceiling.

"Of the jewel's authenticity and general description," Lily opened the desk drawer, drew out the velvet case. "As Bill Sanders will have told you, for personal reasons the client prefers not to share the details of its origin and early provenance that you reasonably would expect under the circumstances. He understands that decision will affect the price. But the jewel fits the description and would appear to fit the age as well."

"Then the original documentation does exist?" Madame LeRoux picked up the box, opened it. "There is a painting in our vaults," she said. "A miniature of a prince of Kashmir with the ruby at his throat. We have no record of his name—company history reports that his brother murdered him to eliminate the competition soon after the painting was made. This is the same stone."

The priest finished with the ceiling and resumed his study of Brad, as if he held the answers to the universe, which he did, more or less. But he didn't want to antagonize the only buyer they had for the ruby, so he waited. Which was a mistake.

"Adiuro te, Satan," the priest said, "hostis humanae salutis..."

I adjure you, Satan, enemy of human salvation...

Father Michel LeRoux was an exorcist. Wonderful.

Chapter 24

"IT'S A LOT OF HOUSE." Carlos Sanchez—*the* Carlos Sanchez, Evan guessed, who would inherit all those rubies when Matt Shields went home—was waiting on the front porch that wrapped the Victorian monstrosity of a house. "You must be Evan Davis. Matt said you might want to talk to me." Sanchez was an inch or two shorter than Evan. Squint lines radiated from the corners of his eyes but didn't give away much about his age—anywhere between forty and sixty, maybe. He had dark hair with no gray in it, neatly trimmed. The mustache, also neatly trimmed, did have a few stray grays. His hands rested casually in the pockets of his Dockers.

Evan nodded, accepting the offer, and mirrored the stance, hands hooked on pockets. "So what was Matt Shields doing here anyway?" he asked.

"General maintenance, minor plumbing jobs, painting. He started on one of my landscape crews, but my son came back from college, wanted to branch out. It's all that fancy business education these days. Diversify, as if the grass will stop growing, or branches will stop falling from the trees." He shook his head, but he was smiling when he said it. "Matt thought he might like to try his hand at that kind of work, and he took to it right away."

Evan nodded back—mirror moves, "we're in synch" moves—to keep Sanchez talking. "Still, there doesn't seem much here to keep him." Shields had a radius of ninety miles to work with, and New York City fell within it.

"Well, there was the girl."

"What girl?"

"Oh, a pretty little thing. Skinny. Rich guys seem to like them scrawny. Skin smooth like milk chocolate." Sanchez got a faraway look in his eyes, not seeing the scenery, Evan figured, and wondered what memory was playing against a ridge of the Catskills rising low in the background. "Kady, I think Matt called her," Sanchez said, "never mentioned a last name. You used to see her in the side gardens sometimes, or passing by an upstairs window. Mr. Donne never let her go far. Never let either of them go far. She disappeared right before Mr. Donne had his heart attack. We never found her. I thought maybe she saw her chance and just left, walked out to the road and hitched a ride to the city. Matt didn't believe it, and he wouldn't leave without her. I told him to call the police, but he wouldn't, begged me not to. I think—"

Sanchez hesitated, and Evan didn't ask him to betray a trust. He'd have to come to that himself. But he offered reassurance, "I've heard pretty much everything in this job—there's nothing you can say that will make me think less of Matt Shields." Didn't say how he felt now, but it was the truth—his father had killed fifty people in a towering rage and he still counted his world fortunate that Brad had pulled his punch, so to speak. Matt Shields couldn't shock him.

Something in the way he said it, or maybe his own long stare into the past, seemed to decide Carlos Sanchez. "I do not want to hurt Matt Shields, you understand, but I think that maybe he and the girl were prostitutes. They'd been here with Mr. Donne a long time. When I found him, he had no clothes. And the girl, she never wore clothes either. After Mr. Donne died, Matt didn't know what to do, had no place to go, so he just stayed on. I gave him a shirt, a pair of pants, a job to keep himself fed. Then, some people from the state came and cleaned out the house. I would have offered him a room, but I have daughters and their reputations to consider. Matt said he'd saved up some money and it was time to get help. My daughter, Marina, drove him to the bus. You're the help he went to find."

Evan felt sick, but he didn't show it. Couldn't afford to let his own dark memories cloud his judgment. "Not prostitutes. They were captives, kidnapped and held against their will."

"I didn't know." Sanchez turned his face away, but not fast enough. Evan caught the shame in his eyes, and in the downturn of his mouth. He hadn't tried to help.

"There was nothing you could do," Evan assured him. "And we don't know what else Donne was into—he might have killed you if you'd tried." It was true, but he felt irrationally angry that Sanchez *hadn't* tried. Six hundred fucking years of people looking the other way—it made him sick to be human.

Sanchez looked up, let Evan see that he appreciated the effort but knew what he should have done. "You think he killed her? Donne, I mean. Did he kill that girl?"

"I can't say." Evan picked his way carefully through an answer, thinking about a screaming box with a daemon inside for sale to the highest bidder. "But I'll do what I can to solve this case for Matt, and for the girl."

Sanchez nodded, one sharp tip of his head, accepting Evan's word as it was given, "Guess you'd better get busy," he said, and dropped the key into Evan's hand. "Leave it on the hook by the kitchen door. I'll be back to pick it up later."

He turned away then, opened the door of the Prius but stopped, his arms crossed over the top of the door. "One day, when I was working in the side garden, Mr. Donne warned me to stay away from the girl, and from Matt. He said they only looked human, but were monsters he was trying to tame. He said they refused even clothing. I told my daughter this, and we decided that Mr. Donne, he's a little crazy, you know? An old man, and maybe he likes boys in his bed, as well as girls, but cannot face his own sins.

"But I ask myself, could it be true, Mr. Davis? Did I bring a monster, like Mr. Donne said, into my business? Let a demon from the pits of Hell work beside my own son—"

"Matt Shields is not a monster," Evan answered quickly, though once he would have thought so. "And he certainly didn't come from the pits of Hell."

"But?" Sanchez prompted. And because Grayson Donne's house was waiting for him, and because Donne had drawn Matt Shields from the second celestial sphere to do unspeakable, degrading things to him, Evan dropped his head and answered as much of the truth as he thought Sanchez might be able to handle. "He's here because someone pulled him out of his home against his will. All he wants is to go home. Can you understand that, Mr. Sanchez?"

"Do you know where I come from, Mr. Davis?"

It was an odd question, and Evan wondered if he'd understood. "Mexico?" he guessed.

"No, Mr. Davis." He looked at the house for a long minute, then he sighed. "They always come for you at night, because no one is watching then. No one can help you.

"There were others. Mostly young. Even pets sometimes, but animals live in the woods and young people leave small towns like ours all the time On the television, they always find bodies, blood—something. We never did. Parents would put up flyers in the nearby towns and in the city, but the ones who disappeared never came home."

Evan didn't know what to say to that. He wasn't in an absolution mood and didn't think Sanchez would accept it if he was.

"Tell Matt I will do anything I can to help." Sanchez tapped the top of the door to the car once, emphasizing his offer, and ducked his head, got in and drove away.

"I will." Evan reached in through the open window of the BMW and grabbed the flashlight and a small digital camera from the front seat. Then he opened the wide front door of Grayson Donne's house of horrors and stepped inside.

Chapter 25

"*DISCEDE AB HOC FAMULO DEI* ..."
Depart from this servant of God ... The exorcism resonated in Brad's human bones and he could feel the air pressure rising like a corona around Lily. He had to stop this before she lost her temper, because he didn't think Claire Murphy would come back to fix the ceiling again. And he knew she couldn't fix the planet if Lily broke it. Evan could make do with a cracked ceiling, but he'd been pretty emphatic about needing the planet in one piece.

The ritual had power, but since they weren't Satan and weren't inhabiting someone else's body, the power didn't go anywhere, just built in urgency with no direction. It was a distinctly human power, and he didn't like touching it, but he figured only a graphic demonstration would stop it. So he took a deep breath, ignoring the impulse to destruction building with the words, and said "*Te adiuro*, Satan," just as Bertrande LeRoux shouted, "Not yet! I don't have the ruby!"

The bodyguards broke through the door, guns in hand. Brad hoped they'd misinterpreted the situation. He was pretty sure there'd be no more chess with Ellen Li if he killed Madame LeRoux, but it might be better than letting the cutthroat world of art theft find out that a priest and a little old lady had tried to rob them and actually got into the house.

"The door was unlocked," Brad pointed out. Maybe they could get Matt Shields to fix it as part of his fee.

The snap of a round chambering reminded Brad that the bodyguards were still reacting to an emergency that didn't exist. Yet. "I don't think that will be necessary," he said, but the driver with the Uzi didn't budge.

Bullets couldn't do him any permanent harm. They did smart, though. Mai Sien Chong's housekeeper had shot him once, and he hadn't liked it. But Lily had regained her sense of humor, if not composure. She patted Madame LeRoux's hand. "It's all right," she said, "Satan isn't here, so no harm is done, but it would be nice if your priest stopped chanting, since it is making your guards nervous. If you don't want the ruby, please say so. In English, French, or Italian—I understand and speak all three tolerably well—but I hadn't counted on Latin."

In fact, Lily's first priest had impressed upon her more Latin than Madame LeRoux's priest would ever know, but it wouldn't help the situation to tell him that.

"My son," Madame LeRoux shook her head. "Michel, it's not working."

The priest buried his face in his hands. "You're not supposed to be able to do that," he muttered between his fingers.

Brad did *not* feel sorry for the man, but he still needed to trade Matt Shields' ruby for his mother's millions. "It was awkward," he offered, though he could have meant in an ordinary way and hoped the damned priest took it that way. He didn't want exorcists showing up on his doorstep on a regular basis.

Michel LeRoux—Father Michel—pulled his head out of his hands to glare at him. "What are you?" He asked it like an order.

Brad just raised an eyebrow. "Detectives?" he said and met more glares, but Madame LeRoux dismissed her fire-power with a wave of a hand.

"We like to think we provide a distinctive service."

Lily followed the bodyguards as far as the credenza against the wall—under the pentagram in the ceiling while Father Michel titled his head back and frowned—and returned with the brandy in one hand and a clutch of snifters dangling from their stems in the other. She poured, handed out drinks. Madame LeRoux took hers, sipped. "A fine brandy calms the nerves and raises the spirits," she approved.

Father Michel didn't touch his drink. Lily left it on the desk and leaned back in her chair, running a finger around the rim of a glass she'd taken for herself.

Brad took a sip, contemplated the rich bouquet while he gathered his thoughts, but Michel LeRoux still looked like he wanted to smite something.

"Why *are* you here?" Father Michel had his hand wrapped around the cross at his neck again. He was using it as a lifeline and Brad wondered what he'd seen, what they hadn't hidden well enough against a spell aimed at commanding them, no matter whose spell or how it was intended against something else entirely.

"It's my house."

"That is no answer."

If Father Michel expected an interdimensional confession he had badly misread the situation. But Madame Le-Roux's money was still not on the table, so Brad tried again with the backstory they had put in place four years ago. "My son was born in this town. He wanted to come home, and it seemed as good a place as any to open a business. Nothing more mysterious than that."

"Evan Davis. We know what happened in New York. We know what was going on in that club—we've been watching him."

Watching? The Black Masque? While Omage tortured and nearly murdered his son? And now this man wanted to *exorcise him?*

"This meeting is over." Brad took a step around the desk. "And if you hurt Evan, your Uzi-toting muscle will not be able to help you." He let a little of what he was show through in the glitter of his eyes. It was stupid, but Evan Davis belonged to Ariton. Brad would not tolerate threats against his Prince.

"Abomination!" Father Michel stood to face Brad eye-to-eye, his shoulders set for a fight he couldn't possibly imagine. "I know what you are. My God will defend against you."

Brad didn't think so, not on either count. Figured he was going to need a new rug.

"I gather, then, that you did *not* come here to purchase the Lyon ruby?" Lily pushed back in her chair, interrupting the brewing disaster. She masked it well, but she was angrier than he was, and for more reasons. He was focused on the threat to Evan and didn't really care about the fucking ruby. Lily still had all the balls in the air even if they were all spitting sparks.

Then Madame LeRoux said, "Sit down, Michel," and tugged on the priest's sleeve. "I apologize for my son. Our own family history shames us, but believe me that we are trying to make amends now."

Lily fluttered blood-red fingertips, dismissing the apology as too little and far too late. "If you are looking for absolution, find a church. If you want the ruby, we need to talk money. Now would be best."

Chapter 26

GRAYSON DONNE'S HOUSE OPENED ON either side of a grand hall painted with murals of pastoral scenes, more or less. An equally grand staircase rose to a gallery with an oak balustrade twined with carved bunches of grapes and a row of portraits watching the door from the upper hall. Bacchus, the grapes meant. He turned the flashlight on, checked to make sure it worked, then turned it off again. He might need the batteries later and was just as glad that the dim light inside the house made it impossible to see what the figures in the murals were doing among their painted trees. The floor was marble, pieced so that the veins of black and rust spread like heart's blood throbbing through the house.

A crystal chandelier hung from the high-beamed ceiling and wall sconces were set at intervals between the murals, enough faux candles to light the room like Times Square for a party. He left them turned off, waited while his eyes adjusted to the shadows.

The woman at the dry cleaner had been right about the feel of the place. In spite of the open hall, the house felt close, guarded. Mostly, Evan couldn't shake the feeling that it was waiting for something. Empty—he was pretty sure of that. Wasn't going to let his guard down, though, not on the uncertain evidence of senses he didn't fully understand. The house could be lying to him.

He first checked the parlor on the left, empty, as he'd

expected, except for the heavy brocaded curtains drawn
over the windows. His footsteps sounded strange in his ears,
heavy and muffled, as if weighed down when he crossed to
open the pocket doors on the right.

Nothing, though the marks on the threadbare Turkish
carpet indicated a desk once stood in front of the curtained
window and the shapes of absent bookcases left bright
holes in the shadows on the walls. Not the library Brad
wanted him to look for, however. These were quiet rooms,
and not just because the furniture was gone. Whatever terrors the house had seen, they hadn't happened here. That
left the stairs, or a hall leading to the back of the house. He
took the hall. Basic rule—know your exits—and he didn't
know why that thought tumbled into his forebrain like a
warning, but he was not stupid and he didn't ignore things
like that.

The light grew stronger as he moved toward the back of
the house. Halfway down the hall the dining room was also
empty, except for a big fireplace with a carved oak mantel
and a small warming cupboard set into the wall above it.
The room had a double door from the hall, and a narrow
one that led from the kitchen. Afternoon light poured in
through a cut-glass window that looked out on a sculpture
garden. He thought the shapes looked familiar, but the
glass fractured the light, distorting the squared hedges so
he couldn't quite process what had set off his back brain.
With a mental note to check it out later, he moved on.

Farther down the hall, the kitchen opened to a back
door with a hook for the key set into the frame. The morning room to the left had no curtains; diffuse light from the
corner windows left no pools of warmth or shadow, but he
figured the morning sun would be pretty spectacular. Pantry on the right. The kitchen had been modernized about
sixty years ago, but now held nothing but rusting appliances
and a narrow pantry staircase snaking up the back way. The
staircase exuded an oily, claustrophobic dread the closer he
got to it. He took that for the clue it was, and started up.

Bedrooms on the second floor—a lot of them—with
doors opening onto a central corridor. The state had taken

out the furniture for auction, but he could see the wear on
the wood where heavy beds had stood, blocks of light and
dark that marked where rugs had lain. Some of the rooms
had plain walls, cream wallpaper over aged plaster. Some
had elaborate decorations of leering satyrs and naked
women with rounded curves who ran with outstretched
arms and horrified glances cast behind them. The satyrs
always caught up above the bright space where the head
of the bed would have stood against the wall. Evan turned
away from depictions that fell somewhere between can-
nibalism and rape, except that satyrs weren't human. The
women were prey.

Sometimes the running figures were naked boys instead,
but the outcome was the same. It didn't tell him anything
he didn't know already. Grayson Donne had been a sick
fuck.

Evan found another staircase going up and took it, to a
round turret room with an orrery suspended from the ceiling. A table or desk had stood under it, and curved shelves
lined the walls. The movers had left behind a few jars, nearly
empty and worthless, based on casual examination. Evan
didn't want to know what left those residues at the bottom
of the jars, or what Donne had used them for.

Between the shelves four windows looked out to the
four quarters and three of them looked down on the formal gardens. He stopped at the west window—from above
he could see the pattern that had nudged at his memory.
The yew hedges formed a maze encircled like a pentacle.
Pebbled walks wandered purposefully through the maze,
where figures of stone and bronze marked the key turn-
ings. With the beds, mostly greenery but some in bloom, the
garden formed a sigil, but not for summoning a daemon, he
was sure of that.

He let his mind go wide-focus, imagined the shelves of
books in the private study at home. He'd seen this mark
before—Agrippa? Paracelsus? No. Then he had it. A con-
founding seal, that prevented the escape of a rebellious
daemon. A daemon couldn't say "no" to a master. He knew
that, to his shame. But a daemon could twist a command

out of true, do something unexpected and unintended with it. Lily had escaped the Russian priest that way, killing him and a small village along the way.

The garden below was meant to punish a daemon or hold it. A prison of sorts, facing west, and Paimon was prince of the west wind in the old lore—odd constraint on creatures that existed in a realm that seemed to have no connection to this one, except that it shared the same space somehow. Destroy a world in the second sphere and it died as surely in this one. Trap a daemon in a box or tangle it in that garden, it wasn't going anywhere. Except that in the garden, Grayson Donne could watch. And Carlos Sanchez said they'd had no clothes. Evan turned away before the rage building behind his eyes turned into something with rain and wind behind it. Losing his temper wouldn't help Matt Shields, so he focused on finding the secrets Donne's turret room still held.

Tucked between the north and west windows, a rectangle of wood floor showed discoloration where a small carpet had worn away the finish. When Donne had lived here, the trapdoor would have been hidden under it. There was no handhold—Evan ran his hands over the braces for the shelves, looking for a mechanical release, and found it on the opposite wall.

Inside, a hidden staircase led down at an angle diagonal to the one he'd come up on. Evan found a switch, of all things, and flipped it. A series of naked bulbs gave little more light than a trail of candles. It was enough of an invitation to keep him moving and enough light to keep him from breaking his neck.

He'd have expected a secret passage to be rough and unfinished, but he found the way filled with paintings here as well—of rape and torture, and he guessed the satyr must be the devil, because other paintings showed Donne himself, or a close relative, naked on a throne above the flaming pit. In his hand he held a scepter of flame, and under his foot groveled the satyr. Evan wondered briefly how things had turned out for Donne in the afterlife, hoped he was burning. He was pretty sure the devil was laughing, Around the

central figure of Grayson Donne milled the demon min-
ions of hell, and at his left and right, other men, the features
too specific to be an allegory. So Donne hadn't been in this
alone. Matt Shields had some explaining to do.

Evan pulled the digital camera out of his pocket and
snapped a few pictures for evidence. He'd thought maybe
he'd go back over the house when he was finished here, get
a few shots of the women in the paintings as well. See if
they could match the faces with missing persons' reports.
Halfway down the first flight inside the walls, he stopped
at a narrow landing. Peepholes let into one of the undeco-
rated bedrooms. On this side of the passage there was no
need for secrecy, and a button glowed with pale electric
light. Evan pushed it, and a panel slid open.

Now that he knew what he was looking for, he easily
found the hidden door between this bedroom and the next,
larger and more elaborately decorated than any of the others he'd seen so far. The master bedroom, Donne's own.
The paintings were evidence, he knew that now, but his
breath tightened in his throat when he looked at them. Torture and rape, women and men both, and for a moment he
thought he saw his own face on the wall, bound by chains
and screaming.

His mind went away, didn't come back until he was gasping for air in the passageway again, teeth clenched against
a keening moan that he would not let go, not even alone.
He was afraid that if he started, he would never stop, so he
counted to ten, a fist pressed to his forehead to remind him
to think, damn it, just put it aside and think. It wasn't him.
Grayson Donne had been miles away when Omage played
his nasty little games. But he recognized his own face,
wouldn't be confused about something like that. Wasn't
going back in that room to check it out, though.

Down. The hidden staircase took him down. And somewhere, right about—yes, there it was, a release hidden in
the eye of the devil in the nearest paintings. Donne hadn't
wanted anyone to stumble on this room uninvited.

Chapter 27

MONEY DIDN'T MAKE AMENDS FOR THE year Evan had spent in chains, driven insane so that his captors could use him as a battering ram between the universes. But Madame LeRoux said, "Ten million," reached into a small but expensive purse and pulled out a Blackberry. "It was all I could raise on such short notice."

Lily looked at the screen. "Euros."

Half again as much—fifteen million—in dollars, so maybe money could make amends. The ruby was worth more but it was enough to fulfill the contract. They didn't expect Donne's box to cost even a fraction of that at auction. Shields didn't plan to stick around to spend the rest, so the price didn't really matter.

Lily entered the agency's account number and returned the Blackberry, brought out the transfer of ownership, and signed it. "You can have your lawyer look this over if you'd like, but it's fairly standard. You agree to the description, but not the provenance."

"Can you lie?" Madame LeRoux asked. Now that the money was on the table, she'd relaxed and simply seemed curious.

"All the time," Lily answered with a raised eyebrow, "but never in a deal."

"Ah, but you can't always trust the truth from the mouth of a stranger, can you?"

Lily shrugged, letting Madame LeRoux think what

she wanted. "There are no promises on this table. Just a wire transfer and a stone."

Father Michel had focused on Brad from the moment he walked in, but Lily had caught Bertrande LeRoux's attention, and not for the usual reasons she turned heads.

"He is kind to you, then? This young man who holds you here?" Not entirely out of the blue, given the exorcism at the start of the meeting, but still not what she'd expected.

"No one holds me here." Brad recognized the bitter smile, the one with the ages of planets in her eyes. Madame LeRoux nodded as if she'd just confirmed something she'd already worked out for herself. Father Michel might have had something unpleasant in his mouth, but Madame LeRoux tapped her cane lightly on her son's knee. "We have what we came for. Let it go."

"The boy—"

"You were wrong," Madame LeRoux rose painfully from her chair. "And it appears I was as well. Let it go."

Father Michel stared at the ceiling again, as if he could shatter the protections there with the power of a glance. Fortunately, he was human, and couldn't. Daemon lords always kept score, though, so Lily added, "We'll send you a bill for the door," which made Madame LeRoux smile. "I always pay my debts," she said, "and look forward to receiving it."

The priest took a breath to object, but Madame LeRoux shook her head. "It's all right," she said. "They are happy here, and they are hurting no one. Leave it alone."

"Their happiness is not my concern. We know the boy is involved."

They had the money, a wire transfer, so they didn't need Madame LeRoux anymore and never had needed Father Michel. It would be worth it to rid the universe of the annoyance. But Lily liked the house.

Chapter 28

H E WAS IN AN OCTAGONAL ROOM, no doors that he could see other than the entrance from the secret passage. No windows. Evan thought he'd gotten used to Donne's idea of art but had to turn away from the painting of a man being torn to pieces by a horned devil with Matt Shields' face. "*We know who the devil in this room was, Mr. Donne,*" he muttered under his breath, but found no relief from the images of rape and murder on any of the eight walls.

No furniture. All of Grayson Donne's worldly possessions were sitting in a gallery at Sotheby's, but Evan saw no indication that this room ever held more than the seal inlaid in parquetry on the floor. A parquetry circle bound the perimeter in black. Not painted, but a darker wood polished to a dull glow. It had been here for a long time. Longer than Grayson Donne. He'd known that going in, but seeing the evidence made those centuries of captivity real.

Inside the circle, the outlines of stars nested like a compass rose, each with a different number of points, each major point touching the circle. Each space held an inlaid symbol—the zodiac on the outer ring, and letters in Greek and Hebrew closer to the center, where the legs of the seal crossed to make a smaller internal ring. At the very center a simple pentagram held a dark, irregular stain. Evan crossed to it, knelt to look closer.

Blood, and not just one stain—they overlaid each

other, soaked into the wood at the center of the pentagram. With nothing to give the room scale, he'd thought the space was smaller. Crouching over the bloodstains, he realized that a human could have lain inside the central pentagram. Iron rings were bolted to the floor, aligned with the four lower points—Grayson Donne's ground zero. Behind him, the secret door snicked shut.

The room gathered power at its bloody center. It raised the hairs on the back of his neck, but he reached out to it anyway. Only the feel of it, solid beneath his fingertips, could make it real, so he brushed his fingers lightly across the bloody stain.

The lights flickered and went out, but he barely noticed them, because a hundred or more screams exploded in his head and no, he hadn't expected that. His hand went down, instinctive move to steady his balance and made full contact with the bloody center of the pentagram.

"*Fuck.*"

He was naked, wrists and ankles clamped to the floor at the center of the pentagram. His swollen wrist hurt like a son of a bitch and the cuts on his arms, his body, ached with the deep throbbing pressure of old infections left untreated, as familiar as if he still carried the wounds.

He'd been here, in this room, drugged when they moved him, so he didn't remember leaving the Black Masque or how he'd gotten here. Hadn't remembered any of it until now, and he didn't think the memory was all his—the room fed him more than he could have known, out of his mind from more than the drugs then. But he saw it all now.

A dozen figures surrounded him, shrouded in robes of scarlet and black with bands of arcane symbols embroidered down the front. Each figure held a candle and each watched him avidly as he struggled to escape the iron rings that held him. They were chanting something—there was always chanting. He didn't recognize any of them, except for Franklin Simpson, who stood at his left side holding the leash of a horned monster with green scales out of his nightmares. Omage, daemon lord of the host of Azmod, wore the form that Franklin Simpson commanded and sat hunched at Simpson's feet.

Impossible. *Not now, not now*. Simpson couldn't be there, couldn't hurt anybody anymore because Evan had killed him, brought a house down on top of him in Venice and watched as they dragged his dead body out of the ruins. Omage had gone home to the second celestial sphere. He was still an enemy, but he owed Evan for killing his master. And he was still quite mad. So it was impossible. But acid dripped from curved fangs to sizzle pinprick holes in the scales of the creature's own clawed feet. Evan could smell it, acid and musk sharp enough to cut through the fetid odor of infection and pain. Green fire simmered low in the daemon's eyes—Simpson had taken everything but rage against his own suffering and the pleasure of tormenting his master's victims. Evan knew Omage who, in his human form as Mac, owner of the Black Masque, had seduced him with promises and secret knowledge—Evan was different, a lord in his father's house. And, oh, yes, he could find the father Evan had never known. The answers were behind the door to Omage's back room. All Evan had to do was walk through it—

Omage hadn't lied. Evan had found answers in that back room—learned all the forms a daemon lord took on the material plane and all the forms of agony an enraged daemon lord could inflict short of killing him, because Simpson had wanted him alive. In human form, Omage had once told Evan how much he loved him, for the way he screamed. A secret between them. The beast reached out a furtive claw, dug a deep gouge in Evan's swollen wrist.

Evan screamed. Of course he screamed; that was the point.

"Enough!" Simpson kicked him in the side. He pulled on the leash too, so Evan counted that a win. But Omage grinned around his sharp, curved fangs.

"My beast has trained the half-daemon well." Simpson was dead, but this was a dream, a memory that bowed to the figure at the head of the pentagram as if he were still alive. "With the proper encouragement, the half-daemon

flies to his heavenly home and returns on command." That
was Evan, half-daemon, half-human, wholly mad. But not
anymore. Simpson was dead, and so was Grayson Donne.
Evan had survived them both, so why was Franklin Simpson still there, in his head?

"He has brought no heavenly treasures back with him
yet, but my beast assures me that it is only a matter of
time." Omage, the beast, reached for him again, but Simpson dropped a hand on the daemon's head, said, "Soon."

Evan caught his breath, moaned, "Nonono."

"But can he escape this room?" The question came from
the top of the pentagram. Evan didn't know the voice,
hadn't even considered the possibility. He didn't control
any of it, wouldn't have known how back then. That came
later, but Simpson said, "My beast has trained him, let us
try."

The leader—Grayson Donne—gave a signal, and Franklin Simpson took a step so that he had a foot on each side
of Evan's head. Then he leaned over and lifted him by his
hair. Candlelight flashed on the silver knife that curved
around his throat and Evan thought, *This time, this time*,
but the knife made only a shallow cut. Simpson caught
blood from the wound and dropped him, left him bleeding
slowly into the old marks on the floor while he smeared
the blood on the beast's snout. Then he leaned over, spread
his hand on the bloodstained floor. "To feed the room," he
said, and returned to Omage, who had begun to whine and
thrash at his leash.

"Send the half-daemon home," Simpson commanded,
"bid it return to this room with treasures." Then he un-
hooked the leash.

Not here, not now. Evan rolled out of the blood-soaked
circle, knew that hadn't been the last of his own blood
spilled there. The room had held him, he hadn't escaped it
then, and . . .

He curled in on himself, wrists held protectively close
while he fought the sense memory of Omage's claws on
him, acid falling on infected wounds and Omage's fangs at
his throat, Omage—

Chapter 29

MATT SHIELDS BURST THROUGH THE door, trailing Madame LeRoux's bodyguards, his eyes snapping fire and a new sports coat flying out behind him. "Evan's in trouble," he said, but Brad had already realized that. Suddenly, Evan was gone. Something had sliced through the connections that had tied Brad to his son with laser precision. No frayed ends or dangling attachments. Evan was dead. There was no reason to pretend to be human anymore. His duty to his Prince and his own folly was finished; he could go home, leave nothing but cinders behind. But first, and it surprised him that it should be so, he wanted to find whatever had murdered his son and kill it, personally.

Shields grabbed his arm before he could do more than form the thought. "Get Sanchez. Don't go in the house. It will trap you too."

Behind him, Lily was escorting Madame LeRoux to the door. "He's excitable," he heard her say, "I am sure everything is fine." The door closed behind them. Gone. Good.

"Why didn't you warn him?" he asked, and Lily followed with the obvious assumption, "Were you looking for a war?"

"I was looking for a way out of here! Without Evan, what are my chances of that? You figure it out! I thought he'd be safe."

"Well, he wasn't." Brad shook off Shields' hand, straightened his jacket. Ariton had made a deal with

Paimon—Evan's deal. He didn't know what would happen to Matt Shields if he destroyed the box, didn't know what would happen to the daemon lord trapped inside it. But if destroying the wretched thing would work, Shields would have done it. So he had to wait until Shields was free or persuade Ariton to break the deal. They were about due for a war anyway.

Lily had abandoned him to his argument, gone home to the second celestial sphere. He should follow her, except that something had just killed his son.

Evan didn't need him anymore, but flying to the rescue had become a habit he wouldn't break now. It was stupid and human and he hated the feeling, but he wouldn't believe it until his human eyes saw the cold dead meat of his son's body. Afterward . . .

Well, Evan didn't need the planet and Brad was well sick of it. Blasting it down to its basalt roots would be a pleasure, but not until he looked into the eyes of the thing that had taken his son. Not until he'd killed it, close up. Intimate. Personal. All those words he'd learned in his time here suddenly took on a clarity of meaning he'd never wanted to feel. He thought Lily might want to play too, but first, he had to find her. He headed home.

In his daemon form, Badad entered the second celestial sphere. He found Lirion easily enough, at the center of a knot of blue flame, a gathering of the host that had not yet reached a quorum in the endless darkness of home. Lords of Amaimon, of Oriens, flickered by in their haste, but did not linger. Azmod counted Evan its personal enemy, but knew to stay away. Evan was Ariton's problem: who had killed him, and how, were now matters of interest only to Ariton.

His death had resonated through the host, a loss of a part of themselves that the daemon lords hadn't expected either. That was Badad's fault. A sane Evan, trained to control his daemon side, had burned as brightly here as any lord of Ariton. Not permanent, he'd always known that, but utterly *present*. For good or ill, his death was a part of them too.

Blue flames twined and merged as Caramos and Sched

touched Badad's mind—curiosity from the one and acceptance from the other. Sched knew humans, knew the inevitability of their deaths. To her, Evan was just another child lost to time and a cruel planet. Her dead outnumbered the stars, but he'd only had the one to lose. He hadn't wanted to be the one who killed it, but he hadn't realized it would matter that much if someone else did. Certainly hadn't known it would matter that much to Lirion.

At the center of the gathering host, she was arguing for war. Evan was Ariton. Paimon's soldier had drawn them into his fight and Evan was dead, which made it a strike against Ariton. Anader was there, willing to go to war or to turn the planet into a wobbling cinder for no special reason at all. He didn't need a reason. Anader the Cruel he was called, cold except when his temper flared hot. Few even among the host chose to attach themselves to Anader. Harumbrub would fight for the pleasure of it. Sched turned her back on him, indifferent to his small loss but Caramos absorbed his sorrow, although he didn't understand the too-human emotions that passed between them. No lord had ever returned from the material world with such regret for the loss of his captor. Sched's regret was cold and distant—a failed experiment, all her dead. She understood loss, but she'd never inhabited a dying body, couldn't comprehend death itself, the pain before and the darkness after. Humans said they saw the light, but Badad hadn't. He wondered which Evan had seen at the last: a human light, or daemon darkness.

They would require a quorum—a battle between Princes was no small thing even when they waged war for sport— did Ariton want Paimon as an enemy? Was the life of one half-human monster worth unsettling the balance of power across a universe in which by nature he existed fleetingly at best? The debate might last millennia by human reckoning.

Badad would be there at the end, but he had scores to settle in human time, and he'd been right—Lirion wanted in on the kill. They followed the imprint of Evan's last presence on his world, searching for the place where he had ceased to exist.

Chapter 30

"**N**O!"
 Omage was gone. Simpson was dead and so was Grayson Donne. Evan got to his knees, groped in the dark for his flashlight, catching it as it rolled out of his grasp. He'd won. It had taken him long enough, but he'd won and no old memory was going to steal his victory.

He got to his feet and tried the flashlight.

Nothing. Shook it to resettle the contacts and tried it again. Better. The light wasn't great but it was there, and he turned in a circle where he stood, looking for the door. No door, but in general, he didn't need one, so he fixed an image in his mind of home.

Didn't go anywhere.

Tried his father's home, the second celestial sphere, instead.

Damn. "In general" had just bitten him in the ass. Hadn't made it out the last time either but he had control now. He knew how to do this. Calmed his breathing and tried to sense what waited for him outside the room. Wouldn't be able to tell a demented magician from the guy driving the FedEx truck, but he should know if he had company. Except he didn't. Hadn't realized how much he'd grown accustomed to the low-level awareness of life around him until it was gone.

His ears popped, air pressure dropping suddenly in the sealed room, and he damped that impulse quickly—

didn't want a tornado in there with him. Another clue, though. Pentacles could contain a daemon's power, or repel it, depending on the way the spell was cast. Grayson Donne's room contained daemonic power, pretty much like the pentacle in the ceiling at home, except that Grayson Donne hadn't given open contracts. So he could use his abilities inside the room—whether he had control of them or not—but he couldn't use them to leave it, which left his feet, he hoped. Pentacles, Seals, Sigils, none of them held human flesh and Evan was as human as he was anything else. So, find the door, walk out.

He knew there was a door because he'd gotten in, and a door that only opened from the outside didn't make sense. Grayson Donne and his cronies were human as far as Evan could tell. They couldn't just vanish at will even if they did own the pentacle. And the bodies—the sacrifices—had to be removed somehow. So there had to be a way to open the door from the inside. Maybe more than one, but the flashlight only gave him a narrow beam of light, which was just as well—the less he saw of the paintings on Donne's walls, the better.

The catch had to be somewhere within the normal reach of the man who owned the room and it was likely close to the door itself, though it didn't have to be. He began to sweep the wall with fingertips at light-switch level for a break that might be the door or for any imperfection that might hide a button.

Nothing. He tried the next wall and the next. In the hazy circle cast by the flashlight, robed figures massed around a child bleeding into a chalice while its mother groveled nearby, tearing her clothes in despair. The memories stayed memories as long as he stayed away from the bloodstains at the center of the room. The scars on his wrists ached, reminders of old pain, old losses. He didn't lose himself in the past again, not even when he saw himself in the claws of the beast painted on the wall, but a familiar rage built inside, burning over his heart.

He forced himself to move on, but a dim blue light followed him like smoke, growing stronger—he heard the snap of flame, felt it playing with the hairs at the back of his neck. The paint on the wall smoked, turned brown and then black in a growing circle of ash.

He was going to burn the house down if he didn't get his temper under control. Not a bad idea really, except that he was still in it. He dropped his gaze to the floor, fought the rising flames under control. Not well, though. The light dropped to a twilight fog and he snapped the flashlight off—might as well save the batteries.

The floor was unmarked by his temper.

Circles, compass rose of pentagrams, zodiac. In the spaces forming the center circle, eight Greek and Hebrew letters aligned with the eight walls. He thought about the hidden staircases, one rising from the kitchen to the tower, the other plunging down through the house inside its walls.

Generations of Donnes had filled the house with their pentagrams, but they'd done more. The house was itself a seal marked out in halls and stairways, in rooms and galleries, and he stood at the very center of it, where the blood of a century and more of victims cursed it at its heart.

Chapter 31

EIGHT GREEK AND HEBREW LETTERS aligned with the eight walls. Evan went to the first letter, an Aleph, and pressed with the toe of his shoe. Nothing. But, there, a catch at the center, not the letter but the empty space between the lines. Behind him, a door slid open. And if his theory was correct—he went to the next letter, Rho, found the catch easily this time because he knew where to look. Another door opened, and another. Eight in all. Some opened onto the passage that led to the hidden staircase, some might enter into a hall or the back stair, or the gallery above the grand hall, connecting the house in a complex seal of magic.

Some of that magic was real—he couldn't escape Donne's ritual room by calling on his daemon nature, for one thing—but some was just easier to do mechanically, using secret passages and hidden latches. Figuring Donne from his house, he wanted to be center stage, controlling things, mystifying. So he'd probably hidden another catch at the center of the seal, under the blood of his sacrifices, which opened and shut all the doors at once. It didn't matter. He was getting out of there, didn't want to go near it again.

But Donne had to keep his victims somewhere. So he braced himself for the flashback and knelt in the blood of those unwilling sacrifices, ran his hand over the stain, heard their voices, but he fought back the burn of acid on his skin, the heat of infected wounds. The catch was there. Donne would have just stepped on it, but he'd have known where it was. Evan pressed it, drew his hand away with flecks of dried blood clinging to his fingertips.

As he'd expected, the doors all closed at once, and a stairway opened in front of him. The smell of damp and earth rose from the cellar below, but not the smell of rotted flesh, which was a relief. He found the switch; another string of dim lights illuminated a small staging area and a tunnel leading away from the house. Evan followed it.

There were no paintings here, just a long, straight run through earth and soft rock, mostly dry, with a few damp patches that had calcite crystals forming in the rock. He figured he was well outside the house when the tunnel veered off at an angle and headed up. He came to the end at a narrow flight of stone steps that led to a locked trapdoor. He was outside the house now, though; could move at will and didn't bother looking for the catch.

The tunnel had let him out in a forest of narrow pines fighting the hardwoods for light. The sun had dropped well into the west, but he still had hours to go before nightfall. Golden threads of dusty light wove their way between the trees, falling on soft needles and rotting leaves.

At his feet, a scatter of small crosses wandered among the knobby roots. He bent down, scraped away the leaf-fall. The earth was darker here, richer. Bodies made good fertilizer.

How many? He couldn't even count the crosses—couldn't see them all, scattered on the floor of the woods. A few looked newer, more were weathered and grimed. Some were right on top of each other—new on top of old.

His cell phone didn't work, blocked by the trees and the mountains, but he thought it might back at the house. It did, and he leaned against the car, thinking 9-1-1 and dialing—

"Philadelphia Police Department. Jaworski speaking."

And, God, just the sound of a familiar voice— "Mike, I'm in New York State, a private estate owned by the late Grayson Donne. I know it's not your jurisdiction, but I need—I think there are bodies here, Mike, a lot of them. He's been killing people for a least half a century and it may be a family enterprise. I don't know how far back some of these graves go." The house was, what, 1840s? No later than the 1870s, and the first Donne who lived here had built the house around that room.

"Are you in any danger?" He heard Jaworski scrabbling for a pencil on the other end of the line, but didn't hear what he said next. The wind had picked up, eddies rising around him, and he didn't think he was doing it.

"Dad?" he said, though he'd never called his father that, never even thought it until now and Badad of the host of Ariton would not appreciate it, on second thought.

Brad appeared in front of him with a snap of blue fire and a crack of thunder. Lily was right behind him, and Evan figured the neighbors must be hiding under their beds. But he hadn't felt this glad to see them since they pulled him out of a different back room, full of its own chains and knives and drugs and rape, where he'd prayed more than once that the daemon Omage would let him die.

Chapter 32

"**D**ON'T CALL ME 'DAD.' It sounds ridiculous."
Brad didn't know what had happened. One minute he was gathering Lily for an assault on the planet, ready to destroy everyone and everything, with a special fate for whatever had killed his son. The next, Evan was just there, every connection humming with life. He'd followed it, expecting to find his son damaged in some way, but found him talking into a cell phone next to the BMW as if he hadn't just been dead to two universes.

For some reason, that made him angry—angry enough that the grass under his feet began to crisp and brown. He'd wanted Evan alive, hadn't he? Or at least, not randomly dead at the hands of an enemy—that was Ariton's prerogative. So why was he angry enough to start a small earthquake when he found Evan not only alive, but well?

Although, not so well, if he looked a little closer. Evan hadn't had that particular look since he'd walked away from the rubble of Ca' DaCosta in Venice. He'd lost his only human friends that day, killed two people and learned his own capacity for destruction all in the space of an afternoon. He didn't want to know what had put that look on his son's face, sharp enough to see through the bruises, but he was pretty sure that Evan was going to tell him anyway.

Evan slid his hand over the phone's pickup. "Don't go in the house—it's a seal. I'd still be in there, but I'm mostly human, found the hidden latch and walked out." And yeah, Matt Shields had said something about that, he knew to stay clear, but a seal didn't erase the presence of a daemon lord. Muted it some, tangled the sense of it, but didn't cut it off completely. Evan wasn't a daemon lord, but his daemon essence was visible to any lord who looked for it.

"It's been consecrated with blood—lots of it. The sick fuck killed hundreds of people here. He buried them in the woods."

Clever man, Grayson Donne. Still too bad he was already dead. There was something else, but Evan wasn't sharing. It had to be about the seal, something that had hidden his existence from his own Prince, because that's when Evan stopped talking. He'd have to spill it before they went much further, but Brad recognized that look, pushing through shock with nothing but stubbornness to keep him moving.

Brad avoided the house, avoided the gardens that opened up a dead, cold space behind his ribs, and went in search of those graves in the woods. He wondered about Matt Shields—Parmatus—though. Could the room have the same effect on a daemon lord? No reason Ariton would notice the absence of a lord not of his own host— they didn't have that connection outside the host and had no reason to be looking for it. Matt Shields was bound here, might not know what effect the house might have on the second celestial sphere. But Paimon—Paimon had to know if a lord or two of its own host passed in and out of existence. That was powerful magic.

Paimon had made the deal, but hadn't told them. So maybe the human side of Evan's nature hid his presence at the dark heart of the house. Or maybe Paimon was hiding information vital to completing the contract.

He had no power to extract the truth from Paimon, but a carefully balanced combination of fear and emotional blackmail worked better than a summoning spell on Evan. He'd give Lily a shot first, because she had that combination calibrated to a fine point. But he wasn't going forward until he at least knew what his son was holding back.

Chapter 33

"EVAN. EVAN! ARE YOU THERE?"

Jaworski was beginning to sound a little desperate. That much got through. But Evan had the backup he needed now and he pulled himself together, answered, "Yeah, I'm here. Sorry. Got distracted, but I'm okay." He didn't mention Lily breathing fire next to him.

"You did the right thing to call me," Jaworski said. "I've got the address and help is on the way—local police should be there in about ten minutes."

"I'm fine, Mike, really. The bodies are buried in the woods northwest of the main house." And it struck him then that Carlos Sanchez had to know about those graves.

Mike Jaworski was still talking, and he tried to focus, difficult to do with his assumptions about this case realigning and Lily standing just out of reach.

"The locals have somebody checking the county records for abandoned cemeteries just to be sure, but they are sending a car to check it out in the meantime. Once they confirm—and I believe you, no question—they'll bring in the FBI. It will take a while to get an investigative team out from the regional office in New York City, but they'll want to talk to you—can you wait for them?"

Jaworski was using that soothing police voice and—huh—it worked. If he didn't know better, Evan would have been happy to leave the whole mess in the hands of the nice policeman. The next question slipped in along his own line of thought, "Your client—Matt Shields, right?—was a victim, wasn't he? The FBI will want to talk to him too."

"Yeah." The police would see it on the wall, no use hiding it now, but Jaworski would call for the shrinks if he told him the truth. "Donne is dead, but he wasn't working alone." With any luck, they could send Shields back where he belonged before the FBI caught up with him, but he was on the loose and unprotected back home.

And Lily—flames snapped, her lips drawn back in a snarl with teeth in it and he thought she was about to yell at him, but all he could think about was how he much he wanted to touch her hair.

"I have something to do first, but I'll be back by the time the FBI arrives. And thanks. I owe you."

He cut the connection, reaching for Lily. Somewhere between his ear and Lily's waist he dropped the phone—he'd have to remember that, eventually, but right now the scent of her hair was in his head and the curve of her spine was the road home.

"What's in the woods?" she asked, her mouth against his lips. Her fingers scraped lightly over his skull, reminder, caress, captivity. "Evan!"

"Nothing." She wasn't buying that. "Graves," he said, "I told you. Just graves." Nothing human moved in his awareness this side of the road—no magicians lurking in the woods to stuff his father in a box. "Nothing that can hurt him."

The reminder of Donne's human sacrifices sent him shivering back into her arms. "Oh, God, Lily, he murdered hundreds of them." He could have been one of them.

"And now he's dead." She didn't say, "He can't hurt you." Dead or not, Donne was still hurting Matt Shields and had somebody locked in a box at Sotheby's. But her arms drew him in, possession and the illusion of safety

She took his mouth. He leaned back against the BMW and let her, just held on tight for the ride because now that they'd gotten started, he wasn't in any shape to lead this dance.

But his father would be coming back from the woods, and he didn't want to be rolling around naked on Grayson Donne's lawn when the police showed up. So he pulled away from her kiss and gasped, "Not here—"

Then kissed her anyway, because he needed the feel of her, needed Lily's breasts and Lily's hands and Lily's long, strong legs wrapped around him—everything she was in the flesh or in bright blue flame meant home to him. Lily. He didn't let the words escape. knew she'd laugh at him if she caught him muttering her name under his breath. He was losing buttons—Carlo would sew on new ones, he always did—but Lily was more focused than he was. He couldn't decide whether to go for the zipper on her slacks or the buttons on her shirt, clenched his throat around a frustrated whimper he *would not* let her hear, because to get to skin at all he'd have to drag his hands back out of her hair, dark as the second celestial sphere and soft like the whisper of her name. God, he loved her hair. But her breasts were right there—he needed to be inside of her, now, in all the human ways and some that weren't—needed her mind in his mind, needed to be a part of her, sharing every molecule. Or something.

"Home," she whispered, and they went, into the darkness.

He couldn't stay here long, not with his body and he wasn't letting that go, shouldn't be here at all. He loved her here and couldn't hide the thought any more than he could hide the way her name was ricocheting off the walls of his mind. She saw his fear, and he saw hers, saw a war just averted when he reappeared and one that might be brewing, because Paimon must have known something and hadn't warned them and she'd thought he was dead. Took that for all the declaration he would ever have. Which, all things considered, was a pretty damned huge declaration of something.

They were attracting a crowd. He flinched as blue flame engulfed him in the darkness. It didn't burn, not like fire, but every nerve buzzed with the electric presence of daemon lords moving through him, taking his mind apart looking for answers he just didn't have. Ariton had agreed to a war over losing him and here he was, as safe as he could get in a place he had no right to exist. He felt the anger of the host, its curiosity. It overwhelmed him, plundering his thoughts to find out where he had gone and what he'd been doing. He knew the questions because he'd already seen them in Lily's mind, in his father's closed-down expression now that he knew to look.

He'd learned to live with nosy relatives—even, apparently, when they wanted to kill him. So he let them in, clamped down hard against the onslaught of violent outrage and showed them a little of what they were looking for, because he could read their thoughts too— "Trap," he showed them, and, "prison."

He hadn't known how completely he'd vanished, and it scared him, the power that meant.

"I didn't know! Daemon flame pried bloodstains from his mind, Grayson Donne's floor wet with sacrificial blood—his own, daemon blood. It fueled the power that lingered in the house long after Donne was dead.

That scared the relatives too, and he'd brought that danger into the spheres. So Anader still wanted war against Paimon, but he also wanted to blast Earth and Evan with it, so it could never happen again.

Evan wanted to live. He wanted his home to live. And Ariton—the host, gathered in quorum, that became its Prince—had made his deal with Paimon to free Matt Shields from Donne's strongbox. So he wanted Matt Shields to live too. But Grayson Donne's box didn't really hold him and slagging the planet wouldn't free him. He let the host see that the seals were just the physical signs of a powerful spell that had to be taken apart piece by piece. He didn't know what would happen if the whole thing went up in a molten ball of lava, but he was pretty sure Matt Shields would be screwed.

A piercing pain shot through his head—Harumbrub, with no subtlety at all, looking for something, and he hadn't credited the lord with that level of interest. Not personal, though.

"Kill him," he said. "His loyalties are divided. He's no different from the others—flesh is not to be trusted."

Daemon lords could have one loyalty—to the host, and through the host, its Prince. Minor loyalties always fell within the host. Evan's loyalty to Earth, to all the things he loved that fell outside Ariton, made him insane by their reckoning. "He'll always be a danger—and he knows our names."

"He's loyal to Ariton," Lirion showed them that part of him—it hadn't changed since the last time—and Sched touched his mind, more gently than Harumbrub. "To Lirion, and to Badad," she agreed. "To Ariton the Prince, but not to the host, which is an impossible thought. But also to his world, to his ties of flesh."

"Not divided." His reaction was too immediate to be anything but real, and they could read his mind anyway. "Two parts. One whole." And he thought that it was even true. He'd didn't feel like a jumble of bits and pieces anymore. It was all just Evan, and he could love his mother *and* his father, feel the same fierce loyalty to Ariton as he did for his home on Earth. He even understood why the host would fight the Prince of a foreign lord who took his life but then want to kill him themselves.

Was he dangerous? Of course. He was Ariton and human—a danger to both and, as he'd been told often enough, the loose end that could bring down all the spheres if he'd a mind or the blind ignorance to do it. But his loyalty was unshakable. His mother was the face in his mirror, but his father was the storm he shaped like clay and flung into the sky. No self-interest could trump either of those things.

Lily was tugging at his mind, though he didn't need the reminder. "Mine." She claimed his body and he needed her eternity after Grayson Donne's trap, needed to wrap himself in the curves of her legs and feel her life between his hands after seeing all those crosses, all Donne's murdered sacrifices. Ariton might go to war or kill him because of his own blood spilled there, but he wasn't letting go of Lily until he was dead.

Could a daemon bind a human? She saw the thought,

curled around it like a hungry cat. "Silk scarves or hand-cuffs?"

"Silk scarf? What do you do—? Oh!" Caramos would have waged war for Evan when it seemed the house had killed him, still would as soon as they figured out who the enemy was. Sched would not, but had regretted his loss a little. She still wanted Evan to find a real girl and leave Lily the hell alone. He liked her anyway, but he didn't want to share his thoughts with every gathered lord of Ariton.

Lily's fire was snapping at his nose. War could wait. He needed the comfort of their own house, the illusion that nothing could touch them His bed shaped itself in his mind and he let the image carry them there. Lily didn't protest, just took the opportunity to shed an outer layer of clothes.

Chapter 34

HIS ROOM WAS A MESS—unmade bed, paints and brushes everywhere—but he didn't care, because she was pushing him down, her palms planted on his shoulders, her back arched, dark hair closing around them.

His mouth found her breast and latched on, familiar taste of Lily and silk. She dragged her fingernails down his neck, pushed his shirt off his shoulders. He kept his mouth where it was but helped her strip off his shirt and managed his own zipper because she couldn't reach. He tipped her over and nestled between her legs, the scent of her mingling with the smell of damp silk, the taste of it, and he gripped her hips and slid the scrap of midnight blue down, followed it, tracing the curve of her leg, the landscape of thigh and knee and ankle. Her toes distracted him, brightly, pinkly, polished nails. Like candy, so he had to give them a lick, and then she laughed, threatened him with dire consequences, and offered other tasty bits, but her calf curved just so. He had to stop and lick it too. She smelled like Lily right there behind her knee and he tasted that as well, salt and sweet and Lily— she tugged him up by his ears because his hair was gone.

"Later," she gasped, imperious as a lord. "I need more now." She never said please, but the hard glitter in her eyes told him everything he needed to know. He kissed her, deep as he could get in his world, his hips moved, and he was home, sinking his hands deep in her hair while she raked hot pink fingernails up his arms, down his back, latched onto his ass tight enough to leave little red half-moons in his flesh.

He thought he could do this forever, but he couldn't, though he managed to hold on until Lily gasped and bit his ear, a little keening sound escaping the almost-clench of her teeth. She'd leave marks, a line of scratches where her nails had slid up his ass, taking skin with them, but he didn't think he'd need an earring.

She rolled over, taking him onto his back, letting him know with one leg wrapped around his thigh that she wasn't done with him yet. Evening was turning indigo in his window. In the corner, Lily laughed at him out of a canvas, half painted and wholly naked. He could feel those lines in his hand, wanted to paint them, wanted to mark her as his own, and smiled.

"Just a minute." He slipped out of bed, found what he wanted—jars, brushes. Paint. It had settled a bit so he mixed the colors with the handle of the brush, then filled the bristles and began to paint. There, on her breast, the swirl of a dark blue leaf, another on her belly, joined by a trailing vine of white paint. She lay still, sighing at the lap of the paint on her flesh, the sweep of the brush, sable, for her—that sound she made when he touched the tip of her nipple with blue was worth every brush he had. A stroke from the base of her breastbone to her navel. The intricate design, like lace, worked from hip to hip across the softness of her belly, brought up her knees, but he couldn't touch, didn't want to smear the paint. Not yet, not until he'd covered every inch of her with abstract flowers, vines and leaves and tendrils, stroke by stroke by stroke, following with kisses carefully placed in the pink and cream between the lines. Aleph, he worked in, and Rho, then obliterated that memory in a tangle of painted flowers while she moaned softly and the sweat bloomed between her legs. Looking at it, his mouth went dry, and so he licked it up, and wanted more, and she was digging her toes into his ass, but not touching him with her arms, left them where he had placed them, stretched out on the bed as if the trailing vines had grown out of the rumpled covers and bound her to the bed.

"Evan," she sighed his name, and her eyes slid shut, focusing inward on the sensations he was giving her. "I did that," he thought. The paint glistened wet on her skin.

He couldn't wait, wanted the liquid slide, slow and easy, because she'd gone soft and languid on the bed and they moved together as if the day had never happened, obliterating the lace he'd made on her skin, sharing paint with the spit and the sweat and all the other things they stained the sheets with. White streaks of paint worked their way into her hair and his heart clenched, knowing he'd never see her hair grow white. She'd outlive him by a billion years and might lose interest tomorrow anyway.

But he had her now, her arms coming up to leave smears of blue and white on his back. He'd gotten paint on his face and shared it with Lily, who laughed at him and wiped a dab off his nose before she put a kiss there—didn't want to know where else that paint was going, but he wasn't going to let her go to find out. They were slippery and wet and the bed was a mess—he'd never get the sheets clean, figured they'd be his favorites after today. Lily managed to get on top, laughed at how difficult it was not to slide right off each other. But she knew what she wanted and he was ready for her, fingers gripping her, counting ribs, thumbs nestled under the slope of her breasts. He was exhausted by the time she was done with him, too tired even to think about clients or graves in the woods or a house with his face on the wall and his blood on the floor.

Before he'd finished debating with himself the value of a shower, he'd fallen asleep.

Chapter 35

MATT SHIELDS HAD LEFT A NOTE ON THE desk: "I locked up before I left. Are we set for the auction?"

Shields took playing human to new levels of ordinary. Brad didn't trust any part of it, but figured that the faster they were done with this case the faster he could stop worrying about deals with Princes not his own. The laptop was open, so he tapped through the labyrinth of passwords Evan had set and checked the agency's account for Shields' transactions.

The money was there, and he shut down again, ignored the phone that rang on the desk. He had to talk to Shields about the trap in Grayson Donne's house— the one he hadn't bothered to mention before it caught Evan—and he wanted to know who was screaming in the box they were supposed to buy. But right now? He wanted coffee and, in the absence of anyone else to do it, wandered back into the kitchen to make a pot.

Evan had left the coffeemaker ready, so he turned it on, pulled down a plain white mug while it gurgled to life. Tried to ignore the agency line ringing through on the kitchen phone and that seemed successful for a minute. Then it started again. Different tone now—the private line.

Brad checked caller ID. He didn't recognize the number, but the exchange was the same as Ellen Li's official cell phone, so he picked up. Didn't say anything, just waited because he hated telephones even more than he hated computers and never gave away the tactical advantage.

"Evan? Is that you? Evan?" Mike Jaworski, half threatening, half cajoling. "Are you hurt?" Scared. It cheered Brad to hear that tone for some reason.

Evan was pumping out residual panic along with about a dozen other emotions that Brad didn't much care to sift through, but he didn't seem hurt. Brad hung up the phone, poured himself a mug of coffee and wandered toward the study to find a book. He had to pass through the living room to get there, and Mike Jaworski was standing in the middle of it, gun drawn.

"I should have known it was you." Jaworski slid the gun into its holster. He had an earpiece on and it all looked rather television to Brad. Jaworski said "Stand down" into the plastic arm that swept his cheek. "Bradley's here. Send in the file." He pulled off the earpiece and turned an exasperated glare on Brad. "Normal people say 'hello' when they answer the phone. 'Fuck you' will do in a pinch, if you don't want the police barreling into your house."

Brad glared back. "When did failing to talk on the telephone become a felony?"

"It's not an arrest—it's a rescue. Have you heard from Evan?"

"Evan's fine. What are you doing here anyway?"

"Rescue," Jaworski repeated, "Ellen set a watch on the house. I called from the corner. Came in through the side gate." He cocked his head, receiving some message from the plastic in his ear. Then he frowned, not angry, but puzzled. "The gate? It's the big iron thing in the middle of the brick wall." A pause, then, "Wait there. I'll be right out." He jabbed a finger at Brad, didn't make contact but still infused it with all the threat that a human with a conscience could muster. "Don't move. We have to talk."

Brad's coffee was getting cold, so he went back to the kitchen, dumped it in the sink and poured another. Mike Jaworski found him there and slapped a file on the breakfast bar.

"Have you *seen* Evan? Are you sure he's all right? He called, reported graves in the woods at Donne's estate. He was supposed to wait and talk to the local police, but he wasn't there when they arrived. His car was parked in front of the house and the police found his cell phone in the grass beside it, so the working assumption is that whoever was working with Donne took Evan."

"He seemed fine when I talked to him a few minutes ago." It was only partly a lie. Evan was in the house, with Lily, but he wouldn't appreciate an interruption. An image of Mai Sien Chong, naked on a sea of green silk, completely blanked his mind for a moment and in that time Jaworski found himself a blue pottery mug and poured himself a cup of coffee. It unnerved Brad that Jaworski knew where the mugs were, and that he'd picked the blue. Evan had broken one that morning, over a conversation they still had to finish. Jaworski had seen the broken pieces and made his own calculations.

Entirely too familiar. Brad considered modifying the wards on the gate, but that would make Ellen Li suspicious, and he was supposed to be playing chess with her husband tonight.

Jaworski set down the mug and opened the file, spread police photos on the breakfast bar. "He was right about the graves. Those people were torn to pieces by some animal and partially eaten, then ritualistically buried in shallow graves." He sorted through the photos, picked out two that showed distinct evidence that something had gnawed on the bones.

Brad's eyes slid shut, but he couldn't hide from the images in his head. Rage. Overpowering rage, rage to destroy worlds. Donne had caged that fury, turned a daemon lord of the second celestial sphere into a ravening mindless beast. He remembered the rage from his own binding but had no cage of human words to stop him now...

"I know it's bad, but I think you need to see this." Jaworski's voice gentled, and Brad wanted to kill him for it.

"You don't know anything at all, Mr. Jaworski."

"I'm sorry." Jaworski didn't offer any false comfort, just

pushed his coffee at him. Brad stared at him for a moment but read concern in Jaworski's furrowed brow. For him, not Evan, this time. For the human shell, the human father of a human friend. He didn't think Jaworski would handle a demonstration of his true nature nearly as well. Wouldn't understand that Brad felt for the daemon lord who had been driven to do those things, not the humans who had died. *Matt Shields,* he thought. Donne had paid in more than rubies.

"Evan is in danger. Donne was into some freaky stuff, and he wasn't working alone. According to the FBI profiler, we're looking at a cult that uses torture and murder in its rituals. We know what they did to their victims. If they have him—"

"They don't." Brad was sure of that. But his temper was starting to create static on the line.

"But they did." Jaworski slid another photograph from the file. "I didn't want to show you this, but the FBI found his fingerprints nearby, so they're pretty sure he saw it."

Just paint this time. Brad recognized Evan in the picture, of course. At some point he'd been held in that house. The horned monster raping him had green scales, so it was probably Omage. Brad had been there, seen that. Another place and time, but Evan had belonged to Franklin Simpson, not Grayson Donne, and Evan never would have taken the case if Paimon's lord had done that to him. They'd be well into the war that the Princes had put on hold.

"We think they wore costumes as part of their sick rituals, and to protect their identities."

The robes were costumes. Omage's material form in the painting was just a bad rendering. He didn't think Jaworski would appreciate the critique.

" . . . Evan may have seen or heard a name, something, that can help us stop them. The FBI wants to talk to him about what was going on there, how he got away."

"Evan didn't escape." Old story. Brad was tired of revisiting it. "Lily and I got him out. But it was a different place, different people who held him and they are as dead as Grayson Donne, so I don't know what help he can be." The pictures gave Evan a motive for murdering Simpson and tied them to the Black Masque. Brad wondered how much money they had stashed in their own offshore account.

Jaworski rubbed at his eyes, buying time while he added it up in his head and came to the same answer Joe Dougherty had. Then he shook it off—probably remembered how they died and figured that a collapsing house made an unlikely murder weapon. But he wasn't finished.

"Knowing what he'd been through, how could you take this case?"

"Evan took the case," Brad pointed out. "I objected. But we didn't know they were connected." Matt Shields must have known, though, and he hadn't said anything.

"Yeah, well. The FBI also wants to talk to your client."

Jaworski shuffled the photographs back into a neat stack, the one with Evan in it tucked into the center, hidden as much as he could make it, and tapped the rim of his coffee cup, reminding Brad of the broken pieces scattered on the floor that morning. He wasn't an expert on the material sphere, but he figured nothing that started this badly ever ended well.

"He may need—you may want to talk to him when he gets back. You really *do* know where he is, don't you?"

"He's with Lily. They're both safe." Which was a lie in ways that Jaworski might even appreciate.

And there it was. A sly smile sneaked across his face. "That's one way to handle it." The smile disappeared as fast as it had come. "A roll in the hay may not be enough this time."

Brad didn't know what hay had to do with anything, but Jaworski didn't explain, just pulled a couple of business cards out of his breast pocket. "These people work with victims. They can help."

Counseling the half-human children of daemons was beyond the scope of any help Jaworski had in his pocket. Brad couldn't quite sort out how much of the conversation was police questioning and how much was the concern of someone Evan was starting to think of as a friend, but that was Evan's problem, not his. He took the card anyway—anything to get the policeman moving and out of his house.

"The FBI's New York office has the car." Jaworski was talking again, settled into the stool at the breakfast bar and not going anywhere. "At the moment they're treating it like evidence of a kidnapping, but they'll release it when Evan confirms that there's been no crime." He looked down at the folder of photographs neatly squared on the granite counter, then backed up and tried again. "At least not this time. He can pick the car up at the impound yard."

Brad didn't care about the car, but he'd had enough of the FBI. "Tell them to keep it. We'll get a new one."

That brought Jaworski's head up with wary surprise. "What did they do to him? I can protect him, but not if you don't tell me what happened to him." Earnest concern, right in Brad's face and he had to take a step back or do something that would complicate all their lives. The damned car.

"He's fine. Nothing happened." The coffeepot was steps away and not a retreat at all. "The FBI won't find anything useful. Nothing has ever happened in that car."

Jaworski huffed, but couldn't quite mask the laugh. "If they find bodily fluids, I assume you don't want to know?"

"Unlikely. Lily likes her comforts."

"Lily likes her Evan. I can't see a stick shift stopping her. But we'll keep that confidential. And I get it, really. 'Grand gestures are us.' The FBI will let you know when you can pick it up." Jaworski took his folder and headed for the door. "I've seen how bad it can get carrying memories like Evan's around. If he needs somebody just to talk to, tell him to give me a call, off the record."

Brad thought "thank you" might be in order, but he did not put himself in the debt of humans. Jaworski shook his head, but kept moving. "You're a stubborn bastard," he said, "But you're welcome anyway."

Brad watched the gate behind him and added a new car to the "to do" list. The BMW was getting old anyway. He wasn't worried. Evan hadn't been kidnapped this time. Caught in a trap set for daemons and found his own way out. Clever boy. And Lily brought him home. She always did. But Jaworski had unsettled him, so he followed the sense of his son to the third-floor studio.

They were in bed together, covered in swirls and smears of blue and white and each other, not quite done with what they'd started. Evan didn't notice him, a human trait he'd once said: to shut out anything but a perceived threat. Lily never lost the awareness of cousins in the room. Perhaps she had a better understanding of danger.

She stretched and smiled, kissed Evan in places that stirred a few new memories of his own. Rolled him over and went with him, a kaleidoscope of blue and white, so that Evan was on his back and Lily was riding him, laughing. Playing like host-cousins in human form. Except that Evan looked at her in a way that set warnings clamoring. Lily's attention span was short, and Evan had already stretched it farther than Brad had thought it would go.

He hadn't come here to watch his son play, and seeing them, he wondered why he *had* come. He had more pressing concerns, and Matt Shields was top of the list. But it was late, and Mai Sien would be waking up soon, which seemed as good an idea as any.

Chapter 36

BRAD HATED PAPERWORK AND AVOIDED it whenever possible. Occasionally it wasn't possible, so he spent half the next afternoon at the computer in the formal office because they still hadn't replaced the desk in the study. He asked himself again why he didn't just fry this little ball of wax and go home. Knew the answer—the IRS would rise from the ashes to find him and he'd still have to do the paperwork. But he was done for the quarter, closed the computer and stretched at the desk. Evan was in San Diego, taking a quick look at the real estate holdings of a senior executive for one of their regular clients, money in the bank. Lily had gone back to Hokkaido for reasons that Evan was better off not knowing, which meant that no one was watching Matt Shields.

They'd left him on his own too long when he'd merited more watching than Evan. Evan was a smart boy and he made good use of his dual nature. Matt Shields had handed them a case like a bright shiny object to chase, and they hadn't questioned his motives beyond the obvious. But the strongbox in Sotheby's galleries screamed when he approached it, and that hadn't been in Shields' story. Not all of Grayson Donne's effects had made it to auction either. You didn't bind daemons without a lot of research—where were the books? And what else had already passed into the hands of the robed figures in Mike Jaworski's photographs?

Brad was restless and he'd been looking for a war, felt cheated when he didn't get one. He thought maybe he'd found one at a pool table on Third. Matt Shields was at Charlie's, a little joint off the beaten track for the club scene, but the front booths and the long, polished bar were already filling up with the local beer-and-a-burger crowd. Brad shrugged his way past the bar, where a bartender in black jeans and tee with a shaved head and a plug in his earlobe looked up but didn't stop wiping down glasses.

In a room at the back, Shields had found a local to relieve of his money. He was studying his shot over a pool table with a bump or two in the worn red felt; his shoulders tensed when Brad walked in behind him, but otherwise he pretended not to notice a daemon lord of a foreign Prince at his back. Allies, after all. Brad took the cue out of the hands of the indignant hipster, his smile pretending an apology that the cold set of his eyes took away again. "He cheats," he said with a little shrug. "Take your money and bring me a Sam Adams."

"Now how am I going to pay for my burger?" Shields looked up, shook his head in mock dismay, but he was smiling, so he'd learned that much about human behavior. He took his shot; the last of the striped balls ricocheted off the cushion and dropped into the corner pocket.

From the front of the house the clink of glass on glass, the din of clashing conversations punctuated by laughter bounced off the walls and sank into the local after-work crowd again. They had the back room to themselves for now, a second table for play and three for drinks and food still empty, but that wouldn't last much longer.

Surprise—the waitress brought him his Sam Adams. She had short hair, purple on one side, and a full-sleeve tattoo crossed by a studded leather bracelet on her right arm. Her piercings made him a little queasy, but Shields smiled like they were old friends and took the Heineken she'd brought him without asking.

"Anything else?"

Somebody to watch my client while I play chess with

Harry Li, Brad thought, but he said "We'll take the other table too."

"That'll be twelve dollars for the tables." She stuck her hand out for the money, drawing her own conclusions about why he wanted privacy in a semi-crowded bar. "We don't allow sex in the bar. It's against the health code and could get us closed down."

"No sex. Got it." Brad pulled a hundred out of his wallet, handed it over, and turned to the table before she could ask if he wanted change. He figured for that much they'd have at least ten minutes without an audience. Maybe more if the house didn't need the tables. He couldn't count on it, but he heard her say "private party" to someone in the arch between the rooms and then she pulled an accordion door halfway across the space.

"Do you know what to do with that stick in your hand, or are you just happy to see me?" Shields goaded him. Brad didn't think he'd ever heard that almost-laugh in his voice before, figured he was about to ruin Shields' day, and didn't much care. The void in the universe where Evan had gone missing in that house had raw edges. The agency had never walked away from a contract and Princes did not break trust with each other when alliances were made, but for Matt Shields, he might still make an exception.

"How hard can it be?"

"Candy from a baby." Shields racked the balls and stepped back. "For a burger and fries, and all the beer we can drink?"

"The money's in the bank. You can buy your own dinner."

"Yeah, but where's the fun in that? I'll even let you go first."

The bar wasn't his kind of place, but Evan and Lily came here sometimes, ran a tab and played a few games, not all of them on the table. "Physics and geometry," Evan said about it. Lily figured that, as a way to observe the limits of the material world in action, it was a lot less painful than driving the car into a tree.

Brad took off his jacket and laid it carefully over the back of a chair, took a swallow of his beer.

He sighted down the cue, hit the white ball, and watched the roll and scatter across the table. "Six," he said, taking solid, and dropped the green into the side pocket. "Where is Donne's library? Who has it, how did they get it, and why?"

Chapter 37

HUNGER DROVE EVAN TO THE KITCHEN. He scarfed down a leftover beignet and wandered through the living room, passed the private study with a mental note to get the damned desk replaced. Maybe he'd call Claire Murphy, see if she could help. Overhead the shower cut on, and he thought, *maybe not*. Lily hadn't been home when he arrived, but that sounded like her bathroom.

Brad was sitting at the desk in the front office, the leather executive desk chair tilted back. "Nothing going on in San Diego," he started. "The guy looks clean so far." But something was off with his father.

"Evan!" The desk chair swiveled left, right, left. "Where have you been? I've been waiting to see you."

Way off. Evan stepped under the seal worked into the plaster and hoped the repairs worked. "Who are you?"

"I'm your father—the Bradley part of Bradley, Ryan, and Davis? Who else would I be?" Brad's lids dropped over blue sparks. So—family.

"That's a good question." Evan relaxed a little. Not too much. Whoever he was, he knew Brad's earthly identity and his relationship with Evan, that they got along reasonably well most of the time, so it wasn't a stranger who'd been stuck in a box like Matt Shields. But there were still lords of his own Prince who wanted him dead.

"You're usually not that suspicious, Evan. I was just

here, and I thought, maybe we could have a little sex, you know, to pass the time until Parmatus ..." The eyes were open again, full of reckless fun and giddy hope.

Parmatus. Matt Shields in the second celestial sphere? But deals between Princes weren't the point of this visit.

"Lily! We've got company!" No panic, just a wave of profound exasperation. "Hello, Caramos. What are you doing here? Wait!" He raised both hands in front of him, to put a stop to that giddy hope. "I am not going to have sex with you. Not now, not ever. How did you get here anyway? I thought only lords who had been summoned at some point could find their own way back."

"I followed you. Got a little lost, but then I just looked for Lily. And here I am."

Help—more or less—arrived. Lily wandered in, still naked from her shower, her hair wrapped in a towel. Neither was necessary. She reshaped the body when she moved through the spheres and only took the shower because she liked the feel of the falling water. And she had plenty of clothes in her closets. "Evan doesn't sleep with his father— Brad asked, Evan said 'no,'—so that body won't work." She kissed him on the chin, gave it a little nip that didn't reassure him.

"Why not? I thought—we're both Ariton and Brad is family, a familiar body. I thought it would be fun."

Caramos' explanation wasn't entirely unexpected. But it wasn't exactly welcome either, and Evan found himself at a loss. Didn't want to upset the relatives when they could take out the block over an unintended insult, but he didn't want to have sex with whoever turned up jonesing for some daemon-on-human action either.

Lily just thought he was funny. "Evan has it all muddled up with two-headed babies, something to do with human genetics," She raised her arms to massage her head with the towel, which brought her breasts up, presented like a gift.

Evan dropped into one of the guest chairs, closed his eyes while he pulled himself together, which was difficult under the circumstances. Lily sat on the desk, still naked, facing Caramos. He could think of better things to do with a naked Lily, but she hadn't stopped talking.

"He's wrong about the two-headed babies, of course. It's really about power. They have stories, literature, full of fathers and sons struggling for power. Sex is a forbidden weapon, because the sons are supposed to win, eventually ..."

"I'm still here! Why are you talking about me as if I left the room?" Evan put a hand over his closed eyes. He didn't want to have this conversation, didn't want to hear this conversation.

"... If the fathers use sex against them, the sons lose, pretty much forever."

Caramos had stopped swinging his chair. He huffed through his nose in a way that Brad never did. "The boy's already lost. He's alive only because his father felt a moment's curiosity. I like him, I really do, but as soon as Badad gets tired of playing the Brad game, the boy is dead. He knows that, right?"

Of course he knew. But he'd learned more, that Caramos might never understand, about the attachments that even a daemon lord could form when it kept to a human shape in the material sphere. He dropped his hand from his eyes, ready to argue the point, but Lily warned him with a twitch of her head. She wanted him to hear this, so he subsided into his chair, waited while Caramos took a breath to speak, let it out, and tried again.

"Does Badad know about this?"

Lily shrugged, but Evan didn't let the shift of muscle under smooth skin distract him. Not while they were tossing his life between them like a live grenade. "He asked, Evan said no. At the time, he wasn't all that interested and Evan wasn't all that sane, so he didn't pursue it."

Caramos had stopped using his name. Lily hadn't, and Evan clung to that. But Caramos was frowning at something none of them could see—Evan had become a cipher in daemon politics, and not a person at all.

"He'll have to do it. He can't let the boy think he's got the upper hand with Ariton. I do like him, Lily; I didn't come

here to break your toys. But he has to bend to the will of his
Prince. Badad cannot let a human will stand against him."

Evan stopped breathing. Inside the circle where he sat,
a wind had risen, but neither Caramos nor Lily could feel it
outside the circle. He had protections, and he ran through
the spells he knew to hold that small foothold against them.
Rejected any that involved binding his relations because
he would not break another promise, no matter what they
did to him. But he knew they were talking about the end of
everything they had together. Lily must know that—

"Badad can't," she said. "If he did, we'd lose Evan, and it
will all have been for nothing."

"It *is* for nothing," Caramos pointed out. "Humans die.
I've seen Sched's memories. They live brief lives and die
brutally and in pain."

"Badad can't. Not against Evan. He's only just learned
the fun of sex. To use it as a weapon would destroy that
pleasure for him forever."

"Ariton does not bow before such creatures, nor does a
daemon lord stand against his own Prince. If he wants to
stay alive—"

Evan had built an image in his mind of this lord as a jolly
old uncle, a bit pervy, but harmless if you were firm. He'd
gotten careless, forgotten the most basic fact about daemons—at their very best they were capricious and dangerous. Caramos, right now, was mostly dangerous. He didn't
look happy, but that wasn't going to stop him.

*Not my father. Anything else, but don't look like my fa-
ther.* He didn't say it aloud, was afraid that anything he said
would flip the switch on the daemon sitting in his office.

"It's all right." Lily reached out, ran fingertips across lips
that *did not* belong to his father, leaned in and followed with
a kiss, stroked the daemon lord's palm before linking her fingers with a hand that was not—*was not*—his father's hand.
"Badad can't, but he isn't the only lord in this house. It's taken
care of. Come on, I'll show you. We can use Evan's room. I
learned a new trick just last night—do you like blue?"

Caramos tugged the towel loose, freeing her hair. "It's
just become my favorite color."

"It will be fun, I promise."

She smiled over her shoulder at him, but Evan couldn't read the smile. Didn't want to. His world wasn't imploding—she'd paraded her lovers in front of him before. Never in his bed, though. But he hadn't understood why she did it before. Knowing carved a hole in his heart. Wondering whether she enjoyed any of it, or simply did what she had to do to keep him alive, made it bleed.

"Or, maybe we'll have ice cream instead. Chocolate ice cream with fudge sauce is better than sex."

"Ice cream? I didn't see ice cream in the human's mind." Caramos followed her eagerly, trusting her with his joy.

"That's because it's the greatest secret of the material world."

She stopped, smiled innocently, and Evan remembered a ruby lost in the garden. So it had been one of her jokes. But not entirely. He'd been in real danger. Caramos would have hurt him, but it would have damaged his own exuberant joy in the universe to do it. Lily wouldn't let that happen to a host-cousin. Not to Caramos, at least.

She'd wanted him to take some lesson from it, but he didn't want to know, would rather feel like a jilted lover. Didn't think that Lily was doing the same thing to him as Omage had, and he'd just been too stupid, too much a slave to his own prick to notice he was being screwed over as well as screwed. Which was unfair all the way down the line. He loved her; she found him amusing. If she had other motives, those two things were still true. And Lily never did anything she didn't want to do. Including, it appeared, sex with Caramos in a bed full of drying paint.

"You'll need clothes," he reminded her weakly. "And Brad is around somewhere. It will confuse the hell out of the neighbors if they see two of him running around."

"I didn't like it much anyway." Caramos frowned, morphed into something a little softer, a little rounder, but still with a family resemblance, especially around the eyes.

"Cousin Ray?" Evan asked.

Caramos grinned. "Cousin Ray. Can I meet your mother?"

Evan paled at the thought, but Lily was there with a rescue.

"Chocolate," she said.

"Ice cream!" Caramos responded. They disappeared, leaving him to his uncomfortable thoughts.

Okay. So, okay. He'd never had any illusions about who was in charge in his relationship with Lily. If that meant Ariton was satisfied that its human monster was properly humbled, so be it. Better than not having her at all. And as an alternative to being dead, well, he'd cope—and when the relatives dropped by to make sure Lily was torturing him enough with all that sex, he'd try to keep the smirk off his face.

It did make him think, though, about relationships and obligations, including that rider to the partnership papers that Brad wanted. He sat down at the desk, opened the computer to their standard contract template for clients, and started to type.

Chapter 38

"WHERE IS DONNE'S LIBRARY? Who has it, how did they get it, and why?"

Shields frowned, not angry but confused. "I don't want the books. I just need the box."

"If Donne wrote down what he was doing, whoever has his books may want the box too." He didn't mention Michel LeRoux, the priest who'd come calling, or the priest's mother, who knew more than she was telling. "Two, side." He missed his shot, deliberately, stepped back to give Shields access to the table—figuring angles might distract him enough to let the truth slip.

"Cyril Van Der Graf has most of the books." Shields studied the table. "He has a house off Park Avenue. He lined up his shot. "Thirteen." Bridged the stick, pale knuckles on felt the color of fresh blood. Over his shoulder a slate board nailed to the cheap paneling gave the beers on special, said, "Take the fighting outside."

"I delivered the library before Donne died, because he commanded it and paid a price in rubies to have his will obeyed. That's the way it worked."

Van Der Graf. Brad knew the name. He had a reputation for being a recluse, and for his collection of modern art. Shields' orange stripe dropped obligingly into the pocket.

"Why send the books to Van Der Graf?"

"Evan's been to Donne's house." Shields spared him a quick glance, "get a clue" in his eyes. "He's seen what passed for art there, So you know Donne wasn't working alone. Not all the time, at least." He took his shot quickly this time, nine in the side, his next moves all planned. Brad had figured it as well, knew where a little intervention would put him back in the game, but not yet. Shields was still talking.

"Donne was getting old. After his son died, he was under pressure to appoint a successor. He still had hopes of producing another heir, but he was ninety years old, and I'd already done all he commanded to keep him alive. It wasn't going to be enough. So he knew he wouldn't live long enough to raise it, figured the group would probably kill it when he died. "Fifteen, side pocket." Shields turned back to the table, took his shot. Waited while the ball rolled, red stripe appearing and disappearing again, until it came to rest at the lip of the cup.

The bar out front was heating up, voices rising to a dull roar. The waitress dropped off a second round, the clink of glass on glass a warning. Brad passed her another twenty, but they didn't have more than a few minutes back here. When she'd taken a few steps out of hearing range, Shields picked up his story.

"Van Der Graf didn't have kids. Didn't want any. Liked them well enough, but not in a good way. He was powerful enough in the group to have a chance of keeping the kid alive, though, so Donne made a deal—raise the kid, make it his heir, and he'd name Van Der Graf his successor. Transferring the library was a good faith gesture. But he never did make that heir, and he never actually named Van Der Graf his successor either. So the rest is up for grabs."

Something in his story sounded false at its core. Brad was pretty sure all the words were true—it was the missing bits that worried him. Donne had died of a heart attack, or it had looked like a heart attack. Natural causes at ninety. Wouldn't have had an autopsy. Brad could have done that, easy.

He called the two, taking the shot he'd missed last time. Sank it and prowled the perimeter choosing his next shot. Pretended not to look at Matt Shields when he asked the question. "Did you kill him?"

"Van Der Graf? As far as I know, he's still alive."

"Donne." Brad flicked him the "don't be an idiot" look he'd perfected on Evan and took his shot.

"He had a heart attack. I would have done it, had a chance once or twice, but I'd still have been stuck with the fucking box."

"And to whatever's inside. I heard it scream." Brad looked up then, wanted to see the effect he'd had. Shields wasn't showing much. Brad missed his next shot.

Shields called the seven, an easy drop, but his voice sounded clipped, efficient in the call. Professional.

"How long has Donne held your contract?" Circle around the burning hole in the middle of Shields' mind. This should have been the more painful question, but it wasn't.

Red fell in the pocket. Shields shifted his weight, went after the twelve. "Forty years." Bad enough, but not the truth. Or, not the right question.

"Not just this Donne. All of them. How long have you been bound to that box?"

"The box was new. He made it to bind me there. Later— later, there was company."

Six hundred years, then, give or take a decade or two. Brad couldn't wrap his mind around it, not as a daemon lord and not the meat brain that ticked away the hours at the base of his skull.

"Did you stay for the killing, or did you just like it in that box?"

The cue stick in Shields' hand burst into flame. Nobody was looking, but just one bike messenger waiting for a table had to turn around and they'd have a panic on their hands. Police called.

Brad suppressed the fire, glared. "Sotheby's tomorrow, or a jail cell for setting the bar on fire? Your options seem limited until we get the box back. Speaking from the other side of a jail cell, I'd think carefully about my answer."

Wrong thing to say—Shields smiled like he'd just won the point. "He put you there, didn't he?"

"Which he? Captain Marsh? Lieutenant Ellen Li? It was a misunderstanding. We all got over it."

"Evan. The other humans couldn't make you stay."

"That was a misunderstanding too." He'd get over it eventually. Not today, though. Didn't want an outsider to see the cracks in their defenses—never give up the tactical advantage—and Shields hadn't answered the question. So he shrugged it off as if it had meant nothing. "It was a mistake. He paid for it, he got the message. Won't be doing it again. Were you in it for the rubies or the killing?"

Shields found another stick, took his shot. "It's a powerful spell. For a century I fought it, but the magicians were smart. Only the owner can command the spell or destroy the box, and ownership passed from father to son. Donne could trade the box, or sell the box, but none of them ever did."

"In 1578 the Donne was murdered by a highwayman who stole the box. Whole generations of Donnes lived and died without knowing it existed, until sometime in the mid seventeenth century the new heir found a description of it in the family records. He summoned me, made me find the box for him. I could have killed him—he didn't know what he was doing, really. But I would have ended up back in the box, so I brought it to him. He's the one who founded the society."

"Did they all have sons?" It seemed unlikely, but Shields just gave a little shrug. "It was part of the spell. They didn't all live, though. I think in 1793 Donne ceded the box to his daughter's son, provided that he took the family name. They were already in England then, and were calling themselves Donne."

He stopped. Still hadn't said who was stuck in the box with him, but Brad figured he could buy the thing with agency money and negotiate ownership once they knew what they were dealing with. It wasn't clear from Shields' story whether buying the box from the state would work at all. Brad thought that a spell based on a bloodline should have ended with the last Donne, but there'd been that cousin in Colorado, so there might be more of them out there. But they could at least keep the spell out of anyone else's hands until they figured out how to break it. Shields sank the ten—last stripe—but he hadn't quite finished.

"For a long time, I was crazy. It's hard to hold onto your-self when there's no hope at all."

The eight ball followed the ten and Brad figured he'd just learned what he had to know. Not who, but the condition of the merchandise, at least. As if the screaming hadn't told him that already. He remembered the interrogation room at Major Crimes. Bad as it had been, he'd had Khadi-jah Flint, a human, fighting for him and Lily. And once Lily pointed out the magnitude of his mistake, Evan had let them go, no strings attached even though he thought it was going to kill him.

He tried to imagine being trapped in a small box, with no one for company but a frantically mad cousin. For cen-turies. It didn't bear thinking.

"Tomorrow we'll have the box," he said, careful not to make promises. The agency had a contract to buy the box for Matt Shields, but it didn't give the time frame, or who they had to buy it from. Throwing the agency into the middle of the transaction stretched the contract to the breaking, but the deal with Paimon called for one freed daemon lord, not two, especially one who was more insane than Omage had been and not inclined to leave reminders behind. It always came down to Evan needing a planet to stand on. So they'd see. Tomorrow.

Until then, somebody had to keep an eye on the client. A new set of players had wandered in—they'd outstayed their money, so he hung up his stick, waited until Shields had done the same, then clapped him on the back. "I don't know about you, but I could use another beer."

"You owe me a burger and fries."

"Burger and fries it is." Or maybe not. Someone had crossed all the protections they'd put in place and had got-ten into the house. Brad felt the intrusion, but he didn't, immediately, sense danger. A host-cousin of Ariton, under no compulsion that he could find, and Lily was there. So maybe he had time for that beer. But, oh, Ariton and all the Princes, it was Caramos, at his most gleefully curious, and Evan was in the house. Brad felt the jolt of fear, followed by amused exasperation, then suddenly Evan was as angry as Brad had ever felt him. Which, in a room with two host-cousins after a narrow decision to take his deal and let him live, was not smart. He considered his options for a discreet exit and decided on the men's room.

"Next time," he said. "We've got company. Evan gave you a card, right? You can charge it to the agency—"

"I know, I know: you'll put it on the bill."

"I owe you a burger, but the beer is on your bill. If you need cash, just draw it off the card. Stop by the agency later; we have to talk about tomorrow."

Shields found a stool at the bar, a smile ready for the girl with purple hair, and waved him off—he would have felt it when Caramos arrived, wouldn't have known where exactly, or who, except that it was Ariton. "Say thanks, for me?" He owed all of Ariton. Still, a deal between Princes didn't mean peace between their lords. Shields would stay clear until the numbers were more in his favor.

Brad left him to his burger and went in search of the men's room.

Chapter 39

"NICE ENTRANCE." Evan looked up from the computer screen to greet his father, who had appeared at the center of the medallion worked into the Aubusson carpet. The light from the window was fading, falling yellow low on the garden wall from the west. So the glinting flames in Brad's eyes were Ariton, not the sun.

"When is Lily going to replace the desk in the study?" Not exactly "hello," but Evan sympathized. They'd set up the office with a few real antiques and an air of cool blue competence to impress their well-heeled clients, but it didn't encourage lingering. He wanted his chair and his books and the homey clutter too, though he knew his father would never admit to needing the human comforts just down the hall. But Evan needed a desk now, and the printer.

"She already bought it: delivery's tomorrow. Mary's coming for the regular cleaning; she said she'll show the furniture movers where to go if we're not home, but this is the last time."

"I don't expect to need another desk," Brad said, which wasn't what Mary had meant. She'd worn a big silver cross around her neck since the first time she'd had to clean up their blood and ruin, and she'd put them on notice every time since. Evan had found little sachets of herbs in the odd corner and he'd left them there, figured they could use all the help they could get.

Brad seemed to relax a little at the news, but he hadn't made a grand entrance over the furniture. "Where's Caramos?"

Ah. "Out with Lily. For ice cream. I'm not sure sex is completely off the table yet, but she's doing a pretty good job of distracting him. I still don't understand how he got here—thought you had to be summoned to make it into the material sphere."

Brad wandered around the desk and peered over Evan's shoulder. "Depends. Desire will work if he had a marked path between the spheres. Sched was invoked by prayer. The prayer marked the way and curiosity provided the desire. But there hasn't been a lot of desire, or much polite asking, since humans crawled out of the mud, more or less. With Caramos, we know what provoked the desire. As for the marked path—"

"I know. He followed me home, but I don't want to keep him."

"He'll go home when he gets bored, which he'll do pretty quickly if he doesn't get what he wants. In the meantime, I have the name and the address where Shields delivered Donne's library. The name's Van Der Graf. Do you know him?"

"I've seen his picture in the paper." Evan pulled up a browser and plugged in Van Der Graf's name.

"Cyril," Brad added over his shoulder, and Evan added that, limiting the search. It didn't take any fancy footwork— the story appeared on the first page of links, and Van Der Graf's picture was in it. "He bought a Braque at auction last year, paid something like twenty-five million for it, but I've never seen his face before. He didn't hang out at the Black Masque, but there were pictures all over Donne's house." He kept his memory to himself. They'd all worn robes with hoods pulled down over their faces anyway. "I don't know what he knows."

"Can you check him out tomorrow? Lily and I can handle the auction."

"I can do it." He hadn't been to New York City more than once or twice since his father had pulled him out of the Black Masque, physically broken and mostly insane. But he wasn't that guy anymore. Refused to be that guy. "I'll take a look around, see what I can find out."

He made a note of the address and closed the window, watched his father's eyes narrow as he read the document on the screen under it.

"Is that the contract we talked about?"

"Yeah." Evan shifted the laptop so that his father could read more easily and paged down to the highlighted sections of their usual client contract. "You can walk away whenever you want. I hold the contract for life, or until you cancel the agreement, if earlier. If I die before you walk away, your contract passes to Ariton, a Family Partnership, and you can still walk away from the contract." He wasn't going to leave them like Matt Shields, bound to a broken contract. Grayson Donne's twisted circle of friends tortured and murdered their victims—they'd given Evan to a daemon lord of an enemy house who had tortured him for almost a year, had come damned close to killing him before his father and Lily had shown up to pull him out of there.

Evan knew he was no hero. If he'd known her then, he'd have given up Lily to make it stop. He'd have given up his father. God help him, but he might have traded his mother if it had gotten him out of Omage's back room. He wasn't proud of it, but he was going to make sure that nothing he said or did could put his father or Lily in their hands. "It should be pretty much leak-proof, but I thought I'd send a copy to Khadijah Flint—she can take a look for loopholes I didn't anticipate." He didn't think there were any, except the big one, that let one side cancel the contract with no penalty.

"She won't like it." His father reached over his shoulder and hit "print."

It took Evan a minute to sort out who "she" was. Khadijah Flint. The contract worked well enough with clients who paid by the hour, but raised questions when you were talking about a partnership. Their lawyer would call him ten kinds of fool and try to build an out for him that he couldn't afford.

"But it should work." He gave the printed sheet a last quick pass and handed it over.

Brad nodded, reading the page. It didn't seem to hurt him to hold it, or to read it, which was a good start. "There's only one way to know if it works. I don't have to sign this in blood or anything, do I?"

It was a joke. Evan was sure it was a joke, but it still sent a tremor through him. "No blood," he said, "just ink." If it didn't work, he'd try again—they had until tomorrow to get it right. The fading light from the garden window failed completely. Evan turned on the desk lamp and signed at the bottom of the page, slid the contract sideways on the desk.

Brad looked at the pen for a moment before he took it. Probably thinking about what had happened to Matt Shields, but nothing else bound his father. Not anymore. So the deal shouldn't hurt—not like it had Matt Shields and not like the last time Evan had bound his relations to protect them. They hadn't had a walk-away clause then, and it turned out that he'd been the one they needed protection from. He'd learned that lesson.

Still, it was all theory until they had a signed contract. He held his breath while the pen scratched out a few quick strokes. Not Badad, the secret name, but Kevin Bradley, the full name his father used in the material world. It had been enough to almost tear Matt Shields to pieces, so he figured it would work.

Waited. Let his breath out when nothing happened.

Brad rubbed at the corner of his brow, like he had a headache, and Evan figured maybe he did. Better than screaming in agony on the carpet, but—

"It doesn't feel any different."

Bad news. "I'll try again. I must have missed something—"

"It worked. I don't think you let go completely the last time."

Which didn't carry quite the kick that a monitor to the head had, but it came close. "You're my father. I never let go of that. But—"

"I didn't let go either. Sched isn't the only fool of Ariton."

"Lily?"

"Is going to be really pissed."

Evan thought about that a minute. Shrugged. At least it didn't hurt. "That's why they call it family. What are we going to do about Caramos?"

"Send him home." Brad thought about his answer, amended it. "Tell Lily to send him home. I'll be playing chess with Harry."

"I don't want to go home. I'm having fun." Caramos appeared on the outside of the plaster pentagram and skirted it carefully before settling in the antique chair in the corner with a sigh. He looked too much like Brad and acted too differently for Evan's comfort. The resemblance felt like an intrusion, the differences a betrayal, which was stupid and beside the point.

"It's going to be dangerous." No point in bothering to repeat any of the conversation, since Caramos appeared to have been listening anyway. "There are traps, and if they find out your name, you could wind up stuck in a box like Matt Shields' friend."

"More than a friend, I'd say." Caramos wiped the fudge sauce from the corner of his mouth and licked it thoughtfully off his finger. "From what Lily says, I gather he has a closer bond with the lord in that box. In fact, it may not be the box holding him here at all."

"Daemon lords fall in love?" It seemed so unlikely that Evan couldn't wrap his brain around it. When he did, he wondered, "Brad and Lily?"

"Don't be a fool," his father snapped, "We are host-cousins, no more than that."

But Caramos was watching Brad with something that could almost be sympathy, except that was a foreign notion to his daemon kin as well. "Not Lily. I didn't think they even liked each other. But—"

"That's enough. It's too dangerous for you to be here. Donne is dead, but he had confederates, and Matt Shields would cheerfully trade you for the contents of that box if he knew you were available for the offer. We can protect ourselves to some extent, but we can't protect you."

"I'm not going anywhere. Lily promised me dinner."

"Where *is* Lily?" Evan listened for footsteps in the hall, but heard nothing.

"She's finding me a dress. I thought that might work better."

Brad set down the pen and appraised his host-cousin with a raised eyebrow. "Not a good look for you," he said, "and it will limit your options for dinner."

Lily appeared in a red silk, narrow to show the curve of her hip and short enough to show off miles of leg. She carried a little black dress on a hanger. "He's decided to be a woman tonight."

Caramos grinned as if he'd done something clever. Already the bone structure in his face had grown more delicate, his hands smaller. "Lily said that Evan prefers women. She herself sometimes prefers them, so they must be the superior species." He didn't waste any more time with a slow transformation.

Evan had seen his relations change their material forms before, and it always disoriented him, but never like seeing Caramos turn into a petite blue-eyed blonde with a bit more breast than she could comfortably balance.

"And then after dinner, when everyone is feeling relaxed and comfortable, I thought we could have some sex."

"Women are the same species," Evan corrected, "and I have already told you, I will not have sex with you."

Caramos pouted, which was a disconcertingly good look on—her. "Don't you think I'm pretty? Tell me what you like. I know you *like* sex. I read your mind, remember?"

His father saved him from answering, or perhaps, from angering a powerful lord of his own host. "Sex is complicated with humans," he explained. "Evan is useless to you, because he is only interested in Lily."

"But I saw another woman in his mind!"

"I was just looking," Evan explained. "We look; it's what we do. Then we make choices. I chose Lily."

Brad took that for confirmation of his point. "You see?

And Lily is useless to you because she is only interested in Lily too."

"That's true," Lily smiled brightly, as if he'd just said something clever. "I am!"

"And I am useless to you because I am playing chess with Harry tonight." He had already started toward the door and Evan saw his last hope of salvation leaving with him. But Brad had one more comment, for which he would doubtless owe him later.

"Matt Shields is drinking alone at Charlie's. We'd better get someone on him, just in case there's trouble."

"I'm on it." Evan was up and following his father before the words were spoken, but Lily caught him by the tie. "You have seen his mind at home. You know she wouldn't hurt you, and it would please her very much."

Lily wasn't human, he reminded himself. Sometimes the differences needed working out. But he couldn't do it today. "You're wrong on both counts. I'm sorry. I can't do it." He kissed her to show that he wasn't angry, but somehow all the hurt and longing and desire for more than just between her legs were there in the kiss, in his hands finding their grip in her hair, no matter how much he tried to keep it to himself. He didn't want to frighten her away, didn't want her to know how much she frightened him, but the desperation was all there anyway. She pushed him back toward the desk and he didn't resist her.

"It's all right," she said. "I'll feed him ice cream for desert and send him home happy."

He thought she meant with the ice cream, but didn't push his luck.

But sending Caramos home was harder than it seemed.

Chapter 40

SOTHEBY'S WAS ALL MODERN GLASS and cream-colored angles, bright morning sunlight filling the front foyer. Brad picked up a catalog at the front desk and tucked it under his arm. Wouldn't ever tell Evan that he liked them as material objects in their own right, but he thought Lily had already figured it out. He had a little collection of them on a shelf in the study, beautifully produced reminders of the conservation of luck in human existence. Apparently the universe contained all the good fortune it ever would and passed it from hand to hand, like the flu.

Upstairs, the Donne auction had started an hour earlier with a few lots of furniture, nineteenth century American and eighteenth century English, mapping the travels of the Donne legacy. Brad had timed their arrival to miss that part of the sale—they had about an hour, more or less, to settle in and scope out the room before their items came up. He followed Lily and took the elevator with the rest of the stragglers to the fifth floor, where he followed a trail of odd-looking modern sculptures exhibited for a sale next week, to the auction room.

He kept his expression casual, preferring to remain unobserved as he crossed the thick cream carpet. At his side, Lily hadn't shut it down at all. Heads turned, a few faces brightened with increased blood flow. One poor soul took a step forward, his feet apparently connected to the wrong brain. Brad shot him a warning glare and kept Lily moving. She liked to play with her food, but they didn't have the time. And he didn't want to call more attention than their presence did already.

He supposed if he were Evan he'd care more about the people buried in Donne's graveyard of sacrifices, but mostly he was annoyed that Evan had called Jaworski when he found them. The bodies had attracted the attention of the FBI. He'd expected to hear about it on the news, to find that the police had halted the sale of Donne's estate and seized his property as evidence, but there had been nothing. His second guess was agents at the auction and, somewhere in the city, a room full of New York's version of Sid Valentine tracking the movements of anyone who showed up or placed a bid by phone. For all he knew, they were checking anyone who had viewed the exhibition on the internet. He imagined the vast reach of Interpol, spreading out worldwide to interrogate every granny with a taste for vulgar furniture. The last thought cheered him, but not enough to make up for the fact that once more they'd have the FBI watching them, or for the past hour and a half spent getting here so they'd have something to watch.

They'd traveled the human way, purchasing train tickets with agency credit cards and chatting with the cab driver about New York traffic and the annoyance of horse-drawn carriages in Central Park, leaving a perfectly ordinary trail for the official investigation to follow. Lily hadn't seemed to mind. She'd abandoned him for a stockbroker commuting to the city from New Jersey and he hadn't seen her for most of the trip.

Madame LeRoux, on the arm of bad-suit boy, approached from a gallery of nineteenth century paintings that would probably sell for less than the odd-looking toilet gracing the pedestal at his elbow. She gave him a nod and a wry half-smile of recognition. He thought they might be spared the presence of Father Michel, but no, he was waiting at the entrance to the sales room and looked ready to detonate when he saw Brad and Lily.

"Discede ab hoc famulo Dei," Brad said conversation-

ally. *Depart from this servant of God*... It itched a bit under the skin when he said the words, but they couldn't hurt
him. The body was his. Not permanent, but he wasn't rent-
ing from a human. Unfortunately, they didn't work on the
priest either. Father Michel glowered and planted his feet
deep in the thick pile of the cream carpet, blocking their
access to the auction. Lily prickled all over and he wondered if Sotheby's allowed panthers in their showrooms,
and if she would make the whole issue moot by ripping out
Michel LeRoux's throat. The FBI agent in the corner, with
the poorly hidden earbud, was looking at them and talking
to someone off in a command center somewhere, never a
good sign. So much for a low profile. It put official attention
on Father Michel as well, which might be useful. But he'd
had enough of the priest's dogged hostility.

He braced himself to nudge his way past, but was inter-
cepted again, this time by LeRoux's mother. "Now, now.
Pretend the picture that nice policeman is taking with his
cell phone will appear in the society pages. All old friends
here. Money always is." Madame LeRoux relinquished her
hold on bad-suit boy and landed a hand firmly on Lily's
arm. She smiled warmly as if she had in fact met her dear-
est friend by happy chance.

"Men will be men," she said. "The collar makes no difference. Mr. Bradley won't do anything precipitous, will
he? Can we safely leave them to bristle and hiss at each
other? I am ready to sit for a while."

"I'm the one Michel has to worry about." Lily wasn't
kidding, and the priest might still not survive the encounter, but Madame LeRoux patted her arm, nudged her forward a step.

"I know you are, child. Come, help me to a chair."

"I am older than you can possibly imagine." Lily's tone
frosted the air, but Ariton fire shone in her eyes. Father
Michel couldn't see it, but Brad held his breath, waiting for
the explosion.

"I know that too." Madame LeRoux slipped her arm
around Lily's waist but kept them walking. Father Michel
turned on his heel and took a few quick steps to catch up,

dismayed with his mother's choice of company. Brad followed because he couldn't think of anything else to do that didn't involve piles of rubble and screaming sirens, which seemed overkill for a change.

"It is a terrible thing, to be far from home. If you needed my help, could you tell me?" Madame LeRoux was giving Lily a look that he'd seen Evan's mother sometimes use on Evan, and Brad was at a loss to explain it here.

A bank of paneled telephone stations, where bidders from around the world called in their bids, wrapped the left side of the room and a bit of the front as well, with two sections of folding chairs filling the middle of the room. The podium stood off to the corner, so the auctioneer had a good view of the phones as well as the room without drawing attention from the center screen where each lot came up for sale. Madame LeRoux turned left and Lily went with her, rounding the section closest to the telephones.

"If I needed help, no, I could not tell you. But if I needed help, why would I trust you to give it?" Lily's smile was very cold. She pulled away, but not outside the circle of that arm. Up close, Lily could kill the old woman without making a fuss, perhaps, but a dead body always complicated a sale.

"It would be foolish of you, wouldn't it? I suggest that you put no faith in me at all. But men like my husband have no right to do the things they did, no right at all. I would make amends if I could. I will help, if you let me."

"If you could be trusted, you wouldn't be here." Lily did break away then, slid into the back row of folding chairs. It gave the best view of the action, and Brad took the aisle seat next to her. Madame LeRoux went no farther than the next row forward. Father Michel argued with small gestures toward the other side of the room, but his mother folded her hands in her lap and tilted her head to watch the screen at the front of the room. Stone-faced, he sat beside her, which put him in front of Brad, his shoulders tense as if he expected a knife between them at any moment. Wasn't a bad idea, but it would spoil the carpet, and at least one FBI agent had come in behind them.

They had a job to do, and Brad kind of liked auctions

anyway, so Michel LeRoux would have to wait. The screen at the front showed a photograph of an eighteenth century desk with the current bid translated into seven different currencies. A few representative pieces from the collection were on display beneath the screen. One of them was Matt Shields' strongbox.

Good photographs for the FBI, he remembered. He opened his catalog with an air of quiet interest and pretended he didn't hear the screaming coming from the front of the room. Lily paled, but she maintained an air of professional calm, at least for the moment, while she scoped out the competition.

Chapter 41

"TELL ME WHAT YOU KNOW about this guy Van Der Graf." Evan hit "enter," speed-read the story that popped up on the screen. He had two things going for him: the FBI had kept the story under wraps and they didn't know about Van Der Graf. And it turned out good things came in threes.

Van Der Graf's Park Avenue mansion was a registered historic landmark, all five stories of it. It wasn't actually on Park Avenue, but around the corner, on 70th. Van Der Graf's restoration had made a splash in *Architectural News*. Evan didn't have to hack anything—the magazine's website had produced a rough plan of each floor, including the third, where the room marked "library" held Grayson Donne's books. Five screens of photographs, before-and-afters, followed the plans—lots of marble and carved pillars on the first floor, and a grand staircase with a wrought iron balustrade sweeping an elegant path upward. Donne and his cronies had a thing for staircases.

So he had a sense of the house, and Van Der Graf's involvement with Donne told him a lot, but he still didn't have a good grasp of the situation he'd be walking into. Unfortunately, Matt Shields was being an asshole.

"Van Der Graf—?" Evan looked up, repeating the question. Shields had dragged a more comfortable chair from the waiting room and sat with his legs stretched in front of him, half in and half out of the protective

seal in the office ceiling. Evan thought he did it just to remind himself that he could. It hadn't made him particularly
cooperative.

"He's an evil son of a bitch just like the rest of them.
What more do you need to know? You, of all people, should
stay away from him."

"That stopped being an option when we made a deal
with Paimon."

"Look—" Shields sat up straight in his chair, leaned forward a little. His hair flopped in his eyes, but they caught
the sun from the garden window anyway, amber sparks a
reminder that Evan had plenty of danger right here.

"—In about three hours I'll own Donne's cursed box
and I'll be gone. You have my bond, and my Prince's, not to
make a mess when I leave. If Van Der Graf hasn't figured
out the secret of Donne's box in the past three years, he
won't crack it in the next three hours.

"But this isn't about Donne's box for you. It's about the
bodies in Donne's woods, and they aren't any part of my
bargain with this agency."

Maybe Shields was right about that, but it didn't make
Evan wrong. And reading the aggression in the daemon
lord's posture didn't mean giving in to it. He leaned forward in his own chair, both hands resting on the desk, in-
stincts older than civilization ready to push him to his feet.
Fight or flight, and he had no intention of running away.

"You killed those people." The effort to stay calm rough-
ened his voice. He knew better than to expect a daemon
lord of any Prince to notice its human dead, but he'd never
met one before who worked so hard at looking like a good
guy, like somebody who might actually give a damn about
the hundred or more graves in Donne's wood. Sometimes
it was hard to remember that Matt Shields, in the most terrifying form a daemon wore, had put them there.

Not today, though. Shields gave him a long stare with
blood and torn flesh in it, and no remorse. "Humans die,"
he said, answering the accusation, and maybe talking about
gambling with Van Der Graf's life expectancy and Donne's
books too. Nothing friendly about him now. "That's what

they do best, every one of them, eventually. I just helped a few of them along."

"You don't have to tell me that human lives mean nothing to you. I know that." And Evan was damned tired of hearing it, really. Not worth shit. Got it. Let's move on. Except that he couldn't move on. "There were children, kids just starting out in the world, and they died in agony." So many crosses, the breath stuck in his throat at the thought. "You had no right. No right at all."

And God, he must be the poster child for posttraumatic stress, because he wasn't talking about Shields or Donne or the dead in that wood anymore. He was in Omage's back room again, in Donne's Octagon, the touch of a daemon's hands, his knife, the body he'd used for rape and other torments, inescapable. Worse, Shields knew it, looked out the window with a pointed little smile.

Being what he was, Shields had to push. "I'm not the only one who filled that graveyard. Fifteen-year-old boys are Cyril's favorites, but they don't stay fifteen, do they? You were what, nineteen when they found you? A little old for his tastes, but he wanted you back then, always started to sweat when they talked about you." Matt Shields was looking straight at him then, mocking.

"Donne wouldn't let him have you. Simpson claimed a nearly grown half-breed heir. Donne wanted one of those as well. That wasn't working out for him, but he had the box and a human son. Van Der Graf had nothing, and Simpson needed the practice. So you are well past your sell-by date for old Cyril, but he'll take you anyway, because he hates to lose at anything. Looks like he'll have to find a new place to put you, now that the FBI is tramping all over their dumping ground."

Banks of angry clouds had cut off the sun, leaving the room in sickly green shadows. Evan's ears popped with the change in pressure. He thought maybe he'd brought it on, but Shields was a lot more upset than he was pretending, so it might have been him. Evan couldn't always tell, not when he was having flashbacks to Omage's back room. One thing for sure, though: a hell of a storm was coming.

He couldn't afford to play this game. But he wasn't a helpless kid anymore, wouldn't be that. Old Cyril didn't really scare him anyway. Maybe once, but he didn't have much to fear from humans anymore. His nightmares all had a daemon lord at their center. And Shields' nightmares had Grayson Donne, who'd wanted a half-daemon heir but had no blood relation to carry one for him.

Carlos Sanchez had said there'd been a girl named Kady with chocolate skin, who'd been a prisoner like Shields. And something was still trapped inside the box that had been Matt Shields' prison.

Oh, God. Lily.

Breathe. The old pervert was dead and he'd never even met Lily. Had never hurt her, and Evan wasn't anything like Grayson Donne. He wouldn't let anything like that happen to Lily. But it made him wonder again if loving her was just another iron-bound box. He needed space, some privacy from a daemon lord who was not a natural ally. Figured he'd pencil in some meltdown time next week, but he didn't have room in his schedule right now. His father was trusting him to take care of Grayson Donne's library.

Shields was looking at him strangely when he pulled it together again.

"You don't even know her." He frowned, like Evan had presented him a new puzzle. Shields wasn't a puzzle kind of guy.

"I know Lily. And just so you know, if she wanted to go home, I wouldn't stop her."

"I'm pretty sure she'd have to kill you."

"Not my first choice. But, yeah. I get that."

Shields looked at the bruises fading at Evan's brow, thinking hard. "I guess you do," he said, but the fight went out of him.

"When Donne died, I was stuck here. I didn't know how to fit into this world, I just knew I didn't want to be what he'd made me—why would I? I hated him.

"Carlos offered something different, and I took it. So I don't have fancy houses in the city, or yachts, or tickets to the opera. I paint houses and repair leaky faucets, and I eat bacon and eggs for breakfast. I haven't been snacking on preschoolers. But I didn't know Carlos back then. Donne called a monster, and that's what he got. Don't expect me to be sorry for any of them, because I won't."

Six hundred years—how many dead, torn to pieces, and buried in gardens across Europe and America? No one had ever put a stop to it.

The desk phone rang then—Shields jerked in his chair, looking for an exit before they both realized what the noise was. Evan's breathing had kicked up a notch as well. They watched it as if they expected it to explode. It didn't, of course. The service would answer if he waited, but each ring shredded nerves a little deeper under the skin, so he picked it up.

"Evan Davis." Tried to keep it civil. Didn't want to frighten the other clients. Or Ellen Li, for that matter, who answered, "How are you, Evan? Harry mentioned that he saw you this week." He could hear the suppressed laughter, remembered Harry walking into the garden. He'd been pretty close to naked at the time, and Lily'd been all the way there. Which he wasn't going to discuss with Lieutenant Ellen Li of Major Crimes, especially in front of Matt Shields. "I'm with a client right now. Can I call you back?"

"Shields?" she asked, and the laughter was gone.

The agency did not share that information without a warrant and she knew that. But she didn't stop to give him a chance to remind her.

"I'm sending Jaworski. The FBI talked to Carlos Sanchez about those bodies you found. Sid passed along the word that he didn't pass the polygraph, said the guy got twitchy whenever Shields' name came up."

"I don't need Jaworski. Matt Shields was a *victim*." It was getting hard to sell that line with the graves in Donne's woods burning a hole in his brain.

"Sometimes good people try to hide innocent secrets from the police," Ellen conceded in her soothing police-voice. "And sometimes even victims commit terrible crimes."

"Donne was ninety years old. He had a heart attack."

"Donne had a heart attack," Ellen agreed. "But the bodies in those graves did not. And the records of Mr. Shields' existence before that time do not hold up under close scrutiny. So perhaps your client is an innocent victim, as you say. But the FBI would like to know who he really is, and how he got involved with Grayson Donne in the first place. And we'd all like to know what he can tell us about the bodies in the woods. If you can bring him in around two, we can do the questioning here. He won't have to go back to New York unless they find something more concrete against him. Of course, if he'd rather deal with his local police, they'll be happy to do the interview there."

"Your office at two." Not a good idea, but Shields would be gone by then.

"You have people on your side if you need help," she said, and it seemed out of the blue, except that she was telling him the client in the room with him might be a killer. Which he was.

He agreed with her right down the line, but they didn't have pentagrams on the ceiling at Major Crimes and much as he hated the 1950s bus station vibe of the place, he didn't want Shields doing any impromptu urban renewal. "I'm fine," he said, thanked her for the information, and promised yet again to bring Shields in for some questions at 2:00, before he disconnected the call.

Shields was waiting, the thunderclouds in the east growing more ominous, so not exactly patiently. "Paimon knows secrets," he said, "including the kind you try to hide on the telephone *in the same room*. I'm not going anywhere but home by 2:00—you can tell your friends the police anything you want after that."

"I figured. But it got her off the phone."

He'd confused Shields again, which was just fine. Ellen Li wasn't his problem right now. Evan knew—he *knew* that the only thing that worked with daemon lords was self-interest.

"The people we're up against aren't stupid. Van Der Graf knows Donne bound at least one daemon, and he'll be looking for a way to take over that part of Donne's estate as well.

It's just a matter of time before he finds your true name in Donne's notes and figures out what to do with it. If he succeeds, it won't matter if we've freed you from the box. He can summon you whenever he wants and he doesn't need Donne's library to do it. A search on the 'net will bring up a dozen workable summoning spells on the first page alone. So we find Donne's notes now, or we do this all over again next year, or in ten or twenty. Call it job security."

Matt Shields had the long gaze past Evan's shoulder. Nothing but a wall and a bathroom on the other side of it, but he didn't think Shields was seeing any of that. "I've told you all you need to know. You were younger when he first saw you, and bloodier. The combination made an impression on Old Cyril. If he catches you, he'll want to torture you to death like he did those boys in Donne's woods. He's still mad he didn't get to do it when you were the right age for it. But he'll figure that he finally won—beat Donne and the Simpsons—so he'll want to gloat first. That's when you kill him."

"I'm not going to kill anyone."

"Has your father mentioned lately that you're a fool?" Shields pushed out of his chair and paced a twitchy circle around the protections at the center of the office. Evan considered the scotch in the credenza, but the hour hand had barely scraped past eleven. Still morning, and that had never worked out well for him. It told him all he needed to know about his mood, though.

"It's an old, leather-bound book in a wooden case." Shields looked up, grimaced when he found himself under the pentacle after all and neatly stepped outside it before going on. "Getting in won't be a problem, but you'll have to walk out. The house isn't as bad as Donne's, but Van Der Graf's no fool, and he's got stuff like that—" he pointed at the ornate plaster, "—all over the house. So escaping through the second sphere won't be an easy option. Any one of the seven Princes would likely kill you for it if you brought the book there anyway."

"With any luck, I'll be out of there before anyone notices me."

"Luck isn't your forte," Shields pointed out. "How do you expect to find it?"

Evan shrugged, swiveled in his chair to keep Shields in his sights. "That's what Ariton does. I thought that's why you hired us."

Shields remembered where the scotch was on his own. Got out a bottle and a glass, filled and downed it without asking if Evan wanted one. "You're not Ariton. You're a jumped-up human with delusions of lordship." So, he might look like a handyman, but he sneered just like a daemon lord of the second celestial sphere. No surprise, and Evan was used to that.

"Half-human," he snapped. "The other half comes with the delusions preinstalled. Have you been to Atlantic City yet? Lights, noise, gambling 24-7, and an ocean if you get bored? Consider yourself on vacation. Just don't go near New York City until I have Donne's notebook." Shields couldn't get past the front office—the deal didn't give him access to the house—so Evan didn't stick around to find out what he planned to do. The floor plan shaped itself in his mind. He focused on the third floor, front, the word "library" in neat print on the drawing. And then he went there.

Chapter 42

OUTSIDE OF HIS OWN CIRCLE, Donne had kept a low profile in his mountains, and furniture didn't bring out the glitter people. Just a scattering of buyers filled a chair here and there at the center of Sotheby's sales room—tourists in sneakers and tennis shorts and a few dealers in golf shirts looking for bargains. Brad figured the three guys in gray hair and suits for Donne's cronies. They sat well apart from each other, expressions closed off and a little bored.

No one else seemed to have noticed the entry of Brad's strange little party, but those three had turned and looked, ignored him, and Lily, except for a brief, speculative glance. But they knew Bertrande LeRoux, seemed to add things up when they saw her, which cast serious doubt on the truth of anything she'd told them. She hadn't told them much, so that was okay. Brad hadn't trusted her anyway, and knew Lily didn't trust anything with a beating heart.

The room was quiet except for the occasional rustle of a page turning and the auctioneer calling the bidding war in the telephone stations that took the desk on the screen to half a million, US dollars. It wasn't a bad desk and, if he hadn't known the provenance, Brad might have bid on it himself. As it was, he made a note of the buyer number but let it go to the telephones well within the valuation range printed in the catalog.

A few lots passed with minimal interest, a table,

some chairs that went for the low end of their appraised value, and a set of bookcases that no one seemed to want. Then the chalice and curved silver knife appeared on the screen. The catalog appraised the items like Donne's furniture, at its historic value—the description didn't mention traces of human blood in the bowl or add to the expected price centuries of murder in its prior use dragging daemon lords out of their home. Didn't have to. One of the gray men opened the bidding, which quickly went to $20,000, then $50,000. Lily had the agency's paddle, but she'd set their limit for the cup at $100,000, a courtesy bid, she'd told him. This was Brad's folly; Shields' contract didn't require clear title to the cup. They could just as easily steal it from whoever won the bid and save the money, or go after it by less subtle routes and destroy it in the rubble if they preferred.

Which would have been fine if the gray men hadn't fallen out of the bidding against Madame LeRoux's son. LeRoux was easy. The Church, a little more complicated. They still had to buy Shields' box for him, so Brad walked away before he brought down the building.

Michel LeRoux caught up with him at the toilet on the pedestal, kept pace to the windows, where Brad turned on him, fire licking at his eyes. LeRoux might have taken it for the afternoon light, but he took a step back, with a tight grip on the silver cross hanging from a thick chain around his neck.

"Your FBI is watching," he warned, as if that would matter to the creature he thought Brad was—the creature Matt Shields had been for Grayson Donne.

"Not mine," Brad pointed out. On the street below, traffic ebbed and flowed with the turning of the light. Red, green. Stop, go under the trees that lined the sidewalk on 72nd Street. Brad had stopped. Go was still an option. Evan needed a planet, but he didn't need this block of it. "My patience is on a short leash. Why did you follow me?"

"Tell your master that he will never own Donne's cup."

"Again, you are mistaken."

"The boy you call 'son,' who dragged you out of hell to

do his bidding. The Church forgives all sinners who repent, but stands unyielding against him while he holds the leash, as you put it."

Which wasn't what Brad had meant. Until two weeks ago, he would have laughed at that description. Then Evan had said "no," and abandoned him to an interrogation room at Major Crimes. That was over now: Evan had a few stitches in his head and Brad had a walk-away contract. And that had all come later anyway.

"No one dragged me out of hell." He didn't think Father Michel would appreciate the news that he'd been sent, so he kept that to himself. "Evan doesn't even know about the cup."

"Then why—"

"To keep it out of the hands of people like you." Glass. Inside, the building was plaster and steel, but the skin was made of glass. The problem with having a body was that it felt its thoughts in muscle and bone. He wanted Father Michel to go away, to leave him his unquiet peace, but he didn't know how to make that happen without bringing the FBI down on him or scattering splinters of glass in all directions. Sunlight flashed off Father Michel's silver cross. He wasn't going anywhere.

"You mean like them. The men like my father, who followed Grayson Donne. I am *not* like them. I have devoted my life to God's work, undoing the damage they have done."

"Are still doing. Some of the graves at Grayson Donne's estate were fresh." Brad didn't mention the box screaming at the front of the sales room. He still didn't know who was in it.

"Put there by monsters out of hell, a hell to which I am determined to return you all."

Brad almost laughed. "It's not exactly hell," he said, "but oddly enough, I'm trying to do the same thing."

"Then you will not mind if I banish you to the depths your black soul deserves!" Father Michel kept his voice low, but fervor drove each word.

"Not the depths, and not today," Brad observed coolly.

"If you are not following in your father's footsteps, why do *you* want the chalice?"

"Each of the cabal has his own vessel to draw the blood of their offerings. As you well know, it is how they call their demons from hell. One was destroyed in this very city. Another, my father's, now rests in the vaults of the Church, where it can cause no further harm. This cup will join it, like the ruby that paid for Satan's services. It is a tragic part of our own family history, but one we will neither shirk nor forget."

"Your Church created Donne and his cult of thugs. You gave them the tools. They nearly killed my son. You watched and did nothing, and now you accuse him of his captor's crimes. So I don't trust your vaults, or your good intentions."

"And what would the devil have me do!" Michel LeRoux had his back to the sales room. He didn't see his mother approaching or hear her halting steps on the plush carpet. So he jumped a little when she said, over his shoulder, "How can I have raised a son who believes so firmly in devils, but denies God's angels?

"Fallen angels, Mother, shorn of their wings."

"They make it hard to ride the subway," Brad pointed out, though he'd never considered wings when shaping his material form. LeRoux mere and fils ignored him.

"It is the angels here who cry for justice. And how did you answer? By watching as their sacred children die? How many times will you stand in the way of the avenging angel and live to tell of it? Give him the cup, and hope your God does not inspire him to strike you down where you stand!"

Brad coughed at the thought of Evan as a sacred child of God. The things he did with Lily were, all in all, pretty profane. He'd become a spectator in his own drama, however. In spite of her cane and her faltering step, Madame LeRoux stood very straight, her chin set and her eyes ablaze with a purely human fire. So this was righteous wrath. He'd read about it, thought the author had exaggerated, but apparently not.

And she was right about the avenging angel. Well, the avenging part, at least. Father Michel was skating the thin edge of disaster, and his mother seemed to know it. Good for her. Especially if it got him that cursed cup.

"You're going to destroy it, aren't you?" she asked him. He took her free hand and lifted it to his lips, kissed it softly. *"Oui, Madame. J'en ai l'intention."*

"Bien." He felt the brush of her lips on the crown of his head, then she was taking a step away, and Father Michel was making disgusted noises low in his throat.

"We'll have it sent to your office by special messenger. You will have it tonight. The Church will need its money back—"

"The Church has no need of the devil's money."

"Make the check out to LeRoux Compagnie. I will repay the Church out of private funds, and everyone is happy." Father Michel was definitely not happy, but she took his arm and led him back to the auction. The strongbox was due up soon, so he went as well. But he wasn't following Madame LeRoux. No, he wasn't.

Chapter 43

SO THE FLOOR PLAN HAD LIED. The third-floor front room had a round table with a bowl of flowers on it, half a dozen antique armchairs with ribbon stripes and tiny roses on cream upholstery, and four built-in cases with a dozen or so books artfully scattered among the expensive bric-a-brac. Two tall windows filled the room with bright sunshine through sheer curtains. Too bright, too open for a collection of antique books and manuscripts. Didn't look like it got much use, though, so that was good. At least Old Cyril hadn't been waiting when he appeared in the middle of that pale marble floor.

"If I were a library, where would I be?" Evan wondered under his breath. The fifth floor was supposed to be a warren of small rooms for the live-in staff. The fourth had bedrooms and baths, with "after" photos in *Architectural News*. But the floor plan had been a little vague about a space at the center of the house on the second floor. So somewhere on this floor or the second. Evan listened at the door, an old habit. Finding human presence wasn't the problem here—people crowded his senses, on the street, in the house. It had been easier at Donne's, where he'd had to reach for a mile or more to find a handful of human lives. With the dense press of humanity in the city it was almost impossible to sort out where any of them were beyond "here." But none of them were looking for him yet, and none of them were on the other side of that door, so he relaxed a little. Opened the door.

An empty hall with more doors on the right. Bathroom, bedroom, bedroom. No cultish paintings on the walls, just the stray modern. Not the Braque, though. A couple of Chagall, no Klee. Cyril reserved his playful side for wearing funny costumes while he murdered fifteen-year-old boys.

He found the back stair and took it, down a level, closer now. Voices behind a door. He opened the next one. It reminded him of home—no windows, lots of books, a desk, a few leather club chairs, and a bar, bigger and better stocked than they bothered with at home.

The books smelled of dust and age, cracked leather and greed. Your garden variety avarice didn't rise to a level he could sense in the wind—the lust that had acquired these books left a trace, tainted sweat that lingered from the countless hands that had stroked those pages. He could almost hear the whisper of the words of binding, imprinted in the air that settled, unmoving, at the center of the room. A library table on a rich Turkish carpet at the center of the room held a single book, leather-bound, in a wooden case. Old Cyril was making it easy.

He looked up and silenced a huff of laughter. The ceiling was a copy of the sixteenth-century paintings from Ca Da'Costa, Alfredo Da'Costa's Venice palazzo. Not well done, but Da'Costa's hawklike face still looked down on him, even if it had lost the piercing gaze of a god that the original had.

The Simpsons had held him prisoner under that ceiling. They hadn't survived the encounter. Unfortunately, neither had CaDa'Costa. The last time he'd seen it, the palazzo had lain in shambles with the Simpsons under the wreckage. You'd have thought Van Der Graf would take a lesson from that.

Apparently not.

"Evan Davis. How exciting to finally meet you. I'm glad you're enjoying the library."

Van Der Graf, and Matt Shields was right. If he'd had a mustache, he'd have been twirling it. Evan dropped a hand casually on the book that held Donne's notes. "I go for the bestsellers myself. Wouldn't mind borrowing this one, though. I'll bring it back next time I visit."

"Ironically, he used to be that much a fool," Van Der Graf said to someone in the doorway. Four more figures moved into the room, wearing the robes Evan had seen in the paintings on Donne's walls. They stopped at the bar, poured amber liquor into crystal glasses and settled into leather club chairs—didn't bother with masks, so no one expected him to survive the afternoon.

Van Der Graf frowned at Evan, examined the fading damages with his fingertips. "A shame about your face. You used to be so pretty. Ah well, I suppose it would have healed, given time." Van Der Graf didn't plan on giving him any time at all, but he wouldn't be the first to make that mistake.

Evan took a step back, glanced up at the ceiling where Alfredo Da'Costa looked down his hawklike nose at him, a reminder. Evan had learned a lot since Venice, about what he was and what he could do. Control, Da'Costa had said, and Evan had control up the wazoo. Or whatever. What he didn't have, yet, was the book.

"I've been watching you for years, Mr. Davis. Care for a drink? A little scotch, perhaps? You used to like Bushmill's, if I remember correctly, but I expect your tastes have grown since then. A lucrative business, I understand. You will have to tell me how you did it.

"I have a nice selection of single malts." He gestured to someone Evan couldn't see, and the sound of ice on glass followed, the splash of liquor on ice.

"No, thank you. I've lost the taste for it." Evan needed a drink now about as bad as he ever had, but he knew suicide when he saw it in a glass and he wasn't buying. Van Der Graf studied him for a moment but didn't question the lie, just waved the glass away.

"Grayson said you were a waste of time, but he's dead now and so is his heir, who turned out to be useless—not even a pretty face. And here you are, still alive, if not as pretty as the last time I saw you. Mac was always careful about your face. Hmmm."

Van Der Graf poked around in the desk, frowned. "I'm out of cocaine, but that never was your drug of choice. I have a full range of hallucinogens. Heroin, of course, and the usual pills for those little ups and downs. If we don't have what you want, I can make a call."

"Actually, the book is enough. Always good to see you, must do it again, I'll be leaving now—"

"I think you'll find that difficult. Leaving, that is. Or doing it again, for that matter."

"He doesn't want the scotch?"

Evan knew that voice. "Joad?" The bouncer from the Black Masque. They used to talk comics and art in the neighborhood—he'd had his own book, an independent with a black superhero—before they'd ever heard of the Black Masque. Joad had stayed on the door, just making the rent that the book didn't cover. He hadn't joined the sick games in Omage's back room.

And he should have been dead. Brad blew up the bar. Fifty people died—it could have been a lot worse, given his father's temper, but Evan still felt sick when he thought about it.

Joad shifted a shoulder, almost apologetic, still holding out the glass. "The drugs were free," he said, as if that explained everything. "I was in the alley shooting up when the place blew. I thought they'd killed you, but then there you were, big businessman in Philly, and Mac was pissed as hell. Then he left, and Cyril needed help. The drugs were still free, so . . ."

"Joad likes cocaine now," Cyril said, "It helps his creativity. But I have anything else you want."

"It'll help," Joad said, "It always did before. A little something in the booze and you won't even care."

"Thanks, but no." Omage had used paralytics. Hallucinogens on occasion, but mostly paralytics. Evan had felt everything.

"All I need is a name," Van Der Graf said. "I'm willing to pay—" He held out his hand, palm up, offering a cushion-cut ruby, about five carats. The gem pulsed in Evan's blood, quickened the beat of his heart and throbbed deeper, in the part of his soul that counted Ariton his father. Hard not to reach for it, and Matt Shields' collection of them made a lot more sense. Lily had taken a ruby about the same size as payment for Matt Shields' case. Not so innocent, then, and he'd been a fool to think it.

A deal in blood, daemon's blood, and he figured if he took that stone he'd die here today, torn to pieces by the contracts at war in his daemon nature. Because he already had a contract with Paimon to free Matt Shields.

"Take it, boy." The robes were sort of a giveaway. He recognized the speaker waving his scotch for emphasis as a well-known California judge. "It's not worth your life."

Except that Evan knew how they called daemons with human blood, how they paid in the flesh and bone of their sacrifices. He didn't plan on being the first in the new burial ground.

"No deal."

The judge shook his head. "This could all be so easy," he said, and Evan wondered for whom.

Van Der Graf sighed dramatically. Withdrew the ruby. "I had hoped we wouldn't have to go in this direction," he said, "I thought maybe we could be friends. But I see that you have been turned against me."

They were all playing a part for his benefit, and doing it badly, as if he hadn't seen all those crosses in Donne's makeshift graveyard. Maybe it even worked on the desperate victims they'd trapped before. Evan considered his options.

Joad wasn't the only guard on Van Der Graf's door, but there were other ways out. He could make an exit through the second celestial sphere, leave his audience gaping and come back later for the book. But Van Der Graf was already close. If he found Matt Shields' true name in there, Evan would have only bad choices: breaking a deal between Princes or committing cold-blooded, premeditated murder. If he destroyed the book first—

He could do this. He thought fire and beneath his hand the book warmed.

"Bring her in," Van Der Graf ordered the guards in the hall, and someone thrust a girl into the room. She had long dark hair and wide dark eyes behind glasses that made her eyes look wider still. He'd seen her before, and recently; couldn't quite—

"Help me!" She ran to him, clung trembling, and he re-membered her voice, giving bad directions to the men's room at the Lea Library at Penn. Too young to be in there between semesters. She'd been reading *Treatise on the Names of the Angels,* so he didn't trust the victim act. But it slowed him down for a minute.

"I'm not sure what you think you know about me," he said to Van Der Graf over the girl's head, "But the last per-son who tried to control me with a girl is dead. And I liked that girl. I don't even know this one."

"I had hoped she would make you more tractable, yes," Van Der Graf conceded, "But I'm not a fool."

Evan felt the prick of the needle and pulled away, but not fast enough. He felt the drug enter his bloodstream, recognized the effect. Shit, shit, shit. Burned like a son of a bitch. Down. The girl had already moved away, so nothing broke his fall. He lay on Van Der Graf's Turkish carpet, eyes wide—they'd stay that way until he cleared the paralytics out of his system—arms and legs useless. So was his mouth, so he knew this had nothing to do with information.

"I did what you asked. Can I go now?" he heard the girl say, and Van Der Graf answered, "Sit down and shut up before I decide you're as useless as the rest."

Joad passed the hypodermic to Van Der Graf. He looked sorrowfully into Evan's too-wide eyes but didn't offer to close them, just hefted from the shoulders while someone Evan couldn't see had his feet, lifted and dumped him on the library table. The book was still there, digging into his hip.

"You should have said yes to the skag." Joad said, and moved away.

"But I'm glad you didn't." Van Der Graf frowned down at him. "Don't worry, I'm not going to kill you yet. I may still need you."

"The box is up next," A voice at the door said. "We have the auction house on the phone." Van Der Graf patted Evan's cheek. "This won't take long. Then we'll all have a little fun."

Chapter 44

EVAN WAS IN TROUBLE. AGAIN. Panic, sharp and clear, settled a sick knot in Brad's stomach. Lily felt it too, looked over nervously at him with a little movement of a shoulder. Shields had warned them not to go into Van Der Graf's house, so Evan would have to handle his end of things on his own. They'd gotten out of the habit of rushing to the rescue anyway, and bidding had started on the iron-bound strongbox.

"Ten thousand." The auctioneer called. Three paddles went up. Brad waited, scoping out the competition.

"Eleven," and the same three paddles. Gray men in gray suits. Fifteen, twenty. Then one of the telephone reps jotted something on a slip of paper and passed it to the auctioneer.

"One hundred thousand," the auctioneer said, reading the slip. "I have a bid of one hundred thousand on the telephones. Do I hear two?"

The same three paddles went up. They weren't part of the art world he usually traveled, so he didn't know them, but he figured them for the faces beneath the hoods, slitting throats and feeding children to the worst aspect of a tortured daemon lord in the paintings Jaworski had shown him.

The one on the far right was sweating already, dropped out at five hundred thousand to the phone, and Brad raised a finger. One.

"One million to the gentleman in the back."

The appraisal set the value at a fraction of that. The room had gone silent with that electric stillness of nervous systems tuning to the same frequency. Even the low mutter of the telephones stopped for a moment. Brad felt exposed, and it made him dangerous. Nobody made a move.

Then the phone rep raised two fingers before the next call, took the attention off him, which made everyone safer, though the tension didn't go out of the air as they bounced up millions for a few bids. They lost the last of the gray men at five. The three of them left the sales room with hurried glances at each other.

Someone on the phones had alerted the offices. The room had gained an audience, including a man with dark-rimmed glasses who furiously took notes and a woman in a trim black suit who stood off to the side, watching with a proprietary eye. Most of the observers crowded at the back, just outside the wide entrance to the sales room, watching silently while the gray men argued in low and angry tones, out of sight among the moderns. The crowd parted to let them through, huddling together with a bid for ten.

The phone raised to fifteen. Brad calculated the house's fee, figured the woman in the corner was doing the same with a great deal more satisfaction, and raised to twenty million—twenty-three with fees. They were well into agency money now; Shields was going to owe them the rest of his rubies. Evan's panic at the back of his mind had subsided, but he was replacing that with some panic of his own. He figured Van Der Graf for the telephone, and even he didn't have limitless resources. But Brad had just made his last bid. The agency could scrape up another few million, but not in time.

Chapter 45

VAN DER GRAF HAD GONE, taking his cronies with him. He'd left the girl sobbing in a leather club chair and Joad on the door. Irony there. Evan wasn't going anywhere. He could deal with the drugs, but he still had to destroy Donne's notes. And he didn't rule out Van Der Graf outbidding the agency. He didn't know what he'd do if Van Der Graf suddenly came into possession of two daemon lords, one of whom was his client. But he'd have to do something.

He'd have a lot better chance of that if he could move, and he blessed old Cyril's kinky heart for withholding drugs that would dull the pain of his games. Paralytics didn't cloud his mind. So he ignored the girl, ignored Joad and the jab in his hip from Donne's book, and turned inward on the drugs flowing through muscle and vein. He'd done this sort of thing before—opened a wound on the palm of his hand and closed it again with the daemon side of his nature. Saw the essence of that daemon nature integrally a part of him, not foreign or unnatural but necessary to the living, breathing person he was. The drugs had suppressed his breathing—black spots danced across his vision—but he saw the chemical mark of it, sterile and insidious, and followed it. Pushed.

He started to sweat, bright beads of salt and drugs standing out on his brow and across his cheekbones. His shirt was soaked and his pants weren't feeling all that great either, but he thought he could move his right index finger. His heart sped up and he realized that he'd gone from barely breathing to hyperventilating while he'd been concentrating on moving his left big toe. Slowed it down, but Joad had noticed, shuffled hesitantly over to stare down into his eyes. Evan slowed his breathing with an effort—don't blink, don't blink.

Joad brushed a thick finger across his forehead, frowned at the moisture he'd collected before wiping it on the leg of his black slacks. "You're OD'ing," he said, and patted Evan's shoulder in an awkward attempt at comfort. "I'll get Mr. Van Der Graf. He'll know what to do."

Cyril's first aid would probably involve speeding up the pain part before Evan could die of the drugs, but it would get Joad out of the room. He held still, ignored the itch fizzing in his sinuses. Couldn't sneeze, not when he was so close—

Joad patted him on the shoulder again, sighed. "You should have stuck around," he said. "Mr. Van Der Graf's not a bad boss."

Which might be true until the moment he decided to kill you. But Joad was heading toward the door, closed it behind him. Evan heard him walking away down the hall and couldn't hold it in any more. He sneezed. Held his breath. Maybe the girl didn't know how the paralytics were supposed to work.

"I know you can move," she said. "I saw you move your finger before Joad came over."

She was standing over him, less sympathetic than Joad, but then she'd caught him at flushing the drugs and Joad hadn't. She had tear tracks on her face, but she look more like she was pissed at him than falling apart.

"Can you sit up?"

Turned out he still didn't have control of his vocal cords, but he managed to turn his head to the side—no. And, shit, he'd better get it together before Cyril got back.

"God." She looked down at him with hope shining in her eyes. "He called you Mr. Davis. Evan Davis? Did you take an antagonist before you came in? Matt said you'd help us. You're not doing a very good job of rescuing me—

are there more of you outside? Cyril left Joad on guard because you couldn't move, but he's got a lot more guards and they are sharper and faster than Joad."

Joad used to be sharp and fast. Joad used to be funny and creative and he used to care about his art and his industry. But he'd been taking drugs from Mac too. Shit.

"Who are you?" he said. Had his voice back, sort of, and he thought he could sit up now, but Van Der Graf would be coming through that door soon and it was still more effort than he could summon at the moment. Considered summoning something else, but this was his part of the job and he'd get it done. In just another minute.

"Alba Sanchez," she said, answering his question. "Matt's friend. He works for my father—well, Rafael now. We found your agency on-line. You were supposed to help us!"

Carlos Sanchez's younger daughter, starting SUNY in the fall. Rafael must be the son, and he'd think about that later. Sanchez's involvement seemed a lot less innocent suddenly, but the dead bodies in Donne's woods now took second place in his scary scenarios involving the Sanchez family.

"You're not sleeping with Matt Shields!" He thought he'd already hit his limit for adrenaline rush, but he'd been wrong. He would not, absolutely would not, play big brother to the half-daemon babies of a foreign prince. Which was a sufficiently not-human thought that it made him queasy. He had some daemon in him, but his mind, his *self* was fully human.

Okay, even he didn't believe that, quite.

But Alba Sanchez was answering, "No!" in an indignant whisper. "I'm not sleeping with anybody, and neither is my sister anymore. She was in love with Grey before he died, but neither of us sleep with Matt!" Grey Donne had died, and his father had followed him less than a year later. He didn't think she could have done it, but she'd been hanging out with daemons and looking through books she shouldn't know existed to find the words that would bind them. So he couldn't be sure.

They were running out of time for this conversation. Somebody'd be coming back to check on Joad's story any minute, and he was better off playing dead until he could do more than stagger to his feet.

Right on cue he heard footsteps coming down the hall. "Van Der Graf," he said.

Alba Sanchez dashed back to her club chair, curled into it and sniffed convincingly, if he didn't know better.

The door opened then, and Van Der Graf appeared, a telephone pressed to his ear and the four men in robes following him, their hoods drawn up now. They formed a semicircle around the table where Evan lay, but their heads turned to watch Van Der Graf. Two guards followed, and the girl was right. They didn't have a history with him, and he doubted their drugs of choice involved any of the stash in that desk drawer. Joad came last and closed the door behind him.

"Fifteen," Van Der Graf said into the phone. He cut a glance at Alba Sanchez weeping in her club chair but seemed satisfied with what he saw.

Evan had stilled, but he'd stopped sweating.

"Are you in there, Evan?" Van Der Graf found the nerves at his elbow and pressed, hard, watched the muscles clench along his arm. Damn.

Van Der Graf couldn't ask for what he wanted while he was on the phone, but he mimed pressing the plunger in a hypodermic, and one of the guards went to the desk, found the drug. Evan saw a hand, not Joad's, pass the hypo across him, then felt the prick of the needle, the burn of the drug moving through his body. He knew the chemical now, knew how to override it, break it down, get rid of it. Which he'd better do right now or it would kill him. Cyril hadn't been careful about the dosage, and he'd mixed something with it this time. Evan could do this. He really could. If he remembered what he was supposed to do.

"Twenty-five," Van Der Graf said to the phone.

Evan knew that was bad, but he was floating now, light as the wind, and he didn't really care.

Chapter 46

THE PHONE TOOK IT TO TWENTY-FIVE. The price of a Braque, and Brad was pretty sure that was Van Der Graf's last bid as well, but it didn't matter. The house fees took it over thirty and that was six million more than he could hand the cashier.

Brad was thinking furiously. He could kill Van Der Graf. The man had heirs somewhere, but pretty far down the family tree. He'd have time to liquidate some assets. Lily could diddle the banks if they had to, but that might be dangerous—ownership would be less clear.

"Twenty-five, to the gentleman in the back. Do I hear thirty?"

In front of them, Madame LeRoux was whispering furiously to her son, and he wished she would just stop talking. The hum of it was a distraction when he needed to think. Van Der Graf had Evan—the panic had faded to a muzzy blur, but Van Der Graf was still at the center of it—so he couldn't flatten the house. Not without warning his son first. And he didn't know what he was going to tell Parmatus—Matt Shields.

The LeRouxs had stopped talking at least. But then Madame LeRoux tapped Lily's hand, curled her fingers around a Blackberry. Brad tried to calculate all the possible outcomes while the auctioneer called, "Going once."

Lily glanced briefly at the screen, showed him the figure. He looked up at Madame LeRoux for confirmation, got it in a single nod. Father Michel looked pale, in that witch-burning way, but he didn't object when Lily punched in the account number.

"Thirty," Brad said.

Matt Shields tapped his shoulder. Short-sleeved broadcloth shirt and a pair of dockers, so he'd had the minimal sense to dress for the occasion. Except for the paint-spattered steel-toes he refused to give up. Lily moved down a seat, Brad did the same. "You aren't supposed to be here."

"Didn't have a choice," Shields whispered. He took the seat next to Brad and listened politely while the auctioneer called for the phone's bid. "He doesn't have the money. The box has owners now, and that complicates things."

Shields was right—the phone was silent as the auctioneer called thirty-five, then thirty-one to the phones.

"If you don't give a command, I'm going to wind up inside it when the hammer falls."

"Well, don't."

"Gone for thirty million dollars to the gentleman in the back."

It seemed to work. Matt Shields hadn't disappeared in a screaming burst of flame, at least.

Now that it was over, the auctioneer seemed stunned. Brad was conscious on some level that the room still hadn't started breathing. The next item up was an ornate ormolu clock. The phone rep hung up, signaling a return to business as usual, and the woman in the suit pulled away from the corner by the row of phones. A buzz of hushed voices erupted, and the auctioneer persisted in the clock, trying to break the kind of spell that everyday humans could weave over each other. But the staff was well-trained, and the crowd at the entrance cleared bit by bit. Brad stood up, suddenly understanding the human need for air in a room chock-full of the stuff. The agency was now part owner of a box of daemon lords who did not belong to the host of his Prince.

He'd have to work out the part-ownership deal with Madame LeRoux, and the consequences to both hosts. If there was a later. Van Der Graf still had Evan.

Right on schedule, Madame LeRoux's cell phone rang. She answered, frowned, and handed him the phone. "It's Cyril," she said, very chummy, and he wondered what he'd gotten them into with a priest and the wife of a dead member of Donne's cabal. "He asked for you."

Brad never used cell phones. The microwaves gave him a headache. But Van Der Graf had something that belonged to Ariton. He took the phone, headed for a quiet space by the windows, out of the path of traffic.

"I want to talk to Evan."

Chapter 47

"EVAN CAN'T COME TO THE PHONE RIGHT now. He's indisposed. But I assure you he's alive. For the moment. He may even stay that way if we can come to an agreement about the object you've recently acquired."

Evan listened to Van Der Graf's side of the conversation. After a short pause, Van Der Graf went to the desk and found a vial, handed it to one of the guards. "Keep him down, I just want him able to speak."

He'd missed the mark there. Evan felt his face relax right on cue, but he could wiggle his toes as well, and liked it. He could do that some more if he just grabbed hold of that molecule and pushed . . .

"Open your eyes." Evan blinked his eyes open, but the light hurt and he closed them again.

"I said, open." Van Der Graf slapped him, left a hand-sized burn of pain on the side of his head. Held the phone closer to Evan's ear. "Summon your daemon," he said. "Tell it to bring the box." Then he hit "speaker."

"Evan?" The disembodied voice of his father filled the room.

"Dad?" Evan giggled, remembered a time when he lay like this on the floor of Omage's back room, helpless and tormented and insane. Remembered that he didn't like it. "Dad!"

Remembered then that his father hated it when he

called him "dad." Too human for a daemon lord, and Evan tried again, "My lord?" But his father wasn't paying attention to forms of address today.

"I can't give him what he wants, Evan. You made a deal we *cannot* break."

"I know. Me or the planet." Maybe next time, he'd just say the hell with it, go for the planet. Should have been a sobering thought, but the drugs took care of that. He couldn't stop laughing, and he thought it must be annoying his father, so he tried, really hard, to get it under control. "Tell Lily that Alfredo's on the ceiling," he said, because his mind kept skittering away. "I'm looking up his nose. Tell her I'm sorry I screwed up." Which was a complete downer.

"You haven't screwed up yet," Brad said through the telephone, "But you're working on it. Why don't you just get out of there?"

"Drugs." Sober for more than four years and he couldn't wait to get off the phone so he could beg old Cyril for another hit. He was sooooo fucked.

He started to cry. Kept it out of his voice, he thought, but tears were running down his stuffy nose, right in front of Cyril Van Der Graf, who'd stalked him and wanted to kill him for the pleasure of it. "I'm a mess."

"You'd think I hadn't taught you a thing."

Evan wanted to protest, he hadn't gone out looking for drugs. He was a prisoner. But his father didn't sound disgusted with him. He sounded . . . like he was talking in code. And, yeah, Evan had already cleared the paralytics once today. Could do it again, only he knew he was going to feel like hell this time. Of course, he'd feel like hell if he didn't, also—old Cyril would make sure of that.

At a gesture from Van Der Graf, two of the robed men left the circle around the table and went to a small cabinet next to the desk. One brought out a glass art deco bowl, the other a long silver knife and carried them ceremoniously to kneel at the table. A third brought a set of robes and held them while Van Der Graf slipped on first one sleeve, then the other, and settled the heavy fabric around him. Evan knew how this worked, felt his heart speed up.

"Don't tell Lily I love her, okay? Especially if I die." He knew Van Der Graf and his cronies could hear him, but this was more important. He didn't know why, it just was.

"You're not going to die, Evan." His father sounded sure, but Evan knew better.

"Yeah, I think this time I am."

"We'll be there." Brad hung up, left Evan alone with Van Der Graf and his glass bowl and the drugs coursing through his body. But his father had said they were coming.

It would take work, and he was stuck with the drug that had already hit the receptors in his brain, but he could clear the rest. He just had to do it faster. One of the hooded men offered up the knife. Heavy black sleeves fell back from his wrists as Van Der Graf took it, held it up on fingertips and examined the blade for sharpness. "I need his throat."

Joad grabbed Evan's shoulders, pulled until his head hung off the table. "Don't fight. It only makes it worse," he whispered. "He's not going to kill you, just wants to draw a little blood."

"He's right." Van Der Graf leaned over him and traced the fading bruise on his cheek with the tip of the knife. "I would enjoy killing you. Very much. But I'll restrain myself. You have a lord to placate."

He didn't usually have a calming effect on the daemons of his acquaintance, but Van Der Graf didn't give him time to explain that. Evan felt the knife open a vein in his neck, felt the blood flow, heard it splash into the glass bowl. Van Der Graf's breathing sped up. Sweat glistened on his upper lip when he traced a finger through the blood at Evan's throat, licked it with a little moan. "Evan, Evan," he whispered, "You used to be so beautiful, such a perfect sacrifice. I would have loved you then. Why did you have to spoil everything by getting old?" He made another cut, and the blood ran again. Again.

"Don't kill him," the robed figure who held the bowl reminded him softly. Evan thought it was the judge, and wondered who was being killed. He ought to be up and to the rescue.

"His daemons will want to do that."

Oh. Him. It wasn't true, though. Evan had finally come to understand that. But it was enough to stop Van Der Graf for the moment.

Chapter 48

"**V**AN DER GRAF HAS EVAN. He wants the box."
Lily had followed him to the windows, but so had the humans. He held together his human shape because he didn't think he'd get what he wanted from Madame LeRoux if he went up in flames in front of her. But it was a close call.

He snapped the cell phone shut, returned it, and shook out his hand. Blisters had formed on his fingertips and he healed them without thinking, raised an eyebrow when Madame LeRoux drew back a little, her gaze darting between the cell phone and his hand. Father Michel had come up behind her and crossed himself.

"Discede ab hoc famulo Dei," he said, to remind the priest. Not human, but not that either. "If you don't want us here, stop dragging us into your world."

Madame LeRoux dropped her head. "We are trying to make amends," she said. But it just made her son angry.

"A waste of time," Father Michel gritted out between clenched teeth. "My father tried to tame a devil and it ripped his heart out and took it with him for a keepsake. Evil must be rooted out, destroyed or banished to the depths of hell."

"And how long did your father bind this 'devil' to his prison, after he had torn it from its home?" Lily asked, calmly enough if you didn't look into her eyes. She stared out the window, at the street below, so Father Mi-

chel wouldn't see the fire twisting there. He wouldn't have
recognized the memories of her own binding flaring hot
and bright with her anger anyway. "What crimes did your
father force a lord of the heavens to commit? Understand
this, *priest*: our kind know nothing of death. We learn murder from you."

Brad didn't need this argument right now. He needed
the co-owner of the box to trust him when common sense
and his own intentions would dictate otherwise. Lily usually did this part of the case, but Evan was *his* liability. And
Lily hated priests.

"Think of us as friendly aliens who don't need a space-
ship," he tried. Not that friendly, and not any version of
Father Michel's universe, but, by Ariton, he would not be
one of Madame LeRoux's angels, fallen or otherwise.

It seemed to snap the priest out of his trancelike fixa-
tion with the blue flames of Lily's eyes reflected in the window. Maybe got him thinking down a different path for a
change.

Lily rewarded him with a wry smile. He'd pay for the
alien thing later, but it took her mind off murder, which
was a good start if he wanted Madame LeRoux's trust.

With the dying of that argument, she had time to ask out
loud the question he'd been asking himself since Van Der
Graf called.

"Why didn't he just leave when Van Der Graf found
him?" Evan was Brad's responsibility but Lily's toy. She
wasn't pleased when someone else broke him—not with
Evan or the person who did the breaking.

"He's drugged. Don't ask how he let anyone close
enough to do it—I don't know."

"The house is full of traps," Matt Shields said. He'd forgotten Matt Shields. How had he done that? But he was
there, making it a party and darting covert murderous
glances at Father Michel.

"Evan knew that." And Brad didn't need the reminder
that he was playing out a family drama in front of a priest
and a lord of a foreign Prince that he'd bound to Ariton
against all sense and the nature of Princes. Contracts made

obligations, not allies and the LeRoux family had been up to its eyebrows in the cabal from the day Donne's ancestor used Matt Shields to wipe out a village. Bertrande LeRoux's decision to switch sides came six hundred years too late to change any of that. The less she knew the better—humans were notorious for changing their minds.

"He said Alfredo was on the ceiling."

LeRoux mere and fils looked puzzled. "Alfredo?" Madame LeRoux asked, but did not wait for an answer. "They must have your young man in the library. It's the only room with figures on the ceiling—it's a copy of the secret apartments of Pope Alexander VI.

Pope Alexander'd had a copy of Alfredo Da'Costa's ceiling in his secret apartments. Brad wondered what the Pope had known about Alfredo.

"Know the house well, do you?" he asked, not quite hostile yet. According to Evan, Van Der Graf had recently renovated the house. So, not as far from the cabal as she'd said.

"I didn't know what any of it meant then, but yes," she said, "Thirty years ago, with my husband. I returned to the house three years ago, when Cyril threw a party to celebrate completion of the renovations. Reconnaissance." She smiled ruefully. "We were trying to undo as much of the damage as possible. The ceiling had been preserved and he'd moved Grayson's library into the room. It's on the second floor. The seals and protections are all in the rooms and grand galleries. You can reach it from the kitchen stair without being seen if you are careful. But you still have to deal with whatever defenses the ceiling represents."

He didn't, actually, but she didn't have to know that. He'd been called under the real thing a few years ago and Evan had sent him away again. Prior contract—the most powerful seals in the universe couldn't hold him if Evan said, "Go," and he'd done just that. Would again if he had to, Brad figured, though this time the contract had better terms. He tried not to think about his options if Evan broke his end of the deal. He could walk away from the contract—that's the way they'd written it—but he'd be left standing in Van Der Graf's trap if he took that out.

Evan was Ariton, had proved that over and over. Had offered his life for his Prince on more than one occasion. No gamble at all, except *that* thinking had banished him from the debate over Evan's deal. The host was wrong. He hadn't grown too human in his thinking. Maybe Evan wasn't that much Ariton either. But maybe he was.

Ariton had taken the deal; now there was only one way to find out. "I want to be seen. I'm taking the box to Van Der Graf."

Father Michel spoke first, not angrier than Matt Shields, but faster to express it. "If you were going to give him the box anyway, why did you spend thirty-five million dollars—fifteen of which did not belong to you!—to buy it? We have a part in this decision!"

The carpet under Matt Shield's feet had begun to smolder, and a wind stirred the air that had nothing to do with the air-conditioning. LeRoux hadn't recognized him for a daemon lord, too caught up in his own anger to notice the change in air pressure, but Lily glared at Shields until he settled uneasily.

"There will be consequences," he said, but the box had an owner—owners—now, and he couldn't do much of anything without an order.

"Stand down," Brad said, made it that order, and in the absence of another command, Shields had no choice. It might mean war at home, but he did it.

"I'm not giving the box to Van Der Graf."

"A ruse," Madame LeRoux guessed. "Which may go very wrong."

"He has my son." Which was not what he'd planned to say.

Father Michel just gave him a disgusted huff, but Madame LeRoux laughed, low and with no joy.

"Children," she said. "We would sacrifice the world for them."

That wasn't it at all, but Matt Shields was looking at her like he actually understood, which was scaring Brad right down to the core of Ariton in him. He didn't have time to pursue it, though. Madame LeRoux gestured at the window. "My car is waiting at the door," she said, "Take it, please. My driver knows this area well."

Lily had started them moving toward the elevators. The gallery had cleared, except for two FBI agents pretending to inspect a piece constructed of fractured glass and wooden clothes hangers at one end and, on her way past the toilet on a pedestal at the other end, a tall and purposeful woman in a trim black suit approaching their unlikely party on a collision course. He'd seen her at the auction, watching from a corner by the phone banks, and she recognized them as well, at least to the extent it involved the auction house.

The box had gone for a shocking amount of money, if you didn't know what was inside. Brad figured she was counting up the millions in buyer's premium to the house in her head and worrying that buyer's remorse—sanity— might set in before she closed the deal. Walking away was not an option, of course, but she didn't know that.

Lily smiled and held out her hand. "Lily Ryan, Bradley, Ryan, and Davis," she said, "Buyer's agent. And Bertrande LeRoux. She will be joining us if you don't mind."

"Jeri Hunt," the auction representative returned the handshake. "We haven't worked together before but I've heard of the company. I'm very glad to finally meet you. And of course, Madame LeRoux. I was once fortunate enough to handle a telephone bid for you. It's a pleasure to meet you in person as well." She turned and headed back toward the elevators. "Your purchase has been moved downstairs. I've come to offer any assistance you may need. If you'd like, we can go to my office . . ."

"Of course." Lily smiled just enough. Madame LeRoux had once again taken her arm and they followed a step behind the auction agent. "Will a wire transfer do?"

"A wire transfer is fine. Once we've taken care of the details, I can have your purchase shipped for you, if you'd like."

"That won't be necessary." Lily assured her. "We'll be taking it with us if everything is satisfactory."

"Of course. I'll have it packed and taken to the loading dock—"

"No packaging, please."

The woman paled a bit. "It might become damaged in transit."

"We'll be careful." Lily smiled too brightly. "We're making a special presentation here in the city."

Shields lagged behind. Lily was an expert at this part, so Brad left her to it and fell in step beside him. "What?" he said.

They were passing an alcove, and Shields nudged him toward the men's room. Brad fought the insistent tug on his sleeve, but he'd asked the question, gave in rather than create more of a scene than they already had. The auction agent was smirking, but he had to deal with Shields, even if it wasn't the way the auction agent thought.

"You can't give Van Der Graf the box," Shields said when the door closed on the empty room. "You don't know what he'd do to her. To me." The last was said too softly for a human to have heard him, but Brad wasn't human, and in fact, he could guess. Van Der Graf liked fifteen-year-old boys. He liked sex with them, and then he liked to murder them in slow and painful ways. With a bound daemon lord or two, he could do both as often as he wanted. No bodies to dispose of, no dangerous forays out to find fresh meat. He could feel the rage building in Shields already. It almost matched his own.

"It won't come to that," he said, clipped, because he had work to do and Matt Shields was in the way of it. "Go—"

"No!" Shields eyes blazed with amber fire before he settled with a low clap of thunder. Toe-to-toe with Brad.

"We still need the planet." A gentle reminder, but he'd made his point. Shields took a step back.

"Please." Not quite supplication, but close enough. "Don't send me away. Please. This is my fight as much as yours."

A daemon lord was screaming in that box, and Caramos had said the two lords had more than the loyalty of the host between them. Shields wasn't free yet either. Couldn't send him home permanently until the papers were signed, and probably couldn't have made an order stick now if Shields didn't want to go.

He wondered if this job could get any worse, and realized it could. Evan was still alive, but that didn't mean he'd stay that way. He felt a lot like Lily did about that. Nobody broke his toys but him. But they'd been gone too long, with too many factions watching.

Brad expected the knock on the door, barred the FBI agent with an apologetic smile as Shields slipped out behind him. "They should really do something about the plumbing," he said. The agent pushed the door open, but there wasn't any blood, just the faint odor of sulfur. Let him wonder. Brad went to find Lily and the strongbox that didn't belong to Grayson Donne anymore.

Chapter 49

"MR. BRADLEY?" A young woman in a flowered dress and really ugly hiking sandals waited to show them the way. Brad sensed Lily three floors up and to the right, but their escort wouldn't know that. They left the FBI behind, still checking out the men's room. Had the elevator to themselves, which was fortunate. The woman's excitement and Matt Shields' agitation didn't leave much room for anything else. He was ready to get out and walk.

The presence of a stranger at least meant he didn't have to talk to Shields. Sharing an enclosed space with a daemon lord not of Ariton made his skin itch. Didn't last long. The doors opened and their escort marched them briskly down a cream-colored hallway to a door that said, "vice president." Bad-suit boy stood next to the door, arms crossed over his chest and back to the wall. Their escort opened the door for them but didn't follow them in.

Lily and Bertrande LeRoux had taken the only guest chairs in the room. Father Michel stood behind his mother with that pursed-up "I knew they were criminals" look that didn't take a translator to figure out. Behind the rosewood waterfall desk, Mike Jaworski toyed impatiently with an art deco penholder. The paperwork for Donne's strongbox lay on the gleaming desktop, the signature lines glaringly blank.

Closing his eyes didn't help. Jaworski was still there

when he opened them again. "Aren't you out of your jurisdiction?"

"The lieutenant gave me a surveillance order. I go where he goes."

"Surveillance on whom?" Brad asked, then wished he could take back the question. There were no good answers, and they had an audience. That didn't stop Jaworski.

"Who do you think? The FBI hasn't cleared your client yet, and Evan's tendency to turn up unconscious at crime scenes has Ellen a little worried."

A glare over Brad's shoulder, and Jaworski's hand drifted under his jacket, fell back at his side.

Beside him, Matt Shields took a step back, palms up, and hit the closed door behind him. "Hey, not me."

"Please don't shoot my client," Brad snapped, because Jaworski wouldn't shoot Matt Shields, but he still might start a war neither Ariton nor Paimon wanted and they didn't have Evan back yet. "What made you think you'd find Evan here?"

"I went to the house to give him some information on the case—a warning about Sanchez and your client. Some guy who said he was your cousin Ray told me Evan had gone to New York. We knew where you had gone and took a chance. But Evan isn't here, is he?"

At the mention of Cousin Ray, Bertrande LeRoux's brows went up and her son's went down. Brad hoped they weren't keeping count.

"Evan is fine." He had a long history of lying well and didn't know why the skill chose *now* to fail him. "Can this wait until we complete our purchase?"

"No, it can't. You've got about thirty seconds before Sid Valentine shows up and takes over this dog and pony show." Jaworski pulled a cell phone out of his pocket. "Funny thing about these things. You can pick a conversation right out of the air if you know to look, and the FBI was looking already."

Sid would have been sitting in a room full of electronics monitoring the key players in the sale. They wouldn't have understood it all, but some of it had been pretty obvious.

"Let's stop playing games, shall we? He's not *fine*." Jaworski tapped the phone to emphasize his point. "He's pretty sure he's going to die in that house, and given the number of bodies we've found so far, it's not a bad assumption. True or not, how long do you want him to think it?"

"He would not have wanted you to hear that." He couldn't kill them all, not and get Evan back. They hadn't signed those papers yet.

"I don't think less of him. Won't. But, Jesus, Bradley, he's in a shitload of trouble right now. Would it kill you to just take the help that's offered?"

"You're in over your head here, officer."

"They call that 'life.' What am I supposed to do? Let him die because you're too stubborn to understand that somebody else gives a damn?"

He wasn't about to explain trust to a human. And they'd used up their thirty seconds anyway. The cell phone on the desk rang and Jaworski answered it, said, "Thanks," and hung up.

"Sid's downstairs. Do you want to stop these guys or not?"

"I do." Matt Shields finally took a step forward. "Evan's not my problem, but Cyril Van Der Graf is."

Lily smiled too broadly. "Sched told Evan to make friends. Apparently he did. So I vote 'yes' too."

Giving up gracefully wasn't in his makeup. He'd expected Lily to stand with him, but she had picked up the pen at least, signed the transfer of ownership with a flourish as the door half-opened, hitting Matt Shields in the back.

"Bradley!"

Jaworski shrugged apologetically. "You're his person of interest. He opened the folder on you weeks ago. At the moment he is considered the expert on your case."

Sid Valentine tried the door again, smacked Matt Shields in the back again. "Bradley! We can play games here or we can get your kid back! What's it going to be?"

"Right now, Evan is waiting to die," Jaworski reminded him.

Probably not. By now he'd be nursing a drug hangover

and waiting to find out what the plan was. But the police complicated things. Brad wanted the bastard Van Der Graf dead.

"By the book," Jaworski said. "We don't let him get away. We don't make Evan celebrate Fathers' Day in the visitors' room of a federal prison." He was looking at Lily when he said it, appealing to her to make Brad see sense.

Shields took his silence as agreement and opened the door.

Valentine gave them all an equal glare. "If you're done singing 'Kumbaya' in here, we've got an appointment with a serial killer." From one hand, he dangled a thin wire ending in a gum patch "Open your shirt, Bradley."

"I'm taking this one." Lily started undoing buttons. "Can't let Brad sit in jail, now, can we?" Which was a pointed reminder of the hours he'd spent handcuffed to an interview room at Major Crimes, and a warning that gave Brad's anger a target. She wasn't worried that he'd kill Van Der Graf—Lily was as likely as anyone to turn the man into a smudge on his own carpet. No, Lily was afraid he'd trade the strongbox for Evan's life, and she wasn't taking that chance.

"I'm not that stupid."

"Of course not." But she didn't give him the wire.

"I'm going where the box goes," Shields stuck his hands in his pockets, stuck out his chin with a daemon lord's stubbornness.

"Not on your life." Valentine was talking to Shields, but he didn't take his eyes off Lily's breasts. "Sanchez has disappeared, and so have his daughters. But we got some background sound off that phone call. There's a woman in the room. Doesn't sound too happy at the moment, but hey, murder can't be all fun and games, can it? I'm not letting you out of my sight."

"The box is heavy. Someone will have to carry it. Van Der Graf won't let a stranger in the front door, but he knows me." Lily could carry the box without touching it. She could probably manage it even if she were human. But Shields was starting to look desperate. He didn't deny that Sanchez was involved, which made sense. You can't plant that many bodies without the gardener figuring it out. Complicated things, though. "You'll be listening on the wire. Where can I go?"

That was going to depend on Evan, but Brad wasn't going to tell Sid that.

Sid waited until Lily had exposed a swath of breast and pale silk. Then he said, "Doesn't matter. We're not sending in a woman. Bradley will do it. If he kills the guy, no skin off my ass. A serial killer will be dead, and I get to put him away. All good however you look at it. And by the way? I didn't say that. You get that, Jaworski?"

But Lily had already snagged the wire and pasted it so that it lay against her breast, well away from her heart. "I'd rather not have Shields there myself," she said, "But he's probably right about Van Der Graf. He won't let one of your people past the door."

Jaworski had listened without interrupting, but he picked up the penholder again. *No talking stick in this room,* Bradley thought bitterly, *spit it out or go home.*

"The phone call gives us cause. We can go in and pull Evan out before things go south."

"Weren't you listening, Detective? Van Der Graf's a murderer and all we've got on him so far is giving drugs to a paranoid with a history of using. You do the math because I ran out of fingers."

Check and mate. Brad had a grudging respect for Mike Jaworski and no liking at all for Sid Valentine. But they needed to get into that house.

Chapter 50

OFF SOMEWHERE DUE SOUTH of the table they'd laid him out on, Alba Sanchez was crying softly, her sobs muffled by the arm of one of the leather club chairs scattered in the library. Van Der Graf told her to shut up and went to the door. Evan couldn't see much in her direction past Alfredo's nose painted on the ceiling, but he had a clear view of Van Der Graf, heard his low-voiced mutter giving instructions to the guards in the hallway.

With Van Der Graf's attention off him for the moment, he tried to think past the drugs. Brad would have a plan. He had faith in that much and he couldn't be lying around bleeding out when his father needed him. So he focused on the cuts Van Der Graf had made at his throat and closed them, one, then the next, and the next. Left a couple that had already clotted so the EMTs would have an explanation for the blood. His whole body screamed at him to hang on to the drugs, but he didn't have the time. Whatever his father wanted him to do, he had to be ready.

The chemical signature felt like an old friend already. He found it, pushed outward until the sweat bloomed, and let it go—bon voyage.

First downside to sober? They'd laid him out on a damned uncomfortable table and Donne's book was leaving a permanent dent in his hip. His father had better have a plan.

Van Der Graf's mansion was just a few blocks from the
auction house. He was still shaking the drugs when the
doorbell chimed. It took no effort at all to sense Lily at
the door, and Matt Shields—what was he doing here? They
had Donne's strongbox with them. Evan heard it screaming even before the sound of footsteps on the stairs told
him they were coming. But where was his father?

Oh. There. A breeze with sparks in it drifted across his
faded bruises, moved on. Safe. He was safe. Absurd to think
it with his whole life at risk under that ceiling. But they'd
come for him. They'd come. For just a moment he let his eyes
drift shut, hiding while he settled that fear at least, that he'd
been wrong to put his trust in them, that they'd leave him
here with Van Der Graf pumping drugs into him until he
died of it and they could go home. He hadn't realized he still
carried that fear, wasn't straight enough, not steady enough
yet, to cope with the relief. Tears gathered in his lashes. *Don't
fall, don't make me look like a fool in front of my father.* But
they slid from the corners of his eyes anyway.

Lily came through the door, and—even through the
blur of drug-induced tears—she took his breath away. Or
maybe it was the adrenaline that rushed in to fill the spaces
where the drugs had muted good sense. She smiled at old
Cyril like a long lost lover, but Evan could see the tension
at the corners of her eyes. No flames yet, but she was in a
dangerous mood.

Shields followed her, carrying the box, his teeth gritted
against the screaming of the daemon inside it. He looked
up, eyes narrowed, and took the step that brought him under Van Der Graf's ceiling, onto the blood-red Turkish carpet. More than just dye in the color, but Evan tried not to
think about that.

At a gesture from Van Der Graf, the robed figures came
forward, almost huddled together. There were seven of
them in their long black robes now, eight including Van
Der Graf. Evan didn't know when that had happened. He'd
lost some time, didn't know how much. But the robed guys
were all bowing to Lily, including the one with the stained
glass bowl clasped in his outstretched hands.

"Welcome, my lord." Van Der Graf said with an exaggerated flourish. "I am honored by your presence. Please, a drink? Our gift."

The bowl held about a pint of his blood, Evan figured. Not more than he'd give at the blood bank, but Lily's eyes glittered ominously. "Don't you have brandy?" She dismissed the bowl and the man with a mildly disgusted wrinkle of her nose and damped the murder simmering in blue flame. "Or scotch."

"Scotch sounds good," Matt Shields agreed. "I never really got the whole blood thing."

"Of course." The judge scurried to the sideboard, leaving Van Der Graf standing awkwardly with a thickening bowl of blood nobody wanted.

Shields scanned the room, caught on Alba Sanchez burrowed into her leather chair, but let his gaze move on. Stopped at Evan. "Shift it. This thing is heavy." He didn't wait, just slipped the box onto the table and moved out of sight.

Evan looked up at Lily, waiting for a signal. She grinned down at him, showing too many teeth over her brandy.

"Is that for me?" She scratched almost absently at a trail of blood drying on his neck, looked for the cut that made it but didn't find any— "Good boy,"—and kissed him.

"Fair recompense for bringing me Donne's daemons," Van Der Graf sounded smugly pleased with himself. "My daemons now."

Evan tasted her brandy, felt it when she licked the drugs off his lips. "Yum," she said; he wasn't sure if she meant him, or the drugs. "I thought I'd mislaid him."

She looked up at the seal painted overhead, and he remembered, it had been a trap once, that pattern on a different ceiling. "What should I do with you?" she asked.

Evan knew then. She needed a command. "Save me?" he said, while Van Der Graf made promises, "Once he's dead, you will be free."

"Is that an order?" With her question, it seemed that the air went out of the room. He had to do it, but he couldn't, not after what he'd done to his father— "Only if you want it to be."

"Foolish boy." She looked up then. Van Der Graf wouldn't know to fear that smile, but Evan did.

"You mean you'll kill Evan for me? And I'll be free of him then?"

"Yes," he said, "Yes. At your command, my lord, with my own hand, or at the tooth and claw of my beast." Behind him, the robed men muttered their assent.

Shields didn't protest, but he flicked a nervous glance at Alba Sanchez, who knew more than she should, but apparently not that. Evan thought his father might materialize with an appropriately showy display of fireworks— surprise! Rescue!

Nope. He had kind of hoped they'd come up with a plan he actually lived through, but it wasn't looking good. Lily seemed to be in charge, and she didn't really grasp the permanence of "dead."

She licked her lips, made a show of it, not looking at him, but she meant the next question for Van Der Graf. "And how do I know you have the skill?"

"You know about Donne's boneyard." Van Der Graf swept his robed arms wide in a gesture that called on his newly acquired disciples to confirm his prowess at murder. "Evan's not my first sacrifice, though he might have been, once. But I've learned a lot since then, practice makes perfect. I can give you countless offerings. The girl, my own men." He was sweating, the gaze he fixed on Evan glazed over with lust and hatred and fanatical fervor. "Let me serve you the bleeding heart of your captor."

"A valentine in June. How sweet," Lily cooed.

Suddenly Van Der Graf's sleeve fell back to reveal the silver knife in his raised hand, poised over Evan's heart.

Lily shaped the air in the palm of her hand and flung it. Van Der Graf's knife thunked on the carpeted floor. He gripped his wrist, pain twisting his face as blood spurted between his clasped fingers.

"What are you doing on that table?" she asked, and Evan decided that maybe she planned to rescue him after all.

"Waiting for my ride." No point in playing dead anymore. He sat up and casually, almost accidentally, dropped a hand on Donne's notes at his side. His head floated in the wrong direction when he moved, but the sensation was clearing fast. The drugs were almost gone, adrenaline holding off the payback.

Van Der Graf's cronies scattered like cockroaches, but the judge picked up the silver knife, which just pissed Evan off. He knocked the knife away with a quick burst of twisting air that blew the judge back off his feet but didn't break his wrist. Didn't have that kind of focus or aim yet. Didn't have the presence of mind to consider what he'd just done it in front of Donne's cabal and Matt Shields' human girlfriend either. Van Der Graf took a step closer, pupils dilated. He seemed almost to have forgotten his broken wrist.

"You've grown into your powers well," he said. "If only you'd come to me younger."

He turned to Matt Shields. "Take this sacrifice, my beast. I own you now; let his blood freely offered seal this contract!"

Matt Shields gave him a wide innocent blink. "If you're trying for an insanity plea, it won't work." He patted the strongbox on the table, gave it a little nudge so that it bumped into Evan's hip. "This belongs to you, by the way."

Okay. So. "Your plan stinks."

"Try telling your father that. Or Bertrande LeRoux for that matter."

"In case you hadn't noticed, they've got a hostage. How do you suggest we get her out of here?"

"Oh, that part's easy."

Shields looked at Lily, shared a rueful smile.

Something crashed into the front door on the floor below.

"We didn't tell you the whole plan."

Chapter 51

LILY PUT A FINGER TO HER LIPS. Brad waited, a damped flame, while she reached into the open vee of her shirt collar and brought out a length of wire "There," she said, as she zapped the tiny microphone with a fingertip. "You can talk now."

Brad took that as his signal to step out of the shadows. "Are we done here?"

Matt Shields looked up from herding the cabal into a corner where they cowered in their robes against the shelves of Grayson Donne's books.

"Don't let it kill us," one said, and Van Der Graf snarled at him over the broken wrist. "They can't hurt you, fool. What do you think that ceiling does? The boy made a stupid mistake. The messengers are inside the circle and we are outside it now."

Time for a quick lesson in the limitations of cabalistic magic, Brad thought. Really quick, because— "That's Sid at the door." A reminder for the rest of them, maybe, but they hadn't gotten around to telling Evan. "The FBI was eavesdropping when you called. They should be through the front door in another bash or two. So if we've got work to do here, we've got less than a minute."

He caught Evan's eye, met fog. The sudden hitch in his breathing meant nothing. Lords of Ariton never showed fear. He could walk away from Evan's contract—it was written that way.

Alfredo Da'Costa looked down from between the

arms of a pentagram. He considered the consequences of breaking his contract, of trusting his son. But Evan had learned that lesson—the graphic demonstration still colored his face.

"I don't need the formula for cold fusion," he prodded, "but there's only one way we're getting out of here." Brad finally got a lock on his Evan's attention.

"Yeah, sorry." Evan wiped a hand across his face. "The usual conditions apply," he said. "Go where you want. Do what you want. Just, and this is a personal favor, not an order. Try not to complicate my life any more than it already is, please?" Which, all in all, was a lot better than the last time they'd been in this kind of situation.

"You don't make that easy, but I'll see what I can do." Brad stepped outside the circle just to show the cabal that he could, while Lily gave Evan a "clever boy" kiss. But Evan wasn't done yet.

"The box is mine?"

"Until we sign it over," Brad confirmed. Wasn't sure why it mattered, unless Evan planned to increase his collection by two, which didn't bear thinking about. "Madame LeRoux put her share in your name, personally. As part of the agreement, so did we. The agency took full possession as your agent."

Ariton could not own Paimon's lords. But Evan had made the bargain, and the second celestial sphere hadn't figured out what to make of him yet. The Princes might accept him as a temporary compromise, unless he decided to make Matt Shields a permanent member of the firm.

Shields stood between the girl in the chair and the cabal in the corner, watching grim-faced as Ariton made plans around him. Downstairs, wood splintered and someone screamed.

"I'm not tracking well enough for this right now," Evan muttered under his breath.

"We're out of time." He could stop this now. Didn't know what it would do to Shields or his damned box, but he could snuff Evan's light like a candle—nothing less complicated than dead. The boy could not wrap his head around contract language to save his life.

Chapter 52

"**O**KAY." EVAN STEADIED HIS VOICE. He knew what he had to do. "Matt? We'll get this done when we're out of here; it's in the contract. The part about not complicating my life—"

Shields waved off Evan's concern. "Heard it already. You've gotta live here. The box—"

"Ritual formula," Evan interrupted, and completed the command. "Go where you want. Do what you want. Don't complicate my life here."

"Don't kill him," his father added, and Evan said, "Yeah, that too." Leave it to his father to interpret his way around that one.

"I can't let her out yet." He nudged the box—the screaming rubbed nerves left raw and vibrating from the drugs—"But I promise, we'll find a way to do it."

Matt Shields nodded, accepting the deal for now. Evan hadn't left him a lot of choices.

He didn't feel the familiar echo in his gut the way he did with his father or Lily, which was a relief. No time to think about it now, though. Heavy footsteps pounded up the stairs.

"I can't be here," Brad said. "Valentine thinks I am drinking tea with Bertrande LeRoux."

"Go." Evan shoved the book at him. "And take this with you. It's the first Donne's notes. Maybe it has something in it that can get us out of this in one piece."

"Got it." Brad picked up the book as the door crashed off its hinges. *One less thing to worry about.* He vanished, just ahead of the police pouring through the shattered door.

Chapter 53

THE FIRST WAVE CAME DRESSED IN BLACK, with Kevlar vests labeled"FBI" and very big guns that said "bang" if Evan wasn't very careful. They ignored Lily and Matt Shields, but one of the guys in black pointed a gun at his heart and kept it there. He blinked lazily at the man, figuring his chances of making it to the second sphere before a bullet hit him. A fog still wrapped his head, though, slowing his reactions. Eyes like ice narrowed at him over the gun. Not the hesitating type. Evan raised his hands slowly. "I'm with her," he said, and nodded his head slowly in Lily's direction.

Lily was busy flirting with an agent in a suit who'd followed the assault team, but Sid Valentine had come in behind them as well, looking like he had indigestion. "That one's mine," he said, and Evan didn't realize Sid was talking about him until the gun pinning him to the table dropped, pointing at the floor. The eyes didn't warm, but he got an acknowledging tilt of the head before the man moved off to join the Kevlar parade leading Donne's robed cronies away. Van Der Graf's now, he supposed. Either way, they were going to jail. It wouldn't be enough to pay for all those graves, but at least they'd stopped it. At last.

He was feeling good about that, and it made him a little light-headed.

"We need a doctor here!" Sid was staring into his

eyes. "You are high as a kite, boy. Have you considered finding a different line of work?"

"Lily likes this one."

Sid shook his head. "Thinking with your dick is going to get you killed, son."

"Not my dick. She gets into my head." Evan knew he needed to shut his mouth, now, but Sid rested a comforting hand on his shoulder, invited confidences, and he'd thought that one was pretty obvious.

"Yeah. They do that." Sid gave him a pat on the shoulder before turning away. "Get an EMT in here. This one needs a hospital—doped to the gills. Remember! He's the vic. Van Der Graf can wait. I don't want them in the same ambulance."

Sid was usually a jerk. He couldn't solve his way out of a paper bag, and Evan worried that he'd feel up Lily one of these days and get himself killed for his trouble. But this part? He was good at this.

An EMT slapped a medical kit down and pulled out a pinlight, flashed an unwelcome beam in Evan's eyes. "When was your last hit?" he asked, and Evan said, "About an hour ago."

"Before that."

"Four years." The EMT kept his expression neutral while he pulled a blood pressure cuff from his medical kit, but Evan knew he didn't believe it.

Evan tried to slide around him. "I don't need a hospital."

"Yes, he does." And what was Mike Jaworski doing there, closing off his escape route? "You'll go in the ambulance and do what they tell you. God knows what they gave you."

"I'm fine."

The EMT had finished with his blood pressure, and they both stood up, Evan with a great deal less success. Jaworski grabbed his arm before he fell, but he had it figured now, found his feet and knew what was upright.

Jaworski didn't let go. "I'll make sure he gets to the ambulance." He waited until the EMT moved out of earshot, then he asked, "How stoned are you, for real?" He was studying Evan's face for truth, and Evan said, "I'm fine. Almost fine. I don't need a hospital."

The fog that had clouded his mind and slowed his body was clearing, and Jaworski seemed to recognize the difference, though Evan didn't like the conclusions he was drawing from it. "I'm not using," he insisted. "Not four years ago either. It was never like that." Which maybe wasn't a hundred percent true, but mostly. "Donne's cronies have been after me since I was nineteen. Maybe earlier, I don't know. But they reeled me in when I was about twenty, fed me a line with the booze and the drugs. When I wanted out, Mac used chains mostly, and paralytics for rituals. If my father hadn't found me, I'd be dead. I haven't touched any of that shit since."

Jaworski flinched. He'd seen the photographs from Donne's house, his graveyard, and would have figured a little of what Evan had done, if not how or why. Evan braced himself for Jaworksi to turn away in disgust. But he managed to just be Mike, a little frustrated, maybe a little angry, but taking it in and not quite believing all of it because they'd had the "I'm an alcoholic" part of this conversation three weeks ago over his refrigerator.

"I have a problem with booze. It hasn't been the whole four years, but I didn't take a drink today." The judge had left his scotch on Van Der Graf's desk. Once Evan noticed it, he couldn't bring himself to look away.

Jaworski saw the glass, stepped into the line of sight. "You're brooding." He snapped his fingers in Evan's face to get his attention. "You're probably too stoned to hear this right now, but maybe your defenses are down far enough to let it sink in. The things those bastards did to you are not your fault. Not then, not now. So get your head out of your ass. We've got them. Not even fucking Sid would let it happen again."

It wasn't exactly a twenty-five-year-old scotch, but Evan let his shoulders sag a little, for the moment letting go of the burden, that he'd been too weak to resist the seduction of Mac's booze and his drugs and his promises.

"Nobody came for Matt." Didn't know why, but he

needed Jaworski to understand about Matt Shields too, who was not kin but shared a kindred scar.

"Yeah. Figured that. Let's get you to a hospital."

Evan took a breath, ready to object, but Jaworski stopped him before he said a word. "Home is not an option. We clear you with the medics and find Lily and your father. You tell Sid everything you know about what happened today and why anybody would pay thirty-five million dollars for an old box, let alone kidnap someone to exchange for it when they lost the bid, and then maybe I'll drive you home, because your car is still in impound."

Jaworski reached for the strongbox, but Evan stopped him. "Thirty-five million dollars."

"And butt-ugly it is, but in your condition you'll never make it down the steps with it."

Which might not be true anymore, but Evan let him take it. Jaworski didn't hear the screaming, which made it a lot easier for him, and Evan wasn't letting the box out of his sight, regardless. "Give it to Lily or Brad, not Matt Shields—he still owes us a hell of a lot of money that we've already spent on this thing. Tell them—I know this sounds stupid, but the words are really important—just tell them to hold it for me. Make it clear that I am not *giving* them the box." And, because it was the only part of the deal that Jaworski would understand, he added, "Lily says that was the agreement with Bertrande LeRoux. If we screw up on this, she'll take the box back to France with her, and Matt Shields will own the agency outright."

Jaworski didn't ask why they'd made a deal like that in the first place, just swung the strongbox up by its handles, oblivious to the screaming soul of a daemon lord inside it, and carried it down the broad marble staircase ahead of Evan, the EMT right behind them.

When they reached the street, he looked for Lily and found her smiling brightly at Sid Valentine. They were facing off under a tree that shaded the pavement in front of the imposing brick-and-sandstone facade of Cyril Van Der Graf's townhouse mansion. 70th Street was narrow and crowded. At the top of the block, two police cars in front of a mid-rise apartment building held back half a dozen news trucks with their dishes extended while their lacquered reporters and not so lacquered camera people jockeyed for position and the best view of the crime scene. At the bottom of the block, a single car guarded a pair of sawhorses that closed off the street. There were more news trucks on standby, but nothing much for them to see.

Overhead, the sound of helicopters racketed off brick and stone and concrete, with chaos below them on the street. The police must have gotten some of the neighbors out before they closed off the block because there were gaps in the line of civilian cars bumped up close to the curb that held patrol cars now, with red lights flashing lazily under the trees. Two black vans blocked the middle of the street, the doors hanging wide while the strike team milled around them, stowing weapons. Van Der Graf's cronies were already gone, but more official vehicles had filled in the close space. On either side of the strike force vans, ambulances with their own flashing lights faced in opposite directions down the one-way street.

He was pretty clear, but not enough for the onslaught of lights and noise. Evan stumbled, reached a hand out for balance, and someone grabbed his arm to steady him. Sid Valentine swore softly under his breath and pulled Evan behind one of the black vans, out of sight of the reporters. "Where's Jaworski?"

"I thought you were with Lily—"

"Now I'm with you." Valentine shook his head like Evan had done something stupid, which he hadn't, really. It wasn't his fault that *Architectural News* had the floor plan wrong. Not his fault Van Der Graf had a hostage to use against him either. He was crap with hostages, had been since the time he'd been one, and didn't want to connect those dots.

"Jaworski," Valentine repeated.

"He was right here," the EMT said before Evan could answer, "I've got this one."

"Well, get him out of here before he collapses on the street."

"I need the detective, sir."

Jaworski was talking to Lily, handing over the box, but Sid glared and the EMT didn't wait.

"This way." He took Evan's arm and steadied him when the flashing lights blew his sense of up and down. Mike Jaworski caught up and climbed in the ambulance after him. Then they took off, quietly heading the wrong way down the street while the second ambulance went the other direction with lights and sirens, pulling the news vans after it.

Evan gave it some thought but couldn't remember any clients on this block. After today, he figured it was going to stay that way.

Chapter 54

DONNE'S BOOK DID NOT TRAVEL WELL. Some material objects, with no intention attached to them, might pass through the second celestial sphere without creating a ripple in the waves of energy that filled the great dark. But magical objects designed to rip daemon lords out of their natural home and pull them into the material sphere created tidal disturbances in the flow of all the universes. Brad moved through that flow in less than the time it took to draw breath in the material sphere, but the book still created eddies in the currents of his own universe. The material sphere would feel those rips and eddies as the bursting to life of a new star cluster, the death of a galaxy far enough away that Evan's world remained secure—he'd made sure of that. The mountains of Earth would be gone to dust when the effects of those actions touched it as starlight and its absence.

The book's presence touched Ariton rather more quickly. Anger crowded him in the streams of darkness, threats against himself, his Prince; mostly against his son, who had caused enough trouble and should have died in the cradle. If Ariton couldn't handle the simple death of a mortal human, then Magot would do it, or Astarot, both allies of Azmod in the gathering of Princes. Amaimon remained silent, but Oriens would have destroyed the planet to be done with it, and Paimon could not speak at all, being torn by the words in the book, two of its own lords held captive by it and only Ariton able to free them. Ariton that would have killed the mortal boy as well, and left Paimon to its own devices, except that contracts had been made. But Badad must go, and take the cursed book with him, destroy it on the human sphere so that it never intruded on the business of Princes again.

He was already heading in that direction, so he went. Not home. He wanted no part of Donne's legacy to taint the place where he grudgingly found comfort in Evan's world. The book had a mind of its own anyway, and drew him to Donne's house, built as a trap for daemons. Brad turned away, resisted its pull, and tumbled on his shoulder into Donne's wood, still marked with police tape. The churned earth of the empty graves softened his fall, until a splinter from the overturned white crosses bit into his upper arm. He plucked it out and closed the wound. Didn't expect company but looked around anyway.

Long shadows crossed each other—pine and oak, hemlock and beech, sunlight shafting low between the trees. He would have picked a more comfortable place to do this, but Evan and his cursed book had left him few choices. So he found a spot under an oak tree that hadn't been turned over and lifted the book from its case.

It took only minutes to uncover the spells of binding in the book—Ariton found things, and the first Donne's notes crawled across their pages like liquid fire. Centuries of Donnes had filled the pages with bindings more terrible than Evan had ever considered. No spells to free a daemon, though, which didn't surprise him when he thought about it. People like Donne and Van Der Graf and the Simpsons never gave up their power willingly. He didn't look forward to telling Evan, but his son was a clever boy. He'd think of something.

In the meantime, Brad would do the universe a favor. He set the book and its wooden case in a shallow hollow where a small body had lain—a fitting place to end this legacy of torment in two universes—and knelt beside it. The wooden case went up in a flash that left the barest trace of ash behind. He could have burned away parchment and leather in an instant as well, but undoing so many years of misery woven into its magic took time. So he rested a hand on the tooled leather cover and thought of flames. Smoke curled between his splayed fingers.

He let the fire grow naturally, according to this world, as it ate ink and parchment and oiled leather. When the cover was crackling in earnest, he leaned back, wrists resting on his thighs, fingers lightly curled over his knees, and watched the flames rise higher, dig deeper into the old parchment leaves. He couldn't tell if the stink of burning flesh came from the book's cover or from the empty grave, or if the corruption of the book gave off its own stench of human misery as it burned.

He watched until the flames lapped low and then broke up the embers with a rotting twig. He'd grown accustomed to the stillness, only the snap of flame and the rustle of leaves on the trees for company, so the brush of a footstep against old pine needles brought his head up, eyes flashing blue fire, quickly suppressed—reflection of the flames dying in the grave at his feet.

A young man, not much older than Evan but shorter, darker, with dark eyes behind aviator glasses, stood framed by two straight beech trees, watching him. In his hand he carried a good-sized stick with most of the deeply grooved bark still clinging to it, not quite threatening yet, but the thought was there. "You're trespassing. The police will be back—"

Carlos Sanchez had the run of the place, and he had a son and two daughters, so it seemed a good bet that this was a Sanchez.

"I'm looking for Carlos Sanchez."

"In the ground?" Nervous, but a challenge. "This is private property, and a crime scene. If you want to see Carlos Sanchez, go to the office and make an appointment."

Sid Valentine said that the father and both daughters had disappeared. They'd brought Alba Sanchez out of Cyril Van Der Graf's library, but that left two of them still missing. The stranger was worried about something, but not that, so he knew where Carlos Sanchez was—at least had reason to think he was alive, which didn't mean he was on Matt Shields' side. Maybe Alba Sanchez had been a prisoner as she said, but maybe not.

Brad didn't trust any of them. Someone had buried Donne's dead, and Brad had never believed the gardener could miss hundreds of marked graves on the property he maintained. So maybe Shields hadn't had a choice about painting houses and trimming shrubberies after all.

With a wary eye on the intruder, he gave the ashes of Donne's book a last stir with the stick, made certain that not a scrap of readable parchment remained, and stood up, brushing the dust off his hands. "I know it's a crime scene. It's my case." Which was true as far as it went, and if he left a more official impression, that was fine. "Who are you and what are you doing here?" Brad infused the questions with a little danger and the authority of a lord of Ariton.

"Rafael Sanchez."

The son, and no surprise there. He frowned, measuring Brad with a quick glance at the grave where smoke still rose from the ashes. "I work here."

"Your employer's been dead for three years," Brad pointed out and wondered briefly if Donne were really dead, though it seemed unlikely that he would hand his possessions to the state if he were alive.

"We have a contract with the state, minor upkeep and lawn maintenance paid out of the estate until they sell the place for taxes." It made sense as far as it went—Evan had said something about it when he'd first checked out the house—but the state had very little to do with Sanchez's presence in the wood today. "You'd know that if you were the police. What are *you* doing here?" Then the pieces came together behind his eyes.

" Are you Bradley, Ryan, or Davis? Not Davis. Alba called, she said the FBI rescued them and sent Evan Davis to the hospital. Is Matt all right?"

"Seemed fine when I left him."

Sanchez nodded, processing the news. "When Matt found the ad, I thought you were con artists. But he seemed sure you were legit, and then Marina found you on the

Web, mentioned in the newspapers for a high-profile case in Vancouver." Marina Sanchez. The other sister—the one still missing. "So I thank God they were right, and I'm glad you're helping Matt, but that doesn't explain why you are trespassing on a crime scene."

"I'm a detective," Brad said, with a twitch of his fingers indicating the graves around him. Sanchez clearly knew more than he'd told the police, but Brad recognized that combination of shock and sorrow that humans reserved for their great tragedies. He may have planted them, but he really didn't seem a likely candidate for membership in Donne's cabal.

"Murder isn't my specialty," he added, pushing a little. "But I can hardly ignore it when it turns up on a job. I can't believe you ignore it when murder turns up on your job either."

"I never killed anyone. Most violent thing I've ever done is set rat traps in the garden. For rats. Haven't done that in ten years or more." Which didn't entirely answer the question.

"Maybe not. Grayson Donne and his friends may have killed them, but he didn't bury them. His kind never do. Leaves his gardener as the most likely candidate."

"I'm not his gardener. I run a contracting company. You want a new wing on your house, you call me. You want a petunia border for your driveway, you call somebody else."

"Your father, then. Did he run from Donne's cabal, or from the police?"

"My father stayed alive. We helped when we could. Mostly we just stayed alive." Sanchez headed back through the trees, toward the house. He stopped, half-turned to add, "I wasn't lying about the police coming back. Unless you want to have this conversation with them, you'll get out of here now."

The book was gone, and it had started to rain, a scattering of fat drops with rumbles of thunder in the distance. Brad waited until Sanchez was out of sight and headed for the house on Spruce Street. But he couldn't shake the feeling that the Sanchez family knew entirely too much about the business of Princes.

Chapter 55

THE DOCTOR DIDN'T BELIEVE he'd been clean
for four days, let alone four years. Sid Fucking Valentine got the drugs and doses out of Joad before they
police took him away and the EMT called them ahead.
So the doctor was waiting for a comatose patient when
they wheeled him in still arguing because he wasn't an
invalid, damn it. He needed to be on his feet, hated
being vulnerable to attack with fight or flight clearing
a lot more slowly than Van Der Graf's drugs in his system. The doctor came to the obvious conclusion, asked
Jaworski to wait outside, then tried the conspiratorial
approach anyway when he wouldn't leave—all just
drug addicts here, must have been cut for shit on the
street, man, 'cause that stuff could put a horse in the
ground. We all just want to help—ignore the policeman in the corner; he's a good guy. Not arresting users
today, right?

Evan's drug history was four years out of date and
he didn't really know what Mac had put in his scotch or
directly into his veins back then. He didn't care what the
doctor or the uniformed policeman waiting in the hall
outside the curtains believed about him. But Mike Jaworski stood in the corner with his professional face on
and Evan had thought he might have had a friend there,
for a while at least.

Ridiculous to care what anybody thought, though,
when the truth would earn him a 72-hour stay in the

psych ward. He tried the logical lie instead. "He must have made a mistake. I'm fine."

The doctor didn't believe him on either count, told him he was lucky to be alive as if he didn't know that already, that the drugs were clearing on their own, but he needed to be under observation. But he was the victim here. They couldn't arrest him, and they couldn't hold him against his will, and he was sick to death of hospitals. So Evan promised to call for the results of his tests and to come back if they found something unexpected in the blood work—wouldn't do either, but he said what they wanted or he'd still be arguing—and he just walked out, a signed release, AMA—against medical advice—in his pocket and Mike Jaworski dogging his footsteps, still not saying a word.

The ambulance had brought him in through the back, a covered level for emergency vehicles only, but the uniform led him out through the front. Jaworski was still with him, still not talking. He knew where he was now—cobbled drive, gardens full of impatiens and low shrubberies—they'd taken him to Cornell. He'd never made it to a hospital the last time—Brad and Lily had taken him back to Philly and detoxed him in an empty house on Spruce Street. They'd bought it just ahead of an open house and wound up living there—but he wouldn't have ended up here. Hadn't lived in the high-rent district then.

Clouds had moved in, so it was dark in spite of the hour. Quieter than he'd expected, all things considered—a few more police around than you might expect, but none of them looking their way. Jaworski led him to a nondescript black sedan illegally parked in front of the door. "I'll take it from here," he told the uniform and walked around to the driver's side. "The news vans followed Van Der Graf's ambulance. By now they know you're not there and they'll be on their way, so if you're not going to stay put like a sensible vic, we've got to get out of here now."

Evan slid into the passenger seat, relieved at his escape—from Van Der Graf, and from the hospital. Jaworski was talking again so he let him; tried to pay attention, but he needed sleep, his own bed and a long walk along Boathouse Row after: river and grass and quiet to think. But he wasn't going to get it.

"Your father seems to have disappeared." Jaworski glanced over, knew right away Evan wasn't surprised. "He's going to have to talk to Sid again when he turns up. Lily's downtown now. That's where we're going. The FBI wants to know why that box is worth thirty-five million dollars, and why Van Der Graf and his cronies would risk a federal kidnapping charge over an empty pine box that doesn't even open. So do I."

"Oak," Evan corrected him, rubbed gunk out of his eyes. Long day, and they were heading into more trouble. Sid Fucking Valentine, when every muscle he had quivered with the need for sleep. The need for something. "Oak and Iron."

"Oak. That makes all the difference, I suppose." Dry as old bone.

"The provenance makes the difference. It's always the provenance," Evan explained, and wished he hadn't.

Jaworski didn't look over this time. Kept it cool. "Provenance. So where's it from?"

"France." Anyone with a catalog knew that much already. Evan pointedly closed his eyes. Hoped it would discourage more questions he hadn't figured out safe answers to. Hoped Sid didn't know the right questions.

When he opened his eyes again, it was raining, and the car had pulled up in front of the house on Spruce Street.

"Make some notes before you forget anything," Jaworski said, "Then get some sleep. Sid can wait until morning." Evan wondering how he was supposed to forget any of the afternoon. But he didn't have to think about it now. Could, at least, try not to let it drive him crazy.

The car pulled away, left him standing alone in the rain. Ellen Li would assign somebody for the night shift, but nobody else in the police department had access to the house. He could look forward to a night interrupted only by his own nightmares.

The streetlamp on the corner gave him enough light to navigate the office, but not enough to see the medallion in the carpet or the pentagram above it. He felt its presence, though, an easing in his shoulders under its protection. Didn't see the daemon lord sitting in his high-backed leather desk chair.

"You made the evening news, but not in a good way. You looked like you'd been dragged backward through a neutron star. They are calling it a Satanic murder cult, complete with pictures of Grayson Donne's graveyard. And you have messages."

The daemon read from a lined tablet, though he hadn't turned on the desk lamp. "Three of them wanted interviews, all local. The FBI hasn't released your name, but they recognized you from local cases. I asked for money and hung up.

"Your mother called. I do a very good you, by the way. She said to come home, you can find a job in the school system. Making all that money is pointless if you don't live to spend it, talk, talk, talk, you never did listen to sense, but let her know if you need anything."

Caramos. Caramos had talked to his mother? Once his heart started again, Evan pushed the thought aside for later. He'd have to call her, but not yet. Couldn't cope with the well-meaning concern when he was feeling this raw and really didn't want to face the fallout from her conversation with a daemon lord. God. What had Caramos said to her?

Unfortunately, there was more. "Your lawyer is not happy that you've been getting yourself damaged again, or that members of this agency may have been talking to the FBI without counsel, or, and she stressed this particularly, with the agency contract you sent her to review. She said that you must not sign it, because it puts you at risk for full liability, including for the thirty-five million dollar box she saw on the television, if your partners decide to walk away from the business. Are your partners likely to walk away?"

Too late not to sign the contracts, but they'd worked—his father had Donne's book, Lily had the box, and they'd all walked away from Van Der Graf's traps.

"If they walk away, I won't be alive to worry about the

business, so it won't matter." That was his life all right—so screwed up that thirty-five million dollars was the least of his problems.

"True. You might want to cancel the appointment tomorrow, then. I penciled her in for ten."

"Tomorrow is Saturday."

"She's charging you extra for that. Someone named Lieutenant Li called for Badad—Brad. Said—" Caramos tilted the tablet, gave up trying to read his own handwriting. He knew it all by heart anyway. Daemon lords never forgot anything. "Said that somebody named Carlos Sanchez has fallen off the radar and they haven't found his older daughter at all—if Brad knows anything, she wants to hear it. Did he kill them?"

"Did Ellen—Lieutenant Li—ask that?"

"No. I was just wondering."

"Wonder about something else. He didn't, and we don't need to raise any more suspicion that we have already. Why are you still here anyway?"

"You made a deal with Paimon. Host-debts are at stake. " Judgment blurred his features, a fuller version of his father's face lit by the unearthly blue flames that he raised around himself.

"I'm here to guarantee the contract you made with a foreign Prince, one way or another." I hope it goes well and we can all celebrate with a hot fudge sundae and go home. But I protect Ariton's interests in this matter.

One way or another.

Evan knew the minds of daemon lords. Caramos was called the Joyful One, but it didn't make him any less dangerous than Anader the Cruel. So he knew what that meant.

"You're here to kill me." He backed away, both hands raised to stop him, though Caramos hadn't moved and couldn't enter the circle of the pentagram in the ceiling.

"Not *me*." Caramos set down the tablet with its messages scrawled in the dark. Fire smoldered in the pits where his eyes had been. "I want to help you."

"Get out of my house. I abjure you."

"If things go badly, you don't want it to be your father, do you? That's why he's here—it's been his appointed task from the day you met him. But I like you, Evan, so I will do this one thing for you. If you cannot fulfill the contract, your father won't have to kill you. I assumed you would want that for him. And you will have your memories of Lily for comfort when the time comes."

"I want you out of my house." Evan didn't give an answer, or wait for one. He needed to sleep off the last of Cyril Van Der Graf's drugs, but he lay awake, staring up into the darkness, for a long time. Lily didn't come home, and just this once, he was glad.

Chapter 56

"I HAD AN APPOINTMENT WITH YOUR SON, but you'll do." The furniture was out of order in the front office—someone had dragged in one of the comfortable chairs from the waiting room and Khadijah Flint homed in on it, settled herself for a long stay. "Is Evan all right? I saw him on the television last night— they were putting him in an ambulance."

"He's fine." Brad met her skepticism with an even stare and tried again, opting for something she'd believe this time. "He'll *be* fine. He just needs sleep. And I thought we canceled this appointment."

He closed the billing file in the accounting program, wished he'd used the private office at the center of the house. But Caramos was in there, playing "Battleships" on Evan's laptop. Evan was still sleeping off the tail end of Cyril Van Der Graf's drugs, and Brad didn't expect to see him until noon. If he'd known Caramos hadn't canceled the appointment, he'd have gone to Singapore. He would at least have worn a suit.

This was going to cost his son; he just didn't know how yet.

Khadijah Flint didn't remark on his shirtsleeves, however. "My office received a call from a Mr. Ray Moss." She didn't move, but her tone left frost on the windows. "He said that, on second thought, your offices didn't need the help of my kind on matters of contracts. I considered whether he meant people of color, or women, or just lawyers in general. But I don't work for Mr. Moss. If you no longer wish my services, you'll have to tell me yourself. And since the contract language Evan asked me to review favors you and Miss Ryan at his expense, I will also have to hear that from your son, personally."

Brittlely formal, she still managed to say "your son" like an accusation. Brad closed the laptop for a distraction, but it didn't work. He hadn't expected it to. "Mr. Moss has reason to distrust lawyers," he said. "He hasn't met you, so he wouldn't have known about the other possible interpretations you might put on his dismissal."

"Am I dismissed, Mr. Bradley?"

"Of course not." He really should have kicked Caramos out of the study. "I assume your current visit means the contract Evan sent is airtight, ironclad, loophole free—the cliché of your choice—it works?"

"The cliché of your choice. I advise against it." She found a folder in the sleek leather bag she carried and slid the contract across the expanse of antique Hepplewhite desk with an expectant cock of her head. She wanted something more from him, and he knew he couldn't give it.

"I can't promise not to walk away," he said, which was the crux of her problem with that contract and the only part that made it livable. Because he knew he would. Someday he would tire of playing respectable businessman, and he wanted a way to just go that didn't require his son creatively dead first. Couldn't tell his lawyer that, and she wouldn't understand the other side of the agreement— that until he chose to walk away, Evan owned him. It made him queasy to think about it.

She looked at him like he'd disappointed her in some profound way. "The news reports said the FBI found hundreds of bodies murdered by the people who held your son hostage yesterday. I gather he would have been the next one. Can't this wait until he's recovered from his ordeal?"

"He was working, and we had him covered. He was never in danger." Cold himself, because Evan wouldn't appreciate being cast as the victim in this drama. He had a job. It hadn't gone exactly as planned, but the job still got done. "It's too late anyway. We've already signed it."

Tight-lipped, she shook her head, reached into the leather bag again and brought out an envelope. "The results of your DNA tests," she said pointedly. "You can destroy the paper they're printed on, but you can't undo the information in the hospital's database."

"Why would I want to do that?" He hadn't needed tests to know Evan was his son. Every daemon lord in existence could taste it on him. Ariton grudgingly acknowledged him. But Evan's mother was human, and she hadn't recognized the body Brad wore now. It had seemed a small concession, and DNA was easy to match. They'd done it with a bloody handshake.

She didn't answer him, just looked at the walk-away contract on the desk between them, not much different from any contract the agency held with its clients, and he reminded himself that she didn't know what it meant to Ariton.

Daemon lords didn't function well in solitude, and it made him uncomfortable to realize that the need for connections was so powerful in exile that he'd substituted an assortment of human associations for his absent host-cousins. He would not willingly give up those associations while he stayed here, but he couldn't promise against his nature to keep them either.

"This isn't about DNA," he said. "Evan's my son. The tests were for his mother. And the agency is solvent." It had been, until they'd dumped eight million dollars into Matt Shields' strongbox. But Shields had plenty of rubies. Carlos Sanchez would not be quitting his day job, but the agency would be in fine shape as soon as they sold a few of those stones.

"Then what *is* it about?" Flint settled herself more comfortably in her chair. "Pardon me for prying. I don't mean to intrude on your private life, but if you tell me what you are trying to do, hopefully, we can find a better way to do it."

"This way works fine. But thank you for the test results."

The question was closed and Flint seemed to read that,

changed the subject. "Do you want me to stay while you look at them?"

"If you wish." Brad slit the top of the envelope and lifted out the single sheet of paper. "All the proof you need," he said, and handed it over. "Evan is my son. Any more questions?"

"Do you still want to go through with this contract?"

"I told you. It was never about that."

Flint shook her head. "It will kill that boy if you walk away from him now."

"No," he said, "It won't." Which made him laugh because, thanks to the contract, it was the truth.

"Then I will have to concede that I don't understand. I just hope that you know what you are doing. As usual."

Khadijah Flint got up to leave and Brad followed. "Thank you," he said. He'd be paying weekend rates and acknowledged no unwelcome debt with the words. "I can't say whether Evan's mother will be pleased, but this should reassure her that we mean no harm to her son."

And then perhaps she could convince Sergeant Joe Dougherty, who might still pull their lives down around them because he'd owed her a favor from high school. But that wasn't a problem his lawyer could solve, so he showed her to the door.

Evan would be asleep for another hour at least. He was going to kick Caramos out of the study and reclaim his tapestried wing chair and his coffee and his book.

Except that Ellen Li was waiting on the other side of the door.

Chapter 57

"**W**E HAVE TO TALK," Ellen said, and he wished she'd sent Jaworski. Jaworski was Evan's associate and didn't require any effort on Brad's part.

"I don't suppose you'd settle for a game of chess?" he asked hopefully. Khadijah Flint moved back into the office.

"Maybe next week, if we can clear this up now. I need to talk to Evan—Captain Marsh persuaded Sid that I could get more out of him than the FBI. Is he all right? Mike said he left the hospital against medical advice.

"He's fine," he tried that answer again, waited for the objection. Ellen just nodded her head and let it lie. She was a cop and knew the answer for what it was—not maimed, still functioning. Best you could expect for the present.

Khadijah Flint sat back down, smiled politely though she hadn't known about the AMA. She was their lawyer and it looked like they were going to need one even if she was angry with him. But he knew he was going to hear about it later.

Ellen Li sat next to Flint, smiled encouragingly. It felt odd, that professional smile. He'd met at least a dozen of her smiles, over the chessboard or dinner with Harry. This was the only one that didn't light her eyes with their own human fire. "Is he here?"

"Sid?" Brad played for time.

"Evan."

"He's asleep."

"Can't this wait until he's recovered a little from his ordeal?" Flint's voice carried just the right amount of professional indignation. Brad knew she really was indignant, at him for not protecting his son and at the police for intruding before Evan regained his feet. He couldn't figure out why she'd want Ellen to think otherwise.

"If I don't come back with something, Sid will be in this office by noon. And he's cranky when he isn't fed regularly." Ellen Li was Brad's associate. He trusted her and so did Evan, which could be dangerous, but he didn't want Sid Valentine anywhere near this house if he could help it. So he stood up with a slight nod to acknowledge the request.

"If you wait here, I'll see if I can wake him."

Once past the office door, he didn't bother with the stairs.

Evan usually sprawled when he slept and he usually did it naked, with at least an arm or a leg wrapped around Lily. But Lily hadn't come home and Evan was sleeping in sweatpants, curled up tight like he was hoping to contain the damage. Even his face looked pinched, waiting for the next blow. The frown line between his eyes deepened as awareness of an intruder penetrated his sleep.

Brad considered waking him, but hesitated. Some wounds Evan carried like a "fuck you" to the world, and some he hid for the weaknesses they were. Brad remembered the photographs that Mike Jaworski had shown him, paintings from the walls of Grayson Donne's house. Remembered the mad, defiant boy he'd dragged out of a bar in the East Village. Those sweatpants hid more than his son's body. They hid wounds he was in no mood to deal with at Khadijah Flint's hourly rate.

He considered stopping for a jacket. Ellen would notice, so he didn't, but he did stop at the study. "If Evan wakes up, tell him Ellen Li is here to see him," he said when Caramos looked up, from a game of solitaire now.

"I could be Evan," he offered, which would have been tempting if Brad didn't want to live here tomorrow.

"It can wait."

Caramos shrugged and went back to his game.

Ellen Li and Khadijah Flint interrupted a discussion of a judge they all knew when he rejoined them. He didn't have to tell them. Ellen took one look at his face and laughed, gently, like he'd proved something to her she'd known for years. "You couldn't wake him."

He didn't answer—didn't have to.

"Mike is worried about him too. I can give you names if he'll accept help."

"He'll be fine," Brad assured her, and didn't think about Evan coiled up tight in his sweatpants. "Was there anything else?"

"Thanks in some part to the efforts of this agency, the FBI safely recovered Alba Sanchez, but Carlos Sanchez and his older daughter, Marina Sanchez, are still missing. If you have any—"

"I don't have them here. I don't know where they went. The agency would help if we could, but I suspect that Sid would find our efforts intrusive." Sid was still angry that they'd solved the theft of the Dowager Empress treasures. Angrier now, Brad figured, and he was right, but not for the reason he'd expect.

"That never stopped you before. Apparently isn't stopping you now. The FBI in New York found recent ashes in one of the overturned graves on Grayson Donne's estate. They questioned Rafael Sanchez, who was on-site at the time. Sanchez said he found someone from this agency burning something in one of the graves. He identified you from your license photo. Sid thinks you were destroying evidence. Were you?"

He didn't answer, felt the pull of associations, his resistance to them as well. Khadijah Flint leaned forward. In the hierarchy of furniture, she had the better chair and Ellen Li did not. "Are you here to arrest my client? Again? This time, we *will* sue."

Ellen waved away Flint's question. "No one thinks Mr. Bradley is involved in these murders, not even Sid. But would your client destroy evidence to protect his son's past from being dragged through the courts? There's not a soul who's ever worked with this agency who'd expect anything else. Even Sid has that figured."

"It was nothing," he said. "An offering for the dead." In a way, it was true.

"My client is innocent." Khadijah Flint straightened her spine where she sat. She supported him coolly, but he was not her favorite flavor today. Brad wondered if she believed him. No question Ellen didn't.

"The FBI will be analyzing the ashes. By Tuesday they'll know what he burned."

Which was the point of this discussion, really. He had until Tuesday to solve the case and put it to bed, then he'd have, at minimum, an obstructing justice charge to deal with.

A noise at the door made them all jump a little, settle again with an embarrassed ruffle of feathers. "Evan," Brad said. "You're awake."

"Sorta." Evan took a sip of his coffee, and Brad wondered if Khadijah Flint could win a case for justifiable homicide if he killed him for it. More of that must have shown on his face than he'd intended, because Evan handed over the big blue mug with a cautionary, "Leave some for me."

Their audience pretended—broadly—not to notice as he handed the mug back. "Ellen wants to ask you some questions. Are you up to it?"

"I'm fine." Evan looked fairly disgusted at his choice of chairs, but he took the spindle-backed reproduction. "Has the FBI exhumed Grayson Donne yet?"

Chapter 58

EVAN STARED INTO HIS NEARLY EMPTY mug. He wasn't exactly in withdrawal from yesterday's drugs, but he couldn't quite shake a lingering hunger for a little something to take the edge off. It heightened his awareness of the bottle of scotch in the credenza.

He'd filled the hole he used to pour the booze into—didn't need it to kill the night terrors or dull the questions about what made him what he was or whether it would kill him someday. It still might, but at least he knew why now. Knew where the flames in the mirror came from. His mind had that figured. His body, though, still wanted the feel of the bottle in his hand, the scent of the scotch and the slide of it down his throat. He craved the numbness that followed the fire in his gut, and set it up again . . .

Coffee wouldn't do much, but it was something to hold, something to pour down his throat, and the kick of caffeine hitting his bloodstream would have to do. He considered going back to the kitchen for the coffeepot and a few more mugs, but figured the faster he answered Ellen's questions the faster he could get the police and his lawyer out of the house. Then—well, then he'd take it one minute at a time and let the case distract him until his hands stopped spasming around an imaginary bottle.

He sat down, rested the mug on the desk, stuck his sneakered foot on the corner, and tilted his chair onto the two back legs. He was wearing a loose pair of Dockers with a Penn sweatshirt—had considered changing into work clothes when Caramos gave him the message, but it was Saturday, and his skin felt like Cyril Fucking Van Der Graf had gone over it with sandpaper. So they'd just have to deal.

At least he'd gotten Ellen Li thinking down the path he wanted her to go.

"Grayson Donne was over ninety years old when he died. Do you have any reason to believe he was murdered?"

"Not that one." Though he wondered, now that he thought about it. Matt Shields had said he'd done everything he could to keep Donne alive. He'd never said why his efforts finally failed. "The younger one. Donne had plans for his son. Van Der Graf said that the cabal had some kind of breeding program. But Alba Sanchez said her sister was in love with him, and Grey Donne wanted to marry her."

Grayson Donne's breeding program involved a captive daemon. Matt Shields had said that the son had refused, and so the father had raped the daemon—Carlos Sanchez had said her name was Kady—repeatedly, in an unsuccessful effort to impregnate her, until she'd gone completely insane. Then he'd died and left her trapped in a box. Evan still had to figure out how to release her without turning the planet into shrapnel, but he had at least until tomorrow for that.

He couldn't tell Ellen Li, of course, but he could point her in a useful direction. "So maybe the son had an accidental fall, or maybe somebody murdered him over his life choices. Maybe it wasn't premeditated—he was no good to any of them dead—but given the number of murders the police uncovered in Donne's woods, I wouldn't bet anything in the family mausoleum died of natural causes either."

"That's not in the transcript of any of the Sanchez interviews." But Ellen looked like she believed him, and she didn't talk to him like he was about to crack. He needed business as usual, and she gave it to him. "As it happens, the FBI agrees with you about not assuming natural causes for any of the deaths related to the Donnes or their cult. Yesterday they filed orders to exhume both of them—father and son.

"But there is one person who might have gained by the death of the younger Donne. Sid thinks that's why Carlos Sanchez ran, that he decided to stop both of the Donnes the only way he knew how, and that your client helped him. He's ready to have your client arrested as an accessory, at least, and possibly for the murders of both Donnes if he can't find Sanchez."

It was sort of ironic that Sid could get that close and still tag Shields for the wrong murders. They knew Donne had orchestrated the deaths that filled his graveyard, but the tooth and claw marks on the bodies, the strength it took to tear them apart while they struggled and breathed, remained a mystery to their forensics experts. They'd never seen Matt Shields take on the monstrous form summoned by Donne's spell.

Brad interrupted then. "Sid always confuses the victim for the suspect. I'm not surprised he's done it again. As for Carlos Sanchez, we have no evidence that he ran from anything. He may have been kidnapped, like his daughter. He may be dead. Or he may wisely have gone into hiding until the police neutralize Donne's group. You spoke to his son—what does he have to say?"

"He said he doesn't know." She didn't believe it.

Neither did Evan. "Sanchez is a political refugee. His daughter was kidnapped by Donne's cronies. It's the same old nightmare back to haunt his family again." The police would already know that, but they hadn't seen Carlos Sanchez staring down the threat of Donne's house of horrors. Which didn't speak to his innocence, but maybe explained why he'd gone to ground.

"It's not the same thing at all." Ellen sounded tired. Disappointed too. "The police are here to help him, not to terrorize his family."

She hadn't expected the need to defend herself here, and Evan hadn't meant her. He trusted Ellen Li, trusted Mike Jaworski, and he even trusted Joe Dougherty to mean well, he really did. But somebody had to have noticed when all those people went missing.

"Where were the police when Grayson Donne and Cyril Van Der Graf were filling Donne's woods with bodies?" He'd meant it as a challenge, but knew he'd lost his professional detachment when Khadijah Flint reached over and patted his hand.

"No one is going to hurt Carlos Sanchez," she said, and Evan cringed at the softness in her voice. Khadijah Flint didn't do soft. And she didn't know Carlos Sanchez, wasn't thinking about him when she said, "He's got the best lawyer in town on his case, and a detective agency that would take on the world for him."

She hadn't seen the pictures from Donne's house, but Ellen Li had, maybe recognized his picture on the wall and no, he hadn't meant, "where were the police when *I* needed rescue from Donne's cabal," but guilt passed fleetingly across her face, so he figured she'd taken it that way. He didn't know whether to apologize for what he hadn't meant in the first place or keep his mouth shut before he dug in any deeper. And maybe he did mean it that way, if he was honest with himself.

Brad didn't say anything, which was worse. Evan knew that look—mayhem simmering behind eyes that had gone completely blank to keep the fire from revealing more than he wanted the police or his lawyer to know. But Evan could see it, just a flicker that could pass for morning light glancing off the blue of his father's eyes.

"Shields may know where to find him," he said, because he had to do something to damp the tension building in the room before the rising air pressure cracked the windows. "I'll talk to him. See what he can tell us."

Paimon's lords knew secrets the way Ariton found things. Between them, they'd have Carlos Sanchez in hand before dinner. They could decide what to do with him later.

"Your client missed his appointment with me yesterday."

"We were tied up." A little irony there. Ropes were about the only thing missing yesterday. "Will Monday do? It's the weekend."

"Too late. Sid wants it, and he's still in New York. You'll be hearing from him." Ellen left it at that, which was a minor miracle. She rose to leave with a smile for his father, but Evan still had a question—*the* question. "We bought a box at Sotheby's yesterday—"

"The FBI has it—that and your car. They've checked them for evidence, and they're ready to release them both to the owner." That would be Evan. "You can pick them up this afternoon in New York. Just bring proof of ownership. But they'll want to know why you were willing to pay thirty-five million dollars for it before they let the box go."

Brad filled in smoothly with: "Eccentric client. The fee was very good."

"The Vatican was bidding against you, then suddenly dropped out. Another bidder, the mother of the priest bidding for the Vatican, combined her bid with yours. I can well believe that the Church would not willingly concede to Cyril Van Der Graf anything it wanted. But that does not explain why they wanted it, or why the Church would defer to you when its resources must be far in excess of your client's, or why the co-owner would sign over full ownership to your son.

"Our objectives were mutual," Brad said, "But the agency had a greater likelihood of success."

Ellen hadn't asked a lot of questions—mostly seemed to be warning them. "It's those objectives the FBI will want to hear. I'd like to hear them myself."

Brad smiled, and Evan knew never to trust that smile. "We just want to unite our client with his property and send him home. It's as simple as that." The first part was true. But simple? Not really.

She didn't confirm chess with his father on Wednesday, so they weren't in the clear yet—they never were until all the pieces shifted into place.

Time to start shifting pieces.

Chapter 59

EVAN FOUND THEM IN THE BACK ROOM at Charlie's. The place had opened for lunch but it was still early, only a diehard or two at the bar as he passed—trying not to look at the bottles displayed on the wall—to the pool tables in the back. Lily was taking a shot while Matt Shields watched her ass with appreciation. "That's Ariton's," Evan said, and really didn't understand the wash of anger and raw challenge that hit him like a tidal surge. He wasn't jealous. Wasn't even sure if he meant Lily or the pool table. Lily hadn't been happy with this case from the start, wanted no part of a contract that tied them to a foreign Prince. She barely tolerated Matt Shields. But this was his place, where he could get a Coke and sink a few balls and flirt with Lily across the felt before they went home to do what they did best any time of day. He didn't want Matt Shields intruding on his fantasies about what he'd like to do with Lily on all that red felt.

Shields laughed at him, which cranked the heat behind his eyes a notch higher. "Just appreciating the human part of the view," Shields said, but there was an edge to it. "While I wait for you to turn over Donne's strongbox, so I can go home."

Which didn't stop the simmer, but did add an anvil to Evan's gut. He had no intention of handing that box over to Matt Shields, not with an insane daemon lord inside. He'd let him go—but he needed the box to do it. And he needed some answers first.

"The police are looking for Carlos Sanchez and his daughter, Marina," he said. "So am I."

"That wasn't part of the deal."

"It became a part of the deal when he disappeared. The FBI thinks Sanchez killed the Donnes. They think maybe you helped him, maybe killed Sanchez yourself. They won't stop looking for him. They won't stop watching us because they think you're involved."

"I don't have a deal with the FBI. Paimon does not have a deal with the FBI. Are you reneging on our agreement, in Ariton's name? War between Princes may mean nothing to you, but Paimon will kill you, and this planet."

Evan darted a glance at the doorway, but no one was close enough to hear the argument over the music.

"No, he's not," Lily said, but Evan refused to listen.

"Paimon won't get the chance. Right now, Ariton's executioner is in my house, playing video games on my laptop." He'd had enough of them all and he was tired of trying to slip through his own life unnoticed by the forces battling for the right to kill him. "But if nobody murders me this week, I still have to live here. If that means the police looking over my shoulder for the foreseeable future, I damned well want a good reason. So you'll get your box when I decide what to do about Carlos Sanchez."

Shields glared with amber flames threatening in his eyes, but he set the cue stick down and brushed the chalk off his hands. "We'll need a car," he said, a reminder that the box bound his movement to the material sphere. Evan had already thought of that. "I've got a rental. You'll take me to Carlos Sanchez, then we'll take the box out somewhere away from breakables, and set you free."

"The box first," Shields said. "Then Sanchez."

It would complicate the pickup. The FBI had doubtless slapped a locator on his car. The rental had a lowjack, but the FBI would have to track it down and he hoped to dump it before they got a good lock on where he'd gone.

"I'll follow you later," Lily promised. Evan hadn't expected her to put up with the hours in a car with a lord of Paimon. She gave him a deep and lingering kiss that swept his tonsils and he gave it back, had wrapped his hands around her thighs to lift her onto the pool table when she broke the kiss, laughing and flushed. "Not now," she whispered, her breath coming quickly, like she'd been running.

"Sanchez can wait—"

But she slipped away, still laughing, and left him uncomfortable in his own skin and alone with Matt Shields. The rental sedan was parked outside, so he turned on a heel and went, expecting Matt Shields to follow, and he did. Neither of them said a word until they hit the Jersey Turnpike.

Chapter 60

THE COMPUTER ON THE NEW DESK made noises he'd never heard before when Evan used it. Brad looked up from his book and glared at Caramos, to no effect. His host-cousin grinned madly at the screen and pumped his fist as another faux explosion rattled tinnily from the speakers.

"If you enjoy explosions so much, why don't you just go blow something up? Cities are off the table—I promised Evan—but there are plenty of underpopulated bits of the globe, and a few planets nobody's using at all."

"It's not the explosions, Cousin. It's the winning!" Caramos grinned and jabbed a key with a thick index finger. "Can we have lunch now? Something Chinese?"

Brad loved Caramos dearly in his daemon form in the second celestial sphere. A brush with his cousin's exuberant joy exhilarated him at home. But he found it exhausting on a Saturday afternoon on Spruce Street, when all he wanted was to sit quietly and read a book until Evan turned up with some answers to Ellen Li's questions.

"In the kitchen," he said. "Local menus in the drawer by the telephone. Evan marked the ones that do lunch. If you have Hong Kong in mind, you'll have to wait for Lily."

As if he'd conjured her by speaking her name, Lily appeared in a gust of wind that swirled a sheaf of loose papers off the corner of the new desk. She took their place, perched next to the computer, and snapped the lid down. Caramos snatched his fingers away and looked up at her with shallow dismay glittering in his eyes. "I was winning!" he said.

"Evan called you Ariton's executioner. He said you're here to kill him," she said.

So. Not the usual family argument then. Brad looked up, waited for an answer.

"Not exactly." Caramos tried to open the computer again.

Lily laid a hand on the cover, held it shut. "How 'not exactly'?"

"I'm here to guarantee the deal. If he doesn't succeed, Paimon will want his life. It's a small price for a broken contract between Princes, but Ariton can't allow Paimon the privilege—the boy belongs to us, after all. It's Ariton's prerogative, so Ariton will do it, details to be worked out between the parties.

"I think, based on my observations, that only one thing will matter to Evan if it comes to that. He believes that killing him will hurt you, and he will not want to cause either of you pain. Ariton agreed and granted him that boon. If it needs to be done, I will do it. No promises for quick and painless—though Ariton will not surrender those bargaining chips easily. But I'll do what I can to make it as easy as possible for him. And you won't have to be involved."

Lily reached for him, grabbed a fistful of his shirt and pulled him closer, so that his lips almost touched hers. "First," she said, "if it comes to that, the only thing that will matter to Evan is staying alive. If you think he will allow you to kill him without a struggle that may bring down universes simply to protect my feelings, you have seriously underestimated him. Second, if anyone is going to break my toys, it will be me. You do not get to play. Do you understand me?"

"But Evan—" Caramos looked to Brad for help.

Brad slipped a finger between the pages of his book to mark his place. "Evan knows your name," he said, and smiled as benignly as he could under the circumstances.

"He knows all our names, and all the spells of summoning and binding that our enemies have used against us for centuries, and he will want to stay alive, as Lily says. So maybe you can kill him, or maybe not. Personally, if I needed him dead, I would go with Lily, because he might hesitate with her. He might not realize until too late what she intended. If *you* try to kill him, you'll probably wind up in a box like Matt Shields."

Caramos paled. "I promised him, on the word of Ariton."

Lily kissed him lightly and released his shirt, teasing with sharp fingernails as she smoothed it back into place. "Perhaps he'll succeed. He usually does. If he doesn't, leave him to me. Because you're right about one thing. He won't want to hurt me. Paimon may have to settle for quick, but I'll have that edge, and I'll get it done."

"It's ridiculous to worry about it," Brad pointed out, annoyed at the interruption. "He owns the box; it's just a matter of working out the details." He opened his book again, found his place. He'd seen the signs in Lily and wasn't surprised, not when Caramos said, "Then I suppose we can have lunch," or when Lily kissed him again, said, "Later. Take me to bed now. Be Evan for me."

Caramos' eyes lit up, blue flame dancing joyfully in their depths. "Sex!" he said, and produced a passable version of Evan before they disappeared in a scatter of windblown papers. He didn't move or think like Evan, but she'd satisfy his curiosity and send him home happy. And he'd satisfy—whatever it was Lily needed when she dressed her lovers up in Evan's body.

It would be safer for all of them when Evan wasn't watching for murder at every bend in the case. Brad considered Singapore. Mai Sien Chong would be sleeping, but she wouldn't mind if he woke her, and he wondered which of his many forms she might prefer. He had once appeared to her as a tiger, which pleased her, but her guardian had shot him in the head, which hadn't worked out quite as he'd intended. He decided to keep the shape he had, because it was comfortable and worked well in her bed.

As it turned out, Mai Sien was not sleeping. She was, however, very happy to see him. When he lost control, erupting in blue scales, with horny claws growing from his hands and feet, shredding the silk on the bed, she stroked him knowingly and called him by his Chinese name—Chu-Jung, god of the south wind—and assured him that she had more sheets.

Chapter 61

ONCE THEY WERE ON THE NEW JERSEY TURNPIKE, it was straight going and mind-numbingly boring, except for the daemon lord of Paimon in the passenger seat. The silence in the rental stretched as far as Trenton, but Evan hated going into anything blind, and he wasn't going into this until Matt Shields gave up some of his secrets.

"There's a rest stop ahead—do you want anything?"

Shields looked over as if he didn't understand the question. He was back in flannel and steel-toes, putting on the identity he had lived with for the past three years. Evan couldn't tell if he was returning to the camouflage Carlos Sanchez knew or just letting go of human comforts before heading home. He didn't want to think about the possibility Shields was taking back the human comforts he knew.

"Coffee?" Evan prodded.

"I'm good, but stop if you want."

He did, got them each a cup. He wanted Shields distracted with something ordinary. However long he'd been stuck in that box before, he'd lived in the material world for three years and understood about coffee. Traffic was light at midday on a Saturday, and Evan merged, took a sip of Starbucks over the wheel.

"So," he said. "Who did kill Grayson Donne?"

"Which one?" Shields looked at him over the plastic lid, not particularly surprised at the question.

"Take your pick."

"Mr. Donne killed Grey. You know Grey was seeing Marina, and that his father had other plans for him. Mr. Donne hated it when anyone crossed him, but especially Grey. They had a fight."

"Was it an accident?"

"No." Shields took a sip, grimaced a little—buying time, Evan figured, though he must have known the questions would come eventually.

"Grey defied him. Mr. Donne manipulated the argument to make it look like an accident, but he murdered his own son."

The way Shields said "his own son" was a big clue-light shining on something. The rental protested the sudden jolt of acceleration with a whine and a rattle and he eased up on the gas. Shields had made his feelings about humans clear and he'd said he hadn't produced any half-daemon offspring. Evan had to take him at his word, because the New Jersey Turnpike didn't give him many options for dealing with a daemon's lie. "Didn't he need his son to produce an heir? You said he wasn't having any luck himself."

The sound of the wind and the steady burr of the tires eating up the road filled his head but couldn't blot out the memory of the daemon screaming in the box. No luck, no luck, no luck, the tires rolled, and the wind screamed a daemon's terror around the windows.

"He was going to leave. Had already found a place in the city, and he'd promised to talk to the police when he got there. He knew the locals would do nothing."

Promised who? Evan wondered. Not the sort of thing he could ask outright and know he had the truth, so he angled toward the question with another one.

"Why *then*? He'd been living in that house, had to know what was going on—if he wasn't a part of it, why did he wait so long?"

Shields said nothing for a long time, just looked out the windshield at the flat New Jersey landscape flying by at eighty miles per, his mouth set in a grim, hard line. Evan was about to try another question when Shields' breath hitched.

"When he was a child, he used to sit with us in the garden. His father told him we were his legacy, his property. His monsters. When Grey got older, he would own us, and he had to learn to control us the way he learned to ride a horse.

"He was afraid of his father, but he defied him anyway, even when he was a kid. Used to bring coats and blankets to cover us, because he said it wasn't civilized to walk around undressed. Donne never gave us anything to wear, of course, and Grey always promised we'd have clothes when his father died—dresses for Kady, and a shirt and trousers for me. Blue jeans for both of us, because that's how people dressed out in the world. He said we'd need to know that when he set us free. But we weren't his monsters. He didn't have the power, and he didn't know what being a monster meant until his father brought him into the circle."

Shields wasn't looking at him. Evan hadn't commanded the truth, but he didn't think Shields was lying, exactly. A daemon lord couldn't lie to its own host. The host shared consciousness, so there was nothing to tell and nowhere to hide a truth, except not to know it. They lied to humans easily enough but didn't usually bother unless there was something to gain from it. Evan didn't see the gain here, but nothing so far explained the regret that poured off Shields in waves. Regret that, really, made no sense.

"He was raised with those paintings on the walls, must have played among those crosses and heard the screams of people being murdered in his house." Evan's hands trembled on the wheel of the rental, tangled in flashbacks—his own picture on Donne's wall, his blood on Donne's floor, on the walls of a back room in the East Village. Lying on a moldy rug in an empty house, listening to his father tell him to pull his sanity together or Lily would kill him, and she didn't know him then, would have done it and sometimes still regretted that she hadn't.

Grey Donne was dead, but Evan was still alive, and he had a job to do if he planned to stay that way. "If he wasn't a part of it, why did he wait so long?"

Shields gave a little shrug, more to the tone than the

questions. "He was in boarding school for a while, and at Yale. Both had arms of the cabal to watch over him. They've been raising their kids to this for centuries. Donne came to it early, eager for the power. People were just so much meat to him—the cabal believe they are a superior order of beings. They're not, by the way. They die just like everybody else."

Evan knew that, but he'd wondered if Matt Shields had. Wasn't surprised that Grayson Donne hadn't gotten the memo. "What about Grey?"

"He resisted, and they gave him a long lead. Kept it to the simpler rituals, lots of sex and liquor and the occasional sacrifice of a little blood until he was out of college. He thought it was a game that his father took one kink too far."

Evan remembered the same rituals, taking the sex and the booze and the drugs, listening to a daemon lord whisper in his ear that he was special, not like the others. Then that lord had snapped a silver collar around his throat and proceeded to drive him mad.

"What changed it for Grey?"

"His senior year in college, Donne brought him into the circle. He saw me tear apart the crossing guard from the local elementary school. He started plotting his escape right then."

"He confided in you after he watched you murder an innocent human being?"

At first Shields said nothing, just stared at the paper cup in his hand. Then he rolled down the window and tossed it out, watching it fall behind in a splatter like blood on the asphalt.

"Donne told him it was me, but Grey didn't believe him at first. He still wanted to free us. I think he loved Kady a little. Not like Marina—more the way he loved thunderstorms in summer. Not something you touched, but you could love it from a distance."

Evan did understand that, felt that way right before he plunged his hands into Lily's hair. So he wasn't entirely convinced about the innocence of Grey Donne's attraction.

"How does Marina Sanchez fit into it?"

"Oh, he fell in love with Marina when he was fourteen. He was home for a few weeks on vacation, and she was helping her father in the garden. It took her until the next year, but they never wavered after that. I think it was Marina who kept him normal. In a way, I guess that's what got him killed. Donne didn't mind when he thought Grey was just taking advantage of the gardener's daughter, but when he found out they were planning to leave together, he flew into a rage. He didn't do it right then, but pretty soon after, Grey had a broken neck. Marina dropped out of school for a year, then she went back and finished her degree."

There'd been less than a year between the deaths. Evan figured he still didn't have the whole truth about what had happened. From his side of the investigation, none of it sounded as innocent as Matt Shields pretended, least of all the Sanchezes.

The rest? Maybe, but the part that the Sanchezes were just innocent bystanders who gave a daemon lord of Paimon a job painting houses? It didn't make sense. For one thing, Alba Sanchez kept turning up in all the wrong places—at the Lea Library at Penn, reading *Treatise on the Names of the Angels* the day after Shields had knocked on his door, and then at Cyril Van Der Graf's Gilded Age mansion, where she happened to be a prisoner during the auction of Donne's daemons?

"Whatever hold the Sanchez family has over you, we can fix. But you have to tell me what it is."

"They're just trying to help." Evan waited for an explanation, but Shields had stopped talking. He could have pushed it. He owned the strongbox and the Donne family had died out, leaving no blood heirs, so he owned Matt Shields. Which made him no better than old Cyril, or Grayson Donne himself.

The hell with that.

The sign ahead pointed them to the Lincoln Tunnel. Sharing time was over anyway.

Chapter 62

SID VALENTINE WAS WAITING in a room with a window looking out onto the hallway. Sid's case—he'd opened the file. The room held two chairs with a desk covered in walnut-grained laminate between them. It could have been any office, except for a mirror with one-way glass across from the window. Sid waited in the chair facing the door, with Donne's strongbox on the desk in front of him.

Evan had left Matt Shields with the rental. Didn't want him near the FBI if he could help it; didn't want him in the room with the screaming strongbox while somebody trained to spot serial killers watched through the one-way glass. Sid couldn't hear the screaming, of course. He wouldn't understand why Evan winced when he walked through the door, but he noticed.

"You should be in the hospital. Doesn't your agency give sick leave?" Sarcasm. Great. Evan had an answer to that—used it up on the last case—but he didn't want to remind Sid of Mai Sien Chong or the alabaster child still missing from the art museum's collection.

Fortunately, Sid's attention had moved on, to the doorway behind him.

"I thought maybe Miss Ryan would be with you. Isn't she usually your keeper?" Okay, not so fortunately.

Evan reached out a mental feeler, got a ping. "She's downstairs, signing out the car." She had the dealer with her, to take it away. Brad had been adamant; they were getting rid of the car. He'd picked a new model—it was probably in their garage already. Lily would find her own way home. "If you have the paperwork, I'll take the strongbox."

"Not so fast." Sid shifted his belt buckle but didn't bother to straighten the shirt that belled above it. "We have some questions. Mr. Van Der Graf admitted that his staff might keep illegal drugs in the house. He said that he suspected one of his bodyguards of using performance enhancing chemicals but that he did not know the nature of the substances. He also said you knew this particular bodyguard and invaded his home—Mr. Van Der Graf's home—looking for drugs and that you were semiconscious when he found you in his library. He would have called the police himself, but at that very moment he was losing a contest with your father over the purchase of this antique strongbox. Bad judgment overtook him, and he decided, since you had landed on his doorstep, so to speak, to trade you for your father's purchase. A momentary lapse, and he swears, through lawyers who will probably cost him the price of that box, that he would neither have harmed you nor gone through with the highly illegal exchange, involving as it would, unlawful imprisonment, extortion, and grand theft. And murder, of course. The wire picked up his confession to murder, which his lawyers characterize as a wrongheaded attempt to claim the killings he's seen on the news as his own in order to frighten Miss Ryan into relinquishing the strongbox."

A part of that was true. Van Der Graf wouldn't have gone through with the exchange. But Evan had no doubt about the murders. Van Der Graf had hoped to keep the box, trap Brad and Lily, and sacrifice Evan himself to the monstrous side of Matt Shields.

"What did Alba Sanchez say?" He sounded like he was fishing for an alibi, probably made him look guilty of something to the eyes behind the glass. But he figured if Sid was giving out information, he'd take what he could get until the well ran dry.

"Oh, Ms. Sanchez supports your story. She insisted that

she was Van Der Graf's prisoner as well—a regular collector, Cyril Van Der Graf." Which was true enough to make Evan wince again, thinking of the graves in Grayson Donne's woods, but didn't necessarily include Alba Sanchez.

"She said you were under guard when they brought her into the room, that they used her as a distraction while Van Der Graf injected the drugs against your will. Who gave you the drugs seems up for grabs, but several of the guards backed up the basic story, including one, a user himself, who said you almost ODed because Van Der Graf didn't know you were clean. You couldn't call any of them a disinterested witness, and nobody was telling the whole truth, but we do have Van Der Graf's own words on the wire, and your blood pretty much everywhere. And, yes, the forensic pathologists working the case have found several distinctive patterns in the murders, including a smaller group of adolescent boys murdered during the past fifteen years that fit the pattern of a sexual predator and serial killer."

Evan's hand went to his neck, where one of the cuts he'd left for evidence rubbed against his collar. Sid followed the movement as if it proved something, and not just about Van Der Graf.

"I know you too well to assume any degree of innocence, but it does seem clear that you weren't there for the drugs. And frankly, Mr. Davis, you may think I'm a fool—I know your cousin does—but Ms. Ryan was ready to kill Cyril Van Der Graf if she had to, to get you back. And she wouldn't let your father go in with the wire because he was ready to kill the people in that room without waiting for another option. I don't trust much about your agency, but I know how your partners act when you are in real trouble. So, no, I don't believe Van Der Graf's story. If we hadn't gotten to you when we did, Cyril Van Der Graf and his cronies would have killed you. He came closer as it was than your father will tolerate, and I suggest you keep your nose clean for a while. Because I'd love to lock up Kevin Bradley for any one of half a dozen felonies he may have committed, but murdering your killer isn't one of them. I'd just as soon not have to stand in the rain while they bury you."

Sid pushed the paperwork across the table. "Sign here, and it's yours." Evan signed, stood up and grabbed the handholds on each side. The daemon inside was shrieking, high and desperate, the sound cutting through Evan's head. He didn't know how he was going to get the box to wherever he needed to take it without collapsing from the pressure of that desperation, and it was going to be worse for the daemon lords involved. And he still hadn't figured out how to keep Matt Shields from killing him when he didn't release the daemon trapped in the strongbox. Not until he'd figured how to keep the planet alive when he did it.

"Can you at least tell us why anyone would pay thirty-five million for it?" Sid was asking him to throw him a bone for the guys behind the glass. Evan knew he wouldn't understand it, or believe it, so he told him the truth. "It's not the box, it's what's inside."

"It's empty."

Evan shrugged. "Maybe."

He could see when the possibility, "poison gas," passed through Sid's mind; when he dismissed it. Even Sid knew the box wasn't airtight, and the FBI had tested it every way it knew without destroying it. But he'd figured out that Evan was telling the truth. "Doesn't matter that it's empty. Van Der Graf's running a cult, and the cult is convinced there's something in there." Evan waited while Sid took the next step. "So is the Church."

"I don't know what the Church thinks," Evan admitted. "But they sure don't want stuff that inspires murderous power cults in the name of medieval religion traded on the open market."

"And the Church trusts you, and your client, not to sell it to the next highest bidder?"

"The mother of this particular representative of the Church trusts Lily."

Which disgusted Sid, and Evan found it pretty damned odd himself. But this conversation could get dangerous fast, so he picked up the box and took the few steps to the door. He had to find Lily, tell her the plan, and then get Matt Shields moving. He wanted Carlos Sanchez by nightfall.

"Try not to get yourself killed." Sid didn't bother getting up. "You father won't do well in prison." Evan knew that. Fortunately, this time Brad had a walk-away contract.

Chapter 63

MAI SIEN CHONG KNEW MANY WAYS to please him, and demanded that Brad please her in return, an unspoken walk-away contract between a reincarnated empress and a daemon lord whose true name she came close enough to guessing to add spice to the transaction. He liked the sex well enough, but he'd missed the part that had brought them together in the first place.

Lily didn't play chess. Evan played like strategy was a foreign concept. Harry and Ellen Li didn't include him at all when the police had their collective eye on the agency. So he smiled at Mai Sien Chong across the chessboard set up on her coffee table, drank her champagne while the lights of Singapore sparkled on the bay, and ate bits of chicken and beef served on elegant dishes between moves.

"You're worried about your son," she said. She wore a silk robe the color of the champagne that she hadn't bothered to tie, so that it fell open when she leaned over and took his bishop. "You play defensively, with little imagination, when Evan is in trouble. And I am reduced to flaunting my breasts to hold your attention!"

"I'm not worried." He'd sacrificed the bishop and made his own move—defensive, she was right about that, but he was doing some distracting of his own. He'd taken on most of his human form again, except for a fine glimmer of blue scales that he'd kept for her pleasure.

He'd rid himself of the fangs and the claws—couldn't get hold of the chess pieces with claws, and they shredded the carpet as well as the sheets—but he'd left the nubs of horns peeking out of his hair. She liked to honor them with little licks of her tongue, and he found he liked that too, very much. The last thing he wanted to think about was Evan on the road with a lord of a foreign Prince. He wasn't in trouble—angry, but not in trouble. But Mai Sien was right about the worry. Something . . .

She left her chair and came to him, stood between his knees and stroked the fine blue scales across his shoulders, down his back, offering her breasts for his mouth as she kissed first one and then the other of the nubs of his horns. She couldn't read his mind, but she knew all the tells he let her see. Her breasts certainly worked as a distraction, though he'd planned his moves well before she'd made her play. But this game wasn't going to end with her robe in tatters.

"You're leaving, aren't you?" she asked, and he sighed.

"I have to go home." He let her think he meant the house on Spruce Street. But that feeling of something wrong had grown, and it didn't come from Philadelphia.

So he went, pulled off course by the will of his Prince before he had fully abandoned the material sphere.

Chapter 64

IN WORDLESS FURY, MATT SHIELDS POINTED out the turn. Flames danced in his hair, raised it at the back of his neck and twisted in his eyes. A thin trail of smoke rose from the upholstery.

Evan tried to ignore it—took the exit, made the next turn. The sign at the crossing read, "Toms River, 5 miles." They went the other way, going deeper into more damned woods, pine trees pressing against the sandy verge on either side of the narrow, two-lane highway. He rolled down the window because oxygen was getting short in the car, but it didn't help. Vision tightened down to a narrow tunnel with black spots clotted at the periphery.

"If I die, the box goes to the Church." Bertrande Le-Roux, actually, in exchange for a hefty contribution to the purchase price, but they all knew where it would end up. Her son would make sure of that. The threat was enough. Shields pulled a little further into himself and Evan felt the oxygen leak back into his lungs.

Not Matt Shields, a regular guy with a problem, he reminded himself. He was driving through the New Jersey Pine Barrens with an enraged daemon lord held this side of devastation by the limits of a binding Evan hadn't asked for but couldn't let go of. Yet.

"We'll take care of this. Nobody's backing out of the deal, but it has to be safe for all of us," he reminded Shields. Parmatus. He'd picked that name up in the second celestial sphere, had found it easier to ignore the knowledge until he'd carried the strongbox out to the rental. Shields had said, "Now," and Evan had said, "No." Shields—Parmatus—hadn't liked the answer.

They turned onto a narrow dirt road with more forest on both sides. Spiky, fast-growing pines with narrow trunks were packed dense and tangled in the needle-strewn sand. A few spindly oaks fought it out until the next fire took them down. The Pines always burned.

Couldn't be far now. The air smelled like brine and marsh grass. A few more miles and they'd hit water. Shields still hadn't said more than, "Turn here," but Evan had to figure there was something at the end of this road, probably the Sanchezes, which went a long way toward explaining why the police hadn't found them in New York. "I thought these people were your friends."

Shields—Parmatus—glared, but said nothing. Not even the usual "humans are worth shit" line he usually got. "You might want to pull in the fangs before we get there," he suggested. "Your disguise is slipping."

"I don't have fangs." But Shields got the point, smothered the flames, and smoothed the rage out of his face. The blank screen that replaced it wasn't much better, but Evan figured it would be easier to paste a smile on. The last turn was a driveway that stopped at a low white house set up on blocks, with asphalt shingles on the roof and a sagging screened porch, front or back, he couldn't tell. Evan got out of the car, propped an arm on the top of the door. Shields let his own door slam behind him.

For a moment, the only sound was the wind in the trees and off to his right a stream, water splashing over rocks. From inside the house, he heard running feet, light quick steps with firmer ones following right behind. A woman's voice called, "Katey!" Then the screen door slammed back against the porch and bounced on its hinges.

"Pappiiii!" A little girl squealed but didn't let up her reckless dash into Matt Shields' legs until she bounced off and landed in the dirt. A joyful amber light glittered in her eyes.

That had been one huge lie.

Chapter 65

THE HOST OF ARITON HAD MERGED in quorum, but the blue flame of Badad's Prince burned low in the vast dark, beset by no normal battle but attack from every quarter.

Azmod pressed forward, flaring indignant green in counterpoint to the light of Paimon's anger smoldering in amber flame. Azmod had its own bitter feud with Ariton, forged in an eternity of battle and its own more recent grudge against Badad, whose son had bested Azmod's lords and had been allowed to live.

Ariton had never planned to keep its bargain, made as it was through a half-mad monster, Magot jeered, attacking in white flames shot with silver, and somewhere a galaxy exploded, suns formed from the dust and caught fire, but the Princes didn't notice. Astarot's indigo pressed and harried Ariton's blue light, igniting knots of energy in the second celestial sphere, igniting worlds in the material plane. Ariton had no allies in this, not even Oriens, whose fire the color of blood and rust licked out, tore bits of blue flame away.

Badad heard and felt and tasted battle as the vortex of the host ripped away his sense of self as a daemon lord, his separate thoughts and voice swallowed by the host-mind as it drew him into the unity of his Prince. No human kept a bargain made with a captive daemon lord—Astarot tore away blue flame, flung it into the darkness—no half-daemon monster survived its heritage with its sanity intact. Badad's son was no exception. What honor had a monster to bind its word?

Paimon believed the lies—he felt it in the touch of the attacking Prince's mind—because Evan had not freed his daemon lords when he took possession of Donne's strongbox. And all the Princes of the second celestial sphere stood with Paimon against Ariton, because Badad had not reduced his twisted offspring to ash when he'd had the chance, because Lirion had shared a human bed with Badad's monster, and had not murdered it in its sleep.

For a moment Badad embraced the growing singularity of the host-mind—then he felt himself repelled, rejected by his own Prince and torn away by green-and-silver flame, by indigo and rust and the gold of Amaimon, who was Ariton's ally in all but this.

Despair! Badad would destroy all of the material sphere to regain the mind of his Prince, his host-cousins.

In the solitude of his own thoughts he found a flicker of blue flame he scarcely recognized as Lirion, trembling and alone in a universe of Princes. Although they were separated from all their kind, he would not merge with her, because he would not share the pain and terror that flickered in her light. But he saw the truth she couldn't hide from him. Her bargain for the box had damned her. If Evan died, it went to Bertrande LeRoux. No choice in that, without the old woman they would have lost the box to Cyril Van Der Graf. But Bertrande LeRoux had ceded her rights to the Church. The Princes could not murder Evan—they needed him to control Donne's spell—but Lirion was banished to the material sphere, forever, if he didn't keep his end of the bargain.

None of it was true. Evan had not betrayed Ariton's bargain with Paimon. Lirion had not chosen her human lover above her Prince. But "wait" had no meaning in a place where time did not exist.

"The monster belongs to me." Paimon reached a careful tongue of flame and stripped blue light from the very center of Ariton. "His world"—another fading strip of blue light fell away. "His universe." Ariton said nothing as the

Princes fell upon him, tearing at the essence of blue flame until there was nothing left but drifting tongues of fire as the host scattered, wailing, into the darkness.

Then Paimon turned its baleful notice on Badad, dragged him in, and forced a merge that made him a prisoner obliterated in the group mind of an enemy Prince. "Where is the boy?" The host picked the knowledge from his thoughts and with it the knowledge of time, and gave him back the torture Paimon would inflict upon his son.

But time echoed through the mind of the Prince, and Badad's memory of midnight, that felt like home even in the material sphere. Paimon thrust him away, disgusted, but the threat followed him. "Until midnight, then. But no one may warn him. He honors his bargain, or he does not."

With that he flung Badad into the material sphere and Lirion after him, screaming as she fell, into the late afternoon sunshine flooding the walled garden of home. Their only home, now, unless Evan fulfilled his contract with Matt Shields. In her human form, Lily said nothing. She wiped tears from her cheeks and went into the house, but she wasn't in the living room or the study, and he didn't follow her upstairs. Couldn't read her thoughts in human form and he was glad. He picked up his book, but put it down again. Paimon said he couldn't warn Evan, but that didn't mean he had to sit here and do nothing.

Chapter 66

"**S**HE'S NOT MINE," SHIELDS SAID TIGHTLY, but he leaned over and scooped up the little girl one-handed, like they were both used to the drill. A woman Evan didn't recognize followed, gave Shields a glance, but she didn't take the girl, just stood with her back pressed against the doorjamb, bare arms crossed over a lime-green camp shirt.

"That's Marina," Shields made the clipped introduction with just a darted glance in her direction. Marina Sanchez. Once he had the name Evan saw the resemblance—her father's dark eyes, her sister's hair, but shorter. He'd expected less hostility—she'd driven Matt to the bus to find him. So here he was, found, and she was examining him with distaste carving a groove between her eyes.

"Why did you bring him here?" She wasn't talking to him.

"The box." His answer had made Marina Sanchez angrier. The little girl in his arms sensed the dangerous mood and squirmed around until she could bury her face in his shoulder. Shields craned his neck to get one of her little ponytails out of his nose.

"I thought you had a deal." She was talking to Shields again, but Evan was getting tired of explaining himself anyway. "I'm not backing out of anything. But it has to be safe for the rest of us." It didn't help that his explanation wouldn't hold up under close scrutiny. Yeah, the planet. But that wasn't why he was standing at the edge of the New Jersey Pine Barrens instead of sitting in his own chair at his own desk back home with Matt and friend long gone.

He had to get Sid Valentine off the agency's back, which meant finding out what killed the Donnes. The answer was in this house, and he'd come here with Matt Shields and his strongbox in tow to find it. At least, that had been the plan when he left the FBI office in New York. The little girl in Matt Shields' arms had just complicated that plan by an order of magnitude. "If she's not yours, then whose?"

Marina Sanchez flinched but pressed her lips together as if she was afraid of what might come spilling out if she let the words come.

"Grey's," Shields said, which explained Marina Sanchez's flinch and dimmed the halo he'd been polishing on the way down. But it didn't really answer the question. The amber flames in the child's eyes had to come from somewhere. If not Matt Shields, he was left with just one option. Made him flinch too, and the daemon saw it.

Marina Sanchez pushed off the doorjamb and turned her back. But, "You might as well come in the house," she said before she disappeared inside. Evan followed, his thoughts scattered. The mad daemon lord trapped in Grayson Donne's box. Lily. He hadn't thought it possible.

Sometimes he imagined, not the Lily he knew carrying his baby, or a kid with the wild light of Ariton in its eyes, but sometimes, that a Lily wholly human could love him. They'd have babies and preschools and a van with car seats in the garage. Awake, he knew he wouldn't trade Lily's spirit for any mortal gain. Knew himself well enough to know he couldn't settle for a purely human life anymore or bring a child into the world cursed with his own dual nature. But in his dreams.

Children like him didn't live. Not sane.

Marina Sanchez led him through a sunny and neat kitchen he scarcely noticed, except that Alba Sanchez was making iced tea over a stainless steel sink, into a living room gleaming with polished wood floors and overstuffed furniture, cottage-y and comfortable in ocean colors. Carlos Sanchez sat in a rocking chair in front of a window with flowered curtains pulled back to let in the afternoon sun. Missing person number three. Check.

Evan dropped into a fat blue club chair, rested his head in his hands for a minute while the pieces of the puzzle tumbled in his head. Matt Shields had put the little girl down and carried the strongbox in from the car. The box had stopped screaming, but Evan felt storm clouds gathering around it. He figured if the daemon got out of that box they'd be picking bits of the solar system out of the Andromeda Galaxy for the next billion years.

He still needed answers to the questions that had brought him here—what had killed the Donnes, father and son—but they came second to the big one he hadn't known about until now. "The girl—"

"Katey," Shields said. He put the box on a driftwood coffee table and sank into the corner of the sofa. Katey crawled up next to him, tucked herself under his arm, and stared suspiciously at Evan.

"If she's Grey's, that makes her Donne's heir."

Shields tilted a shoulder, half a shrug. "He didn't live long enough to acknowledge her, so she has no legal standing unless we fight for it, which we won't do. It would require DNA tests anyway, and Katey's wouldn't stand up to human scrutiny." He gave the little girl a wry smile that she returned with an answering amber light in her eyes.

She was damned cute, but it made Evan a little ill anyway. "The box?"

Shields set the girl on her feet, gave her a pat that set her off in the direction of Marina Sanchez, who hadn't sat down.

"Shall we help Tia Alba make dinner?" she asked, and followed as Katey made a run for the kitchen.

Shields watched as she went, let his shoulders slump when the little girl's high voice rang out, "Tia Alba!" But he waited until Marina returned before he answered the question.

"We don't know. Maybe we'll have to wait until she has a son."

Evan couldn't think about generations of monsters, like him but not his, now. Not as something that little girl might be forced to do or that she might one day choose. He needed professional distance, or he'd get up and walk away from Matt Shields and his girlfriend in a box and his contract with Paimon and leave them to sort out their own mess. Which was about as deadly an idea as he'd ever come up with.

Shields was still working through his options when Evan surfaced from—whatever it had been. "Maybe her heritage changes the spell. Or maybe, if we own the box between us, we can release the spell. We just don't know. And then there's Katey to think about. Only once in the history of your world has a child like Katey made it to adulthood sane." Shields didn't say who that had been, kept Evan's secret, and by extension his father's. "Your ad said, 'cases involving the occult handled with discretion'. I thought maybe after we'd dealt with the box, you'd have some insights on that."

Only once. Evan wondered about Sched's giants, but he didn't mention them. They weren't relevant anyway. No one had forced Sched. They'd had each other and a nearly empty planet to shape to their own intentions. But, "I know the case you mean," he said, hiding his own identity in a fiction of objectivity. "He didn't grow up sane. Someone convinced him it was the only way to stay alive, but reports say he spent the first twenty years of his life confused and terrified. And pretty much crazy."

Katey had looked neither, and Evan's heart ached, because he'd never had that strength and happiness as a child—didn't now, sometimes—and because he couldn't see how Katey would stay that way when Matt Shields went home. With all the best will in the world, the Sanchez family couldn't stand between the child and the forces of the second celestial sphere, not the ones that would want to destroy her or the ones that would shape what she was in two universes. "I can't help you." He knew what Matt was asking, and it killed him to say it. But he had no choice. "That other case belonged to a rival faction."

"I know." Shields looked away, neither of them willing to pursue the politics of Princes with humans in the room. It made Evan a little sick that he put himself on the daemon side of that line, but he'd put himself there when he'd made the deal.

"One thing at a time. Just get us free of this box."

And that put Evan right back on the human side of the equation. "When I have some answers."

Chapter 67

CARLOS SANCHEZ HADN'T SAID ANYTHING
yet, just watched, maybe seeing too much. Evan
wouldn't ask that question—what did Sanchez guess
about Evan himself—because he refused to deal with
the answer, but he had plenty more. Math had never
been his strongest point, but it didn't take Einstein to
count to three.

"Three years ago, Grayson Donne pulled you out of
his box and sent you to deliver his library to Cyril Van
Der Graf," he said to Shields. "Then he died. That much
is true. Everything else has been a lie. So why don't we
start with Grayson Donne's breeding program? Katey's
what, three years old?"

"About," Shields confirmed. He clamped his jaw
down tight, but the fire was building in his eyes. Evan
had almost forgotten Marina Sanchez, until she turned
and made a dash for the kitchen.

"What's wrong, Mami?" Katey's voice, rising with
anxiety, floated through the doorway, then Alba Sanchez
said, "Mami has something in her eye. I think she wants
us to catch some minnows in the bucket for her."

When the screen door had slammed closed behind
them, Marina Sanchez came back, sat on the footstool
next to her father. "I don't want Katey to hear any part
of this. None of it is her fault." She glared at Evan as
though he'd wanted to accuse a toddler of—what?

"I know that. I don't want to hurt her—I *won't* hurt

her. But if we succeed tonight, she'll be hurt." No one was looking at him now, and he figured they already knew that. Matt Shields wasn't just a guy who had taken the place of her dead father—he was the only thing standing between a three-year-old girl and the forces of the universe and her own nature, the like of which had once driven Evan mad. He let out a long sigh, tried to tangle his fingers in hair that wasn't there anymore and pulled his hand away liked his head was on fire—nothing like advertising his unease.

"Grayson Donne's breeding program. You said the old man couldn't, and Grey wouldn't. So what changed that? And how did both of the Donnes wind up dead in the middle of it?"

"Donne was old," Shields gave a little shrug, as if the answers should be obvious. "And nobody every accused him of a healthy lifestyle. He was seventy when Grey was born, and that cost him Lily's ruby." His smile was cold, but he didn't fill in the blanks. Grey's mother was dead.

"A hybrid was harder to manage." Shields voice held no emotion, which was just another kind of lie. But the emotions of a daemon lord seldom offered comfort, so he was glad not to know this time.

"Simpson's wife carried her own. They knew in theory it was possible—there have been stories for centuries. Marnie Simpson liked trying, and she wanted it, was willing to do whatever it took to hold onto that child. Donne hadn't considered it until then. Then he wanted one for himself. He spent years looking for a female relative—there was a third cousin out in Colorado, but she turned out to be sterile. Grey was at Yale." Evan didn't bother asking why the cousin from Colorado hadn't claimed the estate. He figured they'd find her bones with the rest of them in Donne's graveyard.

"That left Kady. No one had ever bound a daemon lord to a female form long enough to give birth to a living half-human child. Donne couldn't have done it without the house—you've been there, you know the place."

Evan remembered the house built as a pentagram, the eight-sided room bound in seals and spells, with shackles and blood at its center. "There was no escaping it," Shields said, and Evan shuddered, remembering that too, his dae-mon nature caught in the complex spell worked into the parquetry seals that covered the floor, and Grayson Donne's shackles on his wrists and ankles. If he hadn't been half human, if he hadn't found the mechanical escape latches worked into the design, he'd have been trapped there again. But—

"You said Donne couldn't, and his son wouldn't."

"Donne couldn't. He was as sterile as that third cousin from Colorado by then, but he tried until even Viagra didn't help, then he called Grey home. But Grey refused."

"I remember that night." Carlos Sanchez spoke softly, not facing his audience but staring into the forest outside his window. He wept openly now, Marina's hand clutched in his white-knuckled grip. It had to hurt, but she didn't free her hand or stop her own tears. "They had a furious fight in the back garden—I think if Mr. Donne hadn't needed Gray to produce an heir of some kind he would have murdered him right then. He forbade Grey to see Marina again and ordered me to drive him back to Yale."

"I was away at school," Marina added, rubbing her free hand across the knee of her jeans in a compulsive gesture Evan recognized—wanting to be clean when the feeling of dirt was all inside. "If I'd been there, he would have killed me. I was just another obstacle to him."

Matt Shields in his daemon form would have torn her to pieces, but the cautious panic that hunched his shoulders meant he'd managed to keep that secret from her.

"It gave him the idea, though." Shields picked up the story, left the humans in the room to their grief. "He forged a letter from Marina, asking Grey to meet her in the gar-den, and sent Kady in Marina's form to meet him there. Kady brought him back into the house, into Donne's room, and did as Donne had commanded. Gray left not knowing what he had done, left Kady trapped there in human form, carrying a human child she could not escape. That's when she started screaming. I was locked up then." In Donne's strongbox. Evan felt the blood leave his face, rubbed at the half-healed bruises to bring it back. Oh, God. He tried to pity the daemon in the box, but all he could think of was Lily. He would never. But, God. Lily.

"I heard her screaming, but there was nothing I could do."

Chapter 68

VOICES FILTERED THROUGH THE WOOD-framed screen door, softened by their passage through the house, but daemon senses picked them up easily enough. Kady—who was Kadalon in her own world—bound to a room and a form, driven mad by an alien thing growing inside her. A bad time to intrude, maybe, but Badad was here and they didn't have much time left.

He considered his options and decided against his daemon form. Only Evan and Paimon's daemons would know he was there, but his motives became more suspect, more tied to the politics of Princes, a fact he'd rather not advertise. As Kevin Bradley, a partner in the firm Shields had hired, the case gave him a reason to be here. He knocked, while off to his right, against the chime of water against rock, a small child's laughter rose to a shrill point that he tried not to connect to the story Shields told beyond that door.

No one answered, but he knew Shields was aware of him, felt a thread of curiosity wind through Evan's focus on the job. He let himself in, passed the stove with a pot simmering on low, into the room where Evan rubbed nervous hands against his battered face. The strongbox sat on a low table in front of an overstuffed sofa. It took a second to figure out what was missing—the screaming had stopped. Human emotions Badad didn't even recognize hit him then. Evan really hated that box, but he wasn't focused on freeing Matt Shields from it, at least not right away.

He looked at his watch—five hours before Paimon owned his son—and introduced himself with a bland smile.

"Kevin Bradley, Bradley, Ryan, and Davis."

"Of course." Marina Sanchez stood up, offered him a chair, playing hostess as if he couldn't see her eyes were leaking.

"Do we need a minute?" Evan asked, expecting some emergency, though not the one they had.

Brad—taking back his human persona with the form— shook his head. He could answer that truthfully at least. "It can wait." Not for long, but Evan, Shields, and the box were all in the same room. He had to figure there was a point to that. "Don't let me interrupt you."

He declined the invitation to sit, chose instead to stand in the arch to the kitchen. Evan looked at him for a long minute, trying, it seemed, to see inside his head—just meat there, boy. Get on with the show.

Evan did. "Donne wanted an heir like Simpson's," he said.

Daemon spawn. And there was a thing. He'd felt the spark, thought it was something of Paimon, which he guessed it was. "Did he get one?" Didn't need to ask the question, now that he knew, but the humans would expect it. Evan said, "We were just getting to that part," and signaled Shields to go on.

He didn't want to, Brad could see that. Had been a fool, got himself and another lord caught for only his own Prince knew how long, stuck in a box and let out for special occasions. If it had been him, Brad would never have shared that story with a lord of a potential enemy. He didn't know what he would do if that lord owned him, and he briefly wondered how much choice Shields really had in telling the story at all. He didn't look coerced, but the box still held the power. Evan owned the box, and he'd use it—was using it now—for whatever reasons he thought good enough to break every bond of loyalty to his Prince and the lords who harbored him.

"Donne couldn't do it," Evan brought him up to speed. "So he tricked his son. And yeah, it worked."

Brad knew what that look from Evan meant—please don't blow up the house. We're sitting in it. Brad had done that once already, and hadn't liked the consequences, but he wasn't going to bring that up in front of strangers. "How long?" he said.

"Not as long as a normal human gestation, I gather," Shields said, carefully neutral. "But long enough. When he knew Kady was carrying a child, he killed Grey. Grey made it easy for him. He found out what his father had done and insisted they stop it right then. But Donne didn't need him anymore—he'd have his own half-daemon heir and Van Der Graf was ready to take it on if his heart gave out, make it as crazy as the Simpsons' heir in their mad notion to invade the spheres."

Shields carefully didn't mention Evan in the short list of the bastard children of two universes driven crazy by their own natures and the cabal's plans for them. "Grey was never going to be any use to him, so Donne caught him at the top of the stairs and fought with him, just words at first, then he pushed him. When the fall didn't kill him, Donne snapped his neck."

A cool look passed between them. There was only one way Shields could know the story in that much detail. Donne may have pushed his own son down the stairs, but he hadn't been strong enough to break a neck with his bare hands. No point in saying it out loud, though. Brad could see that Evan had it figured, and the other humans wouldn't take it well.

That left Grayson Donne the elder, dead a few months later. Matt Shields could have done it, but Brad didn't think so. He'd be stuck in that box if he had.

Chapter 69

GREY DONNE HAD BEFRIENDED THE human forms of his father's daemons, had promised to free them when he came into his father's power. Then he'd impregnated one of them and gotten himself killed by the other one. Evan figured he should feel more about the dead part, but he had a couple of bodies to his own account in the wars humans waged against his daemon kin and on the whole discovered that he was just glad the Donnes were gone. But that still left Old Donne's death unaccounted for.

"I didn't kill him," Sanchez said, not waiting for the obvious question. "I was there, and I would have done it. He deserved to die—I should have killed him long ago. But I didn't, God forgive me. He died of a heart attack."

"Not asleep in his own bed, though," Evan prodded. A heart attack wasn't necessarily murder, but it couldn't have been that hard to push a man Donne's age past where his heart could sustain the strain.

"He was trying to save me." Marina patted her father's hand. She was sitting on the low footstool beside him again, not crying now, just staring down the past like she could see it playing out over the coffee table. "Donne planned to pass the child off as mine, but to do that, I had to disappear. He couldn't have me trying out for the swim team when I was supposed to be seven months pregnant.

"You found the tunnel that runs under the house, so you must have seen the cell below his ritual room, where he kept his victims."

Evan nodded—didn't want to slow her down, but his awareness of his father listening made his skin crawl. Didn't want the reminders of his own prison, and some things shouldn't be shared with the other spheres. Humans hurting other humans was human business. His father's kind had enough reasons to despise them.

"I spent months chained in that hole in the ground, listening to Kady screaming above me, with nothing but the trapdoor in the floor between us. I knew she was wearing my face and my body—Donne showed me. He promised that after it was over Kady would go back in the box and I'd be free to raise Grey's child as my own—in his house, under his control. He called that free.

"I knew he wouldn't leave me alive for long. He blamed me for turning Grey against him, but he needed somebody to take care of the baby, and he didn't trust Kady or Matt—figured they might kill it. By then I'd have done anything to get out of that hole, but I wanted this deal—it was Grey's child. My reward was a locked room at the top of the house. And then Kady had the baby."

"There was a terrible storm." Carlos patted her hand.

Evan said nothing, just gave an encouraging nod that Sanchez, caught in the gathering storm of his own memories, didn't even see.

"No rain, but lightning, and thunder like the end of the world had come. For hours. And then, it just stopped. I sent Raffi to check on the Donne house, and he came back, said half the roof was gone and that he'd seen Marina in an upstairs window.

"We'd had email from school, that she was going away with some friends to try to get over Grey's death. We never guessed that it was forged, but we knew that Marina hated that house, would never willingly go back there. And we knew that Mr. Donne was capable of anything to get what he wanted. So we broke in and found her. We could see that she'd been there a long time. She was distraught.

Raffi took Marina out, and I went to confront Mr. Donne. I found him in the round room, holding a newborn child. There was blood everywhere, but no woman. I didn't know, you understand. I thought—

"I confronted him, threatened him, but he just gloated until he realized that I meant to kill him and take the child. I thought the child was my blood. I could not leave my blood in the hands of such evil. I think, when he knew that all his plans would fail again, just as he had achieved success, his heart no longer had a reason for beating.

"He·died in the center of his own evil. I took the child out and left him there, called the police the next day as if I had just found him. They knew some violent crime had happened, but I had no trace of blood anywhere on my person. Donne had died of natural causes and the police in that town were used to looking away from the evil in that house. We all just hoped that meant an end to it."

"And was it the end?" Evan asked. He meant the three years in between, but Carlos Sanchez gave him an exhausted, ironic smile. "Not then. We had dead to mourn, and a girl—we thought of her that way, you understand—had a child in captivity and disappeared. But the killing stopped. At least, until the State put Mr. Donne's legacy up for auction. And so, here we are."

Marina Sanchez stood up, both hands rubbing down the thighs of her jeans. "I've left dinner alone on the stove too long," she said, signaling the end to the conversation. Evan followed her to his feet with a sharp nod for Matt Shields, because it was his problem.

"We'll fix it," he said, and hoped it was true. He thought he had the box figured, but he didn't know how far Cyril Van Der Graf's reach went, whether he had the power, without Donne's daemon lords, to escape a long prison sentence. Wasn't sure, for that matter, how far Van Der Graf's reach went in this house, but he had to find out.

"Mr. Sanchez said that Marina dropped you off at the bus station to come to Philadelphia."

"That is what happened," Sanchez agreed, and Shields didn't contradict him.

"But I saw Alba at the Lea Library at Penn the next day. Why didn't you come together?"

The air went out of the room—not a metaphor—and Evan cut a sharp glare at Shields. But Shields was looking toward the kitchen, where Alba Sanchez had gathered up a half-human child to catch minnows in a stream.

Chapter 70

"WHAT'S THE LEA LIBRARY?" Shields asked, wary, but breath was moving in and out of human lungs again.

Brad had been reading human reactions since the Sun King, and he'd bet the agency that Marina Sanchez hadn't known. Her father knew something. Not that, though he covered fast. "Research," he said, and Evan answered, "Witchcraft. Esoterica. She was reading *The Names of the Angels.*"

"To find a way to put an end to all this, if you couldn't get Donne's strongbox," Sanchez explained. "Mr. Van Der Graf's people kidnapped her when she went to New York to follow up on her research."

Part of that was true, Brad figured. Research made sense. But Carlos Sanchez hadn't said a thing about the graveyard in Donne's wood, and his daughters had an unfortunate habit of turning up in the houses of Donne's cabal.

Shields was looking to Evan for salvation, but Evan's attention had shifted to the other side of the door.

The child was coming back. Brad sensed the spark of Paimon in motion when he looked for it, knew Evan sensed it as well. Shields hadn't put together what that meant yet, stuck on the realization that the Sanchezes were lying. But soon enough even the humans in the room could hear the high-pitched chatter on the path from the stream. Heads turned; they'd forgotten and the voices surprised them, revealing varying levels of guilt and shock as the two missing members of the party—one obviously innocent, the other less so, closed in on the house.

The little girl was laughing, naming the minnows in her pail while Alba Sanchez warned her gravely that Oscar had to stay in the water, but she could tell Mr. Evan that she would take care of his minnow for him. The clack of the screen door obscured Katey's answer, but the little girl appeared fishless in the living room.

"Tia Alba says dinner is ready, but we have to wash our hands!" she held up her own hands, still pink from the cold of the creek, to demonstrate. Then she noticed Brad and hid behind Matt Shields' legs. "Bad man!" she whispered.

He didn't touch her. Figured he could save himself five hours if he wanted to start a war with Paimon over the half-human bastards of the second celestial sphere right here, but declined. Instead he squatted down until she could see him almost eye-to-eye. She made a better first impression than Evan had—no open wounds or desperate madness. She smelled a little damp from sunshine and the water running in the stream, but like breezes through trees and milk and cookies too.

He kept the fire out of his eyes and just smiled when amber twisted in hers. "I would never hurt a little girl," he said. "I want to help."

Chapter 71

INTERESTING. EVEN AT THREE, KATEY—Sanchez?—had an instinct for recognizing her own Prince and the daemon lords of a possible enemy house. Evan hadn't felt the difference until his father had got him sane and started to teach him how to control his nature. He'd learned to distinguish between threats, but still hadn't figured Ariton for an ally the way Katey clung to Matt Shields.

Shields picked her up, said, "Not a bad man. He's a very good friend. An ally." He took a step toward Brad, and Evan almost laughed as his father took an equal step backward before holding his ground. "This is Mr. Bradley. He helps people. If you are ever in really bad trouble and you can't find me, you go to Mr. Bradley. Not to anybody else. Hear me?"

Brad wasn't happy about that, but he didn't say "No."

Katey agreed with a vigorous nod that bounced the little ponytails pulled up above her ears. "And Mr. Evan?" she asked, and pressed a finger against her lips—keeping their secret.

"Mr. Evan too." Shields dared him to walk away in the look he shot over her head, then he put her back on her feet. "Now wash your hands before Tia Alba eats all your dinner!"

She laughed at him, but ran off through the sunshine that dappled the floor, down a hall that led to the back of the house. Evan watched her go, considering the most pressing threats to that laughter. Alba Sanchez was what, eighteen? Shields had said she was starting SUNY in the fall. Eighteen was a little old for Van Der Graf's taste, and he didn't like girls anyway. But Evan hadn't been much older when Mac—Omage of the host of Azmod—had sucked him into the hell of his back room at the Black Masque.

Alba Sanchez didn't have the spark of a daemon lord in her, but neither had Mac's followers at the Black Masque. Completely human, they'd chained him to the marble floor of the back room and opened his veins to fill Mac's alabaster cup. The symbols they'd painted with his blood on the wall merged in Evan's mind with the symbols on the ceiling in Van Der Graf's mansion, the floor of Donne's inner room. When he sent Paimon's daemon lords home, would Alba Sanchez open the veins of Paimon's half-daemon child? Would she gather Katey's blood in another insane bid to storm the second celestial sphere?

Not his child, not his Prince, not his problem.

Except that he absolutely would not let Donne's cabal make a victim of one more half-daemon child. Especially not this one—the first since Sched's giants to have a chance at a sane life. He'd fight his own Prince for her if he had to.

"Alba's set extra places. You're welcome to stay for dinner." Marina made the offer with her arms in their defensive cross, tucked up over her lime camp shirt like she was holding her sides together, but Evan had no intention of intruding. At least, not on dinner. He wanted out of that house.

"No, thank you."

She relaxed a little; so she wanted him gone as badly as he wanted to go. He had just one more thing to do before he could make them both happy by his absence.

"How far are we here from the closest neighbor?"

"About a quarter mile down the road," Carlos Sanchez said, the first thing he admitted to knowing since he'd lied about his daughter Alba. "The beach is a half mile farther on."

Evan considered that possibility. Probably the safest place if things went wrong—plenty of water, and nothing much to burn—but dismissed it quickly. Too many houses with an ocean view, and they didn't need an audience.

Sanchez seemed to follow the thought. "There are neighbors on the road, but the house backs onto the state park. The stream's part of that—no one for miles back there."

Good as anyplace, then. Evan filled them in on their part of the plan. "We'll wait until after dark, let the hikers clear out." In June it seemed to stay light forever. It was already after seven and he was going to need batteries for the flashlight.

"Say, eleven thirty? Matt, you'll bring the box. We'll bring Katey along, in case." In case the spell required Donne's blood relative. He didn't want to consider that she wasn't a male relative and this might not work at all. "I'll make sure she gets home. The rest of you will stay here, but be ready to evacuate if things don't go as planned."

He could tell Brad didn't like that idea, and neither did the Sanchezes.

"I'll come," Carlos rose from his rocking chair, the set of his jaw made him look more like the man Evan had met at Donne's estate.

"She'll be safe with me," Evan said, because he wasn't leaving the kid to chance and he couldn't trust any one of them to protect her. He frankly didn't think Carlos or Marina Sanchez were involved with Donne's cabal, except in the way the town had been, turning its back on the butchery going on at Grayson Donne's estate. The humans couldn't protect a half-daemon child if the second celestial sphere wanted her dead. He was the best shot she had of living through the night, which maybe gave too much credit to his own influence in the second celestial sphere.

Still, better than nothing, so he insisted. "You can't help with this. There are forces at work here that are angrier, and more powerful, than you can imagine. Your presence will only make them angrier. If I have to worry about the rest of you, I may get distracted and screw up the whole thing." The thought made his blood run a little cold, a truth he'd rather not share. "Take care of your family. Be ready to run."

"Katey *is* our family." Sanchez would have fought him on it, but Matt Shields said, "She's my family too. I won't let anything hurt her."

Which appeased Carlos Sanchez, even if it wasn't true.

Nothing left but to get out of there, so he clapped Matt Shields on the arm and said, "Rest if you can. Wear white if you've got it." White for purity. With Katey in the mix, they had a shot at the protection of innocence. "I expect we'll have a wild ride, but we'll have you home and free by midnight. The witching hour." He tried to make a joke of the hour, thought there might be something to it. His father didn't look happy, that was sure, and he hadn't seen Lily at all.

Matt walked them to the door like he belonged there, said, "I'll be ready. Thanks." Then somehow the door was closed behind him and he was alone with his father and the damned forest.

Chapter 72

"IS THAT YOUR CAR?" Brad raised an eyebrow at the rental sagging on the edge of a drainage ditch in the gravel driveway of the Sanchez house. Distraction. Wouldn't work for long. Evan had that look on his face, like the only thing that had stopped the questions so far was the gridlock between his brain and his mouth.

Evan gave the comment its due—"It doesn't call attention to itself. Not like the new BMW you've got stashed in the garage"—then went on the attack. "Where's Lily?"

Brad shrugged. "Not here. Were you expecting her?" This was Evan's part of the job—neither of them had planned to show up. He still wasn't sure why he'd come.

"Not really." Evan stared out into the woods, toward the sound of rushing water. Adding things up and coming to conclusions. "But I didn't expect you either, and here you are."

It never took him long to clear the traffic jam. Smart boy. Brad hoped he was smart enough to keep his mouth shut.

"So I have to figure something went wrong. Are you going to tell me what it is, or do we play guess-the-catastrophe until I hit it?"

So much for hope. The question pulled at his gut, an old, familiar knot. He didn't immediately figure where it had come from this time, until he tried to dismiss the question. "I'm . . ." He knew the answer he needed to give— "Nothing wrong, nothing to tell, move along" —but couldn't force it past his closing throat.

"Nothing I can fix," he finally said, too much truth hanging out there with nothing useful in it. He'd lied to Evan before, kept secrets from him without even thinking about it. Couldn't now, no matter how much he wanted to, and it hurt to try, tore him into fragments of blue flame and Evan took a step back, hands up in front of him.

"Whoa, whoa," he said, "I take it back. What's the matter?"

Brad couldn't answer that one either—all his explanations led back to a geas placed on him by all the Princes, not to speak of Paimon's deadline. Evan freed Matt Shields and the daemon lord in the strongbox by midnight, or Paimon owned him, would torture him to death without even realizing he'd exceeded the capacity of a human body to absorb the damage until it was too late. The box would still hold its prisoners, and the Princes would have nothing but his son's dead body to show for it. And one little girl as dead as Evan, or as crazy as he used to be, if she got caught up in the struggle. Except that Paimon wouldn't let the crazy happen. Wouldn't let her live that long.

He didn't count out that Evan might free Paimon's lords in time, winning a host-debt for his own Prince. In typical Evan style, he was calling it suicidally close on his own schedule, but Brad *could not* warn him about Paimon's deadline or the consequences of not meeting it.

"I don't know what I've done, but whatever it is, I take it back." Evan had gotten close, right inside his defenses, with a hand on a shoulder that kept trying to flicker out of existence.

"God. Father, what's the matter?" He had his head lowered so he could look up at Brad, studying his face for a sign. Nonthreatening, except that every word tore Brad apart. "I can't do anything about it if you don't tell me—"

The contract. Stupid, stupid. A walk-away, supposed to be harmless, but he'd seen what it did to Matt Shields when it came into conflict with Grayson Donne's binding spell. Once he had it figured, the answer was simple.

"The contract," he said, got Evan's attention off the rage and pain he couldn't hide and onto what he was saying. "I'm walking away."

Evan pulled his hand away like Brad had burned 'him. Reached out, but didn't quite make contact. "What did I do?" he asked.

Shock always made his son's voice husky—Brad remembered that, just weeks ago, in a hospital. Evan's bruises were almost gone, but they served as a reminder now that he wasn't torn by the conflicting demands of the Princes and a contract he never should have signed.

"Not a thing." A lie, but it didn't hurt with the contract broken. He couldn't help the grin that followed. The truth would only throw Evan off his game anyway. His son had survived the Princes before. He'd survived Alfredo Da'Costa and the kind of madness that had driven the Simpson's half-human monster to suicide at the very moment of his rescue. This time he had Matt Shields on his side, which broke every rule between Princes but for some reason didn't seem to matter. Evan would succeed. He always did. But just once it would be nice if he didn't wait until the very last minute.

"You didn't do anything."

Brad wasn't welcome in the second celestial sphere, but he hadn't been banished so completely that he couldn't pass through on his way back to Spruce Street. So he left Evan to his rental car and his bargain with Princes. Maybe he'd be back to watch. Or, maybe he wouldn't.

Chapter 73

ALMOST MIDNIGHT. THE MOON HAD RISEN, nearly full, but none of that light made it through the dense pack of pine branches to the forest floor. Not a good place for a midnight stroll—they hadn't met anyone since they'd plunged into the woods behind the Sanchez shore house. It didn't help their own movement, though, and Evan figured he was going to need stitches on that elbow—he'd smacked it twice already—but couldn't pull his arms in, had the strongbox by its handles with three short, fat candles balanced on top.

In front of him, Shields recited Frost in a singsong voice— "The woods are lovely, dark and deep" —bouncing Katey in his arms in time to the meter of the poem. They both wore white as Evan had told them, and Marina had sent a woman's summery white dress because Grey Donne had promised clothing to the daemon in the box. Shields carried the dress over his arm, wrapping Katey in a cascade of white ruffles. Evan figured the bouncing was going to make her sick all over it, but Katey cocked an ear, listening to the poem while she pointed the flashlight ahead of them. She couldn't carry all of the weight of it, but balanced it on the crook of Matt Shields' elbow. The beam of light bounced with her, keeping time to the poem while she peered through the darkness, serious, full of the responsibility for lighting their path.

"Whose idea was this anyway?" Evan muttered. He'd

never cared which of the many interpretations his teachers had put on Frost's "promises to keep." He figured anybody who used "woods" and "lovely" in the same sentence had nothing to say to him.

"Yours." Matt Shields could be dry as old bones when he wanted.

He hadn't come up with a better option, not unless they wanted an audience. But the woods offered no clear line of sight. Attack could come from anywhere and he had both hands full of an iron-and-oak strongbox. Not that he expected attack. Figured he'd have to invoke it, which was never a good idea.

And, okay, maybe he should have stopped for a burger and fries while he waited for the sun to go down, but in the grimoires he'd read the magicians always fasted. He didn't usually bother with a lot of ritual at home, not with family. But Paimon was not his Prince. He figured it couldn't hurt to go through the motions, so he hadn't eaten, and he'd worn white too, more or less—a white dress shirt and khaki pants, which he figured was close enough. Fresh running water would help—another symbol of purity—so they were sticking to the stream.

Katey came a little too close to the innocent child the old guys used to invoke daemons for his comfort. The books never said what happened to the child afterward, but Grayson Donne had drawn his own conclusions, filling his graveyard with his innocents. Not this time, though. Not this child. He had Matt Shields beside him, and Kady in the box, so he figured he had something to bargain with.

And he was angry already, with his father, which helped when he went up against the Princes. if he was feeling sensible, he might not do it at all. Now all they had to do was follow the stream, far enough away from the house to give the Sanchez family a running start if the Princes were feeling less than cooperative.

"Where's Brad?" Shields asked, and Evan had to remind himself that the daemon lord couldn't read his mind.

"He didn't say."

"Do we have a problem?" The question shouldn't have

surprised him. It didn't take much insight to hear the anger in his voice. Shields glanced over, not daring to ask for more. They were both conscious of the child craning around his shoulder to watch them with amber sparks in her eyes.

Evan shook his head. "He just broke his contract and left. He's still got a stake in this, but not for the agency." Ariton had Paimon's host-debt coming out of the bargain. He didn't understand why his father had walked away from everything they'd built in the past four years, but they were still on the same side. At least on this one. There wasn't much to say after that, so Shields turned back to the girl, substituting Doctor Seuss for Robert Frost. Evan liked *The Cat in the Hat* better anyway.

Chapter 74

COPPERHEADS AND RATTLESNAKES. Deer ticks with Lyme disease. Mosquitoes with West Nile. Evan had made a litany of the dangers he couldn't see, but the surface roots snaking over the forest floor finally got him. He hopped a step to catch his balance and realized first that the box had overbalanced him, and second that he didn't have to be there for the fall. Quick as the thought he moved sideways through the second celestial sphere.

The Princes were waiting to rip him to pieces, friends and enemies of Ariton both—he was not a popular guy with anyone right now. He figured he was damned lucky to make it out again on the other side. Gathering up the thick white candles and the strongbox where it had fallen among the damp pine needles, he wished the flashlight would point at the ground and stop bouncing light off the branches, because he wasn't doing that again until this was over, not if he fell over the side of a cliff. Which seemed his only unlikely fate on this walk, given that the Jersey Pine Barrens were flat as a pancake, but still—

"Does this place have a name?" Sanchez had said it was a state park.

Shields said nothing.

He'd figured from the start this might be a setup to kill him or turn him over to the cabal. Hoped not, but planned for contingencies.

But Shields finally heaved a put-upon sigh. "Double

Trouble Park," he said, and Evan could tell he was waiting for the blow to fall.

"You have to be kidding me." Wasn't what he meant to say, but Katey was watching him. Somebody else could enlighten her on the many and varied uses of the term "shit," but not today.

Shields laughed, and Evan could see him shake his head, just a shadow backlit by the beam of the flashlight.

"Trouble!" Katey said, and giggled.

Yeah. Trouble, all right. But they had come to a widening in the stream, and Matt Shields raised a questioning eyebrow, stopped when he set the strongbox down.

Evan dropped on top of the box and looked out over the moonlight cutting a path across the stream. He couldn't see the stars under the low canopy of the pines, but above the clearing the sky was thick and clotted with light like spattered paint. It reminded him, for a moment, of the infinite cold of the second celestial sphere, and he remembered the energy of stars passing through him, wide as the universe. For just a moment, it felt almost like home.

Shields set Katey down, almost hidden in the ferns that crowded the base of an old cedar, and Evan let the low rumble of his voice ground him in this reality. "Don't move from this spot, and try not to talk until Mr. Evan or I tell you it's okay."

Then he turned to Evan. "What now?"

"We call Paimon," Evan managed to sound confident in spite of how he felt—a little light-headed from hunger and the adrenaline from the fight, or whatever it had been. His father had disappeared before they got to the fight part, which probably explained why frustrated arguments still buzzed in his bloodstream.

He couldn't let his father screw with his head. Couldn't let worry about Lily cloud his focus. He'd patch his own relations later—right now he had a job to do, and Matt Shields' eyes had gone as wide as Katey's.

"You're going to *what*?"

"This'll work. Promise." A burst of air knocked the back of his head—hard. Not the wind. His father. Okay. O . . .

kay. Got no sense of Lily's presence, but he'd sort that out later. Right now it was time to rock.

"Hide her eyes," he said, jutting his chin at Katey by her tree. "Protect her as much as you can until I get things settled with the Princes. Then, we'll sort this out together."

"Princes? Plural?" Matt Shields looked shaken. "You're crazier than Grayson Donne."

"Yeah, Probably," he agreed.

Shields wasn't happy, but he had only two choices— Evan was one, and the other one ended in an iron-bound box. So he sat with his back against the cedar and held Katey tight among the ferns. "Don't look," he said, "I won't let anything hurt you." Which was as much a lie from a daemon lord of Paimon as it was from Evan, but they both meant it anyway.

Chapter 75

TIME TO GET THIS PARTY STARTED.

Evan had never summoned a Prince before, but he'd called his own relations and got a Prince instead on one memorable occasion. So he figured the invocation would work. A pentagram would have offered some protection, but he couldn't rely on one here, where a falling branch or a scuttling mouse might break the circle. He counted on the child and the running water to keep him alive long enough to consummate the deal.

Didn't expect it to be enough, but there were all kinds of sacred shapes and all kinds of ways to make them real. For this, Evan chose the shape that fit the tools at hand. Katey, with Matt Shields, anchoring that point in the white of purity, sat by an old cedar about six feet from the water's edge. Evan moved the strongbox so that it formed the second point of a triangle, draped it in the ruffled white dress that Marina Sanchez had sent, and put a candle on top of that. Lit it with a snap of his fingers, something he'd learned early in his father's training. Handed the next one to Shields, who lit that one and turned off the flashlight. He took for himself the third point, at the edge of the stream, in his own less than perfect white. Noticed as he set flame to wick that the last candle had a smudge on it from the fall. Fitting. He was the least pure in his motives, but he hoped the running water made up for his lack.

Across from him the child represented innocence,

and the box stood for the deal. A pyramid, if he thought of
the second celestial sphere as the fourth orientation point
of a three-dimensional space. So he did—stood next to the
running stream opposite the daemon lords that held down
each of the other points. With his arms outstretched and
his palms up in supplication he called the Princes of the
heavens.

"With a tranquil heart, and trusting in the Living and
Only God, omnipotent and all-powerful, all-seeing and all-
knowing, I conjure you, Paimon, Prince of the West, the
whisperer of secrets, and you, Ariton, Prince of the North,
who reveals all things hidden, to appear before me. You are
summoned by the Honor and Glory of God, by my Honor
that I shall cause you to do no harm or injury to others,
to honor the bargain you have made for the freedom of
your servant lords, Parmatus and Kadylon of the host of
Paimon. Appear before me now, for the greater glory of
all creation both in the physical sphere and in the second
celestial sphere."

The wind picked up twigs and bits of bark, spun them
in eddies that skirted Evan's pyramid and came too close
to the child who made the second point. He had to trust
Shields to protect her, didn't dare move from his anchor
point. Not if he wanted any of them alive at the end of the
night.

He waited, but not too long.

"This is not multiple choice. You are summoned in ac-
cordance with contracts freely given. Appear before me to
answer for your contracts! Paimon, who knows all secrets—
to free your servants, the lords Parmatus and Kaydalon,
appear before me! Ariton, Prince of all things hidden—to
claim host-debt, appear to witness the consummation of
your contract!"

Thunder rattled in the distance—a storm was coming.
Of course. I called the damned thing. Evan shuddered and
set aside the thought as clouds boiled across the sky, eating
the stars and replacing their steady light with flashes of blue
and green, amber and gold. More than he'd called by name,
then. Evan clapped his hands over his ears, closed his eyes

against the sound and light of the Princes of the spheres storming one small planet to answer his command.

Lightning struck just outside his pyramid, and again, and he flinched, felt his heart stutter while he braced himself with his eyes pinched shut. Didn't realize he'd been deafened until he heard Katey's screams. Her voice, muffled by Shields' shoulder and his own shocked ears, sounded raw, like she'd been at it a while.

Parmatus. Not Matt Shields. And Kadylon—the box had started to scream again. He had to think of them by their true names if this was going to work.

Paimon was standing at the center of the pyramid when Evan opened his eyes. Amber scales rippled in tongues of amber flame. "Vermin," the Prince rumbled, and plucked the cedar from the ground where Matt Shields sat curled around the daemon child.

"Necessary," Evan warned the daemon Prince. "If you hurt her, the contract is void."

"So you remember your contract." Paimon threw down the tree. The earth shook and Evan reached for a handhold to steady himself, felt scales instead of bark across the palm of his hand. Not a tree, then.

"Ariton." He gathered himself and made a formal bow, first to his own Prince, who glowered above him—that had been a leg he'd grabbed for balance— and then to Paimon. Both Princes towered above the forest, and the storm clouds still shot angry bolts of lightning at him, but he couldn't think about that now or he'd curl up in a gibbering ball of terror.

"We have a contract," he said instead. He'd thought about this part too. Summoning spells had to follow certain sound patterns to work, so he'd used the one he knew, a contract language of its own that did the least harm of the ones he thought might work. The books also had spells to release daemons. Historically, none of them worked very well for the humans involved, but once you had a daemon's attention, you could use any language you wanted. Legal was best, because they were a legalistic bunch. So he didn't bother with the mystical mumbo jumbo now that he had them. They had a contract, and he spelled it out, starting from the language that protected the house. Hoped he hadn't forgotten something that got him killed, but he thought he had it.

"Before we begin, I need your oath to take no retribution on this world or the life it sustains, or the universe it resides in. Your own enemies are your business, but your oath, to deal with them in the second sphere. Don't make it our problem."

"The child is our business." Paimon's words rolled like thunder. Matt Shields—Parmatus—stood up, the child in his arms.

"No," Evan said, and briefly closed his eyes. He'd known since the moment he'd seen the amber light in her eyes that he'd die before he gave up another child like himself to the monsters of his nightmares, had known this would probably be the time. Come to it, he wasn't as scared as he'd thought he'd be.

But Matt Shields said, "No," as well. Then, because it was impossible for a daemon lord, even one bound to the material sphere, to defy his Prince, Shields said, "She's Donne's legacy. We need her to set us free."

"She's the closest relative Donne had." Evan explained. He'd worked that out, figured he could keep them all alive until he broke the spell on the strongbox, but now he had to make a bargain for the life of Paimon's little monster as well. "I can't break the curse on the box without her. And I *won't* break the curse unless I have your oath that she will not be harmed in any way after the contract is satisfied." He thought he'd get an argument from Matt Shields, but the daemon lord stuck out his jaw and held on to Katey. "It's fair," Shields said, close as he could come to rebellion.

Paimon said, "It's midnight. You belong to me, human. Your own Prince has rid himself of you. Free my lords or die screaming. I'll eat your agony like ancient sins."

The threats didn't bother him much—Evan was used to that, and figured he'd make it out of these woods on his own wits or die trying: same old, same old. But Princes never ceded rights to their own. He'd thought he'd gotten past that with Ariton. Apparently not.

"Penalty for a broken contract, but no contract has been broken here." Ariton had not spoken until now, and when he did, he rumbled with Brad's voice, which Evan found more comforting than was reasonable under the circumstances. "Ariton's own monster invoked the conditions of the contract before midnight. Paimon's monster required further negotiation."

"Paimon will not negotiate."

"Just as well," Evan snapped, "Because she's not negotiable, and she falls under the contract as given—no harm to this world or the life it sustains. As long as this world sustains her, she's covered. But, good faith, moratorium is declared on the question until we free your daemon lords."

"Until my lords are returned to me." Paimon agreed to nothing but a five-minute wait.

It would have to be enough. Evan started the simple ritual to release the daemon.

"Parmatus, come forward. Bring the child with you."

Parmatus did. Didn't have any choice, given the binding, but he seemed eager enough to do it and Evan smiled at Katey, held out his arms. "Your papi needs our help. Will you help me free your papi?" She stared at him with her wide amber eyes and he asked, "Do you understand?"

Katey shook her head, no, but she held out her arms to him and clung to him when he took her up on his hip. He carried her to the box where wax melted into the ruffles of Kadylon's white dress and bent on one knee, Katey propped on the other.

"Goodwill," he said, and to Matt Shields, who waited with tension darting flames in his eyes, "Same agreement as we had before." Paimon had already sworn, but Matt Shields had taken the oath conditional on his binding to Donne's strongbox. This would be for keeps. "Do you swear not to harm this world or the people who live in it, or their connections freely given? Do you swear to take no retribution on this world or the universe it resides in? Your own enemies are your business, but only to the extent you can limit the damage as previously sworn?"

"Yeah. I swear." Shields had started to sweat. Evan pretended not to notice. He smiled at Katey and pressed her hand lightly over the iron lock on the strongbox, covered it with his own.

"Repeat after me," he said, and she did, though she struggled with the unfamiliar names. "Parmatus, of the host of Paimon, and excepting only your oath to do no harm, you are free of this spell. Iron and oak have no power over you. Go where you wish, bound only by the will of your Prince, as it has always been."

Parmatus disappeared with his own thunderclap. Katey burst into tears, and the box wailed as if the world was coming to an end—or would when Kadylon got out of there.

Paimon said. "You have kept only half your bargain."

Chapter 76

"PARMATUS WAS EASY, because he wasn't crazy," Evan explained, though he suspected that wasn't true. Parmatus was just crazy in a different way that made it easier to deal with him. Paimon didn't seem nearly as happy with his daemon lord, but that was Paimon's problem. Evan still had the daemon in the box to worry about.

"She can't take the oath." No question what the oath was; Paimon had already taken it. "And I can't release her without it."

Lightning fell around them, amber, but also indigo and gold and green. Of course, the green of Azmod, Evan's personal enemy, waiting for a chance to avenge old grievances. From off to his left he heard the crack of a pine tree hit by lightning, the snap of flame catching. Katey sobbed snot into his shirt, and he figured it was going in the trash after tonight. But he still had a daemon to free, and quickly, before a forest fire did what twenty-some years of enemies in the second celestial sphere had failed to do—turn him into a little pile of greasy ash.

"You've taken the oath," he said to Paimon. "Swear now that your daemon will honor that oath, and I will set her free."

"And if she is, as you say, mad?"

"Azmod can give you pointers." Omage, Azmod's daemon lord, had been mad as a hatter by human standards, but sly and sadistic with it. He figured Azmod hardly noticed, but that Prince took offense anyway and blasted something. Evan heard the whoosh of flame rising in living sap and ducked his head, figured he didn't have long until the fire got to him.

"If I free her, can you absorb her into the host before she can do any damage? Can you get her out of here and honor your oath?"

Paimon stared down at him, three eyes baleful above the treetops. "I can."

Not exactly a promise. "Do you swear?"

More hostility, but the forest was already burning.

"I swear."

Evan peeled Katey away from his shirt. "It will be shorter this time. Can you do it?" She shook her head, no, but held out her hand and he took it, smiled as comfortingly as he could under the circumstances, and once more pressed their hands together against the iron that bound and locked the oak strongbox. Then he adapted on the fly.

"Kadylon of the host of Paimon, and excepting only your Prince's oath to do no harm, you are free of this spell. Iron and oak have no power over you. Go where the will of your Prince commands you, as it has always been."

Paimon had sworn to take her up, but he hadn't said when. Wind rose with the sound of an approaching freight train, stirring up the fire burning in the pines and forming a visible funnel that enclosed them but could not penetrate the ritual pyramid. The lock on Donne's strongbox turned a dull, angry red. Katey screamed in pain and Evan snatched their joined hands away. Not quickly enough—the glowing iron had branded her tiny palm with the seal that bound the lock.

"Oh, my God, baby." Evan didn't know how to comfort her, couldn't make it better, and there was no escape with a tornado right on top of them and the Princes of the second celestial sphere surrounding them.

The strongbox had protected them from Kadylon's madness, but not any longer. The seals and defenses of every iron band pulsed with an angry glow and oak slats crisped and blackened around the edges. Something—Kadylon, he assumed—screamed one high, piercing tone that knocked him back on his heels. And then the box exploded in a storm of splinters.

Evan curled protectively around the little girl—Kadylon's personal monster—felt a splinter the size of a dagger carve a chunk out of his side. A hail of smaller slivers jabbed him with a hundred or more bloody cuts, and he was pretty sure he had another fucking concussion, but he held on.

Kadylon rose on a desperate shriek, shredded the white dress. The wind snatched up the tatters of ruffled cotton, added them to the sticks and leaves and pine needles and a mouse or two whirling over their heads. Centuries of faces she'd been made to wear twisted in a column of amber flame at the very center of the whirlwind—the beauties and grotesques that generations of Donnes had forced on her. He saw the girl with the pale chocolate skin who had walked naked in Grayson Donne's garden, and Marina Sanchez, the face she'd worn when Grayson Donne forced a human child on her.

Katey peered over his protective elbow, called, "Mami," through her tears, and Kadylon attacked.

Evan felt his arm break, but he had another one, and he'd already made his choices. Didn't mean he wouldn't fight back.

"WE HAD A BARGAIN! YOU SWORE!" He screamed to be heard over the freight train of the wind, but Paimon just looked down at him with that baleful three-eyed stare.

"So I did, monster. But as you say, she is mad."

Kadylon was proving that by trying to reach Katey through his back. She'd already torn a strip off him, he could feel air on raw muscle, knew she'd reached bone. Paimon might limit the destruction, he thought the tornado might be doing that, but a couple of half-human monsters were just collateral damage, conveniently rid of.

Except that Evan was not a child, and he'd done the homework years ago.

"I know your *NAME!*" Almost hoarse now, he still shouted above the havoc around them. "*I KNOW YOUR NAME!*"

Kadylon reached fingers of flame through his torn flesh, wrapped around verterbrae, and Evan said, "Kadylon of the host of Paimon, you have been summoned by the Honor and Glory of God . . ."

No need for volume, he just needed the words, but his voice grew stronger as the binding took shape. Words had their own power. "By this I demand your oath: that whenever and every time you shall be summoned, by whatever word or sign or deed, in whatever time or place, and for whatever occasion or service, you will appear immediately and without delay."

She stopped pulling bits of him apart to reach the girl, but the binding hurt like hell, and Evan shared that pain, pulsed with it in the flames she had wrapped through his body. He figured it for a close call, whether he passed out before or after he finished the binding.

"You will obey the commands set for you in whatever form they shall be conveyed. In all things, my will shall become your will, and I will you to stop. Swear."

Kadylon tore away from him, but the binding had her and she left all his bits in place. Bleeding in strange places, but all there, and once this was over he would gather himself up and put the worst of it back together.

Now he had to put and end to this with Kadylon, who twisted like a tormented thing, which she was. His fault, and he leaned over, threw up in the underbrush, not making a good showing of it. Couldn't wipe his mouth without letting go of Paimon's, child and he wouldn't do that if it killed him. But he brought his head up, said, "Swear." And hoped that none of the Princes heard him whisper "I'm sorry," because he'd already shown enough weakness, and Ariton hadn't stepped in, had just watched like the rest of them.

But Paimon rumbled, "Enough," like thunder, swallowed up Kadylon and her desolate screams in a rage of amber flames. "The Princes are not finished with you," he vowed, and vanished, taking the storm of Princes with him.

Kadylon hadn't sworn, but Evan called, "I release you, I release you," after her. He could do that much, having won. More or less. If he didn't do some patching, he was going to bleed out right here. If he didn't do it fast, they'd burn to death anyway.

Chapter 77

HE DIDN'T KNOW ENOUGH ABOUT anatomy to do a thorough job of it, but he managed to seal the worst of the bleeders and struggle to his feet anyway. His back hurt like hell, but he didn't have time to deal with it—staggered to the stream and dunked them both because sparks were already landing in the clearing, but that was no way out. The stream wasn't big enough to stop the fire even if he could manage the rushing water with a kid and a broken arm, which he couldn't. Turned and ran with his good arm wrapped around Katey and the broken one tucked into his shirt for support.

The fire had spread, arching from treetop to treetop and forming rivulets of flame along the ground, eating the undergrowth. There was no way out, and running just meant heading into burning scrub pine whichever way he looked. Evan could feel the heat of it blistering his skin, hear the fizz and pop of sap exploding and the crack of flame. The fire was sucking the oxygen out of the air damned fast, replacing it with thick black smoke. He coughed and coughed, which got him bleeding again in places he hadn't mended yet and made his broken arm hurt so bad he'd have cut it off given a sharp enough knife.

They were pretty much surrounded, and he figured they were going to die here anyway, after all his efforts to keep the kid alive. They had one way out, something he hadn't done until he was nineteen and driven crazy by drugs and booze and captivity and torture. Hadn't done it with a body until later than that. Certainly never contemplated trying it with a small child not of his prince in his one good arm. Give me a choice, he thought, but knew he didn't have one.

"Close your eyes," he said, "I won't let you go, no matter what." And then he moved into the second celestial sphere.

There was a war going on—the princes moved fast where grudges were concerned, but he figured it wouldn't last long. Paimon owed Ariton, and Azmod might be insulted but even princes couldn't hide the truth from each other here. Evan just hoped it didn't cost Ariton the host-debt he'd earned for his prince. He thought they'd make it through while the princes were occupied with their own affairs, but Katey was attracting attention. So he got out quick, just ahead of a curl of amber flame that reached for the girl.

He brought her out under the pentagram in the front office of the house on Spruce Street because, child or not, she belonged to a foreign prince. She was still sniveling a bit, but appeared to have hit overload before their last jaunt. So she hadn't quite noticed that they'd been turned inside out and back again passing between the spheres. Vaguely he wondered if the blood smears on her dress were his, or whether she was hurt worse than he'd thought. Had to get her to a doctor. But she wasn't the only one in shock, which came as a surprise, right before he passed out.

Chapter 78

BRAD SAT BEHIND THE ANTIQUE Hepple-white desk and considered the blood soaking into the carpet. "Do you suppose we can put another one on Matt Shields' bill?" he asked the room at large. Lily shaped her preferred body out of thought and air, answered, "He's not here to object, and the rubies are in the safe. Is he dead?"

The second "he" meant Evan. Brad peered over the desk, considering the question. Two human shapes making a mess of his new carpet, not just one. "He'd better not be. He's still got to answer for that."

"Why did he bring her here?" Lily was on the far side of caring, almost gone already, but she peered down at the girl as if she were trying to solve a puzzle with some of the pieces missing.

Brad followed her gaze and shrugged. He'd read that the helplessness of the young was supposed to resonate with humans. Didn't do a thing to him. Then she opened her eyes, the amber flames of Paimon stirring as she looked around the strange room.

The hairs on the back of his neck came to attention. He remembered something Harry Li once said to him about Evan— "Danger, Will Robinson." Still didn't know the reference, but he recognized danger when he saw it. Katey Sanchez, or Shields, or whatever they called her, might be young even by human reckoning, but she'd made it through the second celestial sphere alive and no worse off than when she entered it, which warranted some thought.

"She's Paimon's problem, not ours," he argued anyway, and wished Evan would wake up. He needed to do something about this before it escalated into an incident between Princes.

The little girl crawled out of the protective hollow that Evan had curled around her before he lost consciousness and used her one good hand to try to wipe at the blood and soot smeared on her torn white dress. She seemed upset that it didn't help, but climbed up on her knees on a guest chair and stretched her damaged hand across the desk to him.

The pentagram didn't hold her. He'd wondered about that. Evan's mother had been human, and so his flesh was of this world. He'd thought it might not have worked the other way, but apparently it had.

"Hurts," she said, and opened her small brown fingers to show him the mark of the lock that had bound her mother to Donne's box.

He cringed a little when she wiped her nose on the back of her good hand, wasn't at all affected by the tears running down her cheeks. But he wondered what she could do, so he took the tiny injured hand and held the fingers open, let the blue fire of Ariton flicker in his eyes, and said, "You can fix it if you want."

Three years old. He wondered if she could.

But she said, "How?" and he said, "Let me show you," and laid her damaged hand against his palm. He took the unmarked one gingerly between the fingertips of his free hand, turned it over so both lay palm up. "You just have to make the hurt one look like the other one."

She searched his face—trying, he figured, to find the joke—and he didn't move. Let her look, decide for herself.

"Okay," she said, and pinched up her face in a display of concentration too huge for her small body. But the red was fading, the marks growing paler. Not scarring, he could see the mending below the surface. Burned skin sloughed away until the damaged hand was as pink and fresh as the other one. Fresher, since she hadn't been wiping her nose with it.

"Very good," he said, and wished that Evan would wake up, because if he called the police to take her away, Ellen Li would show up, probably with Mike Jaworski in tow, and she'd want to know why they were in the business office instead of the house, letting the kid sleep on their nice, clean couch. And he didn't want to explain Evan lying unconscious and bleeding on his own—expensive—carpet again.

Apparently, at least part of that wouldn't be a problem. Evan stirred, moaned, and realized that he no longer had the girl tucked safely near.

"Katey!" He sat up, grunted and made a grab for his alarmingly swollen arm. Then he screamed, as much in surprise as from the pain itself, Brad thought.

Katey scrambled back off her chair. Standing, she was able to stare right into Evan's glazed eyes, and she did, her own expression solemn and a little anxious. "You can fix it," she said, "I'll show you."

"Jesus," he said, "I thought I'd lost you."

"I'm right here." She patted his good shoulder, leaned in so close that her forehead rested against his.

Brad watched as the fight went out of Evan and he opened up completely to the child. She wasn't Ariton, and no one of his Prince should ever let down their guard so thoroughly in the presence of any manifestation of another host. Brad wondered if he should stop it, if Paimon meant them harm with this child. But he knew that arm had to hurt, and that for the moment, Evan didn't feel it at all. He'd have to do something if Evan couldn't, but for the moment he let it go, and wondered what Evan meant by it when he said, "Thank God, thank God."

"She has a point," he said, "If you don't patch yourself up, you'll be explaining your condition to the police and Jefferson Hospital's finest trauma surgeons." He didn't have to mention that it was a little soon after the last time. Questions would doubtless be raised.

Evan shook his head. "I took care of the internal stuff, and patched my back while we were in transit." Bodies were more mutable in the second celestial sphere, where they existed only by the will of the wearer, and Evan had healed soft tissue before. "I'll live, but bone's more difficult. The arm's gonna need a cast."

Which was maybe true, and maybe not, but Brad didn't feel helpful, and the child didn't know how to heal bone either. "What do you plan to do with her?"

"Call Carlos Sanchez. His cell's in the file. Make sure they made it out alive and tell them where to find her." He staggered to his feet, and paled under the dawn light coming in through the office window. Brad hadn't noticed when daylight had happened. Evan still hadn't, he thought.

"Damn, Lily, can you get me something to wrap this arm? It hurts like a bitch."

"No, it doesn't," she said, and snaked an arm around his neck, pulled him in, and kissed him hard, leaving a single drop of blood marking the bite on his lower lip. "*That* hurts like a bitch." She laughed, and kissed him again. "I'm going home," she said. "I'm going home."

She'd picked her moment well, because Evan wasn't tracking, and didn't know that she'd briefly been stripped of her power to move in the second sphere at all, or that he'd won them release from their Prince's command to watch him that had bound them here since the first time Brad had refused to kill him. Not trust, exactly. The Princes would never trust him, but they'd won. Evan was no longer a prisoner. Could become one fast enough, but for the moment, they were all free, no longer bound to his half-human monster or the little ball of dirt he called home. He didn't think Evan would appreciate the honor, but by the time it came to counting up losses, it would all be old news.

In the meantime, they had Paimon's own monster to contend with, and he didn't think Evan was going to do the sensible thing and kill it. "You passed through the spheres with her, and she's healed her own hand just by wanting to. What will the Sanchez family do when she goes for a stroll between the spheres on her own? What will the Princes do?"

Chapter 79

EVAN KNEW ALL THAT, ran his good hand over the top of his head, wished he hadn't, then wished he still had his hair to hide his nerves in. "I thought he'd come back for her."

"Matt Shields? What made you think he cared?" Brad asked, and Lily added, more mystified than his father, "He's free now. He's gone. Why would he come back?"

Shields had cared. He'd come as close to defying his Prince over her as he possibly could. "Caring doesn't mean able," Evan pointed out. "Maybe he can't *get* back."

"We couldn't."

Come back, his father meant, and Evan wondered if he realized the admission he'd just made. He was tracking through the pain in his arm, a little slow, but he got there. Years ago. War between the Princes had swept Brad and Lily both up and Evan had brought them out again, invoked a binding he'd meant to protect them. It had, that time.

Figured what he had to do. The oath Parmatus had sworn didn't bind him to anything but the promise to do no harm, but it left traces. He wouldn't tell his father that. Didn't want to find out where the thought might lead, if he wasn't careful, didn't even know if he could do it. His arm hurt like a stone cold—

"Lily, could you—" She'd relented, drifted silk around his neck, and he cradled the broken arm in the vee of blue the color of her eyes that crossed his chest. "Thank you," he breathed, "but I meant, will you call Sanchez? In case we need him?"

"Ingrate." But she went to the desk, turned on the computer, and picked up the phone.

"Katey, I'm going to need your help again," he said, soft as he could. She was half asleep, curled in the guest chair, but she raised her head, considered the option. "Will it hurt?" she whispered back, like they shared a secret. The question broke his heart.

"It shouldn't," he said. "We're going to find your papi."

She thought about it a minute, then nodded solemnly, scrambled up on her chair, and reached out for him to pick her up.

"I can hold her, but I can't lift her, and I'll need that." He flicked a glance at his father, asking for help with the look. Brad wasn't happy about it, but he came around the desk and picked her up.

She reached for Evan, wrapped herself around him like a blanket when he held out his arm. His father turned away, but not before he caught something a little terrifying in his eyes. He'd think about that later, when he had a cast on his arm and maybe one for his head as well. Katey settled and he looked up, at the design worked into the ceiling.

"Good a place as any," he said, and began the summoning spell.

"With a tranquil heart, and trusting in the Living and Only God, omnipotent and all-powerful, all-seeing and all-knowing, I conjure you, Parmatus of the host of Paimon, to appear before me ... Appear before me now, for the greater glory of all creation both in the physical sphere and in the second sphere."

"You know you're a damned fool." Shields appeared inside the circle, which he would, Evan figured—he hadn't specified, and Shields had been here before.

"Been told that." So, all right, maybe he should have stood outside it when he'd made the call, but he hoped to keep this friendly. Shields was looking dangerous, though. He was back in a flannel shirt and jeans, with his steel-toed boots on. Probably a good sign, all in all, but conflicted, which was never a good look on a daemon lord. And Katey was reaching for him, making grabby hands and whimpering for her papi. Which he wasn't.

"Am I going to have to kill you?"

"Hope not. I didn't summon you to bind you here."

Katey squirmed to get free and Evan almost fainted. His father, he noticed, had put his feet up on the desk and was watching with some wary interest and a great deal of amusement.

"Then what am I doing here?" Shields took the girl from him in disgust and snugged her up under his arm, muttered, "Mi nena,"— my little girl—into her hair to quiet her. Evan thought, *You're here for exactly that,* but he kept it to himself.

"Think of it as an interdimensional phone call. You're free to go whenever you want, usual rates apply."

Lily hung up the phone, and Evan wondered if she'd picked her moment for dramatic effect. "The Sanchezes lost the house in New Jersey, but they made it out alive," she said. "They'll be here in an hour."

Evan gave a quick nod, hadn't thought how it would pull on the muscles around his broken arm to do that, but managed to stay on his feet. Never show weakness to a daemon lord, but he figured he wasn't hiding anything. "I thought you'd want to know that. You can wait, or go back to the second celestial sphere, whatever you want." He didn't mention Katey. Didn't think he had to.

Shields nodded once, accepting what he said, then looked out into the distance for a minute, as if he were doing some complex calculation in his head. "It never was Marina," he said. "You asked about that once, if I had slept with Marina. But she and Grey belonged to each other. I was never a part of that. Alba . . ." he kissed Katey absently on the top of her head. "Carlos didn't know, but I think Cyril Van Der Graf figured it out. That's why he took her."

Alba. Shit. Evan sank into a chair, jostled his arm, and the world went white for a while. When the room came back into focus, Matt Shields was there, and so was Mike Jaworski, staring down at him.

"Got a call on the radio," Jaworski said, exasperated. "What have you done to yourself now?"

"Forest fire in New Jersey," Brad said, "Managed to walk out, but he broke his arm in the process, and I think he hit his head. Again. Someone picked him up on the highway and gave him a ride home. Didn't do his arm any good."

"Head neither, I'd guess. You really need to get him into another line of work." Jaworski pulled up a lid to check Evan's pupils, and Evan bleared back at him. "It was an accident."

"Always is, with you. But this time looks like you bought yourself a three-month vacation. Who's the kid?"

"That is Carlos Sanchez's secret." Evan smiled in triumph, mostly because it jogged Jaworski off the topic of Evan's arm. And his head.

"Marina Sanchez and Grey Donne, the son, had a kid?"

"There's no will, they don't want the money. But, yeah." As lies went, this one rolled easy.

"Hunh." Jaworski didn't seem surprised. In fact, he seemed pleased. "Sid Valentine owes me twenty bucks."

"You knew?"

"Could have been murder. There was plenty of that going around. But we knew they'd had an affair, and Cyril Van Der Graf was looking for something. If he'd found the kid, he could have used her to claim Donne's estate. He'd have had the whole thing, including the house and the graveyard, and it wouldn't have cost him a thing." Close enough, and the truth wasn't an option. But Van Der Graf had known. Donne had already set it up. Then Donne was dead and there was no child. Damned right he'd been looking.

It wasn't over yet. "The FBI want Carlos Sanchez for questioning, and New York will probably want to try him as an accessory. No way he didn't know about the bodies in Donne's woods, and he looks good for planting them. But the old man died of a bad heart—kind of a miracle he lived as long as he did according to the ME—so he doesn't look good for a murder charge."

"The whole town knew what Grayson Donne was doing in that house and looked the other way," Evan pointed out.

The police had plenty of evidence of what happened to people who crossed Grayson Donne—a whole graveyard of bodies torn to pieces. Matt Shields didn't say it, not in front of Katey. Not when he'd put them there. He kept the amber light in his eyes to a low smolder that didn't attract attention.

Jaworski had a hand under the elbow of Evan's good arm, guiding him to his feet, and there were EMTs crowding the office. He heard Jaworski say, "Is that all Evan's blood, or is the little girl hurt too?"

His father answered for him, "It's all Evan's. The girl is tired, but otherwise fine."

"They'll take her to CHOP—Children's Hospital—to be on the safe side, have her checked out. You a relative?" Jaworski asked, but he was looking at Matt Shields.

"Her father, since Grey died. Not blood, but . . . Her mother is on the way."

Irony there, Evan thought. Not blood, no, but Matt Shields was related on her daemon side and the Sanchezes weren't blood relations at all. He figured his father could show them how to fix that. Worked for him, at any rate, but in the meantime, Jaworski accepted the story. "Good enough. You can ride along—they'll want you there to keep her calm."

"Evan will be at Jeff," he added, "They've got a bed with his name on it at Emergency, and this will give the docs a chance to see how he's doing from the last time."

"Three months," Brad answered the accusation. "He'll be on the desk for the next three months. Don't count him out, though. He could still catch his hand in a paper shredder."

"Don't doubt it."

Then there was a gurney that Evan resisted. Jaworski said "Cuts four hours off the wait," and so he let them push him down.

"No drugs," he heard Jaworski tell the the EMTs, hadn't thought of it himself, but he was glad Mike had. Then he was out anyway, didn't need the God-damned drugs, he was that tired.

Matt Shields was free. Last thought before he let the world fade away, just too damned tired to keep his eyes open. Matt Shields was free and in love with Alba Sanchez. He would have laughed except it hurt too much.

Lily had said good-bye.

Epilogue

EVAN FUMBLED THE PHONE, his head still deep in a provenance search for an art dealer in Melbourne. In three more days the cast came off. He'd figured out bone sometime in the third week, gave the arm a little boost just to make sure things were healing all right, but otherwise left it to a natural progression that wouldn't leave red flags in his medical records. Not that kind, at least, though the whole "accident prone" excuse was wearing thin at Jefferson, where he was on first-name terms with the triage nurse on the eleven-to-seven shift.

But by next week, he'd mostly have his life back. He had an appointment for physical therapy and another to see a private collector in Chicago about a Brancusi that had gone missing without raising a blip on the state-of-the-art security system. Life would be great just as soon as he learned how to breathe again.

Lily was gone. He'd known it would hurt, but damn. At least, with Cyril Van Der Graf, he'd gotten the good drugs. Which was just plain stupid, that he'd gladly offer up a cup of his own blood to feel the drugs hit his veins again. Maybe this time—

Stupid, stupid, and he had a client waiting for him on the phone.

"Evan?" Carlos Sanchez. Not a client, then. Sanchez was out on bail.

"Yeah, it's me. What can I do for you?"

"To begin, you can accept my thanks. The state's attorney is not happy, but it appears he will drop the charges in the next day or two."

"No thanks are necessary, but I'm glad to hear it." Khadijah Flint had recommended a lawyer in New York who was, she said, almost as good as she was. But in the two months since they arrested Donne's cabal, the FBI had found no hard evidence that Sanchez had been involved at all. So the state might have made a case that he'd known about Donne's activities, but so did the whole town, going back more than a century. They'd kept quiet or died in Grayson Dunne's secret room—Donne had held Marina Sanchez prisoner in a hole in the ground under his house for seven months, clear evidence of duress. Thanks to Khadijah Flint, the court had seen the sense in that as well.

They had plenty of evidence against the cabal. The FBI had uncovered connections that went higher than anyone wanted to bring to an open courtroom. He expected the whole case to disappear any day now.

"Are you still there, Evan?"

"Yeah, I'm here. Is Katey okay?"

"She's fine. Made a picture for your refrigerator. You can pick it up when you come—"

"I can't—" No explaining to the man the relationships between hosts of different Princes, but he had no intention of visiting Katey Sanchez. Paimon still wanted them both dead.

"The house is up for auction. Matt thought you'd want to know."

And wasn't that a kick in the head. Matt Shields had stayed, for Alba Sanchez and a little girl who had his eyes. But the house—

The house was a festering wound eating at the back of his mind. "I'll be there."

Matt Shields was waiting at dusk in the clearing in front of the house. He had the little girl in his arms, but was otherwise alone. Didn't say anything at first and Evan respected the distance. The contract was closed; they had nothing in common but an uneasy truce between their Princes and a shared focus for old pain. Best to leave it at that. They'd told the Sanchezes they were coming back for one last look before the place changed hands.

Katey squealed and reached out to him, her pigtails bouncing against the tiny silver crosses in her ears. Not his kid, not his place, but it was hard to turn away. Matt Shields huffed an exasperated snort through his nose and gave the cast a pointed stare. "She's getting heavy," he said, but held her out anyway, and Evan didn't have much choice. He tucked her against his side with his good arm, trying not to flash back to the night they'd run through a burning forest like this. He figured it was going to get worse before it got better. They were alone at the edge of Donne's woods, the town locked down tight as storms rolled over the hills and crashed over their heads.

Matt Shields held the rain to the west, but storm clouds rumbled overhead. "I hate this house," he said, and Evan nodded, had his own reasons to want it gone. The wind whipped up and lightning flashed. Katey wanted her papi, and Evan was glad to let her go, waited until he had cradled her face against his shoulder, then gave an abrupt nod. Shields drew the storm down on them, and Evan added wind to the rain and the lightning. The roof bristled with lightning rods, but he listened for the sound of a freight train, nudged it, felt the tearing in his chest as the air pressure dipped. Hail fell around them, and lightning flashed in clouds turned green and purple. Evan pushed.

Together they watched the roof go, the windows blow. The door flew past, a post from the porch, and the house was down. Vulnerable. Shields reached out, became flame and thunder with Katey wrapped up safe at its center, brought down flames. Not lightning. The ground was saturated; a lightning strike would kill Evan and maybe Katey, which would end a lot of conflicts in the second celestial sphere, but he wasn't feeling sacrificial today and Paimon's lord retained an interest in the child.

They watched until the house had crumbled and sirens wailed, growing nearer, then headed for their respective cars. Shields had a four-wheel-drive something now. They were quiet until he'd settled Katey to a few wounded sniffles.

"She didn't leave *you*, you know." Lily. And not Paimon's business.

"Whatever. She left." Evan didn't want to die a crispy critter, so he didn't remind Shields that he'd been living in a box for six hundred years, so his advice on the sex lives of daemons and half-human hybrids was maybe not the most relevant. But that didn't stop him.

"It wasn't about you, Evan." And that was sharper, and he wondered what was going on in Shields' head, what was going to happen to Katey if he'd tired of playing human already. Evan had been grown when he found his father and Lily. He'd needed some training, some assurance that he was sane, but he could manage on his own. Katey was stronger and still had puberty ahead of her. But that wasn't where Shields was going.

"If she were a human girl, would it be a deal breaker for you if she wanted to live in her hometown instead of yours?"

"But she's not human." And he couldn't live in her hometown.

"Well, that's your problem, isn't it?" And maybe that was part of it.

Shields left him to his own thoughts until they had reached the cars, but there was something else on his mind.

"What is it?"

"There's a guy, name of Da'Costa, that's been nosing around. Do you know him?"

No daemon lord should look that comfortable putting a toddler in a car seat, but Evan didn't let that distract him from the question. He'd been pretty well sick of Alfredo Da'Costa since the first time he'd laid eyes on him. "Yeah. Is he giving you a problem?"

"He likes to make threats. I'm just not sure whether he's another crazy or something to be really worried about."

The crazies had been worth the worry, but Evan figured he knew what Shields meant. Da'Costa's threats usually

involved the deaths of universes, and always the death of
Evan. If he was threatening Katey, well. "He's dangerous.
Keep Katey away from him—he really doesn't like our
kind. But I'll talk to him."

He found Alfredo Da'Costa in a garden in Paris. Not one of
the usual ones you'd find in a tourist guide, but high above
the city, tiers of paths paved in cut stone blocks and plazas
carved into a hillside among the beds of grass and flowers
beneath the trees. The neighborhood was slightly shabby,
fading into age with moderate grace, but Paris spread like
a banquet in front of them: Sacre Coeur floated above the
city in the distance, and the Eiffel Tower almost disappeared in the evening haze beyond the maze of slate roofs
and chimney pots.

Evan joined him at the stone railing, pretended to an
appreciation of the view that another day would have cap-
tured his imagination with angles and light and the lone
figure juggling in front of a fountain a level below them in
the park. A ball fell, and Evan figured he wasn't going to let
that happen to him.

"About the girl," he said

Da'Costa raised a patrician eyebrow. "Which one?" he
asked. "Paris has so many." But his dark and ageless eyes
studied Evan as if he were a puzzle he'd grown tired of.

Evan was done with games. "Katey. Don't hurt her.
Don't interfere."

"The humans can't teach her what she needs to know.
What will you do when Matt Shields gets tired of playing
happy houses and goes home? Bring her back to Spruce
Street? Neither of your partners would allow it—she is not
of your Prince."

"Lily's gone." And, God, bad enough she left—he could
have handled that she just got tired of him and wandered
away in time. He'd expected it of her, knew Brad was surprised every time she dragged him off to bed. But she'd
vanished the moment the Princes had let her go, and that
made him doubt every assumption he'd made about the
past four years.

"And because your masculinity has been offended, you would stand against Ariton? Against your father?"

Da'Costa turned back to the city and Evan figured he was supposed to take a lesson from that—he could lose this too. But the Guardian really never had understood Evan. This wasn't about Lily, or Ariton, or even humans. He was tired of lessons that ended with all of creation better off if his kind weren't in it. His kind—neither daemon nor human but distinctly themselves. The last time he'd fought for one of "his kind" had been a disaster. But Katey Sanchez wasn't like that. She was happy and sane, and gave Evan more hope than he had any right to consider.

"What makes you think I care about a universe that can exist only if my kind doesn't?"

"If she were Ariton—"

But Evan wasn't listening. "If you hurt her, I'll bring it all down. A universe that would destroy us just for living doesn't deserve to exist."

Da'Costa had tried to kill him before, and Evan braced for a fight, figured it for the last one, but Da'Costa just gave a slow nod. "We'll talk again," he said. "But today, we're in Paris. Are you hungry?"

Da'Costa was alone here too—a Guardian and the only one of his kind on the planet. He didn't like to think that they had anything in common, but Da'Costa did understand at least that much about him.

"I could use a bite," he agreed. "There's this great little Moroccan place—"